ARGYGIR99

DATE DUE

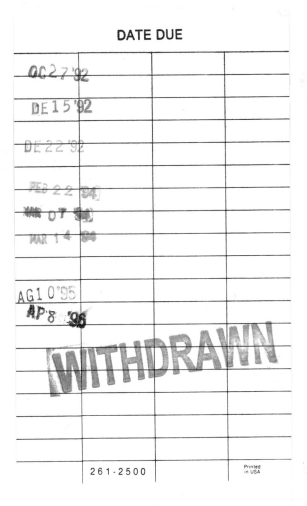

THE YANKEE GIRL

Books by Ellen Argo

JEWEL OF THE SEAS
THE CRYSTAL STAR
THE YANKEE GIRL

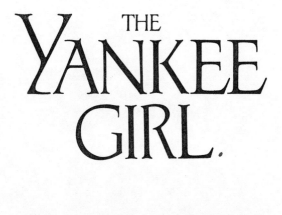

THE YANKEE GIRL

ELLEN ARGO

G.P. Putnam's Sons, New York

fiction

13.95
B.+T.

Library of Congress Cataloging in Publication Data

Argo, Ellen.
   The Yankee girl.

   The last volume of the author's trilogy, continuing
Jewel of the seas and The Crystal Star.
   I. Title.
PZ4.A69Yan [PS3551.R417] 813'.54   80-14388
ISBN 0-399-12528-0

PRINTED IN THE UNITED STATES OF AMERICA

62047

For Mimi,
My sister, my friend

The Yankee Girl

Chapter One

1850

Leaning on the starboard rail, Julia watched rose-touched golden clouds trail across the sky as the sun set behind the three hills of Boston. It was quiet aboard the *Crystal Star*, for there were only five members of the crew besides the cook and steward, the sailmaker and carpenter on the ship. The cook was quietly singing a forecastle song to himself as he washed up in the small deckhouse that was his galley, and the others were either silent or gossiping around the foremast. The only other person on the quarterdeck besides Julia was the second mate, a silent young man named Clyde Rawlings, who stood on the larboard side and watched the idle crew.

She remembered how impatient to set sail she had been when she'd been younger. Now, knowing what could lie ahead, she was content to watch the light dwindle over this peaceful harbor. She thought of nothing except the things that presented themselves to her eyes: the terns and gulls settling themselves on any handy object after their final evening flight, the lights that had begun to appear on the vessels that swung in the harbor, the darkening waves that washed gently by the ship.

Her husband, Stephen Logan, and the first mate, Homer Evans, came from below where they had been going over some final details for the voyage. Turning to watch them mount the quarterdeck, Julia looked at the mate as impersonally as she had watched the clouds and birds and waves. Yet she did not find him peaceful.

Grim, she decided, was the word that best described him. There was a silence in him; a coiled silence, hard and cold. His eyes were of such a light blue, they almost seemed colorless around the small dark pupil, and his chin might have appeared weak if you'd been able to ignore the sharp beaked nose above thin lips that never seemed to smile. Julia wondered if he had learned to smile and had forgotten. Had silence been taught to him by his trade or had he been born silent? More than anything, he reminded her of a snake, always poised and tightly curled, ready to strike without a warning whisper.

"It's time to be on your way, Mister Evans," Stephen was saying. "Take whomever you need with you. And don't forget I want a full crew on board by midnight. We'll sail with the tide."

"Aye, aye, sir." The mate touched one finger to his cap and immediately left the quarterdeck. The men on the main deck watched him warily as he approached. They had not been aboard long enough to know him, but to know his reputation was enough.

When the men had left the ship with Evans, Julia moved to stand beside her husband and watch the longboat as the men rowed towards shore.

"Where are you going to get a crew at this time of night, Stephen? I'd think you'd do better by day."

"You know where I'm going to get them," he said curtly.

"You said you wouldn't deal with shanghaiers!" she protested.

"I'm not. They wouldn't produce what I want. However, there are a couple of boardinghouse keepers who've told Evans they'll supply us with sailors, real sailors."

"Stephen, they're just as bad. You know they'll find men who've only been ashore a few hours, drug them, rob them, and turn them over to you for their so-called expenses . . . which you'll take out of their wages."

"Julia!" He whirled to face her. Even in the dim light she could see his grey eyes flash with the steel of anger. "Who is master of this ship?"

"You are, of course."

"Then you'll oblige me by remembering it. I'll run this ship as I see fit, and if the only way I can obtain a crew is through the boardinghouses, then that's the way I'll obtain a crew. I am not going to take you and this ship around the Horn with only green hands aboard."

"Well, I bet if you'd wait just a few more days, you'd find some sailors who are willing, not forced, to sign the Articles."

"I have waited. The notice has been tacked on the board ever since I returned to Boston. What you see down there is the result."

Julia looked at the few men who remained aboard. It was true that neither in their attire nor in their attitude did they suggest that they had ever seen a ship before. She pressed her lips together.

"Well, it's going to be a long voyage, isn't it?"

"About four months to California if we're lucky."

"I mean in more ways than time."

"It'll be the same as any other voyage," he said tersely.

"No two voyages are ever the same." She looked towards the waterfront where lights were beginning to shine against the coming dark. It was the last time she would see them or the lights of any harbor for months to come. Once they set sail, the only people who would populate her world would be the men aboard the *Crystal Star*. Even now some of them were innocently drinking in boardinghouse bars, flirting with girls, and planning the days of freedom that lay ahead of them. They didn't realize that freedom would never be theirs. She said slowly, "With Homer Evans aboard, I have a feeling that this is going to be a very different kind of voyage."

8

Stephen followed the direction of her eyes. He knew what she was thinking, but he couldn't afford to be swayed by her emotions. He didn't like this business any more than she, but it had become a matter of survival. A ship could not live without a crew.

"You were prejudiced against the man before you ever met him," he said impatiently.

"Maybe I was, but even if I hadn't been, meeting him would have been enough. I intend to stay well clear of Mister Homer Evans, and I'm sure the crew will wish they could do the same."

"I wouldn't worry about him if I were you. After all, you *are* the captain's wife. There's no need for you to have anything to do with him or he with you. Besides I understand he doesn't care for women."

"Oh?" She looked at him curiously. She'd spent too many years observing seamen in port not to know their habits. "What does he do when he goes ashore then?"

"He drinks, but as long as he doesn't do it aboard, that doesn't concern me." Stephen drummed his fingers on the rail. There were more important things to be considered than the predilections of his mate.

"I just wish you hadn't hired him. Something's going to go wrong. I know it."

"Your crystal ball again?" he said curtly.

Full night had finally come, and the lanterns of the surrounding vessels dipped and swayed, leaving small paths of light on the waves. The glow of street lamps rose up the hills of Boston, but the darkness seemed a little sinister on this moonless night. She shivered.

"Maybe it is my crystal ball. If you'll excuse me, I'm going below."

"You're going to bed now? A little early, isn't it?"

"I don't know whether I'm going to bed or not, but I don't want to be on deck when they start hauling the bodies on board."

What a rotten ending to a day that had begun so well, Julia thought as she struggled out of her clothes in the small captain's cabin that adjoined the saloon. When a steam tug passed close to the *Crystal Star*, the gimbaled lamp swung wavering shadows across the ivory walls, and shapeless clothes swayed on their pegs. The brass-rimmed porthole, which had not been properly secured, swung closed with a clang, shutting off the cool breeze. Impatiently, Julia knelt on the wide feather bed and bolted it open again. As she began to let her hair down in front of the mirror above the built-in mahogany washstand, her thoughts returned to the late morning.

It had been nearly noon when the Dennis packet had approached the wharves of Boston.

9

* * *

Aboard the schooner, there was the screech of blocks, the voice of the mate shouting out orders, and the clapping of sails as they were lowered. Passengers, armed with umbrellas and portmanteaus, elbowed their way to the rail. However, when Julia spotted Stephen on the crowded granite wharf, all the rest of the world fell away and only he existed.

Despite eight years of marriage, the sight of that electrically vital man had the power to leave her momentarily breathless. And that smile! The welcoming joy of it flowed across the water.

The gap between the schooner and the wharf closed, and as the lines were heaved ashore, Stephen replaced the tall silk hat he had been waving with such enthusiasm. The instant the gangway touched the wharf, he sprang aboard and pushed his way through the disembarking passengers. She had time to take only one step towards him and she was in his arms. Their kiss was brief but it was filled with warmth and with the memory of longer kisses shared in a privacy not to be found on the deck of any vessel.

"Julia!" He grinned down at her. The eagerness with which he searched her face was so intense it might have been two years and not two weeks that had separated them. As always the sea breeze had loosened her blue-black hair, and springy tendrils, dampened by the heat, clung to her forehead beneath her straw bonnet. Her cheeks were flushed and her eyes, which had so often reminded him of the dark blue waters of the Gulf Stream, were sparkling with excitement.

Nine years had passed since he had first strolled into her father's shipyard and found her in a rough dress working beside the men. Yet in his eyes, the years had changed her very little. He thought she was even more beautiful than she had been at twenty-one. And it was still a wonder to him that she was his. There had been times when he'd thought that he had lost her, but from the love that now shone on her face, he knew that she cared for him as much as he did for her. He resolved once again that this time nothing would come between them.

"Ah, Julia, I'm glad you've come."

"Of course I've come. I promised, didn't I?" she said gaily, but she was scarcely aware of her own words. She was too busy examining the face that was so dear to her. Stephen's forehead was imprinted with lines from the years of command, and small wrinkles beside his grey eyes showed the marks of sun and wind. At thirty-seven, he was every inch the captain, but now the squareness of his jaw was softened by his smile.

The deck was almost clear of passengers and the crew had set to work opening the hatches when Stephen finally glanced around.

10

"Where's Clara?" he asked, surprised that he could have forgotten his small daughter. "Did you leave her below?"

"No." Julia's smile faded as she thought of Clara. "She was sick again, Stephen. Very sick. Soon as I told her she didn't have to go to sea, she recovered."

He drew a sharp breath as he looked down at the deck. The small valise that lay beside the full skirts of her blue muslin dress could never contain the wardrobe necessary for a long voyage.

"Julia, you just said you were keeping your promise. You are sailing with me, aren't you?"

"Yes, Stephen. I'm sailing with you. That bag was just for the trip down to Boston. The rest of my luggage is below."

"And Clara?" Taking a step away from her, he smoothed back the sun-bleached brown hair that had fallen over his forehead. Settling his hat in place, he examined her face as though to find there some hard truth he might not hear from her lips. "You're really going to be able to go off and leave her with no regrets?"

"Well, of course I have a few regrets," she said as unbidden pictures of Clara playing with her cousins, sleeping in the moonlight, standing small and delicate on the Dennis wharf to wave good-bye flashed through her mind. Yet she was able to keep all sign of wistfulness from her voice as she continued.

"I gave it a lot of thought after you left, Stephen, and I'm very certain now that where I belong is with you. I'm only sorry Clara wasn't built for a life at sea. I'd like to have her with us, but she's happier and healthier at home with Mama and Papa. Doctor Willett agrees and Aunt Martha promised to keep an eye on her."

"I never thought you'd be able to leave her," he said softly. "We'll be gone a long time, Julie."

"I know, but Clara has to be Clara, and I have to be me," she said with quiet assurance. Then because the moment was too serious and because she could see the doubt that still filled his eyes, she laughed. "You wouldn't by any chance be trying to get rid of me, would you, Stephen?"

"Oh, no, my lady." His grin was wide and young once more as he took her hand and firmly clamped it under his arm. "I'm not going to let you out of my sight. Never again. I'll arrange to have the rest of your luggage sent over to the ship, but I'm going to get you on board the *Crystal Star* before you have another chance to change your mind. And as soon as all your things are aboard, I'm taking her out into the harbor. The cargo's already been loaded. The mate's out rounding up a crew now. It won't be long before I have you safe at sea."

As Stephen hurried her past the tightly packed tall buildings that lined the wharves, Julia was too busy avoiding the cracks in the granite paving to notice what changes had occurred in Boston in the past few months. Yet it would have been difficult to ignore the numbers of young men in high boots and slouch hats who swaggered among the brightly clad sailors and the more soberly dressed merchants and their clerks. The promise of gold was luring ever increasing numbers of men to California.

However, as they approached the *Crystal Star*, Julia had eyes for nothing but the ship. With her launching eight years in the past, she had long since been outdesigned, and though well past her prime, she wore her years well. From her mainmast, the house flag, a white star blazing on a royal blue background, fluttered in the breeze. Her paint shone like black satin, and the broad white waist that outlined her gunports gleamed as though freshly scrubbed.

Glistening with a fresh coat of paint, the figurehead rode serenely beneath the soaring bowsprit. Her long blond tresses were sharply outlined against the whiteness of her gown, and the crown of stars that encircled her head sparkled in the sunlight. With her blue eyes turned up towards the sky, her smile seemed to be filled with anticipation of the voyage to come. A little soot clung to the folds of her gown, but the first squall they encountered would rinse that clean.

The decks were scuffed and grimy from the recent loading of cargo. However, that would soon be remedied. A few days at sea with the men hard at work would return them to their holystoned purity.

Once they had boarded, Stephen opened the companionway door and the ship's strong aroma, intensified by the heat, blasted out at them. The fragrance of teas and spices was overlaid by the sourness of stale bilgewater and the richness of oakum and tar. It was a familiar aroma that brought memories of past voyages.

As they descended into the heat below, it was obvious to Julia that the officers' quarters had been closed since the latest spell of hot July weather had set in. All of the mahogany doors spaced along the ivory walls of the passageway were shut. As she passed the door that led into the small cabin that had once been Clara's, she almost paused, but then she resolutely brushed on past it.

When Stephen threw open the door to the main cabin and fresh air swept through the room from the open stern windows, the warm welcome in his eyes added strength to her determination. This was where she was most wanted, where she was most needed. By his side. She smiled at him appreciatively but said nothing as she entered the room.

Laying her parasol on the table, she loosened the blue silk ribbons of her straw bonnet and glanced around to see what changes had been made during the eighteen months she had spent ashore. For six years she had watched water-reflected sunlight play over the curly walnut paneling and ivory-painted walls as it did now. The gleaming brass and the well-packed bookshelves were just as they had been when she had left them.

The freshly upholstered red velvet settee made the Brussels carpet seem faded and worn. Hours of pacing across its once rich surface had left their mark. The room seemed a little dimmer than she remembered. When she glanced up at the skylight, she understood why. The soot and dirt of Boston had grimed its outer surface. It needed a good hosing down.

She tossed her bonnet onto the settee and smoothed the black curls the wind had teased loose from her chignon during her trip on the packet.

"It's good to be home," she said with a contented sigh.

"It's where you belong." Stephen's answering smile was just a little crooked. "Welcome home, my lady."

"How soon do we sail?"

"Never could wait to get to sea, could you?" His smile widened into a grin. "Well, I hope it won't be long."

"You said the mate's ashore trying to sign on a crew?"

"Yes. If he can find them," he said more soberly, rubbing his clean-shaven chin. For the moment, he seemed to have forgotten his joy in her presence. "I've been offering the highest wages to anyone who's ever been to sea, but all I've been getting are tailors, clerks, and carpenters who don't know the mainmast from the taffrail. And I know what they want. Free passage to California."

"Well, you can't take them. That's certain." Her arched eyebrows drew together in a frown and her deep blue eyes were troubled. She had heard that it was becoming more and more difficult to find an experienced crew, but until now she hadn't realized just how serious the situation was. "If you did take them . . . Well, even if you could whip them into shape before we doubled the Horn, you'd lose them the minute we arrived in San Francisco. Then who's going to sail this ship to China?"

"Oh, I don't believe I'll have much trouble on that score." Amusement glimmered in his grey eyes. "Once I've got them aboard, that's where they'll stay."

"How do you figure that? If the whole crew decides to desert, I doubt even you'll be able to keep them aboard."

"There's a way. It's worked for other masters before me." He strolled to the stern windows and looked down at a group of men, dressed in the typical garb of the gold seekers, who were going from vessel to vessel as they tried to book passage to California. "I've found two good mates, and I'm fairly sure I can trust the steward. Perhaps one of the royal boys. That's all I'll need to get the anchor down and the sails furled. The rest of the crew are going to be locked below in the foc'sle from the time we sail through the Golden Gate until we sail out again."

"Stephen! You'll have a mutiny on your hands."

"I've been through mutinies before and no doubt I'll go through them again. A few days in irons does wonders for cooling the hottest tempers.

13

Besides . . ." He looked at her speculatively for a moment before he said, "Homer Evans will be first mate."

The name came as a shock and she gasped. "Not the one who was tried along with the master of the *Wild Swan* for brutality to the crew?"

"That's the one."

She sat down suddenly on the settee. Unconsciously pleating the silk and lace of her parasol, she considered what it would be like to sail with a man whose notorious cruelty had been denounced in every newspaper in the country.

"Do you really have to?" she finally asked.

"I have to." His voice was firm and all trace of amusement had vanished from his face. "You've already mentioned the possibility of mutiny and you're not far wrong."

"Well, I doubt the likes of Homer Evans will go far towards quelling a mutiny. Most likely just having him aboard will be enough to instigate one."

"I can control him. After thirty days in jail, no one else would take him on, so he's grateful to me. Extremely grateful. And I've given him explicit instructions. There's to be no repetition of his actions aboard the *Wild Swan*, but his name alone should enforce some kind of discipline."

"So we've come to this."

"Everyone has," he said a little impatiently. Julia was usually so quick to grasp any situation. Why couldn't she understand the present circumstances? "At least be thankful we don't have to resort to the worst of the shanghaiers. Then we'd end up with some of the lowest scum to litter a waterfront. It's what masters of older and less famous ships than the *Crystal Star* are being driven to take."

Julia slowly shook her head. It seemed strange that conditions could have changed so in the short time she had been away from the sea. Strange, but she couldn't doubt Stephen. He did know his business. Yet there must be some other way.

While she silently pondered the problem, Stephen went to the built-in cabinet and unlocked a small, private drawer. He withdrew an elaborate gilt framed picture and looked at her for a moment, as though searching for a reaction which could not yet be there. Then he handed it to her.

"It's a daguerreotype," he said.

The man staring out of the frame with a reckless air of defiance resembled Stephen, yet it was a Stephen she had never seen before. He was neatly groomed as always, with none of the whiskers she had heard the forty-niners grew, but the large brimmed hat pushed back on his head, the racy angle of his knotted neckerchief, the loose rough jacket he was wearing, and most of all the pistol that was stuck so casually in his broad leather belt, were completely uncharacteristic of him. As was the pick he held centered before him like a royal scepter.

14

"Perhaps that will help explain why we have to take extreme measures. You can see for yourself what gold fever can do to a man," he said.

"Why didn't you show this to me before?" she asked in astonishment. "Why didn't you bring it to the Cape with you?"

"I had.to be sure of you, sure that you were coming back to sea with me." He took the picture from her and looked at it as though he had never seen it before. "That's the man I was for a few months, the man I might have become permanently."

Oh, please, Stephen, she thought. Please don't bring up the past and allow it to spoil everything.

She felt a lump growing in her throat as she watched her husband, who seemed to be living in another world. The lost and lonely months of their separation were too recent for the pain to be forgotten. During that time, she'd had no word from him, no letter, despite the many she had sent. He had left her in anger, refusing to understand that, after her father's stroke, she was the only one who could hold the shipyard together. Her constant fear that she would never see him again still lingered.

"You considered remaining in California? You never mentioned that while you were home," she said sadly and wondered if the scars of their dispute would ever heal. She had so looked forward to this new beginning. She believed he had, too. If they were to make it work, she would have to make more of an effort to understand him than she had in the past. "You never even hinted at the possibility."

"No. I didn't. Once I saw you . . . Well, I put all that behind me. I really hadn't planned to ever mention it, but you have to understand what effect the scent of gold has on a man once he sets eyes on the hills of California. Look at those men out there." He nodded towards the stern windows. "They haven't even seen California, but they've thrown up everything they value in life to get there."

She gazed up at him, and as she examined his cleanly chiseled features, she tried to reconcile his face with that of the man in the daguerreotype.

"You look rather happy in that picture, Stephen. And yet from what you've told me, I thought you didn't like the place."

"I told you what was wrong with it." Stephen took a last look at the picture, then folded a length of flannel around it to protect the glass. He carefully placed it in the drawer. There was a finality about the way he turned the key. "I didn't tell you what was right."

"What *was* right about it?" she asked quietly.

"The excitement. Striking a lode and making a claim." At first his words were slow and thoughtful, but as he continued, he began to pace the length of the saloon, and the enthusiasm that enriched his voice was underlined by the rhythm of his steps.

"Watching a town being built where there had been practically nothing before. The newness of everything. The incredible feeling that, with each

15

panful of rocks and dirt you wash, you may find a fortune. And it's luck that controls everything. The poorest, hungriest man today may be the one who winds up the richest tomorrow."

"Is that the life you'd like now, Stephen? The life of a gambler? It's what you said you hated about California."

"I am a gambler. Any man who takes a ship to sea has to be a born gambler. The gaming tables are another thing. Only the professionals know the cards well enough to win at faro or *vingt-et-un*. And I wouldn't have gone back to the gold fields, either, though despite the aches and pains they gave me, they treated me well enough. No. I would have set up a business, become a merchant. I'd be willing to gamble on San Francisco. It's going to become a city so vast, it'll cover all the hills. It'll be larger than Boston someday."

Julia glanced at the locked drawer and thought about the stranger in the picture.

"If that's what you really want now, Stephen . . ."

"No. I don't know." He stuck his hands in his pockets and looked down at her thoughtfully. "It's one of those possibilities life sometimes offers. If I were a younger man, a poorer man, if I had no responsibilities, I might find it to my liking."

"And now . . . when you're no longer so young or so poor?"

He didn't answer but returned to the stern windows where he stared broodingly down at the swirling water that was filled with refuse. Julia watching him, realized that, for the first time since they had met, he'd had a dream that he hadn't shared with her. The gap between them might be closing, but it still existed. San Francisco. Well?

"If that's what you want, Stephen, then you ought to do it. You've put in your share of time at sea. We could find some place to live and then send for Clara."

"And the shipyard?" There was a touch of resentment in his voice as he turned away from the window to look at her.

She shrugged.

"Are you going to be able to leave it all behind, Julia? Your little empire? I suppose it will be yours when your father dies."

"Most likely. But what difference does that make? Papa's going to be around for years to come. Meanwhile, we have our own lives to lead." As she thought of the new life they might be able to lead in that new land, her eyes began to sparkle. Ashore she could have both her husband and her daughter with her. It was only a dread of the sea that caused Clara's illnesses. "If you want to try your luck in San Francisco, why not?"

Her sudden enthusiasm did nothing to brighten Stephen's face. Shaking his head ruefully, he banished what had in reality been only an idle dream. He was enough of a realist to know that he was a man of the sea and that he must follow the course he had charted so many years ago.

16

"It's no place for you and Clara, Julie. There aren't many decent women out there."

"Well, it can't be all that bad," she said briskly. "Aboard ship, I go for months on end without seeing another woman. I can't see the difference."

"Oh, there are women. They started pouring in as soon as word of gold reached them. The Sonorans and Chileñas. French women from the colonies at Lima and Santiago. A couple of months before I left, a ship even arrived from Marseille with about two hundred of them aboard."

"So there *are* women."

"Not the sort you could associate with." He returned to her side and reached out to stroke her hair as though he would protect her. "When I first arrived, any woman, no matter how homely, who walked down the street would empty the saloons. I don't want to put you into a situation where you're apt to be molested."

"Oh, Stephen, you know I wouldn't flaunt myself on the streets, and there must be some decent women out there. We'll just have to find a place to live that's not too close to the saloons." She slipped her hand around his back and looked up at him earnestly. "Let's do it."

His lips twisted in a smile but once again he shook his head. "Julie, you just don't understand. There's practically nothing there *but* saloons."

"From what you've told me, things change fast in California. A year could make a lot of difference. Why don't you wait till we get there before you make up your mind."

"It's already made up."

"And the man in the picture? You're going to keep him locked in a drawer the rest of your life?"

"Perhaps." He pulled out his watch and looked at it. "Damn! What's keeping the men with your trunks? I've arranged for a steam tug to tow us out into the harbor in half an hour."

"I imagine they're somewhere between here and the packet. They'll be along soon."

"I'd better go and check on them."

"And the man in the drawer?"

"Let's forget about the man in the drawer." He cupped her chin in his hand and tilted her head so that he could look deep into her eyes. Then with a smile that was gentle with love, he brushed his lips lightly across hers. "He's not the one who's important."

Julia drifted off to sleep, but some part of her mind remained alert, waiting for the sounds. When they came she wanted to roll over and bury

17

her head under the pillow, muffling out the world. Instead she rose and pulled her white silk dressing gown on over her nightgown.

The companionway door was open because the night was so hot. Mounting the narrow steps, Julia heard a heavy thud on deck, followed by a man softly cursing. She stopped before she reached the top of the steps. With her arms resting on the coaming, she tried to distinguish the shadows that moved on the moonlit deck.

Julia recognized Homer Evans standing not far from her with his arms folded. When a shape moved slowly just beyond the mainmast, she thought it must be the young second mate. However, she could recognize neither the two men bending over a dark bundle on the deck nor the man climbing over the rail to leave the ship. Stephen was nowhere in sight, but she sensed his presence nearby. Someone shifted position on the quarterdeck almost directly above her head. It had to be Stephen. She could imagine him standing there watching silently, but taking no part in what was happening aboard his ship.

Does he think he can keep his hands clean that way? she thought with a flash of anger. But then she realized that as captain, he was as much a participant as any man on the main deck, and he would recognize that just as fully as she.

"Any more?" Homer Evans snapped.

"We got another in the boat," one of the men, who was straightening up from the body on deck, said roughly.

"Well, hurry it up. We don't have all night." As the two men made for the rail, Homer Evans turned towards the crew, who stood quietly near the forecastle. "Two of you get this man below."

When there was no movement from the silent group, he started forward, menace in his quick walk. "You heard what I drecking well said."

Before he reached the waiting men, they moved aft towards him in a body. Evans stopped, and Julia could see his hand raised towards them. Something he held glinted in the moonlight.

The men had obviously seen it, too, for three of them broke away from the others and went to the figure that lay unmoving on the deck. They handled him roughly, hauling him across the deck to the forecastle hatch. The man's head lolled as though his neck had been fractured, and the sound of his feet dragging in the silence of the night scraped across Julia's nerves.

The next newly enlisted sailor could be heard before he appeared, his body banging repeatedly against the hull during his ascent. When the men on deck hauled him over the rail, Julia could see that a rope, twisted around his body and passed under his arms, was the simple device used to raise him. When they rolled him onto the deck and began untying his bonds, he appeared to be as lifeless as his predecessor. He, too, was rapidly dispatched to the forecastle, and this time the crew moved more quickly.

18

One of the men who had brought the sailors aboard started aft, and Julia ducked her head and slipped down a few steps.

"Well, sir," he began. He must be addressing Stephen. "I'll be giving you their names, and you'll be giving me the balance due."

"I thought there were to be more," Stephen said.

"They'll be along shortly, sir, but we may as well settle up as agreed on these here ones."

"No. Not until you've delivered all you promised."

"Now, Mister Browser, he won't be liking that. We always get paid on delivery, as you know, sir. Cash on the barrelhead as you might say, and Mister Browser, he might not be so willing to send any more along."

"Get on with you and stop your bloody whining," Homer Evans' voice rasped close by. "Browser's already been paid enough to cover those two. You'll get your money when and if we have enough men by midnight. Those were the terms, and tell Browser if he don't deliver, I got some interesting evidence the magistrate might enjoy discussing with him."

"I don't know what you're talking about, but I'll tell Browser." The stranger's voice was sullen, but evidently he had decided to go without further payment, for Julia could hear his footsteps retreating.

"You'd better go with them, Mister Evans," Stephen said, "just to make sure they keep to terms."

"There's a couple promised from another source, sir. Browser will deliver, but these others . . . they're the kind to slip you a dead body if you're not careful."

"Very well. Carry on and call me when the next consignment arrives."

When Stephen's footsteps sounded on the ladder leading down from the quarterdeck, Julia quickly descended the companionway steps and ran along the passage to find the shelter of her cabin. But she was too late, for even as she entered the saloon, she heard Stephen's voice calling her name. She didn't stop. She had no wish to see him or talk to him after the scene she had just witnessed.

However, she had no sooner closed the cabin door behind her and climbed into bed than Stephen opened it again. He didn't enter the room, but stood framed in the doorway with the lamp from the saloon turning him into a black and solid figure.

"If you want to watch what's going on, get dressed and come up on the quarterdeck, but don't go running around the ship in your night-clothes."

"No one saw me," she said defensively and then hated herself for being defensive. *She* wasn't the one who was in the wrong this night. "I was hidden in the companionway."

"Well, you weren't hidden very well. Evans just told me he saw you, and if he did, God knows who else was aware of you."

"Tell him he's seeing ghosts," she snapped.

"I doubt he's got enough imagination to see even the figment of a ghost. You're welcome to watch what goes on. I'm not hiding it from you, but I don't want you to go putting any ideas in the men's heads."

"It's evil, Stephen!" She jumped out of bed and faced him with her hands on her hips. "No good can come to us when we sink to these depths to obtain a crew."

"I'm not going to argue with you, Julia," he said curtly. "If you want to discuss it calmly, come out into the saloon. I'm going to have a drink."

He turned abruptly and walked back into the main cabin and she followed close behind him. When she saw him take a decanter from the specially fitted mahogany liquor chest, she was shocked. While Stephen had always enjoyed a drink, she had never before seen him take one just before setting sail. Watching him pour the golden brandy into a small crystal snifter, she almost said something about it. Then as she remembered her earlier resolution, she bit back the words. Nagging him about drinking would not help strengthen their marriage.

"You wanted to discuss the crew?" he said as he slumped down into an armchair that was bolted to the deck.

In the lamplight, she could see that his eyes were weary with a pain he could not conceal. She realized that the necessity for using these methods to obtain a crew troubled him far more deeply than she had suspected. All of her anger vanished and she felt only compassion for him. She slipped into a chair opposite him.

"What's happening to the world?" she asked. "There was a time when men would fight for a place on a good ship like the *Crystal Star*. I can't believe it's changed all that fast."

"Julia, you're still thinking in terms of a day that has gone, vanished. Men want higher wages than we can pay, especially to a green hand. So they've disappeared into the mills or they've gone West to make their own fortunes. They're rushing to the gold fields. The sea is no longer the only place that offers an opportunity to men, and there are safer, more comfortable ways of making a living. So we're left with the dregs."

"It's not right," she sad sadly. "The ships are more beautiful than anyone ever before dreamed they could be, and now you have to force men to sail them."

"Yes." He took a deep breath and suddenly looked much older. "The worst crews will sail the most beautiful ships. That's the way of life, Julie. We never thought we'd have to resort to the practices of other nations, but now we do."

"I just can't believe it." She raised her hands to push back her hair and then rested her face on her lifted palms. "There are so many honorable men who've been masters for years. How can they do it?"

"Honorable men. Yes, for the most part. At least we tried to be. But now . . . The last time I saw your cousin, William Thacher, he was complaining about the same thing. And since the *Neptune's Dragon* is a larger ship, he has more berths to fill. He says that those who come aboard willingly come aboard drunk, and those who don't come willingly . . ." He shook his head.

"You saw Cousin William? Where?"

"In Whampoa, in London. He told me that, the last time he tried to sail from New York, he had to put back for another crew before he even reached Sandy Point. The one he had originally signed on refused to obey a single order and started smashing up the ship when the mates tried to get some work out of them. For the most part, that's what we're getting. The scum."

"But in the past, 'twas only masters with reputations as bullies who had to settle for crews like that." She bit her thumb and almost felt like crying. "Now you and Cousin William. You've both always been known for your fairness."

"I suppose it still brings us the few good men left, but they're so few." He took another sip from his glass and swished the burning liquid in his mouth before he swallowed it. "And I don't like the situation any better than you do. The most we can do is pay our men higher wages than most. That's the advantage of owning what you sail. Some I've talked to, the hired shipmasters, can't even do that. The owners want every cent they can squeeze out of a vessel, and it's the men who pay."

"What about Hiram Richardson?" Julia asked as she thought about David Baxter. Master of Richardson's ship, the *Free Wind*, David was like a brother to her.

"He's an owner and he's out for a profit."

"And yet he buys the best ships. He paid top dollar for the *Free Wind* when we built her for him."

"Of course he does. Because they're the fastest. He pays his masters well, too. Offers them all sorts of bonuses for a fast passage. But he's quick in his dismissals when a master doesn't live up to his famous expectations."

"Captain Logan." Homer Evans was standing at the door. When he noticed Julia sitting there in her dressing gown, he stiffened and turned his head.

"Damn it, man!" Stephen exploded. "Don't you know enough to knock before you enter my private quarters?"

"Beg pardon, sir, but the door was open." The mate was staring woodenly at the paneling of the passageway.

"Then get the hell out of here when you see I don't want to be disturbed."

"Yes, sir. You told me to call you when the next load arrived. They're coming alongside now, sir."

21

"Well, get up on deck and see to it, Mister. What do you think I'm paying you for?"

"Aye, aye, sir." Evans vanished as quickly as he had appeared.

Stephen drained his glass, then glared at Julia. "And you sitting around here like that."

"You invited me."

"Well, from now on, get dressed or close the damned door." He picked up his cap, and striding out of the saloon, slammed the door behind him.

The sharp burst of anger that Stephen's words evoked in her dissipated quickly. Julia was far too disturbed to feel provoked with him. Never since their maiden voyage aboard the *Crystal Star*, Stephen's first command, had she seen him so tense about his ship or the men who sailed her.

And it wasn't just Stephen. All of her life she had looked up to and respected Cousin William. He had been to her the epitome of the wise and honorable shipmaster. David Baxter, too. It was almost impossible to believe that quiet, easygoing David, who could drive a ship across a sea as well as any other man, was also forced to resort to such practices. Yet if Stephen said David did, then he did. And all the other fine men she knew who sailed the seven seas, she thought sadly.

Entire crews, from the cabin boy up, who had sailed with those masters, had eventually risen to become masters in their own right. It was on ships like the *Crystal Star* that they had learned seamanship, navigation, and finally command. Her father had risen through that chain as had most of the captains she knew. Only Stephen and a very few others had come through the cabin window instead of through the hawse hole.

If the boys and the young men didn't continue to follow the sea, then who would command the ships of the future? She thought of the clippers that were now being built in her father's shipyard. To attain the speeds for which they were designed they would need the best of masters; men who'd had long and arduous training at sea. There would probably be enough such men available for the next ten or twenty years, but after that what?

The sounds on deck continued, but she had no need to look now. She had seen what she had no wish to witness ever again. All that she could do was go to bed and pray that the voyage, which she had so eagerly anticipated, would not turn out as badly as she feared.

Chapter Two

1850

Three weeks after they sailed the first man pulled a knife on Homer Evans. Despite Julia's misgivings, the voyage had not begun badly. Once they had put to sea and Stephen had sized up the crew, he began to relax. The mates he had chosen appeared to be well qualified, and the Atlantic brought fair summer weather with only occasional light storms. Although Stephen was ever alert to the problems of navigation and kept a vigilant eye on the ship, he was usually able to leave the actual running of it to his officers.

The sailors whom the boardinghouse crimps had brought aboard awoke that first morning with aching heads to find themselves at sea. When they learned that their chests had been brought aboard and that they were headed for golden California, most grinned ruefully over the memory of their last drink ashore and set to work willingly enough. There were only two who did not.

One was a brown-haired Dane named Barney, who looked at the world through uncomprehending blue eyes. The other was an Englishman whose sharp black eyes saw everything. He was known as Fair Henry, although his hair was black and there was nothing fair about his pockmarked face.

At first, Barney was indistinguishable from the landlubbers, who looked blank when given an order, as though listening to a foreign tongue. However, under Homer Evans' tutelage they soon learned the language of the sea. The Dane continued to look at the world around him as one who had been stunned.

Fair Henry was short, bandy-legged, and wiry. His greatest talent seemed to be his ability to vanish whenever a general order was given, but the mate's eye was quick to find his place of concealment. At first Evans used his fists, but soon he was stalking Fair Henry with a belaying pin. For some reason, the Englishman preferred blows to work.

As for the rest of the crew, the mate was impartial with his discipline. Anyone who did not move quickly enough or who did not perform his duties to the mate's liking would feel the same weight of the fist or the same flick from the end of a rope. But Barney and Fair Henry drove Evans into a frenzied rage.

During the leisurely hours, which had been so bleak when Stephen had sailed without Julia, he and she resumed the habits born of many voyages. By day, there were observations to be taken of the noon-high sun and of Venus, when the planet appeared as the Evening Star in the western sky

23

soon after sunset. On moonless, cloudless nights, after checking the Pole Star, they would trace the other stars to form the northern constellations of the Little and Big Dippers, the Swan and the Lyre, the Herdsman and Hercules, all of which they greeted as old friends.

At other times they walked the deck and talked of all the things that had happened during their long separation. They made plans for the future when they would sail on the new ship, which Julia had designed and which her father would begin building come autumn. They watched the wonders of the sea. The waves that changed as sun, cloud shadows, and wind played over them. The rainbows and far-off waterspouts. Often they would choose a favorite book, which Stephen would read aloud in the seclusion of the saloon while Julia sewed.

It was a comforting time, a happy time when they slowly grew back together. Scars began to heal and the bond of their marriage strengthened. In the darkness of the nights, they found once again the exciting, yet soothing familiarity of bodies well fitted together and skilled after years of practice.

Julia found herself detesting Homer Evans. Though she spent most of her time leaning on the taffrail watching their wake in order to avoid seeing what went on forward, she had to admit that she sometimes found the actions of the mate and Fair Henry diverting. She fully realized that Henry was a lazy and crafty man, but secretly she smiled when she watched him hide behind the chicken coops or conceal himself under a sheet of canvas the sailmaker had been working on. She would hold her breath whenever Evans neared the hiding place in his search for Fair Henry. She wondered if the rest of the crew felt as she did, knowing that if they did, it would shatter the much needed discipline, for they were an ill-assorted and generally incompetent lot.

The day on which the mate found Henry hiding behind the galley house was a day of high headwinds, and everyone's nerves were on edge from the constant buffeting. Julia had seen the Englishman slip around the galley. For once, she hoped that Evans would find him soon. She was on the brink of pointing him out to Stephen when the mate discovered Fair Henry.

Homer Evans raised his belaying pin in his most threatening manner as he rounded the corner to meet Henry face to face.

"You foul, sogering Limey. This is the last time you'll shirk your duties," he yelled at the man as his weapon descended.

At that instant Fair Henry slipped a knife out of his sleeve and sank it into the mate's arm. Homer Evans lost all control. The belaying pin had gone flying with Henry's thrust, but the mate didn't pause to find another. His two fists were all he really needed. In one swift motion, he had disarmed the Englishman, sent the knife skittering across the deck, and knocked Fair Henry flat on his back. After kicking twice at the man's head, Evans hauled him to his feet. While holding him with one hand, he proceeded to smash Fair Henry's face with the other. So great was his rage he didn't notice a few of the crew moving towards him. Nor was he aware that the Dane was behind him until Barney's huge hands were locked around his throat.

"Get that dumb Dane off him," Stephen shouted as he nearly catapulted from the quarterdeck onto the deck below.

The men, who had been mesmerized by the sight, now quickly surrounded the Dane. Although he shook the first three of them off like drops of water without releasing his hold on the mate, they were eventually able to break his grip around Evans' neck. The mate slumped to the deck just as Stephen reached them.

When Barney saw the captain, he stopped struggling with the men who held him and the fury in his eyes gave way to bewilderment.

The wind had picked up and Julia saw that the helmsman was having difficulty at the wheel. She glanced at the compass, noticed its swing, and ran below to get the second mate, who was off watch.

"Mister Rawlings," she shouted as she pounded on his cabin door. "Mister Rawlings! Come at once!"

The door opened so quickly she almost hit the square-faced young man with her raised hand. He wore only trousers and had obviously just sprung up from his bunk.

"Mrs. Logan!" Clyde Rawlings stammered when he saw her. He smoothed down his rumpled dark brown hair, then reached for his shirt.

"You don't have time for that," she said impatiently. "Come up on deck immediately. There's been a fight and Mister Evans is hurt."

"Should I get the guns?" He looked at her uncertainly as though he were still asleep.

"No. Just get on deck!" When she saw him glance at his shoes, she grabbed his arm, which he had just slipped into his shirt. "You don't need shoes. For heaven's sake!"

Finally convinced of her urgency, he pushed past her and ran through the passageway and up the steps to the deck. Julia wasn't far behind him.

As soon as Stephen saw them he said to the second mate, "Put that Dane in irons. He'll be flogged tomorrow morning along with his friend here . . . if he ever wakes up." Stephen nudged Fair Henry with the tip of his shoe. "As soon as you have that brute locked in, give this one the same treatment."

"Shouldn't you see what condition he's in, sir?" the second mate asked as he approached Fair Henry.

"I said take him below, Mister!" Stephen's voice was cold with controlled anger. "The carpenter can look him over once he's under restraint."

While the men were talking, Julia bent over the mate and felt for his heart. Though it was still beating, she could see the blood that was soaking his shirt and the deck beneath him. It seemed incredible that a man could lose so much blood and still live. Turning her back on the men, she started to take off one of her many petticoats when she felt Stephen's hand clamp on her arm.

"No, Julia. I'll take care of it. Rawlings, give me your shirt. Granville," he said to the steward, "go get my medical chest."

Rawlings stripped off the shirt, which he had not yet buttoned, and handed it to Stephen. Then he ordered the sailors, who still held Barney, to take the man below.

As Stephen knelt beside the mate Julia noticed the forgotten knife lying in the scuppers. She picked it up and saw that the bloody tip was sharp and pointed.

"Look," she said, handing it to Stephen. "I thought the points had been broken off all the knives."

"They were." He barely glanced at the knife before he used it to cut the bloody part of the sleeve away from the mate's arm. "Tell the helmsman to keep a steady course."

She looked up at the quarterdeck and saw that the seaman was struggling with the wheel.

"He's having a hard time of it. The wind's coming up."

"Then tell him to bear away two points."

As Julia went aft to relay Stephen's order to the helmsman, she thought about the knife. The day after they had sailed, Stephen had had all the men assembled on deck. While he had given the usual speech with which he inaugurated every voyage, the second mate and the steward had gone into the forecastle and searched the men's belongings for weapons which they had brought up on deck. The points had been broken off all the knives before they were returned to their owners. Obviously, they had either missed Fair Henry's knife during their inspection or else he had honed it back to a point. She worried as she wondered how many of the crew had followed Henry's example.

The wind increased rapidly and to the northeast lightning blazed down from ragged black clouds to strike an empty grey sea. Even before Fair Henry was in irons or the mate taken to his berth below, Stephen ordered all the crew up on deck to shorten sail. He had no choice but to take his place on the quarterdeck. Two men were ordered to carry Mister Evans to his cabin.

Julia followed them. Whether Stephen disapproved or not, someone would have to tend to the man. After the sailors had slung the mate roughly onto his bunk and stomped off, she looked at his waxy features and

26

wondered if anyone could help him. Stephen had stopped the bleeding, at least temporarily, but a man could lose only so much blood and still hope to recover. She gathered up extra blankets and piled them on top of him, but then she felt rather helpless.

The sailmaker would normally sew up the long deep gash, but he was aloft with the others. Hot broth might give Evans some strength, but with all hands called in the face of the gathering storm, the cook was also needed to work the ship. Besides she doubted that she could force liquid down his throat while he was unconscious. It was one thing to take care of a sick child, but it was altogether different when it came to a grown man. All that Julia knew to do was to sit beside him and make sure he didn't start to bleed again.

The excitement had left her feeling drained. The storm-darkened cabin gave the illusion of impending night and through the porthole, she could see spume flying off the tops of ever larger waves. The pitching of the ship and the stuffiness of the cabin made her drowsy.

Things changed so quickly at sea. Only yesterday life had been tranquil. Although the air had been relatively light, it had been strong enough to keep all the sails taut against the lift lines. The knots had reeled off behind them as they flew over sun-sparkled blue waves. It had been a happy day. The men had moved with a spring to their step as they went about their duties.

Then suddenly there was the mirage. A golden city appeared high above the sea. The details of its minarets and domes were so perfect it was hard to believe that it was composed only of sunlight and air. Too far away to see if ghosts of people walked its streets, the city gave the illusion of complete peace.

The seamen paused in their work to gape at it and no one hurried them on. The officers were also hypnotized by the apparition.

Even Stephen was drawn to the rail to stand beside Julia. She was scarcely aware of his presence until he spoke.

"There it is, Julie," he whispered. "Ombedia. I told you it existed."

She glanced away from the floating vision to look at him. The visor of his cap was pulled low on his forehead, but it couldn't conceal the excitement of the dream in his eyes. His whole face was softened with the wonder of it.

"Aye." Her voice was low as she reached out to touch the hand that was gripping the rail beside her. "I've never seen a mirage so beautiful. I'm almost afraid to breathe. It might disappear."

"Sometimes it does, but this time I think we'll keep it," he said huskily, and she knew he was thinking of the magic land he had told her about on their wedding night. She had always thought he had invented Ombedia only for her amusement, but now she realized how much he, too, wanted to believe in that fabled country.

Ombedia was to be their own private domain where they would reign as king and queen forever. He had told her that its turrets soared up into clouds and, from the topmost walls, he had promised her a view of heaven. The streets were of gold and filled with the sound of the sea. From its highest towers you could hear the ethereal music of the angels. Happiness and laughter so filled the land, there was no room for tears or pain or sorrow.

Now the dream hovered before them. It seemed only a few miles away.

"If we tacked ship, I could almost believe that we'd reach it," she said in a voice filled with yearning.

"I know." He turned his hand so that it held hers, but he never took his eyes from the vision. "We must be happy from now on, Julie. We must be."

"We are, Stephen. We will be. The mirage. It's rather like a promise, isn't it?"

"Yes." He squeezed her hand. "A promise."

The mirage seemed so substantial and remained hanging before them for such a long time, it was a shock to see it gradually fade until only the clear sky existed where the city had once been. Yet the vision left a peace on the ship as each man held the memory of it in his mind.

Later, after they had walked the evening deck and had seen the rising of the moon, Julia and Stephen went below. Since the vision had first appeared, they had spoken little. There was a deep contentment in their silence. Julia was still remembering the radiance of the mirage as she sat on the bed in her white ruffled nightgown, pulling her hair into a thick, loose braid.

As he turned from hanging up his shirt on a peg, Stephen saw that her blue eyes were unfocused, as though she were gazing on some inward thing, and that her lips were curved in a soft smile. The black stream of her hair was pushed upwards by the full breasts that were hidden by the white of her gown. He felt the hot tightening of his groin.

"Don't braid your hair tonight," he said thickly.

"Why not?" The happiness of her reverie still lingered on her face as she looked up at him.

"Because . . ." With one step, he was in front of her. He swept the loose ends of her hair out of her hands. "Because you look more like my young queen with it loose."

"The one who rules those castles in the sky?" Her smile was teasing, but there was temptation in her eyes.

"That's not the only place she rules." Unbuckling his belt, he swiftly pushed his trousers down and kicked them aside. He looked down with mocking ruefulness at his swollen stiffness.

Then he was on the bed beside her. His grey eyes smoked with blue as he pulled her to him. With one hand, he reached around her back and loosened the hair she had already braided. His hold on her was so tight, she could feel his heart pounding against her breasts, and yet when his lips met hers, his kiss was gentle.

When he pushed her down against the pillow and spread her hair across it, she could feel the first melting of her body, the liquid fire that flowed through her veins. The beginning of that golden city of Ombedia.

Homer Evans' voice brought her rudely out of her memories.

"Mary," he mumbled, his voice harsher than ever, as though the Dane had mangled his vocal cords.

"It's not Mary, Mister Evans. It's Mrs. Logan." She touched his hand to calm him, and he grasped her hand in his.

"Mary . . . don't . . ."

With her other hand, Julia felt his forehead. It was hot and dry. His grip on her hand became tighter, and she could see that his eyes were partially open and that he was looking at her. It was more like looking through her, she thought as she repressed a shudder.

"Mary . . ." he said once more and then closed his eyes. Slowly his hand relaxed its hold on hers, and his breathing resumed its shallow but regular rhythm. Julia leaned back in her chair and watched him.

She wished that Stephen, the steward, someone, would come, and she wondered if she was keeping vigil at a deathbed. She thought back to the injuries she had seen in the shipyard, the ones that had occurred during their years at sea.

The ship heaved and groaned as the full weight of the storm struck. After she had put up the bunk boards to keep the mate from rolling out, Julia began to wonder about him. Who was Mary? Stephen had said that Evans didn't care for women, and certainly his attitude towards her had confirmed her husband's opinion.

The mate had never been openly rude, but she had sensed his hostility from that first night. He never looked directly at her. If she chanced to remark on the weather, he would say, "Yes, ma'am," and move as far away from her as possible. Since general conversation with the officers was something Stephen frowned on, it hadn't really disturbed her, and since she could never bring herself to like the man, she was happy to be relieved of his company.

Now it was she who sat and watched beside his bed. Mary, she thought again. A sister? A girl he had loved? Or still did love? It didn't seem

29

possible that this man could ever have cared for anyone. Maybe he hadn't always been this way. Maybe he *had* once loved a girl, and she had jilted him to marry someone else while he was at sea. Such things often happened, but they didn't usually have such a terrible effect. Was Mary the cause of his cruelty? Was she the one he thought of when he seemed to absolutely relish tormenting the crew?

Julia shook herself. Just because the man was lying there helpless, perhaps dying, just because he had mentioned a woman's name, was no reason to romanticize him. When the square-cut, compact figure of Clyde Raw-·lings appeared in the doorway, she was more than happy to see him.

"The captain sent me to see how Mister Evans is doing, ma'am," he shouted to make himself heard over the thunder of overtaking waves. Pulling off his southwester, he shook the water from it onto the deck.

"No change," Julia shouted back. "He mumbled something once, but I doubt he was conscious."

The second mate lurched over to the bunk and pulled the blankets down from Evans' injured arm. After he had inspected the dressings, he felt the mate's bruised and swollen throat, then shook his head.

"Can't you do anything for him?" Julia asked.

"No, ma'am," Rawlings said as he unhitched a piece of line from his oilskins and proceeded to lash the mate into the bunk so that he wouldn't be tossed out of it by waves that were slamming the ship with increasing fury. "Not now. All we can do is hope he hangs on till the weather abates."

Julia rose and went to stand beside Rawlings so that she could look down at the pallid, sharp-beaked face that even in sleep seemed cruel.

"Somebody's got to help him," she yelled after a moment. "We need him."

Clyde Rawlings' brown eyes were expressionless as he looked at her from beneath dark eyebrows that ran in a straight line across his face.

"We need everyone, ma'am, and with Mister Evans out of action and two men in irons, we're too shorthanded to help anyone but the ship."

"There must be something I can do. If someone would just tell me what's best for him. I feel so *damned* useless."

His brows jumped when he heard her swear and he looked at her in shocked surprise. Up until now, he'd considered the captain's wife a perfect lady. He quickly recovered his composure and his voice betrayed no emotion when he shouted back.

"Not much to be done. You try to sew up that wound without help in this weather, like as not you'll only open it again."

A rogue wave slammed against the side of the ship. Though Julia clutched at the bunk boards, she was thrown up against the young man. His normally fresh color heightened as he tightened the last knot. Then he quickly moved towards the door.

"Is that all you're going to do?" Julia shouted at him in alarm.

"Yes, ma'am." He put his southwester on and squared the brim. "I've got to get back on deck. The captain said not to be long."

Julia spent that stormy night and part of the following morning at her solitary vigil. From time to time the steward would look in but, for the most part, she was alone. The ship would shudder and heave upright as she slid into the deep troughs where high walls of water cut off the wind. Then as the seas overtook her and lifted her to the crest of each following wave, she would be slammed on her side again.

Sleep became impossible even on the mattress the steward had laid on the cabin deck. Instead Julia sat in a straight chair that was lashed to the wall and clung to it with both her hands. Even so, she was occassionally flung onto the deck, but she was determined to continue her watch.

In the dark she could see nothing except the white foam of the hissing sea that often covered the porthole. She felt that it was too dangerous to light a lamp. Each time she rose to check on the mate, she could only moisten his lips, listen to his breathing, and lightly touch the linen that bound his wound. Once the blood on it seemed sticky, but the next time she examined it she was sure it was dry and caked. When the dim light of morning finally came, she could find no change in his condition. Perhaps his breathing was lighter than it had been before.

It seemed an eternity before Stephen finally came below. As always during rough weather, she was relieved to see him, for the dangers of the deck were never far from her mind. He looked tired and haggard, but he had survived the night with no injuries. Although he glanced at her with a tight smile, his first thought was for the mate.

"See it hasn't opened up again," he shouted as he leaned over the bunk. "Any signs of consciousness?"

"I don't think so." She rose to stand beside him, just to be near him. His dripping oilskins didn't matter. The cabin was so cold and clammy, and her clothes so heavy with moisture, the damp chill penetrated through her dress to the flesh beneath. "It's hard to tell. 'Twas too dark. Not long after they brought him down, he said something. Sounded like a girl's name. Mary."

"A girl?" He checked the lashings that held the mate in place. "Not likely. Could have been anything. I've got to get back on deck. I'll send the sailmaker below with Mister Rawlings. You can go when they arrive."

"I'll stay and help." She used the excuse of a particularly rough wave to sway against him and then cling to him. It wasn't so much that she wanted to detain him as to reassure herself of his solidity.

31

"No." He squeezed her heartily with one arm and then turned to go. "Not enough room in here for three people."

"Just send the sailmaker. I'll help him. You need Mister Rawlings on deck."

"Do as I tell you, Julie," he shouted. "You don't have the strength to hold him down if he starts thrashing about. And it's not your place to nurse the men."

"Some masters' wives do it."

"Well, my wife doesn't! When they come below, get out of here."

There was no anger in his eyes, only a great weariness. The loss of the mate had made the night doubly hard for him, and until Mister Evans recovered, the days ahead wouldn't be much better, Julia reminded herself.

"Sorry. I just wanted to help," she said as amiably as she could while shouting at the top of her lungs. "What happened to Fair Henry?"

"God knows!" He shoved himself away from the bunk and grabbed the door frame as he fought the list of the ship. "He's the last thing that concerns me."

When the sailmaker and the second mate arrived, Julia was happy enough to leave. It was a relief to lie down in the hammock the steward had slung in her cabin and burrow into the quilts while she tried to forget the events of the last thirty hours. She was glad the fury of the wind and waves, the creaking groans of the hull, and the screaming of the masts and yards made it impossible to hear any sounds from the mate's cabin. Why had she ever wanted to go to sea? she wondered. The men who preferred the factories and the gold fields were certainly saner than she was.

The punishment of Barney and Fair Henry was delayed for another day, but once the sea had grown calmer, Stephen had the company assembled and the two men brought on deck. With the mate disabled and still hovering on the edge of death, the mood aboard ship had grown uglier. Rawlings tried, but he didn't have the control. When it came to moving men along with blows, he didn't bring the swiftness or relish to the job that Evans did. A lot of the men tended to linger over their duties, which brought resentment from the men who didn't.

There was no turning back for a new mate or a fresh crew. Knowing that something had to be done immediately, Stephen made two decisions. The first was that discipline would have to be enforced by stronger means than cuffs and blows. Now the first two men who would feel the weight of his decision stood before him.

"Well, what do you have to say for yourself?" Stephen asked as he stared at Fair Henry.

"He were going ter 'it me, Mister Evans were. I were jest defendin' meself." The man stared malignantly back. Aside from a few bruises and cuts on his face, Fair Henry seemed undamaged.

"You were attacking an officer with a knife," Stephen said sternly. "When you signed the Articles, you knew what the penalty for that would be."

"I din' sign no h'Articles."

"There's an X below your name, witnessed and attested to. How do you explain that?"

"I din' sign nothink. Were someone else."

"You were drunk when you signed them. It's no wonder you can't remember. Now listen to me. You are here to work this ship, and work it you shall if I have to drive you every step of the way."

"Oh, stop yer nattering and git h'it over with. You know yer're going ter 'ave me flogged. I know yer're going to ter 'ave me flogged. So le's be done with h'it."

"So you're insolent as well as lazy and vicious. Well, if flogging's what you want, flogging's what you'll get. You heard him ask for it, men?" Stephen looked at the sailors one by one until each nodded his head. "Very well. You'll have your flogging, and I want you men to watch carefully. It won't be the last you'll see. I've been too easy on you, but now that's come to an end. Any man who shirks his duty, any man who displays insolence to an officer, that man is going to feel the taste of the rope or worse. Mueller, Hogan, seize that man up."

Two of the largest sailors stepped up to the condemned man and removed his jacket and shirt. When they led him towards the shrouds, Julia could see the lines that crossed his back, old scars that bore witness that this was far from his first flogging. While Mueller and Hogan placed Fair Henry against the shrouds and bound his wrists to them, Stephen examined the faces of the crew. Among them there had to be one who hated the Englishman, and then Stephen found him. Most of the sailors stood by with faces as blank as they could manage, but one young man, who had not so long ago been a farmboy, wasn't able to hide the smile that tugged at the corner of his lips.

"Cooper, pick up that rope." Stephen pointed at the short length that lay at his feet.

"Me, sir?" There was no longer any semblance of a smile. In fact, the young man looked frightened.

"Yes, you." Stephen watched as the sailor picked up the thick, strong rope, which had been unraveled at one end. "Now get over there and see what you can do with it."

"You want me to hit him, sir?"

"That's what I had in mind."

"I've never done anything like that before, sir."

33

"You'll learn. Get on with it if you don't want to earn a few strokes for yourself."

"Aye, aye, sir." The young man stumbled in his haste. When he reached the shrouds, he glanced back uncertainly at the captain.

"Get on with it," Stephen ordered.

"I don't mean nothing by it, Henry," the young man said.

"You heered what the cap'n said. Git h'it over with," Henry snarled at him.

Raising the rope over his head, Cooper brought it awkwardly down on Henry's back.

"Not like that!" Stephen shouted and strode across the deck to rip the rope from the man's hands. "Like this," he said and brought the rope whistling down on the back that was bared in front of him. The Englishman jerked and his feet left the deck, but he made no sound. Stephen handed the rope back to Cooper.

This time, the seaman applied the rope so hard it broke the skin, and he looked back at the captain for approval.

Stephen nodded at him. "Again."

By the time the seventh stroke had been applied, there were trickles of blood flowing down Fair Henry's back. Julia turned away from the scene to go to the taffrail and stare at the clean wake that flattened the waves astern of them. The man deserved it. She knew he did. Especially when she thought of Homer Evans lying below in a semistupor. Yet even that thought didn't make the sounds of the rope any easier to bear. When the Englishman began to scream on the tenth stroke, Julia wanted to run and hide in her cabin, but if she did, she would have to pass close to the scene of punishment. It was better to stand here with her hands clutching the rail and her throat held tight to keep her breakfast from rising.

Finally she heard Stephen say, "Cut him down and get him out of my sight. Bring that Dane here."

When the noises on deck indicated that they had gotten the Englishman below, Julia turned, ready to flee to her cabin and hide there until it was all over, but the sight of Barney's face arrested her.

He stood abjectly with his head hanging so that his brown hair almost obscured eyes that peered up at the captain with the unreasoning fear of a dog who is being punished but does not know why.

"Do you have anything to say for yourself?" Stephen asked him.

For all the reaction Barney had to his words, Stephen might never have spoken. Not a muscle of his body, not a blink of those blue eyes betrayed anything but stupefied terror.

"You're charged with assaulting an officer with intent to kill." Stephen watched the man for a moment, and then said impatiently, "Speak up, man." When there was still no response, he nodded. "Seize him up."

As they began to strip him, Julia slipped quickly down the steps and went below. Seeing Fair Henry flogged was bad enough, but to see a man who was little better than some dumb animal afforded the same treatment was more than she could stand.

To remind herself of the reason for the punishment that was being carried out, Julia rapped on the door of the mate's cabin. When there was no answer, she pushed the door open and found that the man was alone. As she leaned over the bunk to check his bandage, he opened his eyes and looked at her. It was the first time she had seen him truly conscious since he'd been wounded.

"Water," he croaked.

She found a partially filled glass on the built-in chest opposite his bunk and picked up a towel that was lying on the back of the chair. After she had laid the towel under his chin, she held the glass to his lips. He managed a couple of sips, and then started choking. She tried to raise his head on the pillow with one arm, but he suddenly snatched the glass out of her hand. After taking a long swallow, he dropped the glass over the side of the bed, wetting Julia's skirt with the last of the water.

"Is there anything else I can get you, Mister Evans?" she asked after she had picked up the glass.

"What?" He pointed overhead.

She looked at him perplexed for a moment, but then when he gestured forward, she understood. The howlings of the Dane were all too audible.

"The men who attacked you are being flogged," she said.

"Got . . ." he muttered unintelligibly as he struggled to sit upright.

"You mustn't do that, Mister Evans. You've lost a lot of blood and you're very weak."

He managed to push the bedclothes away from his body, and Julia suddenly realized that he had nothing on. After the first glance she firmly pulled the covers up and pushed him back onto the bed.

"You mustn't do that!" she repeated sternly as she would to a child. "You might open that wound again, and you've lost quite enough blood already." When he still persisted in trying to move, she added, "Mary wouldn't like it if you damaged yourself."

"Mary!" He stared at her in horror and then pulled the bedclothes up over his head.

If he would just stay like that, she thought as she quickly left the cabin, he would be all right, but he had seemed determined to go on deck to witness the punishment of his assailants. Someone should have been left to watch the mate. Much as she hated the thought of it, she would have to go to fetch help. As she passed the steward's pantry, she heard a noise and went in to investigate. The steward was leaning against the counter with a bottle raised to his lips.

"Granville! What are you doing?"

35

She was shocked, for the *Crystal Star* was supposed to be a dry ship, and no member of the crew was allowed to drink while aboard. What startled her even more was to find Granville doing such a thing. He was the oldest member of the crew, as his bushy thatch of grey hair attested. Having quickly risen to become an able-bodied seaman, he had never been capable of filling even a third mate's berth, but he could still hand, reef, and steer with the best of them. However, he had chosen to follow the less arduous life of a steward. Over the years he had drifted from vessel to vessel, and according to all reports, he was reliable and loyal.

"Medicine," Granville said as he slowly lowered the bottle and looked at her speculatively to see if she believed him. "Just a little medicine, Mrs. Logan."

"What do you need medicine for?" she asked suspiciously. "You're not sick."

"I'm sick of what's going on up on deck," he said defensively.

"Where did you get that bottle?"

When he didn't answer, she looked at it more closely. "I believe that brandy belongs to the captain, Granville. You'd best put it back before he finds out. I've half a mind to go up and tell him."

"No. Please, Mrs. Logan." The steward's eyes were filled with sudden fear as he quickly corked the bottle. "He'd have me hitched up to the shrouds next. It's bad enough listening to them."

"Well you wouldn't have to listen if you were where you belong," Julia said with disgust. "Did Captain Logan tell you to stay with Mister Evans?"

"Just told me to keep an eye on him," Granville mumbled, hastily returning the bottle to a cabinet to which only he and the captain had keys.

"Well, you're not keeping an eye on him!" Julia was becoming completely angry with the man. "I was just in Mister Evans' cabin, and he's trying to get out of bed. You'd best get in there fast and stop him, or I'm going to the captain with the whole story." She glanced at the cabinet, which he had just completed locking. "Brandy and all."

The steward quickly pocketed the keys and beat a swift retreat out of the pantry without another word. As soon as he had disappeared into the mate's cabin, Julia went to the bottom of the companionway steps and listened. She could hear Stephen's voice, but there was no other human sound. They must have finished with the Dane.

"Now if any of you have never seen a flogging before, I've added to your education. The next man who strikes an officer, indeed the next man who speaks back to an officer, or is found to be shirking his duties, will be asking for a taste of food from the same table," Stephen was saying. "And if any of you men don't know what hazing is, ask your shipmates, for if this ship isn't sailed perfectly and kept in trig condition, hazing will become standard procedure."

He paced up and down in front of the men who stood assembled before him. As he passed each man, he looked at his face as though he were making a judgment. When he resumed his place, he said, "Since the mate is temporarily incapacitated, I need a third mate, and I want you men to choose one from among yourselves."

There was silence from the crew. They knew it was only a formality. By offering to let them make their own choice, the captain was following tradition, but they would under no circumstances choose the man they would have to obey.

"Well, speak up," Stephen said. He waited another moment, and then said, "Joe Smithers, step up here."

A tall and lanky, rawboned young man moved aft. He was a Yankee who had sailed before the mast for five years, ever since he had turned thirteen. He had been one of the few members of the crew with any experience who had voluntarily signed the Articles. Stephen nodded at him, then looked at the other men again.

"Mister Smithers is your third mate. You are to obey him and accord him the respect due an officer, and don't forget that he now has a handle to his name. *Mister* Smithers, pack your gear and move aft to the officers' quarters."

"Aye, aye, sir." Joe Smithers looked honored by the compliment, but he seemed uncomfortable with his new status.

"And you'll come below with me now. Mister Rawlings, carry on."

"Well, Mister Smithers, so you've become an officer," Stephen said as he seated himself behind the table in the saloon.

"As you wish, sir," the sandy-haired young man said. He held his shoulders stiffly back and tried to feel like an officer.

"Do you think you can give orders as well as take them?" Stephen's eyes cooly searched the young man's windburned, sun-reddened face as he wondered if he had made the right choice. Unfortunately, there was no other member of the crew he could trust to fill the job. However, it wouldn't do to let Smithers guess there was no one else.

"Yes, sir, I believe so, but . . ." Smithers nervously clasped and unclasped his hands behind his back.

"But what?" Stephen shot at him. "If you have any doubts about your ability, I want to hear them now. I can find another man to replace you."

Smithers swallowed. This was the chance he had waited for for so long, yet it had come in such a strange way. He wasn't replacing another man. He would just be standing in for him.

"It's just that it's going to be difficult, sir."

"Difficult?" Stephen barked at him. "Of course it'll be difficult. There's no such thing as an easy life at sea."

"Yes, sir, but you see, in my case, when Mister Evans recovers and I return to the forecastle, the men won't exactly welcome me back with good will."

"Who said anything about returning to the forecastle?"

"I just presumed, sir."

"Then don't presume. You're not being paid to presume. Unless you fail to handle the duties of second mate properly, you won't be going back. I can use you even after Mister Evans is on his feet again. If you aren't able to perform the duties of an officer, then I'll have no choice but to return you, will I, Mister Smithers?"

"No, sir." The newly appointed third mate fought hard to repress a grin. So it was true. He really had made it to the quarterdeck! If he performed his duties well and pleased the captain, then most likely he would never have to sail before the mast again. His place would be aft.

"Now you know where your loyalty lies," Stephen said firmly. He understood the trend of his new junior officer's thoughts, and was reassured that he had chosen the right man. The only thing that disturbed him was the transparency of Smithers' face. Well, he would learn. "Your loyalty is no longer with your former shipmates, no matter what friends they were of yours in the past. Do you understand me?"

"Yes, sir," Smithers said briskly. "It's an honor, sir."

"We'll see how much of an honor it is." Getting up and going to a locked cabinet, Stephen selected a key from the ring he carried. The time had come to implement his second decision. He opened the cabinet and chose a pistol.

"Here," he said as he handed the weapon to the third mate. "Carry this with you at all times."

Smithers took the gun and stuck it through his belt, but the question he dared not ask showed plainly in his sky-blue eyes.

"You know the mood forward of the mast?"

"Yes, sir."

"What do you think of it?"

"There's some good men, sir."

"But not many?" Stephen looked at him penetratingly.

"No, sir. Not many."

"Then I think you should realize even more than I do why it's necessary for you to be armed."

"Yes, sir." Smithers fingered the butt of the pistol and wondered if he would ever actually have to use it. He didn't relish the thought.

"You *can* shoot, can't you?" Stephen asked, sensing the young man's apprehensions.

"Oh, yes, sir."

"Do you feel you're capable of taking the quarterdeck alone for half an hour?"

"Now, sir?"

"Yes, now. Did you think I meant next year?"

"No, sir. I'm sure I can, sir."

"Then convey my regards to Mister Rawlings and ask him to come below."

After discussing matters with Rawlings and arming him, Stephen went to his cabin, where Julia was sitting with her sewing in her lap. Rather than stitching, she had been listening to the interviews through the crack in the door.

"You're aware of what's happening?" Stephen asked her.

"You're expecting a mutiny," she said flatly.

"I don't know whether there'll be one or not, but we have to plan for one."

"And we're only three weeks out."

"Yes. As you said in the beginning, it's going to be a long voyage." He handed her the pistol he had carried into the cabin. "Keep it with you at all times, and if you have to use it, I hope your aim is as good as it was in China."

She took it from him and examined it thoughtfully. "It was one thing to shoot a Chinese pirate," she said, "but it's going to be another to turn it on one of our own men."

"When the time comes, it won't matter what color his skin is. All you have to do is realize that he's going to kill you if you don't act first. You'll do it. I'm more sure of you than I am of young Smithers. It's a pity you aren't a man. I'd make you an officer."

"Just as well I'm not." She tried to put last night's memories into her smile, to do anything to lighten this awful day. "Besides I doubt I'd be much good when it came to discipline."

"Then how did you manage to run a shipyard?" He cocked one tawny brow and his grin was not so half-hearted as hers had been.

"That was different." She sighed as she carefully laid the gun on the bed beside her with its muzzle pointed at the bulkhead. "The flogging, the hazing . . . Stephen, that Dane. I don't think he can speak any English. He simply doesn't know what's wanted of him."

"He knew enough to throttle Evans," he said brusquely.

"Yes, I saw it. It's the first time I've ever seen him react to anything. Do you think he's insane?"

39

"Do you?"

"I think so. I've watched him. Do you know, even if he could speak English, I don't think he'd understand. I have a feeling he was shanghaied in Denmark when he was a boy and that he's been sailing around the world ever since, dumped from ship to ship."

"You think he was born that way?" He glanced at her quizzically.

"Born that way or beaten into it. I think he's the most dangerous man on this ship."

"He doesn't have the brains to be dangerous." Stephen glanced up at the telltale compass that was directly above the bed. They were on course. "Frankly, it's some of the others I'm worried about, especially that Fair Henry."

"But Fair Henry's predictable!" She impatiently pushed her sewing away. "You know what he might do. Barney could break out at any moment over nothing. And he's strong."

"I can't keep the man in irons for the rest of the trip. As you say, he's strong. I need him."

"Didn't you see the look in his eyes?" she persisted. "He didn't know why he was going to be flogged."

"But he knew he was going to be flogged."

"Only because he saw it happen to Henry."

"Well, what do you suggest, Julia? One minute you say he's dangerous. The next, you hint that he shouldn't have been flogged because he's not responsible. What can I do with him? Shoot him?"

"Maybe you could lock him up."

"Don't you think that's crueler than a flogging?" He took the few steps to the stern windows that were caulked shut for the duration of the voyage. The dark blue summer sea of the Atlantic was again rolling along smoothly beneath its white crests, as if the storm had never happened. "Think of it. Never to breathe fresh air, never to see anything but the dark walls of one small room for over three months."

Julia looked past him at a shoal of flying fish that shot across their wake. She thought of how the sailors loved to capture the creatures and flatter the cook into preparing the fish for them. She'd seen Barney capering around deck in pursuit of them.

"But what can you do with him?" she asked helplessly. "Haven't you ever run into this sort of thing before?"

"Yes. Once. The man killed one of his shipmates and then jumped overboard. We tried to save him, but he fought off all attempts at rescue. Eventually a shark got him."

"So long as Barney's free, no one's safe," she warned him.

"We'll just have to keep an eye on him. I'll see to it that he's put on solitary jobs," he tried to reassure her. Putting his arm protectively around her shoulders, he pulled her to him.

40

"I'm just glad Clara's not aboard," she said, her voice muffled in the folds of his shirt.

"Yes." Stephen sighed and stroked the handle of the pistol which he had tucked into his belt. "So am I."

Chapter Three
1850

The mate's recovery was slow, but as soon as he could rise from his bunk, he insisted on going on deck. There he watched the two junior officers as well as the rest of the crew with a malevolent eye. Though he didn't have the strength to use belaying pins or fists with his former zealous fervor, his hand often rested on the butt of the pistol he carried at his waist.

With his return, the tensions aboard ship, which had never relaxed, grew greater, but at last Stephen was able to get some sleep. While the mate had been confined to his cabin, Stephen had been on deck almost twenty-four hours a day through all vicissitudes of weather. His short naps had been snatched while lying fully clothed on the settee in the saloon with his gun near at hand.

Stephen had never encouraged his officers to use the saloon for more than meals. Now he welcomed them. They were, he felt, additional protection for Julia. Usually, the second and third mates fell exhausted into their bunks during their few hours off duty. Only Homer Evans availed himself of the saloon privilege. When the weather was unpleasant, Julia would take refuge there with her sewing or a book. She often wondered what Homer Evans thought about.

He would sit staring into space with his arms crossed against his chest and his legs stretched out before him, never speaking unless someone addressed him first. There was something unnerving about his colorless eyes with their strange small pupils. His gaze wasn't absent. He actually seemed to be seeing something. Sometimes Julia was aware that his eyes rested on her when she was immersed in a book, and she felt especially uneasy.

One day he spoke, which made Julia practically jump out of her chair, she had grown so used to his silence.

"Did I talk much when I was out?" he asked in his harsh voice.

"What?" Julia looked at him in surprise.

"When I was unconscious, what did I say?"

"Why, I wasn't with you that long. I don't know what you said."

"You heard me say something. What was it?"

She couldn't decide whether his expression was one of anger, fear, or embarrassment. "You just mentioned a girl's name. That's all."

"Mary?"

"Yes. Your sister?"

"Sister!" For the first time, she heard the mate laugh, and even that was grating. "She's no sister of mine. She's a limb of Satan."

Julia found that she preferred the mate's silences to his conversation and decided to put an end to it. Picking up her needle, she concentrated on guiding a piece of thread through the eye.

"I didn't say anything else?"

"No, Mister Evans, not to my knowledge."

"She wasn't human. She married my father, but she must have bewitched him."

"Then she was your mother?" Julia found herself drawn into the conversation out of curiosity.

"No mother of mine. She wanted me to call her mother, but young as I was, I knew my mother was in her grave."

"I'm sorry to hear that, Mister Evans."

"Sorry. That's what they all say. Women." From the way he looked at her, Julia knew that he included her in his contempt.

She thought about going on deck, but they were beset with headwinds again. The motion of the ship told her that spray would be blowing aft to soak the quarterdeck. There was her cabin, but she didn't feel like being cooped up in the smaller space. There seemed to be nothing to do but stay in the saloon and hope that the mate would lapse into silent contemplation again. She was soon disappointed.

"Did your mother beat you when you were little?" He leaned forward with his arms on his bony knees and watched her intently.

"Occasionally. When I was bad." She turned the cloth and examined a patch she was putting on an old but warm skirt.

"What did she use?"

"Her hand, though I remember once when she used her hairbrush."

"Did she hit you hard?"

"No, not really."

"Mary did. She hit me with a heavy stick. All over, especially the place . . . places it hurt most. Sometimes she beat me until I was unconscious."

"That's terrible!" She glanced at him and saw that the lips beneath his beaked nose were grimmer than ever. "Didn't your father stop her?"

"My father was away at sea. He was a mate, like me. When he was due home, she'd only hit me where the bruises wouldn't show, and she'd threaten to kill me if I told him. She would have, too."

"How awful." Could his story possibly be true or was this just another one of those tall tales sailors often invented to spin away the long hours at sea? No. She vividly remembered his look of terror the day Fair Henry and Barney were flogged. "Wasn't there someone you could go to? Someone who could help you?"

"No one. Then my father died when I was ten, and she shipped me off to follow him. I was glad to go. It was safe at sea. No one could ever haze me as bad as she did."

"Where is she now?" Julia asked, for she could see that the vicious woman still haunted him.

"Dead. Murdered. No one ever found out who did it."

"Oh?" Julia didn't know what else to say. She couldn't very well ask him if he'd done it.

"She's waiting for me, though. Sometimes at night she comes to me, but I'm ready for her. I'm bigger than she is now, and I know more tricks than she ever thought of. They say she screamed a lot when she was being murdered, but no one could hear her." There was actually a smile on those taut lips.

My God! Julia thought. How many madmen do we have aboard this ship?

"I'm sure she won't trouble you anymore," she said soothingly.

"No, she won't nor will anyone else who wants to make trouble for me. But I'll protect you, Mrs. Logan. I won't let anyone hurt you, not even Mary."

"Well, thank you. I appreciate that." She tried not to look at his gun, but she was aware that his hand now rested on it. "I hope it won't be necessary."

She surreptitiously slipped her hand into the heavy pocket she had stitched onto her skirt to carry her pistol, concealed and yet always ready. The metal felt warm and reassuring to her fingers.

The mate lapsed back into silence and folded his arms across his chest again. Julia relaxed, but she was afraid to leave the room now. She couldn't let him sense her fear. If she went on deck, he might think she was running to Stephen for protection. If she went into her cabin, he would know that she was hiding from him. She tried to look calm as she returned to her sewing, but her stitches were clumsy and she pricked her finger more than once.

Finally Stephen came below and told the mate to take a turn on deck. Julia wanted to blurt out the story, but seeing the complete exhaustion on her husband's face, she hesitated. In that moment Stephen went into their cabin, lay down, and went immediately to sleep.

* * *

43

Several days passed before she felt she could disturb Stephen with the matter. Then one morning she awakened with the firm resolution that today she would tell him. Soon they would be closing in on Cape Horn, and her chance would be gone until they reached the Pacific.

However, this was also the day when Homer Evans decided once more to break his silence. She had been so involved in *The Old Curiosity Shop*, which she was reading for the first time, she had actually been able to forget the mate's presence for a while.

"You didn't say anything to the captain, did you?" His voice grated above the song of the ship, which was running sweetly before the wind.

"Anything about what?" She decided to treat their previous conversation as though it had never happened.

"About Mary."

"No. I thought if you wanted him to know, you'd tell him yourself." She continued to look resolutely down at her book. She had no desire whatsoever to discuss anything with him, especially Mary.

"That's good. I've been watching him." He dropped his voice into a rasping whisper. "If you'd gone to him, I'd have known. You're safe as long as you don't repeat what I told you. So's the captain."

"Safe?" This was getting worse all the time. He was actually threatening her.

"Safe from Mary. She makes me do things sometimes."

"It's all right, Mister Evans." Julia had had enough. She decided to try a threat of her own. If he had been going to sea since he was ten, he was bound to be superstitious. She put a marker in her book and put it on her lap to cover her gun pocket. Then she narrowed her eyes and said in a hushed voice. "It's the *Crystal Star*, you see. She won't let Mary hurt me."

"What?" It was his turn to look surprised.

"Didn't you know I helped my father design and build this ship?"

"No. No woman ever did that." He clamped his thin mouth shut in absolute disbelief.

"I did." Staring at him intently, she challenged those pale eyes to contradict her again.

"I believe you," he said finally.

"And you do know that ships have souls, don't you?" Her smile was more savage than any he'd ever seen on a lady's face, and he moved uneasily in his chair.

"Some say they do."

"They do. I'm certain you've heard of the vessel that avoided going on the rocks by refusing to answer the helm. And what about the one that sailed herself into a safe harbor when all the crew were incapacitated by scurvy?"

"I've heard of them. Knew a man that was on the first one."

"Well, the *Crystal Star* has a soul. I know because she takes care of me. You see . . . nothing can happen to me as long as I'm on board her, and if anyone tries to harm me or anyone who belongs to me, she'll punish them. You know a ship can do all kinds of things, don't you, Mister Evans? A line can break, a block can whip loose very suddenly, a rail can let go when you're least expecting it."

"Yes." Homer Evans stared at her with almost the same sort of horror he had shown when she had first mentioned the name Mary. He quickly rose and picked up his cap. "I'm going up on deck. The captain could most likely use some sleep."

"I think he could, Mister Evans," she said sweetly. "You wouldn't want him to suspect you of sogering, would you?"

After the mate had beat his hasty retreat, Julia rested her head against the back of the settee and stared at the overhead. Now she was doubly afraid to tell her husband about the man. Stephen was sure to give it all away by a questioning glance, a sharp look. It would be impossible to put Evans in irons now. They would need the mate until after they'd gained the Pacific. The man was dangerous. There was no doubting that. If he suspected Stephen knew and planned to take steps against him, Evans was quite capable of causing what would appear to have been an accident in the vicious elements the Horn would loosen on them.

Afterwards, she thought. I'll tell Stephen afterwards. In the meantime, I only hope Evans believed me about the ship. He's mad enough to believe almost anything, but if it's necessary, I'll have to arrange some sort of "proof."

However, as it turned out, it wasn't necessary to arrange the proof. The proof arranged itself.

As they neared Cape Horn, more and more vessels were sighted. In the past, they had counted themselves lucky if they spoke another vessel more often than once a week in these dangerous waters. Now Julia was astonished to see the sails of as many as twenty vessels surrounding them at any one time. They were of all rigs and conditions. Occasionally, a grand clipper would appear, skimming the surface of the sea as she slowly overtook and passed the *Crystal Star*, but more often the *Crystal Star* swiftly overtook and passed the segments of this motley fleet. They were hogged brigs and fast barks, Baltimore clippers and schooners, all racing to get their argonauts to San Francisco. Vessels that had never been designed with Cape Horn in mind were cheered on by their passengers each time they approached another vessel.

Sailing by the Falkland Islands, where in the past, the only sounds to be heard were the deep, long breathings of shoals of whales and grampuses as they broke the surface of the sea, they now heard men's voices filling the air. A thick, heavy fog rolled over them just after they passed Staten Island, and Stephen had Julia dress in her warmest clothes and prepare for a night on deck.

With the coming of the fog, the wind died, and the ship rolled with slatting sails in the slick sea. Oil lamps were lit and attached to the shrouds as beacons to warn away any vessel that approached them too closely even though, by the time the lights were seen, it would probably be too late. As a further signal, the ship's bell was rung at one-minute intervals. Occasionally other bells could be heard, but sounds traveling through the wandering tunnels of fog were unpredictable, and there was no way to tell how close the other bell might be or, indeed, from which direction it had come.

Here, where there had always been danger to spare from the wind and sea, the hazard of being rammed was now added. Despite their precautions, a strange vessel might loom up at any moment. If her appearance were accompanied by one of the sudden winds that swept these latitudes, the damage could well be irreparable. Julia thought of how the *Jewel of the Seas* had been lost in the crowded anchorage at Hong Kong when another ship had rammed her. Here there was no forgiving beach to salvage any errors, and no man could survive these freezing waters for more than a minute or two. She shivered as she huddled in a corner of the quarterdeck and burrowed deeper into her furs and blankets.

Stephen had considered anchoring to wait out the fog, but then had decided against it. Too many of the other vessels were in inexperienced hands, and there might be no time to slip the cable in order to run for safety.

Most of the men had elected to spend the night on deck rather than run the risk of being trapped in the ship and carried to an icy grave. Few words were spoken as everyone strained to hear the least sound that might give warning of impending peril. What noises the ship herself made were almost completely blotted out by the heavy fog. When men passed near Julia, it was as though they had walked out of a wall of white, and even then their forms were insubstantial. Unless he stayed close to another, each man felt that he was alone.

Despite hours of intense listening, Julia felt herself growing drowsy and knew it was the cold. To fight its effects, she thought she'd better make an effort to walk around the quarterdeck. As she was about to rise, she was aware of an indistinct form crouched near her. Danger seemed to fill the thick air between them. Without thinking, she screamed, "Stephen!"

Immediately Stephen and the first and second mates were at her side. Where the form had been, there were now two locked together. Clyde Rawlings sprang forward with his gun drawn, and the fog lightened enough to reveal the third mate, Joe Smithers, tangling with a Portuguese sailor who wore a golden hoop in one ear. When Rawlings stuck his pistol into the man's ribs, the Portuguese let his hands fall and allowed the two mates to shove him towards Stephen.

"He had this, sir," Smithers said as he handed a knife to Stephen.

"Damn it!" Stephen exploded after he had examined the point that had been honed on the knife. "How many times do we have to collect the knives and break them? Tell the men that the next one caught with a pointed knife in his possession is going to be seized high up on the rigging and doused with water."

"He'd freeze to death, sir." Rawlings looked nervous.

"Yes, he would, wouldn't he?" Stephen said caustically.

"What do you want done with this scum?" Evans asked, his thin smile sadistic with anticipation.

"Did he have the knife drawn?" Stephen asked the third mate.

"Yes, sir," Smithers said.

Stephen grabbed the man by the front of his tattered jacket. "What were you going to do with that knife?"

"No understand," the man moaned.

"You understand. What were you doing up here on the quarterdeck?" He hit the Portuguese in the face with the flat of his hand.

"No understand."

"Put him in irons." Stephen gave the man a final shake and pushed him towards Smithers. "He'll understand them well enough."

"No. Please, Captain." The man tried to sink to his knees, but Smithers pulled him up sharply. "Justa want talk to lady. Warna her."

"With a knife in your hand?" Stephen balanced it on his palm. "What kind of talking did you have in mind?"

Tears rolled down his brown cheeks as he started to wail. "No, Captain. Please no, Captain."

"Take him below," Stephen said in disgust. "I'll decide what to do with him later. Get back to your posts," he added to the first and second mates.

When they had disappeared through the fog, he turned to Julia. "What did he do to you?"

"Nothing." Julia shivered and she was sure it was only from the cold. "I'd almost fallen asleep, and when I went to get up, he was crouching there. 'Twas just so sudden, he frightened me."

"Did he pull his knife on you?"

"I don't know. He wasn't close enough to see very clearly." She thought of the terror the Portuguese, knowing full well the dangers of this night, would suffer while in chains below. "Maybe all he did want was to speak to me."

"With a knife?" He looked at it once more and slipped it into the pocket of his oilskins. "He was probably after your gun."

"He could have pulled the knife when he tried to run away," she suggested. If only she hadn't screamed.

"Has he ever tried to speak to you before?"

"No. Never. I wonder what he could possibly have wanted to warn me about."

"Do you want to go below and find out?" he asked grimly.

"No." Julia shivered again. "Not tonight."

"Well, stay near me or Evans until the fog lifts." When he slipped an arm around her waist, he could feel the tremors that ran through her body. He looked at her with concern and wondered once again how wise he was to expose her to the hazards of the sea. If anything were to happen to her . . . Yet what would he have done without her during the past few weeks? So often just the sight of her smile, the touch of her hand had refreshed him and given him the strength to go on. He smiled gently at her. "You're half frozen."

"I guess I am." She tried to smile at him, but her lips were stiff with cold.

"Come over near the wheel, and I'll have the steward bring you a hot cup of coffee laced with rum."

Fortunately, the fog thinned out a little before daylight, and when the wind came up, they were well clear of any other vessels. Julia went below and tried to sleep, but she was awakened after only a few hours by the condensation from the overhead dripping on her face. She burrowed deeper into the quilts and tensed her body against the cold. Instinctively she tried not to move, to do nothing to disturb the small cocoon of warmth her body had built up. She slept only to wake again. After a while, her body was cramped by aches and pains. No matter how she turned, no position was comfortable for long. The icy water outside the hull radiated its clammy chill through the bulkhead. She sighed and gave up all attempts to sleep. How easy it was to forget the misery of Cape Horn once you left it behind, but how familiar it was when you returned.

She tried to count the number of times she had rounded the Horn, and then she realized her mind was as cramped as her body and gave it up. Pulling the quilts around her, she got up and went out into the saloon, where she rang for the steward and ordered hot stew and coffee. If she couldn't warm herself from the outside, she could try doing it internally.

She was pacing up and down the saloon, trailing the quilts behind her, trying to exercise her stiff body, when Homer Evans came in. He sat down at the table without speaking to her and waited in silence until the steward brought two large bowls of stew and a pot of coffee.

Julia had no desire to eat with the man, but if she waited until he was gone everything would be cold, and she needed heat so desperately.

"So the Portugee tried to knife you," the mate said when she sat down opposite him.

"Did he?" she said icily and picked up her spoon.

"Seemed like it."

"Did you have anything to do with it, Mister Evans?" Her indigo eyes were hostile and she looked at him without wavering.

"Me?" His mouth fell open in the midst of his chewing. Then he hastily swallowed his food. "Why would you think a thing like that?"

"Well, perhaps it was Mary," she said, her tone as sharply edged as the cold air around them.

"No!" He looked frightened and hunched closer over his bowl. After shoveling several spoonfuls into his mouth, he said, "I told you I wouldn't let her . . . or anyone . . . hurt you, Mrs. Logan."

"Well, I just hope you don't . . . for your own sake, Mister Evans." The stew was getting colder by the minute and she concentrated her attention on it until she could feel its warmth spreading through her body. Then she asked, "What happened to the Portuguese?"

"Flogged for carrying a pointed knife and sent back to work." Wiping his mouth with the back of his hand, he shouted for Granville and ordered him to bring more stew. When the steward had gone, he said, "I wouldn't have let that dago loose if I'd been the captain, but then maybe I think more of you than the captain does."

"I doubt that very much." She was happy to see Granville reappear almost immediately with more stew. If only the mate would eat his fill and get out of here.

Instead of instantly pitching into his food, Homer Evans continued to stare at her with a peculiar expression until Granville had gone. Only then did he speak.

"Captain says we need every able-bodied seaman to pull his share since we've got so many landlubbers aboard, but I wouldn't have taken the chance if I'd been him."

"Well, maybe that's why he's master and you're mate. And if you continue to talk against him, 'twouldn't surprise me if you're not even that much longer."

"You plan on reporting me to him?" He peered at her suspiciously from under his scraggly brows.

"No, but if you keep it up, I won't have any other choice, will I, Mister Evans?"

The door to the saloon slammed open and the steward stuck his grey thatched head in. "Man overboard, Mister Evans! Captain wants you on deck."

The mate threw his spoon into his bowl with disgust. "Never even get a chance to eat aboard this bloody ship."

After he had gone, Julia quickly finished her bowl of stew and drained the last of the rapidly cooling coffee from her cup. Then she wrapped a heavy blue wool scarf around her head, gathered the quilts around herself, and went on deck to see what was happening. It seemed strange that a man

49

should have fallen overboard. The wind was high, but not of the force they would soon meet.

When she opened the door of the companionway, the cold struck her as though it were liquid, but she forced herself out into the fresh air. They were speeding along faster than she had realized when she'd been below. She could see there were hands aloft reefing sails. A few of the men gathered at the leeward rail were staring at the wake.

She knew better than to ask questions while on the quarterdeck, but Stephen turned to her immediately. She was the only one aboard who would be able to read the anguish he concealed behind impassive grey eyes, and only she would understand the pain each man's death cost him.

"It was the Portuguese," he said, clipping his words. "He was aloft. The man next to him said that his feet just seemed to slip out of the footrope. He hung on with his hands, but before the men could get to him, he let go."

Julia took a deep breath and the cold seared her lungs. "Is there any hope?"

He shook his head. "No. Not unless he was picked up by another vessel. If we'd tacked ship and gone back for him, he would have been dead before we could have reached him."

"I know," Julia said with sad understanding. "Maybe somebody picked him up."

But when she looked aft at the sails that were scattered backwards to the horizon, she knew that none of them could have been close enough. The poor man, she thought. I doubt he meant me any harm. If he hadn't been flogged, maybe he would have had the strength to hold on till help reached him. And as she wondered if he'd had a wife or family, her regret for her part in the affair quickened into remorse.

"Probably someone did pick him up," Stephen agreed, although he didn't believe it. He could guess what was going through her mind. "Don't blame yourself. You know these things happen. Will you enter it in the log? He went over at approximately two twenty."

She nodded and mutely turned away from him. As she approached the steps, she saw that Homer Evans was staring at her. When she glanced at him, he turned white and hastily bent to inspect a line. Her feelings of guilt over the death of the Portuguese lashed into anger at the mate. She was almost certain that he'd had something to do with the sailor being on the quarterdeck last night.

She went out of her way to walk by him, and as she passed, she said in a low voice, "You see how the *Crystal Star* looks after her own, Mister Evans?"

She didn't linger to see what effect her words would have, but she could hear his sputtering cough behind her.

After that, the mate kept well clear of her, and his silence in her presence was complete. Once they had fought clear of the Horn and left the albatrosses with their soaring wings far behind, Julia decided there was no need to speak to Stephen about Evans. She didn't think that the man, with his mad superstitions, would ever again be a threat to either herself or Stephen, not after the accidental death of the Portuguese. Besides, the mate was badly needed to administer discipline, for with each additional mile, the mood of the crew grew uglier, and the floggings and hazings were increased.

When they sighted the bare, sandy hills of California, hovering above a thick blue haze, the lookouts were not the only ones who scanned the shoreline for the gap that would lead into San Francisco Bay. No matter what his duty, every man aboard found numerous occasions to cast a surreptitious glance towards the land of golden promise and freedom. However, it wasn't necessary to search the coast, because the mass of sails that soon appeared on the horizon was signpost enough.

Although they'd found the passage around Cape Horn crowded with shipping, the fleet they encountered waiting for a pilot outside the Golden Gate was enormous. Julia was able to count forty-three vessels, and it was obvious which were destined for abandonment and oblivion and which would leave San Francisco to sail on a new venture. Many, like the *Crystal Star*, glistened with fresh coats of paint, their decks sanded a gleaming white, and their rigging freshly tarred, as was traditional for a proper vessel entering a port. Others told all too well the story of a long and arduous voyage with their chipped and weathered paint, their broken rails and smashed boats, and their roughly patched sails. On several, a quarantine flag whipped in the strong wind.

Later, they were to hear tales of storm-wracked vessels which had almost run out of food and water, where ship's fever raged and scurvy claimed almost every soul aboard. Some had taken eight to ten months or more to reach California. Julia felt a pang of guilt as she remembered the antiquated vessels she had sold for her father and hoped that they had all survived to see this coast.

After watching one weatherbeaten bark, on which emaciated men attempted to furl their tattered upper main topsail, Julia turned her attention to the northern end of the gap, where tall mountains plunged directly into the foaming sea. As they crossed the strait where the current boiled out of a three- or four-mile span, she could see the grey-white rock island of Alcatraz gleaming in the morning sun. A new land and a strange one, she thought. The thrill of setting her foot on the western edge of this great continent swept over her. Here there was space for man to live and breathe, with only a few settlements for his convenience. In this land, a freedom almost as great as that of the sea might be found.

She was leaning on the rail and dreaming of what it might be like to live in California, to grow with a land far from the entrenched ways of Massachusetts, when Stephen touched her arm.

"Julia, do you have your gun?" he asked quietly.

Her hand went to the weight in her pocket. "Yes."

"Then go all the way aft and stay there. Be prepared to fire, but don't show the gun until I pull out mine."

So the moment had come. She nodded and quickly made her way to the taffrail.

Once she was there, Stephen signaled to the three mates and the steward. At the same instant, all five of them drew their pistols. While Stephen and the steward cleared the men from the quarterdeck, the three mates advanced on the remainder of the watch on the main deck.

"Get below. Get below!" Homer Evans shouted.

Most of the sailors were baffled and stood staring at the officers with incomprehension, but Fair Henry understood the situation immediately.

"They're going ter lock us in," he shrieked. "They ain't going ter let us see Californiay. We come all the way 'ere fer gold, and they ain't going ter let us 'ave none." He made a dive for Smithers' gun, but the third mate was too quick for him, and in an instant, Fair Henry was lying on the deck.

Julia, now alone on the quarterdeck with a young Swedish sailor named Knudson, who had the wheel, looked quickly for Barney. If he had come to Fair Henry's defense once, he might very well do it again. When she spotted him, he was standing apathetically near the forecastle hatch with his hands hanging loosely at his sides. Despite her forebodings, he had been one of the most docile men aboard ever since his flogging. Still she worried that the officers' move on the men might trigger him off. When she saw that Clyde Rawlings was training his gun on the Dane, she turned her attention again to the helmsman. She knew that Stephen felt he was a man to be trusted, but in a situation like this, Julia felt it was best to trust no one.

Meanwhile, the rest of the crew, triggered by Fair Henry's warning, stood obstinately still or edged away from the guns that were pointed at them, but no one made a move towards the forecastle. A few, who had been standing near each other, gathered in a knot and muttered together.

"You heard me, you dreckers," the mate's grating voice rang out again. "Below with you. The last man down will earn ten stripes from the rope."

" 'E can't do it. 'E can't flog yer no more," Fair Henry, who was still lying on the deck, yelled. "We'll be in port afore 'e can do nothing."

Just as Smithers' foot connected with Fair Henry's head, Stephen raised his pistol, shot it over the heads of the men, and quickly took out another he had concealed in his jacket.

"There'll be no mutiny aboard this ship," he said, his voice cold and calm. "When the mate gives you the order to get below, you'll get below.

52

You two." He motioned at a couple of sailors who stood near Henry's now unconscious body. "Pick up that vermin and take him with you."

More frightened of the ice they saw in the captain's eyes than of the guns he held in his hands, the men hurried to lift their unconscious shipmate and carried him towards the forecastle. As the officers continued to advance and encircle them, the rest of the men lost their spirit and allowed themselves to be herded towards the forecastle hatch. Suddenly there was a rush for the ladder that led down into their quarters, and the two men who had carried Henry simply dumped his body down the hole and disappeared quickly after it. When the last man's head had vanished, the second and third mates slammed the hatch cover shut and bolted it.

The short, rotund cook strolled calmly out of the galley house, and the first mate raised the gun he had started to return to his belt. "What are you doing on deck?" he barked. "You heard the orders. Get below with the rest of them." He motioned towards the forward part of the ship.

"I don't take orders from no one but the captain," the cook said blandly, "and he didn't invite me to join the party."

The mate looked at the captain, who shook his head.

"What do you want, Jones?" Stephen asked.

"I wanted to ask what you'd like for supper, sir. We still have three of the hens we picked up in Valparaiso left."

"Supper! I don't give a damn what you fix for supper, but it'll have to be cold. From now until we anchor in San Francisco Bay, you're going to be spending most of your time aloft."

"Aye, aye, sir," the cook said and grinned at the mate.

"That includes all of you. There'll be no sleep for anyone until we're safe in the harbor. There's only one watch, and I'm in charge of it. Do you understand me?" He looked sternly at each mate in turn and then at the steward and the cook.

"Aye, aye, sir," came the quick chorus.

Stephen relieved Knudson at the helm and sent the sailor to join the others in their work on the main deck. Although Julia relaxed, she was still not reassured.

"How do you know you can trust Knudson?" she asked Stephen in a low voice as she went to stand beside him.

"Simple," he said, spinning the wheel to avoid a battered Bristol schooner that seemed to be out of control. "I promised that, when we put in, he could leave the ship with a bonus in his pockets. It'll be enough for him to outfit himself."

"You don't think he'll try to release the others?"

"No. He cares more about gold than he does about his shipmates. Here comes a pilot boat. I think he's heading in our direction."

"I hope so. The sooner, the better." She looked aloft at the weather-stained sails. Although a number of them were furled, there still remained the jibs, squaresails, a few staysails, and the spanker. It would be a lot of work for the few men who remained free, especially if a sudden squall were to hit before they reached the safety of the harbor.

"We can do it," Stephen said, aware of the direction of her thoughts.

"What can I do to help?"

"Just stay out of the way."

"It's not right!" she protested as she watched the men who were furling the lower main topsail. "I may not be as strong as a man, but I can at least haul on a line."

Stephen resolutely didn't answer. It was one of the habits he had recently acquired. He simply substituted silence for discussion, and it meant a definite no. Therefore, she was surprised when later, as the pilot boarded the ship, he nodded at the main deck. "If you think you can help, go ahead, but stay out of the rigging."

Julia didn't wait for him to change his mind, but quickly went below to her cabin to rid herself of a couple of bothersome petticoats and her crinoline. She paused for a moment by an extra pair of Stephen's trousers, which she sometimes wore under her skirts in cold weather, but she hurried on past them. She knew Stephen wouldn't stand for her appearance in unskirted pants.

She only had time for a glance to starboard at the small fort with its surrounding trees as they passed through the narrowest part of the strait. A few minutes later, when she looked again Yerba Buena Island had appeared. Between it and Alcatraz Island, the anchorage, though not the city of San Francisco, became visible. Above the mist of the land, she could see the distant tawny mountains that drowsed like lazy lions in the autumn sunlight. Monte Diablo, she thought as she lowered her eyes to the line in her hands. Stephen had said that one of the most magnificent sights when you went through the Golden Gate was Monte Diablo.

The next time she raised her head, they were through the strait and heading for Yerba Buena Island. To the south and west the harbor opened up revealing so many vessels, Julia almost dropped the line in her astonishment. Three tall hills rose around the curving shore cradling randomly scattered buildings. The total impression was one of impermanence. Man would perch here for as long as the gold held out and then he would leave those fluttering tents, those hastily thrown up houses of planks, canvas, and adobe to the ducks and pelicans that circled overhead and to the spouting whales and the porpoise that gamboled about the ship.

By the time the first mate went forward and struck away the one pin that held the stopper around the anchor at the cathead, Julia straightened up and found that she was exhausted. Examining the blisters on her hands, she realized she had never before appreciated how hard the work must be for men who came aboard a ship for the first time.

54

No sooner had they anchored than they were besieged by a flock of Whitehall boats. Grasping stray lines and even the anchor rode, a gang of runners and crimps from the sailors' boardinghouses swarmed aboard. Finding the forecastle hatch chained and padlocked and the few men on deck indifferent to either their bad whiskey or their promises, the runners were infuriated and advanced menacingly on the ship's officers.

Once again it was necessary for Stephen and the mates to draw their weapons as some of their unwelcome guests came at them with belaying pins, capstan handles, and anything else they could find. Others used the same instruments as they tried to break the chain and padlocks which held the crew prisoner. Meanwhile, the sailors below had started shouting as soon as they heard the splash of the anchor. With the intruders above them yelling reassurances, there was complete bedlam aboard. Stephen fired a shot into the air to get the attention of those forward and to warn off the advancing mob.

With that, one of the crimps jumped clear of the others. He pulled a pistol out of his pocket and aimed it at Stephen. A shot rang out, and the crimp fell to the deck.

"Any more of you got ideas?" Evans said quietly in the silence that followed.

"Over the side and take your friend with you," Stephen said, aiming at the largest and roughest-looking of the intruders.

One of the runners bent over the fallen man and then straightened up. "He's dead," he said. "You might as well leave us have the crew, for the police'll be out here soon enough."

"It won't be soon enough for me. Leave him and get off my ship." Stephen swung his gun to aim at the speaker.

"Come on, Jim," called an unshaven man in a slouch hat. "The law'll take care of him, and we can come back for the crew without some madmen shooting off guns."

Amazingly enough, the crimps and runners did leave. The last man to clamber over the side shouted defiantly, "When you get set to sail, don't come to us. All the gold in Frisco won't buy *you* a crew."

Stephen had lowered his gun, but with this he raised it again and aimed at the man's head until the crimp quickly vanished. "Run up the police flag," he said grimly to the second mate.

"I don't know how much good that's going to do you." The pilot, who had taken refuge below when the guns had been pulled, now came strolling on deck. "There's only a few police, and they'll not likely bother with another dead crimp."

"I don't give a damn whether they bother with him or not. I want some protection for my ship from those parasites." Stephen stomped to the rail and looked out over the water at the Whitehall boats that were heading like a swarm of bees for a barkentine that was just about to drop her anchor.

"I'm afraid you won't get it." The pilot was round and sleek, and with his bristling mustache, appeared to be related to the seals that lay basking in the sunshine on the Bay's rocky islands. "The police turn the other way when it's the boardinghouses involved. To tell the truth, that gang is too rough for the police, Captain. You'd have done better if you'd let them have your crew and then bought them back again when you're ready to sail."

"So much for civilization in San Francisco," Stephen said in disgust. "What about longshoremen? Are there any available?"

"Aye." The pilot nodded. "There's plenty of those. Miners looking for another grubstake will do anything you want except ship out with you. Have to pay for them though. They expect anywhere from three to five dollars an hour."

"That's robbery!" Stephen's grey eyes flashed with anger.

"Worse than that," the pilot said, sleekly smiling. He'd had the same conversation with master after master during the past few months, but he never ceased to find their reactions amusing. "Worse than that. They'll heave up your anchor and get your ship alongside the wharf. Even stow your sails, clean up your decks, and unload your cargo, but they won't be in any hurry about it. Not when they're getting that much an hour."

"We'll see about that," Homer Evans growled.

"Mister!" Stephen snapped. "I didn't ask for your opinion. Go ashore with the pilot and find some longshoremen and a berth for us. And speak nicely while you're about it. We have to get this ship unloaded and out of here as soon as possible." He turned to the pilot. "I hope you won't object to taking Mister Evans along as a passenger. He'll have to find his own way back out. We can't spare anyone to man a boat."

"Not at all," the pilot answered smoothly, "but what about him?" He pointed at the body of the crimp, whom everyone had forgotten.

"Perhaps if I made it worth your while, you'd take him ashore, too?" Stephen suggested.

"Wait a minute." Evans was leaning over the prostrate form. "There's nothing dead about this one. Not yet."

"Are you sure?" Stephen strode towards the fallen crimp.

"There's a lot of blood," Evans said and pushed at the inert form with the toe of his boot. "But he's still breathing."

"Then it's doubly important to get him ashore, if you don't mind, sir?" Stephen said to the pilot. Despite the lines of worry and weariness in his face, he was able to make his smile charming.

"I'll take the lot of you ashore if you're willing to pay for it."

"No. That won't be necessary. Just Mister Evans and that one."

They lowered the wounded man over the side in a net, and Evans followed him.

Chapter Four

1850

It was two days before they could get a berth at the wharf. Despite years filled with storms, doldrums, headwinds, and attempted mutinies, Julia thought those two days were the worst she had ever spent aboard a ship. The men who were locked below alternated between periods of relative quiet and those of complete cacophony. They used not only their voices, but their tin plates, their feet, and their fists to add to the din. And yet the quiet times were often worse. Who knew what they were doing?

At mealtimes, all the ship's officers stood around the hatch with their weapons in hand while the cook handed down pots of food and water. Twice it was necessary to fire, but fortunately no one was hurt. At night sleep became an impossibility for those on deck, for they quickly discovered that the crimps and runners used the dark to cover their attempts to slip aboard. By day at least, a boat could be spotted before it reached the *Crystal Star*, and only then were they able to post two men while the others rested.

For Stephen and for those who manned his boat, however, the day was a time for work, for going ashore to talk to the merchants whose goods they carried, and for trying to find men who would sign the Articles to replace the Portuguese and Knudson.

On his first day ashore, Knudson disappeared without even waiting for his pay or his bonus, which left only seven of them. It was necessary for Julia to stand watch with the men who remained aboard when Stephen made his trips ashore. Even he had to acknowledge that two of the things she could do as well as any man were to stand guard and shoot, so she spent the days anxiously scanning the crowded anchorage for any suspicious-looking craft.

Her duties gave her a great opportunity for examining San Francisco and its bay. It was almost impossible to see the lower part of the city, for the masts of abandoned vessels that filled Yerba Buena Cove and hugged the shoreline were so thick they completely obstructed the view. The sight of so many craft left to sink or rot away depressed her as she thought of the many hours and loving craftsmanship that had gone into building those

57

vessels. She preferred to look up the hills where the blue haze of cooking fires was more translucent than the fog that often obscured the lower levels. New structures were rapidly rising among the tents there, but she could spare them only an occasional glance. Danger would come from either the water or the forecastle.

Finally a berth opened up at Long Wharf, and a small paddle steamer was engaged to tow them in. With the help of just a few longshoremen, they weighed anchor and were soon tied up among a strange assortment of bay launches, river steamboats, and an auxiliary steamer. Late in the day, the last line was made fast. With neighbors close at hand to help beat off any attackers, Stephen ordered everyone but the second mate and the steward to catch up on their sleep after dinner. At midnight, they would double the watch. On the following day, the forecastle hatch would have to be carefully guarded while the cargo was unloaded, but for the moment, he felt that they were relatively safe.

They lay down fully clothed, prepared for any emergency, but sleep came instantly to all those below. Although three hours had passed, it seemed that only a few minutes had gone by when Julia was pulled out of an overwhelming sleep by raucous shouts and whoops in the distance. She jerked her head off the pillow and reached out to waken Stephen. Although the sheets were still warm from his body, he was gone.

Jumping out of bed, she grabbed her woolen shawl and groped in the dark to find her pistols. She laid her hand immediately on one and was still searching for the other when she heard voices shouting closer to the cabin. One of them was Stephen's. Then came the sound of loud hammering. Gripping her pistol tightly, she cautiously tiptoed through the cabin and the saloon half expecting to find that the sequestered crew had burst out of the forecastle and were bent upon wreaking vengeance on the men who had put them there. The thought of meeting a wrathful Fair Henry or a deranged Barney made her cringe even while she forced herself onward.

She peered around the saloon door. At the other end of the passage on the steps that led to the companionway door, she could see Evans and Smithers trying to batter their way through with their shoulders. Quickly she ran to join them.

"Hold on!" Stephen came up behind her just as she reached the two men. Somehow she must have passed him in the dark. In one hand, he was carrying two knives. Handing one to each of the men, he said, "Pry the hinges loose."

"What's happened?" Julia asked.

"It's obvious, isn't it?" Stephen practically snarled at her. "Someone's locked us in and let the men go."

With the sound of splintering wood, the door gave way, and both mates ran out on deck with their pistols cocked. Stephen was immediately behind them, and Julia picked up her skirts and followed.

They were just in time to see dark forms fleeing up the wharf and to hear the pounding of many feet on the wooden planking. Homer Evans raised his arm and fired a shot at their backs, but Stephen grabbed his arm.

"You fool! It won't help if you hit someone now. It will only land you in jail."

"I'd like to get just one of those bastards," Evans growled menacingly.

"Forget it." He released the mate's arm and walked slowly towards the galley house, where a crumpled form lay on the deck. Dropping down on one knee, he rolled the man over to see his face. "It's the cook. Unconscious, but I think that's all. Where are the steward and Rawlings?"

As the men scattered over the main deck to begin their search, Julia went up to the quarterdeck. She knew that she was afraid, actually terrified of finding a dead man, but she forced herself to conduct a thorough search. She was peering over the rail down at the water when she heard Evans shout, "Here he is!"

She hurried down the steps to find the men handing the second mate out of the forecastle. When they laid him on the deck, he moaned. Julia plucked the lantern out of the companionway and took it forward to the men.

"How bad . . ." she began, but then was silent as the yellow glow of the lantern revealed dark stains of blood on his slashed clothes. Bruised welts covered his square face.

Stephen took the lantern from her and knelt on the deck beside the unconscious man. With tender hands, he began to examine Clyde Rawlings. As he felt the man's chest, Rawlings opened his eyes.

"The steward . . ." he gasped and tried to push himself up.

"That's all right, Mister Rawlings," Stephen said. Putting his hand gently on the second's blood-caked chestnut hair, he forced Rawlings' head back onto the deck. "Lie still until we get you fixed up."

"Granville . . . said he heard a noise and when I went to . . . investigate, he struck me from behind." Rawlings continued as though Stephen had never spoken.

"Sliced you up, too," Evans said with apparent satisfaction.

"No . . . the men . . . did that." Clyde Rawlings closed his brown eyes which were rapidly swelling shut.

"Be quiet," Stephen said sternly, and began to cut the second mate's clothes away from his chest. "You can tell us your story later."

"May not be any later," Evans rasped ominously as he looked at the many cuts that lacerated Rawlings' body.

"Hold your tongue," Stephen rounded on him. "When I want your opinion, Mister, I'll ask for it."

The third mate brought some hot water as well as the medicine chest,

59

and Stephen soaked the blood-caked cloth away from the wounds. While the others handed him implements and supplies, he washed and cleansed the cuts with alcohol, and then wound bandages around them. By the time he had finished, the last-quarter moon had risen and was shining on the hills of San Francisco. There were fewer lights in the buildings and ships along the waterfront, and only a few sprinkled campfires could be seen in the heights. The night was well advanced.

Stephen stood up wearily and stretched. Then he shook his head. "None of the cuts go that deep, but he's lost a lot of blood. Help me get him below."

For all his square, compact frame, Clyde Rawlings was surprisingly heavy. It took all three men to lift him and carry him to his own bunk. After they had him comfortably settled, Stephen sent the first and third mates on deck to keep watch and attend to the cook. Then he went into the saloon, where he slumped down in a chair with a glass and the brandy decanter on the table in front of him.

"Do you want some?" he asked Julia when she sat down opposite him.

"No. I'm so bone tired, 'twould just put me to sleep." She was torn between an almost overwhelming desire to go into their cabin to lie down and the wish to be here in case Stephen needed someone to talk to.

He took a sip from his glass, then put it down on the table and pushed it away from him. He stared at Julia or through her, she wasn't sure which. His eyes were empty and hopeless.

"That does it," he finally said.

"You knew it might happen," she answered softly.

"No." His sigh was heavy burdened. "I thought I could prevent it. Others have."

"Luck?" Julia suggested, and then she remembered the day of the first flogging. "Granville! I should have told you before. I caught him drinking your brandy one day."

"By God, you didn't!" Stephen straightened up and slammed the gimbaled table so hard with the flat of his hand, some of the liquid sloshed out of his glass. "Why didn't you tell me?"

"I guess I forgot." And it was true. She had never caught the steward at it again, and so many more serious things had happened since then. "It was a couple of days after Barney and Fair Henry attacked Mister Evans. There was so much else to think about. The mate wounded. The men mutinous. The last thing I thought was important was the fact that the steward was nipping from your bottle."

"You should have thought about it when I decided to trust him and let him remain free." He glowered at her.

"Maybe I should have," she said sadly, looking down at her hands. "But the two things don't seem to be connected. Why should his drinking have anything to do with letting the men go?"

"Perhaps he was at it again tonight?"

"Could be. When I caught him before, he was really terrified that I'd tell you."

"Well, whatever his reasons, it's past now." He leaned his elbows on the table and his eyes hardened to granite. "You do realize that you may have cost us the ship?"

"Oh, Stephen!" She lifted her chin and resentment flickered in her dark blue eyes. "Hardly that."

"Yes. That," he said, his eyes accusing her. "Without a crew, we're not going to sail out of San Francisco. Did you get a good look at those derelicts? That's what the *Crystal Star* will look like a year from now."

She reached across the table and touched his arm.

"You can get another crew," she said earnestly. "You know you can. You did it last year."

"And it cost me a fortune."

He seemed not to have noticed her hand resting on his arm as he continued to stare at her unforgivingly.

"You saw that pack of jackals. Those crimps and runners. Well, they weren't here in such force a year ago, and now they control all the sailors on the waterfront. When that ruffian said they wouldn't supply me with a crew, it wasn't an empty threat, Julia. He meant it."

She pressed her lips together and stared defiantly back at him. She was not going to take the blame for their loss of a crew. 'Twas his own fault. If he hadn't locked the men up, he could easily have gotten a fresh crew.

"If you're going to lay these things on my shoulders, then I'd best tell you about Evans, too."

"Evans? What about Evans?" He looked at her with surprise. "Don't tell me he's been swigging."

"No. But he's mad."

"Julia, you don't know what you're talking about." He rubbed his forehead with the tips of his fingers to ease the tension that threatened to turn into a headache. "I know you don't like the man. You've never liked him. But he's loyal to me. He helped get us here, and he'll help get us out of here. Just because you don't like his methods of discipline, it doesn't mean he's mad."

"I do know what I'm talking about and it has nothing to do with his methods."

"All right. Since you're determined to tell me, go ahead."

"I . . ." Julia glanced away from him as she tried to find the words to tell him about Evans' ravings, when she saw the man himself standing in

61

the open doorway. How long had he been there? "Mister Evans is here to see you," she said quickly.

"Well, Mister?" Stephen barked, swiveling around in his chair. "Why aren't you on deck?"

"The cook's come to, sir. I thought you'd want to hear his report . . . if there's any truth in it."

"And what makes you think there isn't?"

When the mate didn't answer, Stephen said impatiently, "Very well. Since you can't seem to distinguish between truth and prevarication, I'll have to question the man myself. Get back on deck before someone decides to relieve us of our cargo as well as of our crew."

"Aye, aye, sir." Evans whipped around and was gone, but with the last glimpse she had of his face, Julia did not think he looked particularly loyal.

Stephen sighed and got up wearily. As he passed behind her chair, he placed his hands on her shoulders and squeezed them gently.

"I'm sorry, Julie. I don't mean to take things out on you. I know that none of this is your fault. It's mine. Part of my job is to know who to trust, and obviously I made a mistake with Granville. Looking back, I realize now that there were signs." He sighed again. "Well, hindsight's a wonderful thing."

Julia reached up and curled her fingers around his hand.

"You have more foresight than most," she said affectionately. "You can't expect to be perfect all the time."

"Maybe not, but that's what a captain's supposed to be. Perfect." He caught her hand and carried it to his lips. "Well, I'd better go see to Doc."

Julia sat on after he had left. It was more of an effort to get up and go to bed than it was to remain where she was. With so few on board, the ship was very quiet. Waves lapped lightly at the hull and a few planks creaked and groaned as they adjusted to the changing night temperature. Somewhere a line that had not been properly secured was tapping against a mast or yardarm.

The events of the voyage flickered without pattern through Julia's mind. The terrified Portuguese shaking in the night fog, Joe Smithers' obvious happiness during his first few days on the quarterdeck, Homer Evans' cold, glittering eyes as he pummeled the men into moving quickly, Stephen's face radiating delight as they rediscovered their joy in each other, Barney's dumbly questioning looks, Clyde Rawlings lying bruised and bleeding on the deck. And now it was over. If they couldn't find a crew, it was *all* over.

They had to find a crew.

There must be a way. There always was if you just looked hard enough.

When Stephen returned below, he found her staring blankly at the far bulkhead. He could see the same exhaustion, which ached in his bones, inscribed on her face. Dark shadows smudged beneath her indigo eyes. Faint lines bracketed her mouth.

"Come on, Julia," he said as he went to stand over her. "It's time to sleep now. There's nothing more we can do, and it's only a few hours until morning."

"Is it really as hopeless as it seems?" she asked as she looked up at him.

"I don't know. We'll find out tomorrow." He glanced at the brass clock that was mounted on the bulkhead. "Today. It's already tomorrow."

She pushed at the arms of the chair and began to rise. Then she sank down in the chair again.

"I think I'll sleep right here," she said.

"No." He leaned over, and grasping her wrists, he pulled her up. "You won't get any rest that way. It's just a few steps to bed."

With their arms around each other's waists, they stumbled into the cabin. Without pausing long enough to remove their shoes, they fell onto the bed, and with their arms still around each other, they instantly entered a deep sleep.

The next morning Stephen went one way to contact the merchants to whom the cargo was consigned and the mate went another to round up longshoremen to unload the holds. The cook, whose only damage was a large knot on the back of his head, had been sent to find a doctor for Clyde Rawlings. Only Joe Smithers remained on deck when Julia went up to inspect the day.

Earlier she had dressed in one of her best woolen dresses and a cashmere shawl, in the hope that Stephen would take her with him when he went ashore. After he had refused, saying that she would only delay him, she hadn't bothered to change. Perhaps there would be a chance to visit the town later on. For the moment, she entertained herself by watching the activity on the wharf.

Hand barrows and mule carts loaded with sacks, parcels, and crates trundeled their freight over the wide planks. Sailors and longshoremen mixed with bearded miners in patched flannel shirts, once multi-colored, but now faded to grey. The miners, some towing protesting mules in their wake, bumped and pushed against each other in their attempt to be among the first to board the river steamer. Already clouds of black smoke were belching from her smokestack as she prepared for her journey up the Bay to Benicia and Sacramento.

After the steamer left, spewing soot all over the decks of her neighbors,

Julia grew restless. Once they had begun discharging cargo from the *Crystal Star*, she would have to stay out of the way. The thought of spending a day confined below decided her. The sun was cutting through the fog and cold of the early morning, and it promised to be beautiful later. She would go exploring on her own.

As she adjusted her bonnet and raised her parasol, she called to Mister Smithers, "When Captain Logan comes back, tell him I've gone to take a look at the town."

"Mrs. Logan," Smithers said as he hurried down from the quarterdeck, where he had been idly watching the busy life of the wharf. "It isn't safe for a lady to go ashore alone. Captain Logan won't like it."

She looked at the young man's anxious face with amusement. "Don't worry, Mister Smithers. I've been in worse places than San Francisco can possibly be. It's part of the United States now, you know."

"Aye, but it hasn't been that way for long. Remember what happened last night." His sandy eyebrows puckered above his honest blue eyes.

"Well, I doubt much can happen to me in broad daylight." Then she relented. "I won't go far. I just want to stretch my legs."

"I'd go with you, Mrs. Logan, but I can't leave the ship."

"I know that." She gave his arm a light pat. "You watch out for the ship, and I'll watch out for myself. Most likely I'll be back before the captain is."

She purposefully made her way to the gangplank and went down to the teeming wharf, which was almost a town unto itself. It stretched two thousand feet out into the Bay, and as she neared the shoreward end, she found that abandoned vessels had been turned into hotels, stores, auction rooms, and storage houses.

Here prosperous-looking merchants in their dark wool suits and high silk hats mingled with Chinese coolies carrying their hugh baskets, Chileans clad in broad sombreros and colorful serapes, and the inevitable miners. Everyone was in a hurry and pure energy radiated from the throng among which there was not a single grey head. Nor was there a woman or child to be seen.

As the crowd increased, Julia almost turned back. She had visions of herself being pushed into the water or under the wheels of a wagon. However, she found that a path of men opened up for her, which made her progress easier, but she was uncomfortably aware of the speculative eyes that followed her.

As she stepped into Commercial Street, she could see why so much business was done on the wharf. Although an attempt had been made to pave the street with wood, black, evil-smelling mire oozed up between the cracks and caked the surface. The sidewalks weren't much better. Barrel staves had been nailed to supports that were driven into the mud. It did form a sort of bridge across the worst of it, but the walks sagged and arched in uneven lines and hundreds of feet had brought the filth to cover it. She just hoped it would come off her skirts after they dried. As for her shoes, she would most likely have to abandon them after they left the town.

But it wasn't a town, she realized as she looked up at the brick buildings, tightly packed side by side with wooden ones. Among them were vessels, which had been dragged up on shore and had superstructures added onto their decks. It was a city, but certainly the most peculiar city she had ever seen.

The din was worse than in any city she had ever visited, she thought as she ducked across the intersection onto Kearny Street. Everywhere was the sound of men's boisterous voices shouting, laughing, arguing, swearing. Hammers and saws sounded from every direction, and invisible animals were barking, neighing, and cackling.

She had almost made it to the sidewalk when two women drove by in an elegant carriage, whose sleek horses were finding the going almost as difficult as were the pedestrians. When the mud from the hooves and wheels splattered her skirts, she decided that the women of San Francisco had no better manners than the men, for they didn't even take the trouble to glance at her or apologize. Instead, they drove haughtily on.

She had decided to turn back after walking to the end of the block, but when she reached it, she found herself on a plaza. At least, that was what she supposed they called it, but a more bleak and less verdant public square was hard to imagine.

An enormous old adobe building sedately presided over the upper side of the square, but the other three sides were packed with buildings and a few scattered large tents that proclaimed themselves hotels and saloons.

The signs were not really necessary, for even this early in the day, the noise that poured from them was incredible. Voices shouting in half a dozen languages competed with a cacophony of music. Each establishment seemed to have its own specialty; the strains of Mendelssohn could be heard in counterpoint to the latest fox trot from a neighboring establishment.

The doors and windows of the saloons were wide open, and tables loaded with stacks of gold and silver coins glittered with temptation. It was easy for Julia to see into their well-lighted and surprisingly elegant interiors, but the gilt-framed pictures that hung on their walls made her blush and hurry on. They were almost exclusively of female nudes.

And here there were females on the street as well, though there weren't many in the horde of men. Women were far outnumbered by businessmen dressed in impeccable Prince Albert frock coats, mountaineers in fringed buckskin, pale men in dark suits with diamonds above their flamboyantly brocaded waistcoats, farmers in nutmeg-colored rough homespun, Frenchmen in the latest Paris fashions, and Chinese in blue pajama suits and broad coolie hats. Drunken sailors staggered from saloon to saloon with

65

dark-haired girls clinging to their arms, girls, who wore their frilled, multi-colored dresses as a bird wears its plumage. There were also Chinese girls with expensive brocaded satin jackets over their long trousers. And there were the ladies.

Never in Boston, New York, Hong Kong, or Cape Town had she seen so many elegantly clothed ladies in one place, especially by day. As they strolled languidly around the square, their parasols twirled lightly in accompaniment to their swaying crinolines. Luxurious shawls were draped to draw attention to daring décolletages, and lace handkerchiefs fluttered from dainty fingers. Suddenly the wealth of California became a very tangible thing to Julia, for in the shape of pearls and diamonds, opals and amethysts, it adorned these ladies.

She was thinking that their husbands must have done extremely well in the gold fields when she passed two haughty beauties, twittering together in French. As she turned to watch them pass the pair was accosted by a couple of grubby miners. Julia watched, fascinated, as the miners opened small buckskin sacks and showed the contents to the ladies. Immediately, any disdain the women had shown disappeared. As each took the arm of a miner, their faces were animated with laughter and their eyes sparkled with a luster Julia would not have believed possible two minutes earlier.

Rather stunned, she watched them enter the Bella Union, from which she could hear gamblers' voices calling the play above the strains of a Strauss waltz. She turned her back on the saloons as she fought to suppress a smile. So these were the "soiled doves" Stephen had told her about. And he had made them sound so drab and desperate!

The chant of an auctioneer in the middle of the square drew her attention to a large crowd gathering around a man in a rather worn black coat and blue trousers, who was standing on an upturned crate. She waited until a team of gaily caparisoned, bell-jingling mules, which were pulling a large cart, had passed, and then she crossed the street to see what he was selling. Once she had joined the edge of the crowd, she found that it was almost impossible to see over the heads of the men in front of her.

She raised herself on her toes, but still she could see nothing. As she lowered herself, she found that she was tightly packed in by the crowd. Men's bodies were pressing at her from both sides, and a rough hand from behind, catching at her waist, squashed her against a Spaniard, who wore tight-fitting black velveteen trousers and a short, snug jacket. When he turned to glance over his shoulder, she saw that his dark eyes glittered dangerously beneath the shadow of his glazed hat while his black mustache lifted to reveal a growing smile. She tried to turn, but the man behind her stood as firmly rooted as an oak. She felt immersed in the throng, captured by it, suffocated by it.

"Please," she said to the lanky man in homespun clothes and a fur cap who stood at her right. Panic caught at her throat and her words were not much more than a husky whisper. "Please help me get out."

He seemed oblivious to her words, but a thin smile appeared on his lips as he stared straight ahead. How could he not hear her when his body was hot at her side and she could smell his rank odors even over the unwashed smell that rose from the crowd?

She became even more frightened when she looked at the large, burly, denim-clad man on her left. He was not ignoring her, but was looking at her with a sly satisfaction that left no doubt as to what he had on his mind. How could this happen in broad daylight in a public place? What would happen to her?

Her terror mounted as the hand from behind encircled her waist more firmly. Breaking loose, she whirled around and managed to jab at him with the handle of her parasol. Using it as a weapon, she flailed at the obstructing bodies. If only she could clear a path back to the street! They had to let her through. They had to!

"Miss Julia!" A tall, red-bearded man roughly pushed his way through the mob and put an arm protectively around her. "Miss Julia, what are you doin' here?"

She didn't recognize the man nor was his voice familiar, but she felt that with him lay a relative safety.

"It's Paul, ma'am. Paul Kelley," he said as he realized from her blank expression that she couldn't recall who he was.

"Thank God, Paul," she gasped. "Please get me out of this."

" 'Twill only be a minute," he reassured her as he held her close by his side and, with his heavy left shoulder, opened up a path for them.

Once they were in the clear, she leaned against him for a moment and then straightened up to take a look at him. He had only been a boy when he had left the Cape last year, but now it was a man who stood before her dressed in rough denim trousers, high seaman's boots, and a slouch hat. A dusty red handkerchief was tied around his neck above the collar of his checked wool shirt.

"Paul, I don't know how to thank you," she said, still a little stunned by her experience.

"Ma'am, how'd you get yourself caught like that?" He shook his head in wonder as he looked at her pale face. "Don't you know women have to take care out here?"

"I'm just beginning to find that out." She laughed weakly. "It seemed so safe, and I was curious about that auction."

"Don't pay to get too curious out here, Miss Julia," he said almost sternly. "Where's Captain Logan?"

"Back at the ship, I guess." What was Stephen going to say if he heard what had happened to her? That was something she could wait a long time to hear. Forever.

"You shouldn't be wanderin' about alone," Paul said firmly.

"I suppose you're right." She had to smile at this lecture from a young man who had been her employee such a short time ago. But this was almost a different man, she thought as she looked at his broad shoulders and rugged face. "You've really changed, Paul. I didn't recognize you at first."

"Yes, ma'am." He was suddenly less the man of the world as his freckled face reddened under her scrutiny.

Taking a deep breath, she tried to put the frightening experience out of her mind and think of other things. Gradually she felt her composure returning.

"I'm glad to see you got here safe," she said. "I was right worried about that old bark you bought. I've often thought I shouldn't have sold it to you."

"Oh, she was sound enough, ma'am." He grinned at her ruefully. "'Twasn't as easy as we thought, though. Took us eight months, but we made it. Least, most of us did."

"And you're still all together? The East Dennis Mining and Trading Company?" She remembered the enthusiastic group of young men from the shipyard and the surrounding villages who had banded together to buy a vessel and sail to the land of gold. They had planned to stay together for protection and to share the profits of their venture, no matter who actually found the gold.

"No, ma'am. Worked well enough on the voyage. Equal votes and equal work, and for the most part we got along. But out here, it don't work that way. 'Twas hard work and a lot of sickness when we got up in the hills, and those of us who wasn't sick spent all our time tendin' those who was. Had to split up a couple of weeks after we got here. Most of us has a partner or two. That's about it."

"And have you made your fortune yet?" she asked as she watched him pick up a rope that was attached to a grey, lop-eared mule. The animal's back was loaded with bundles, blankets, and hardware.

"Not a fortune, but I've done right well." His attempt at modesty was marred by the obvious pride he couldn't quite suppress. "Had my fill of prospectin', though. I'm goin' back to what I do best."

"Then you're going home? To the shipyard? If you'd stayed, 'twouldn't have been long before you'd have been made a master carpenter," she said hopefully. Perhaps she could persuade him to sail with them. His trip out should have taught him something about seamanship, and he couldn't be any worse than some of the crew they had just lost. That was certain.

"No, ma'am. Not home. I still aim to make my pile of gold. I'm just goin' to let others dig it out for me. What they really need out here are buildings of all kinds. There's a real fortune waitin' for the man who puts them up. No reason why that man shouldn't be me."

"I suppose not. You always were a few steps ahead of the others. I remember when you were a little boy and tried building a boat out of scraps of lumber from the yard. I couldn't let on at the time, but even your first attempt wasn't half bad. So now it's buildings?"

"Yes, ma'am." Suddenly a homesick hunger lit his blue eyes. "How are my family, ma'am? Uncle Daniel and Uncle Philip? Are they all right? And have you heard anything about my mother or the rest of my family?"

"They were all fine when I left," she reassured him. "We brought some letters out for you, but I think Captain Logan's already taken them to the post office."

"Are you sure, ma'am?" Paul looked suddenly disappointed. "I stopped by there first thing when I hit town this morning, and there wasn't nothin' for me."

"Well, I'm positive," Julia admitted. "Why don't you check again later, and if there's still nothing for you, come on down to the ship this evening. We're at Long Wharf. Captain Logan may have taken them into town this morning, though."

"I'll do that, ma'am." He reached inside his shirt and drew out a deerskin bag. "Would you mind takin' some gold home to my family for me? Just to prove how well I'm doin'?"

"I'd be glad to," she said, looking nervously at the bag. "But I'd rather you didn't give it to me here. It doesn't look like the safest place in the world to be carrying gold."

"Just stay out of crowds like that one, Miss Julia," Paul said and grinned at her. " 'Twouldn't hurt none to stay out of the saloons, neither."

"Paul! You know I'd never go into a saloon!" she said indignantly, but when she saw the twinkle in his eyes, she had to laugh. As he joined in her laughter, she looked at him even more carefully than she had before. His eyes were clear and he looked happy as well as healthy. Daniel and Philip often worried about him, she knew. It would be good to be able to lay their fears to rest. "I'm not certain you should entrust me with that gold, though."

"You, Miss Julia? There's no one on earth I'd rather trust."

"It's not a matter of trust, Paul. It's just that I'm not all that certain when we'll be sailing or even if we *will* be sailing. You see, we lost our crew."

"There's . . . there's ways of gettin' one," he said, looking down at his muddy boots in embarrassment. "There's certain houses that has got a reputation. 'Tis best to stay clear of them, but there's them that gets lured in."

"I know, Paul, but I'm afraid we're not going to be able to recruit a crew that way even if we wanted to." As she told him the story of the past few days, he frowned and nodded.

69

"You do have a problem, ma'am, but there's a couple of ways around it, I think."

"Oh?" Julia raised one eyebrow as she looked at him. This was certainly not the naive young man who had left Massachusetts. "What are they?"

"Well, there's some get discouraged easy and would just as soon go home." He grinned at her. "They call it seeing the elephant, you know. Now they've seen it, they're not much interested anymore. I know a few fellows. Might come up with a couple for you."

"I'm afraid a couple isn't going to be enough." She sighed.

"No, ma'am, but there's another kind . . . in hiding. They'd do most anything to get out of California."

"In hiding?"

"Yes, ma'am. The kind that don't always see eye to eye with the law."

"You mean criminals?" She shook her head. "I hope they're not friends of yours."

"Not exactly friends. And I reckon if you want to call them criminals, that's what they are. Sometimes the law gets a mite mixed up when it comes to a fight where there's a knifing. Up in the hills, we've got our own laws, and things are pretty quiet. If we don't like the cut of a man's jib, we drive him out of camp, but there's some places . . . well, they're not the same. If you want, I could put out the word, and maybe some of those as would just as soon be gone will slip down and sign the Articles if you'll hide them till you sail."

"Well, I don't know. That would be up to Captain Logan. Come down to the ship this evening whether you get your letters or not. You can talk to him then."

"I'll be there," he promised and tugged on the lead of the mule who had been standing patiently cropping at the few blades of grass that grew in the plaza. "Will you take my gold for me then?"

"If we get a crew."

"You'll get a crew, Miss Julia, and I'd be a lot happier knowin' the gold's in your keeping. Most likely I won't be here when you sail. I might get a contract on a house up in Placerville."

"Mrs. Logan?" An elegant young woman, dressed more conservatively than any Julia had so far seen, was sitting in a six-seat surrey that was pulled by a team of mules. The black driver had reined in beside the rough sidewalk near Julia. The young woman was smiling at her, but was obviously a little puzzled. She said, "You are Mrs. Logan, aren't you?"

"Yes, I am," Julia answered, confused. She *knew* she had never seen this woman before. No one who had would ever forget those bright, deep-set brown eyes or the rich high color and creamy complexion of that oval face.

"Permit me to introduce myself. I'm Olivia Courtney. Mrs. Edward

70

Courtney. My husband told me that you were aboard the *Crystal Star*, and I thought you might enjoy a chance to come ashore. I was just on my way down to Long Wharf to meet you."

"Why, thank you," Julia said, still a little surprised. Although this young woman was a stranger, the names of Edward and Olivia Courtney were certainly familiar. Julia had eagerly read the reports of Colonel Courtney's expeditions of exploration into the West. His survey of the trail to Oregon had aided hundreds of settlers to find their way in relative safety to the newly opened territory. Then his descriptions of the unknown land from Oregon south and east, over the Sierra Nevadas, and into California had been avidly read by the entire nation. When he and Commodore Stockton had completed the conquest of California in 1847, there were very few in the United States who did not know his name.

Julia immediately went over to the surrey and offered her hand to Olivia Courtney. "It's very kind of you. I was beginning to feel a little out of place here." She almost told this sympathetic stranger about her recent predicament, but then found that she was ashamed to admit to it.

"Oh, I know that feeling only too well." Olivia Courtney laughed with warm understanding. "But it's something you become accustomed to after you've been out here awhile. When I first arrived last year, there were only sixteen women I could even speak to, and things haven't improved very much since then. You can't imagine how excited I was when I heard you'd accompanied your husband. So few wives do. Won't you come home with me for a visit and a cup of tea?"

"I'd love it," Julia said with real gratitude. She'd had quite enough of the plaza and had been contemplating the walk back to the ship alone with a growing sense of dread. Besides, she was curious about this woman who, though a few years younger than herself, had accomplished so much. Turning to Paul, she said, "Good-bye, Paul. Till this evening. You will come down to the wharf, won't you?"

"I'll be there," he promised as he handed her up into the surrey.

"And don't tell Captain Logan about the auction."

"No, ma'am." There was an understanding complicity in his smile.

Chapter Five

1850

As Julia settled down under the surrey's striped awning beside the attractive, dark-haired young woman, she closed her parasol and asked, "How on earth did you ever guess who I was?"

"Oh, that wasn't difficult." Olivia smiled and nodded at the driver, who flicked his long whip in the air over the backs of the mules. "I've been out here for over a year, and eventually you acquire a sixth sense."

"Well, it's a good thing you have one. I wouldn't have had the least idea who you were if you hadn't introduced yourself. Of course, I've read the accounts you wrote with your husband about his expeditions through the West, but I never expected to meet you. Somehow, I didn't picture you out here in California."

"The Senator's daughter in the land of the desperadoes?" Olivia's voice would have been mocking if it hadn't been lit with laughter. "It does sound like something from a rather melodramatic novel, doesn't it?"

"I didn't mean it that way." Julia was a little flustered. She really didn't know what to make of Mrs. Courtney, and she wondered how wise she'd been to accept this invitation from a stranger. "I can understand that, if your husband is here, you'd naturally want to be with him."

"Yes, I suppose *you'd* understand." Olivia glanced in the direction of the waterfront which could be seen as they rattled across a crowded intersection, and then her eyes returned to Julia. "But not everyone does. However, this is home for us now. We have no desire to go back East again, not after the disgraceful manner in which President Polk treated Colonel Courtney following the court-martial. You've read about that, I suppose?"

"Yes, I have." Julia was rather taken aback by Olivia Courtney's frank manner. After all, the court-martial had been a national scandal. "It was in all the newspapers, but I thought President Polk reversed the findings of the court and cleared Colonel Courtney."

"No." Olivia's coral lips tightened and she held her head high as she stared straight ahead. "He cleared him of all charges of *mutiny* . . . as if there could ever have been any question of that! But President Polk was 'of the opinion that the second and third charges are sustained by *proof.*' In other words, he was found guilty of disobedience of the lawful command of his superior officer and also of conduct to the prejudice of good order and military discipline."

Julia drew a deep breath. She could see the white anger that lay beneath her new friend's calm composure. "But Colonel Courtney was the hero of California! Why, everyone knows that, without him, there would have been terrible bloodshed here between us and the Mexicans. Instead, I understand there was a fairly peaceful settlement."

"That's true. It's peaceful enough, and thanks to Ned, the Mexicans who remained in California are treated with every courtesy." Feeling Julia's warm sympathy, Olivia relaxed a little. "But you see, Ned was caught between the Navy and the Army. Commodore Stockton was here first and Ned naturally followed his orders. Then General Kearny arrived with contradictory orders, but he didn't take the trouble to show the papers from Washington that authorized him to assume command. Since Ned had received his commission from Commodore Stockton, he continued to follow the Commodore's wishes in setting up a proper government in California. At least he did until General Kearny had him arrested. Well, it's over now and Ned and I are determined not to allow bitterness to mar our lives."

" 'Twould be difficult not to be bitter," Julia said.

"Oh, perhaps back in the States, it might be difficult, but we're building our lives all over again in California. It's such a big, beautiful country, and the native Californians are so kind." Olivia smiled as they left the wood-paved streets to follow a narrow road between stands of live oak and pine. "You see, not all of California is like Portsmouth Square. This is Happy Valley. It's where we're making our home."

"In a tent!" Julia gasped as she saw tent after tent mixed amongst the small shacks that filled the rolling hills.

"No." Olivia laughed as they drew up in front of a tiny wooden cottage that overlooked San Francisco Bay. It had a strangely Oriental cast to it. The roof was almost flat and the windows were made from sheets of thin tortoise shell. Gray paint covered the exterior while the door and the window frames were of a deep, rich vermilion. A path leading up to the door was made up of rough boards. Beside it, there grew chrysanthemums in glowing autumn colors. "We may not have much room, but at least we have a roof and four walls, and it's clean. It's more than many people have, and we'll build something larger here later on."

A small girl flew out of the house. Her hair, worn in long braids, was as dark as Olivia's and her enormous eyes were brown, but there was something about her that reminded Julia of her own blond-haired, grey-eyed Clara. She felt tears sting her eyes as she watched the child dancing towards the surrey with her arms raised up to Olivia.

"Mama! Mama! You're home. Angela said you wouldn't be long, but you were."

"Oh, it wasn't that long," Olivia said as she jumped down from the surrey and hugged her daughter enthusiastically. "And as you can see, I brought a new friend to visit. Mrs. Logan, this is Lucy."

"Hello, Lucy," Julia said.

As her guest stepped onto the grass, Olivia released her daughter. The little girl went gravely to Julia. When she judged she was just the right distance, she lifted her skirts in both hands and made a graceful curtsey.

"How do you do, Mrs. Logan," she said. "We're very pleased you could come to call."

Julia laughed and held out her hand. "And I'm very pleased to be here. I have a little girl, though I'd judge that she's younger than you are. Clara's only five."

"Yes. She is younger," the child said as she took Julia's hand and looked

73

up at her with enthusiastic interest. "I had my eighth birthday last month, but I'd still like very much to meet her. Is she on your ship?"

"No," Julia said a little sadly. "She wasn't well enough to come to California with us and so she had to stay home."

"Oh." Lucy's face lost the look of eager anticipation. "That's too bad. There aren't many children out here. It would be nice to have someone to play with."

"Well, perhaps next time we come, we'll bring her."

Julia glanced over at Olivia Courtney and found a sympathetic warmth in her large brown eyes.

"Won't you come in?" Olivia said quickly and led the way to the small sliding door. "I'm afraid we lead a rather Spartan existence here, but we do have a few chairs and a table."

As they entered the house, Julia realized that it contained only two miniature rooms. Through the open door of the back room, she could see a plump Mexican girl pounding some meat on a wooden shelf. Looking around the front room, Julia wondered where the family slept. Mexican serapes with woven designs of red and black covered the floor. There were the table and chairs that Olivia Courtney had promised as well as cupboards and shelves that lined the walls, but there was no sign of a bed.

"Lucy," Olivia said as she took a china doll from a lower shelf. "Why don't you take Mandy out for some fresh air and sunshine? I don't believe she's been out today."

The child looked from her mother to Julia and then back at her mother again. It was obvious that she was disappointed.

"I'll call you when we're ready for tea," Olivia promised, "and you may join us then."

"Yes, Mama," the child said docilely as she took the doll from her mother. After Lucy had gone through the door into the sunshine, Olivia went to the kitchen, where she spoke to the Mexican girl in rapid Spanish. As she turned back to Julia, she indicated a comfortable wooden armchair with red-and-black-striped cushions.

"Please, won't you sit down? Angela will have tea ready in a few minutes." Olivia removed her wide-brimmed straw hat and put it on an open shelf. Then she sat down near her guest. Sensing Julia's curiosity, she continued, "Isn't this a fascinating house? It's put together so cleverly that the only nails in it are the ones that hold the shingles on the roof."

"But that's amazing," Julia said as she looked around the room with a professional eye. The walls seemed solid enough, but it was true she couldn't see the sign of a single nail. "How was it done?"

"Well, the house was originally built in China. Then they took it all apart and shipped it to California."

"A ready-made house," Julia nodded with understanding. "We have some in our cargo that were built in Massachusetts, but I know for a fact that nails must be used when they're put together. And I've never seen anything like it in China."

"You've been to China? Oh, how I'd love to go there, but I must finish exploring California first. It's such a wonderful place." Olivia Courtney carried herself with a sedate elegance. When she spoke, however, it was with such warmth, she seemed vivacious. "To answer your question about the house, though, everything was grooved to perfection. I watched the men while they were erecting it. It was like a giant puzzle box. When they found two pieces that fit, everything just slid together. As you can see, all the doors and windows slide open and shut so there's no need for hinges."

"It is a marvel," Julia agreed, "but where do you sleep?" Then she bit her lip as she realized how rude she must seem.

However, Olivia Courtney seemed to find her question a natural one, for she smiled before she answered.

"We use hammocks." She pointed high up on the walls. "We sling our hammocks from those hooks. And often my husband and our man, Charles, sleep in the surrey."

"Well, sometimes I sleep in a hammock aboard ship in rough weather," Julia said doubtfully, "but I'm not certain I'd care for it as a constant diet."

"But that's part of the fun of living out here!" Olivia laughed when she saw that Julia obviously didn't consider it such a treat. "I'll have to tell you the truth. We use this house when we're in San Francisco, but we do have very luxurious quarters in a wing of the old governor's residence in Monterey, and also Ned has built a very nice two-story frame house for us at our ranch in Bear Valley."

"You've been here just over a year, and already you have three homes?" Julia thought of the wealth that gossip claimed Colonel Courtney had amassed from his mines. Evidently there was some truth to the rumors.

"Well, they're convenient, but they're not essential. The important thing is that we're all together. Those years of the expeditions; they were exciting, but they were often lonely."

"Yes, I know how that can be," Julia said sympathetically, and then she thought of Clara. The Courtneys might have suffered disgrace, but they were obviously happy now in the life they had built. And how fortunate they were to have their little girl with them.

"You miss your daughter, don't you?" Olivia said with a quick sensitivity which startled Julia.

"Yes, I do," she said quietly. "I didn't realize how much till I saw your Lucy. I reckon I was envying you. It's almost five months since I've seen my Clara, and I don't know how she is. I was hoping for a letter from my family when we arrived here, but there was nothing at the post office. If we leave here with no word, it could well be several more months before I hear anything about her. Whether she misses me. How her health is."

"It must be very difficult," Olivia said with gentle understanding.

"I was thinking that California might be the answer for us. At the beginning of the voyage, my husband and I talked about it, but he dismissed the idea. But now that we're here and we've lost our crew . . ." She looked wistfully around the room. Despite the smallness of it, the workmanship was magnificent. "I wouldn't mind living like this if it meant that we could all be together again."

"It would be wonderful!" Olivia said with a rush of enthusiasm that brightened her color. "Then Lucy would have someone to play with, and I'd have a little more company. It would be delightful to have someone respectable here so near my own age. You could come and visit us at Monterey and out at the ranch. There's so much of California I'd like to show you! It isn't all like San Francisco. You should see the wildflowers that cover the slopes in the spring. And the butterfly tulips in the golden grass in summer. There are towering pines near our house, and we can catch our own salmon in the streams."

"It sounds like a lovely dream," Julia said.

"Oh, but that's what's so wonderful about it! It isn't a dream. It's real." Olivia rose and went to the window. Looking out, she saw that Lucy was playing quietly in the grass beside the house, building something out of the twigs she'd found strewn on the ground. "I really would like to find some friends for Lucy. She spends all of her time with adults, and she's far too precocious for her age. The men out here spoil her, too. They come blocks out of their way just on the chance that they'll be able to see her."

"Good heavens, aren't you afraid for her safety?" Julia asked with alarm. She certainly wouldn't want to see Clara in that sort of situation.

"No. They'd *never* harm her. Not even the roughest of them. It's just that there are so few children out here, and she reminds them of their homes and families. Sometimes they give her a nugget or a coin or a little gold dust. I try to discourage it, and I've instructed her not to accept anything, but some of them have actually put it on the ground next to her and then just walked off. I've seen them do it. All they really want is to look at her, perhaps hear her voice."

"That's so sad," Julia said. "All these men out here so rootless, so homeless."

"It won't be that way long!" Olivia seemed to see a world beyond the small room and her large brown eyes glowed with golden lights. "Soon their families will be on the way, and when that happens, California is going to be a different place. There's room for everyone out here, and when the women and children arrive, the men are going to become more responsible. They'll build towns and cities that will last and all the temporary shacks and tents will be forgotten."

"Maybe we'll stay," Julia said dreamily. Olivia Courtney's vision was so real, Julia could see it. "We could send for Clara and settle down here. It would be fun to help build a new land. I'll talk to Captain Logan about it again when I get back to the ship. I'll tell him what you've said. That might sway him."

When Julia returned to the bedlam of Long Wharf, she could see that steam winches had been brought alongside the *Crystal Star*, and she knew that they had begun unloading. Even before she reached the ship, she could hear Homer Evans' harsh voice above the tumult of the crowd. The unending streak of profanity was the worst she had yet heard from his lips. After waiting for a pause in the stream of cargo, she hurried aboard, dodging the bales and boxes that were being hoisted out of the holds and over the side.

Stephen looked up from the manifest he was holding long enough to glare at her and say, despite the presence of the three gentlemen who stood beside him on the quarterdeck, "Where the hell have you been?"

"I just went for a walk. Didn't Mister Smithers tell you?" She tried to keep her voice pleasant despite the irritation his words had provoked. How dare he speak to her like that in the presence of others!

"He told me, and he spent half the morning looking for you. As though I could spare a man at this time! He came back with the report that someone had seen you get into a surrey with some woman. Do you have any idea how dangerous that could have been?"

"The *woman* was Mrs. Edward Courtney, and surely the wife of the man who blazed the trails to the West could hardly be considered dangerous. She also happens to be Senator Packard's daughter."

"She *said* she was Mrs. Courtney. She could have been anyone."

"Stephen, don't be ridiculous. I do know the difference between a lady and a . . ." She put her hand to her mouth to stop the words from coming out. What would these men, who were obviously prosperous merchants, think of her?

A tall, amiable-looking man, whose gold watch chain hung across his comfortable paunch, chuckled and she could have sworn that he winked at her, too. He swept off his silk hat and bowed.

"You see, Captain Logan. There was really nothing to be concerned about. The only woman in San Francisco who has a surrey of that description is Mrs. Courtney, and you can take my word for it, she is most respectable."

"Mr. Bigelow, Mrs. Logan," Stephen said curtly. There was no softening of the anger that still showed in the steel grey hardness of his eyes and in the tightness around his mouth.

"Mr. Bigelow," Julia said. She tried to ignore Stephen as she extended her hand to the gentleman.

"And my associates, Mr. Hazleton and Mr. Moser." Mr. Bigelow gestured towards the other two men, who doffed their tall hats and bowed.

Julia bowed to them in return, aware that Stephen was shifting from foot to foot in his impatience for her to leave the quarterdeck so that he could return to his business.

She sketched a smile in the direction of the three men. "It's been a pleasure meeting you, gentlemen. If you'll excuse me, I have a few things I must attend to below."

The short November day was nearing its end and the fog was beginning to roll in from the sea before Stephen came below. When he did, he seemed to have forgotten his anger. He slapped a sheaf of papers on the table and then sank down into a chair to stare at them. Julia, who had been in their cabin when he arrived, watched him for a moment through the open door and then came into the saloon.

"Is something wrong?" she asked.

"Damned right there's something wrong," he said wearily. He closed his eyes and rubbed his face with the palms of both hands. At last he opened his eyes again and looked at the papers as though by the very act he could change them. "That pretty gentleman you saw on deck, that Mr. Moser, has refused the lumber he ordered. He simply says there's no market for it, and that it's not worth the shipping charges."

"But he can't do that!" Julia said aghast. "Once an order has been shipped, the buyer can't refuse it!"

"Well, it seems that out here they can do anything they damn well choose. Hundreds of thousands of feet of the best Maine fir and white pine! What in the holy, bleeding hell am I supposed to do with it? Just dump it over the side and take the loss?"

"That's ridiculous! Of course you can't dump it over the side." She went to stand behind him and massaged his tense shoulders. When he had relaxed enough to lean his head back against her, she said, "Stephen, I ran into Paul Kelley while I was in town. You know, Daniel and Philip Sears' nephew, the one who was a carpenter at the shipyard till he took off for California."

"I can't really say that I remember him," Stephen answered absently, his mind too concerned with his other worries to really listen to her.

"Oh? Well, at any rate, he says there's a lot of money to be made in

78

building now. More than in the mines. What are they going to build out of if they don't use lumber?"

"Bricks, I suppose. Bigelow didn't refuse the load we brought out for him. They tell me that there have been several catastrophic fires since I was here, and no one wants to erect a wooden structure anymore." He pulled away from her and leaned forward again with his elbows on the table, and his chin resting on his fists.

"What about the ready-made houses?" She dreaded to hear more bad news; her eyes left her husband as she groped for the chair next to him and sat down.

He dropped his hands and looked at her, but there was no more optimism in his eyes than there had been before. "Hazleton accepted them. Grudgingly, but he accepted them. Said he thought he could dispose of them, but doubted he could make much of a profit. Probably only took them because he wanted the rest of his goods, and he knew I'd never release them unless he took the houses."

"Whether he makes a profit or not, it's not your problem!" Julia fumed as she thought of the arrogance of these so-called men of business. "Your problem was getting them here, and your responsibility should end there. 'Tisn't as though you brought the goods out on your own speculation."

"I know, Julia," he said quietly. "But anger isn't going to solve anything. What we have to do is figure out how we're going to dispose of that lumber with a minimum loss."

"Auctions!" Julia brightened, delighted to find a San Francisco solution to a San Francisco problem. "Everywhere I went today, there were auctions. In storerooms, in the middle of the plaza, even on the sidewalks. They auction off everything here, from house lots to clothing to mining supplies and household furniture."

"If there's no market for lumber, then we'd just add the cost of an auctioneer to our losses," he said gloomily.

"Stephen, this just isn't like you!" She couldn't bear this negative approach to the only idea that had presented itself. If he could come up with a better one, well and good, but the least he could do was think on this one. "Why not auction it off yourself? We can advertise that the sale will be made from the decks of the *Crystal Star*. The cost of printing a few handbills can't be very much. How much can we lose by trying?"

"More than we can afford. Nothing comes cheap in San Francisco. Nothing except lumber."

"But Mrs. Courtney told me it varies widely from day to day. She said that one day a pineapple may cost a dollar-fifty and the very next you can buy three for a quarter. If it's true of pineapples, why couldn't it be true of lumber?"

"Because even for pineapples, you'd have to be a fortune teller to predict the right day. And I don't believe the market for lumber will be as elastic as the market for pineapples," he explained patiently as though to a child. "If the market's depressed, it will stay depressed for a good period of time. Who knows how many vessels will be arriving in the next few days with cargoes of lumber? If people want brick, you're not going to sell them lumber. And we can't continue to pay wharf fees while waiting for the market to rise. Do you realize what we're paying for every hour we lie here?"

"Yes, I do, and that's why we should get those handbills printed and distributed tomorrow morning and have an auction tomorrow afternoon. Everything out here moves so fast, we might as well move with it."

Before Stephen had a chance to reply, Homer Evans suddenly materialized at the saloon door in his usual stealthy manner.

"Captain, there's a ruffian leading a mule here looking for you. Claims Mrs. Logan told him to come down to the ship, but I don't put much stock in that."

"Did he give his name?" Julia snapped at him.

"*Said* his name was Kelley, sir." Evans kept his eyes fixed on Stephen, acting as though Julia were a voiceless, invisible entity.

"That's Paul!" Julia said to Stephen. "I'd completely forgotten he was coming. Seems his letters weren't in the post office, and I told him to come down and check with us this evening."

"Well show him below, Mister Evans . . . politely, if you can manage it," Stephen ordered in his coldest voice.

Once Julia was sure the mate had gone, she said quickly, "He might be able to help us with a crew, Stephen, so please be nice to him."

"When aren't I nice?" He cocked one tawny eyebrow as he challenged her.

"Well, sometimes when you have as much on your mind as you do now . . . He might have some ideas on the lumber, too."

"You make him sound like some sort of miracle worker, Julia. He is only a boy, isn't he?"

"No. He's a man now. You'll see."

When Paul Kelley clumped into the saloon in his high sea boots, with his slouch hat in his hand, Stephen did see. The young man had shaved since she had last seen him. His bushy red beard was gone, and his clothing, though damp from the fog, looked neater than it had that morning. She felt complimented that he had freshened himself up for this visit.

"Paul," she said as she rose to meet him. "I'm so glad you remembered to come."

"Yes, ma'am. I wouldn't forget that. Captain Logan, sir." He nodded at Stephen.

Stephen managed a smile. "Sit down, sit down. I'm sorry, but I have nothing for you. I took your letters ashore with the rest of the mail the day after we arrived. You should have found them at the post office."

"Reckon they sent them on to Sacramento then." Paul looked disappointed but not overly concerned as he sat down.

"Did you get your contract?" Julia asked.

"Yes, ma'am. I got it." Paul's freckled young face glowed with enthusiasm. "I had a meeting with a merchant this morning. I'm going to put up a new building for him up in Placerville. Got three more to boot. Mr. Fanning introduced me to a few of his friends. I spent the afternoon roundin' up some carpenters to help me. They're comin' down from the mines now that the rains have started. If I do a good job on those four houses and get them up in double-quick time, I'll be set."

"I'm glad, Paul," Julia said with genuine pleasure.

"What material will you be using?" Stephen asked, suddenly alert. "Wood or brick?"

"Oh, 'tis wood. Once you get away from this town, that's what they want. With a few good men, I can raise a two-story house in twenty-four hours. Speed. They like speed. Take a good substantial wood house, put some wheels under it, and a merchant can follow the miners to a new lode and set up in comfort. Can't build fast in brick and can't move it, neither."

"You have your contracts and you've found a few men," Stephen said as he studied their guest intently. "What about lumber?"

"Haven't looked into that yet. Tomorrow's time enough. Got to get me a couple of more wagons to cart the supplies around in."

"Would you care for a drink, Mr. Kelley?" Stephen asked smoothly, pushing back his chair. Before Paul had time to answer, Stephen had a decanter of rum and two glasses on the table.

"I'd take that kindly, sir," Paul said as he relaxed. Somehow he knew that something good was going to come from this meeting.

"Well, it just so happens I have a load of lumber," Stephen said casually after he had poured rum into the glasses and shoved a pitcher of water in the young man's direction. He went on to explain his problem to his guest, who was becoming more interested with the telling. Stephen finished by saying, "Can you think of any solution?"

"Yes, sir, I think I can," Paul said, suddenly excited. " 'Twon't be goin' cheap for long. I'm not the only one who's thinkin' on buildin' up in the hills. And Mr. Fanning and his friends ain't the only ones who want it. Don't matter how much lumber there is in Francisco right this minute, 'twon't be enough."

"And what do you propose I do about it?" Stephen watched the young man carefully. He liked his initiative and daring in going into business for himself rather than taking the easier route of working for another man. If he himself were any judge of men, then a lot of shrewdness lay behind that honest, open face.

"Well, sir, you can anchor out in the harbor and wait for prices to rise

81

or . . ." Paul paused as he appraised the captain's face. Then he added in a rush, "Or you can go partners with me."

"Partners?" With his glass suspended in midair, Stephen stared at Paul Kelley. "Just what do you mean by partners?"

"Doubt you want to cool your heels sittin' round here. Most likely, you're frettin' to be on your way," Paul said with a candidly innocent air.

Stephen swallowed his drink and studied Paul Kelley skeptically. How far could he trust this young man and just how much trust would be demanded?

"That's true enough," he said calmly. "But I don't intend to leave here a loser."

"No, sir. I think you can be a winner. I've got a lot up in Sacramento, and with some of that lumber, I can build a long shed, put up a fence, and hire a watchman. No one can afford to hold things like that in San Francisco. Now what I'm suggestin' is that you sail me up to Benicia long with the lumber. Then I'll take a steamer from there to Sacramento. 'Twill save us some on the shippin' costs. You know it costs as much to ship goods from San Francisco to Sacramento as it sometimes does to ship them from Boston to San Francisco?"

"And then what?"

"I pay the shippin' costs from Benicia to Sacramento, build what's needed, and pay the watchman. You throw in the lumber."

"The profit. Where's the profit in that?"

"We wait till the prices go up, and in Sacramento, they're always a good sight higher than they are in Francisco. Sometimes twice as much. Soon as it looks like it's gettin' near the top, we sell and split the profit. Meanwhile, we check out prices on lumber tomorrow, and I pay you the market price for lumber enough to put up my four buildings."

"According to Mr. Moser, it's not worth what it cost to ship it out here," Stephen said with mounting suspicion. "In fact, it's beginning to sound as though I'm going to be the loser and not the winner in this game."

"No, sir! That's just the beginning." Paul slapped the table with the flat of his hand, giving vent to his feelings. "No point my buyin' someone else's lumber and shippin' it up there, is it? Not when I'm shippin' yours. Later, when I need lumber, I pay the goin' San Francisco price to the partnership. It's the others we're goin' to make the profit on."

"The question is are there going to be others?" Stephen said and the beginnings of a frown appeared around the corners of his eyes. "Or is this just going to be your own private store?"

"There'll be others. That I promise you, Captain Logan. Ask Miss Julia. She knows my word's good."

Stephen glanced at Julia and she nodded.

"His word is good, Stephen."

"Better be." Paul grinned at her. He knew his scheme would succeed. "If I was to break my word to Miss Julia, Uncle Daniel wouldn't bother with any kind of vessel. He'd purely *fly* out here and skin me."

"What can you lose, Stephen?" Julia asked. "You can't get much for it now, and if you wait for prices to rise, we likely won't be in China in time for the new tea crop." She hesitated for a moment as she thought of her morning conversation with Olivia Courtney. This might be the ideal time to broach the subject. "Could be you'd rather consider California, though. If we made this our home, we could afford to wait. Mrs. Courtney says there's a lot of opportunity out here."

"You'd never be happy out here," Stephen replied sharply.

"But I would," Julia said earnestly. "We could get Paul to build us a house, and then we could send for Clara . . ."

"That's all you're thinking about," Stephen said firmly. "Clara! Once you got her here and had a house built, you'd be itching to get back to sea or to go home. Just because Mrs. Courtney's happy here, doesn't mean you would be. I'd give you exactly one month back in the hills someplace, and all I'd hear from you would be how much you miss the water."

"I've never been what you might call grumbly, Stephen. You know that." If only he would listen to her. Her arms ached for want of Clara.

"No, not in so many words, but when things don't suit you, I can see it written all over your face. And I'm not going to have you moping around with that wistful look in your eyes. You've never in your life spent an entire day away from the sea, and at thirty, you're too old to start now."

"San Francisco's near the water." Please, Stephen, she whispered in her mind.

"We can't live in San Francisco. I will not have my daughter brought up in these surroundings. And that's final. We're going on to China, and the more I consider Mr. Kelley's scheme, the more merit I find in it."

Paul had become increasingly uncomfortable during this household discussion, but now he brightened.

"You won't be the loser, Captain Logan. I guarantee that. And after your lumber's sold, I'll either send you a draft for the full amount or you can continue in partnership with me. 'Twill be up to you. A lumber business should do right well out here. Later on, we might consider a sawmill. There's plenty of trees up in the hills that's just crying out for a saw and plane."

"Well, first things first," Stephen said and permitted himself a smile. He found that he really did like Paul Kelley. He would have made a good mate and eventually a fine master if he'd followed the sea. But perhaps the direction he was taking was the best for him. "Before we can take you and the lumber up to Benicia, however, I'm going to have to find a crew. Mrs. Logan said you had a few ideas on that score."

"Aye. While I was lookin' for my carpenters I did a little checkin' on men who might want to ship out. Can't vouch for them, nor their experience, neither, for that matter, but I found a few. I sort of let it be known that you weren't too choosy as to a man's background, too. Word will get around."

"How soon, though? I can't afford to wait for long."

" 'Twon't be long. I'll see if I can't help speed things up . . . now that it's to my interest, too." Paul grinned and held out his glass in response to the decanter Stephen waved towards him. "I've got to get my men and my lumber up to Placerville right smart. If I've got to stop off at Sacramento to do a bit of construction on the way, then we should be out of here in no more than a couple of days."

However, Paul was destined to be disappointed, for it took a full week before enough men appeared to fill out the crew for the *Crystal Star*. A few dejected ragged men, owning nothing but the clothes they wore, drifted down from the hills in search of a berth. And there were others. The ones who would skulk down the always crowded wharf in the dark and come silently aboard. Stephen took them all, and with the addition of two men the police handed over as being undesirable to the city of San Francisco, the ship's company was complete.

The passage to Benicia was a nightmare of fog and rain that took all day, and the time required to tack the ship with the untried, untrained crew made the ordeal complete. Julia had been looking forward to the trip farther inland and to the sights of San Pablo Bay as well as the more northern reaches of San Francisco Bay, but the damp chill was so penetrating, she stayed below close to the luxury of the cast-iron stove, which would be dismantled before they sailed out through the Golden Gate.

The next morning when she went on deck to watch the hasty unloading of the lumber, however, she found that the sun was shining and she felt that she was seeing the country truly for the first time. Unlike San Francisco, there were no more than a hundred houses scattered on the southern slope of the golden mountain range, and these were not the ramshackle shacks and motley buildings of the city they had just left. Neat, well finished, and painted in a rainbow of colors, they gave an air of permanence to the new state.

If it hadn't been for an almost complete lack of trees, Julia thought she would have been happy to build a new life in these surroundings. Here the waters were clean as they lapped at the banks and beaches of Carquinez Strait. No raw sewage poured from streets and camps as it had in San Francisco, and the air was fresh with the scent of new-scrubbed earth.

To make the scene complete, she could see the ribs of a vessel rising just down the shore from the wharf, and the sounds of hammer, adze, and saw combined with the rich, familiar shipyard smells of fresh cut oak, pitch, and turpentine to bring back memories of home. How Papa would love to see this, she thought. And there was room for a yard to expand here, an impossibility on the narrow banks of Sesuit Creek, which were enclosed by marsh and sand.

She longed to go ashore and explore, to see what they were erecting on the ways, to talk about the future of shipbuilding in California. Yet the lumber was being unloaded so quickly, she wouldn't have time to take advantage of this last chance to stretch her legs upon the earth for several weeks. There was a need for haste since the Pacific Mail Steamship Company, at whose wharf they had tied up, was expecting the steamship *Oregon* later that day. When the *Oregon* sailed, Paul, his men, and his lumber would be aboard.

It was a little before noon when the last of their cargo had been swung onto the wharf. The final load of ballast had been stored in the holds and Homer Evans was supervising the battening down of the hatches when Paul Kelley broke away from his six men and swung aboard the *Crystal Star*.

"Miss Julia," he said as he came up onto the quarterdeck, "will you tell my family not to fret for me? Tell them I miss them, but when I come home, I'm goin' to have enough gold stacked up in the bank to give us all a life of ease for the rest of our days."

"I'll tell them, Paul, and I'll see that they get your gold and your letters."

"Good-bye, sir," he said to Stephen. "I hope you make out all right with those men."

"Oh, don't worry. We'll whip them into shape." Stephen couldn't suppress a grin at the younger man's ebullient confidence as he shook his hand. "I'll expect a strict accounting from you to be waiting for me when we get home."

"Yes, sir. It'll be there. And about a lumber company after this stock runs out . . ."

"First the accounting. Then we'll consider whether I want to leave the money with you."

"Yes, sir. I'll do my best for you."

"See that you do." Stephen clapped him on the shoulder. "And good luck."

As they were towed out through Carquinez Strait by a small paddle-wheel steamer and the pilot took charge of the quarterdeck, Julia stood at the rail and waved to Paul until they rounded a bend and the wharf was gone from sight. When she turned, she found that Stephen was standing behind her. He, too, had been watching the party on the wharf.

"That's what this country needs." There was a mixture of longing and regret in his voice. "Youth. I've never felt so old as I have these past couple of weeks."

"Good heavens, Stephen," she said in amazement as she looked at him. With his cap pulled low on his forehead, he looked as young to her as he ever had. "You're not old. Why, you just turned thirty-eight a couple of months ago. What are you going to be saying when you're fifty-eight?"

Seeing his reflection in her eyes, he smiled, but then shook his head rather sadly.

"I may not be old by other standards, but in California, I am. Can't you see, Julie, that's why I couldn't stay. Paul probably *will* make his fortune. He has the vigor and stamina that I seem to have lost somewhere along the way."

"What nonsense! How can you even think such a thing? I've seen you go for days on end with only an occasional hour or two of sleep."

"I endure because it's a way of life I've followed all these years, but I don't have the energy to carve a new life out of a wilderness."

He left her side to move restlessly forward, where he critically watched Homer Evans directing the operations for casting off the steamer as they left the restricting waters of Carquinez Strait. Once they had entered the broader reaches of San Pablo Bay and had the wind on their quarter, he returned to stand beside her next to the windward rail. They were silent for a few minutes as they watched flocks of ducks and wild swans rising from the nearer shore to fly across the green waters of the bay. It was Stephen who finally spoke.

"I know why you wanted to settle here, Julie. I know how much you've missed Clara, even if you thought I wasn't aware of it. But can't you see how impossible a dream it is? We're tied to the sea, you and I, and to the ways of Massachusetts. Family. Responsibilities. However, if I can afford it, I'll probably leave my money with Paul Kelley. It will make me feel that I have some small stake in California."

"Yes. I'd like that," she agreed. "To have some small stake in California."

The next day, as they sailed past the Farallon Islands with their noisy population of birds and sea lions, Julia's attention was constantly distracted by the fumblings of the makeshift crew. This time Mister Evans really had his work cut out for him, she thought. If he was ever to make sailors of them, it would be the eighth wonder of the world.

Stephen turned the watch over to Joe Smithers, who was once again acting as second mate, and came to lean on the rail beside Julia.

"Well, that's the last land we'll see for a few weeks," he said, nodding at the islands, "and I'm glad to finally leave it behind. For a while there, I thought we'd never get to sea again."

"Yes," she said idly as she watched Smithers berating a couple of bewildered men. "You know, Stephen, I really can't believe this crew!"

"I can't believe them, either, but they're better than nothing. At least, we've got a few who have sailed before. Four helmsmen. That's what I call real luck."

Julia frowned as she watched the confusion on the main deck grow worse. "I didn't think we could possibly have found a worse crew than the one we brought out, but we seem to have managed it."

"They'll shape up," Stephen said lazily with no more than a glance at the men before he raised his eyes to watch the sails, stretched taut with a good following breeze. The sight of their brightness and curved shadows against a blue sky was one he could never tire of. "As soon as we get Rawlings back on his feet, it's going to be a picnic."

"I'm glad you feel so sure of it," Julia said dubiously. "At least we've lost Fair Henry."

"Oh, there's probably another like him aboard. He just hasn't shown himself yet. Until he does, I'm not going to worry about him."

"Stephen, how can you be so relaxed!" His lack of concern was beginning to irritate her. " 'Twill be more than a month before we reach China, and the only member of the crew you know you can rely on is the cook."

"And the officers. And you." He reached out and took her hand. As he squeezed it, he smiled reassuringly at her. "Julie, it's something we're going to have to get used to. We'll keep a sharp watch on the men, but until something happens, it's useless to worry about them. Meanwhile, let's enjoy life."

"If we can." She looked down at the main deck once more and wondered what was going to happen. Who would be the man to start the trouble? If their last passage was any indication, it was bound to happen soon.

Chapter Six

1851

Despite Julia's premonitions, all remained calm as the *Crystal Star* crossed the Pacific, carried westward by strong favoring winds over long, rolling dark blue waves crested with white. The men settled down to their work with only the normal amount of restiveness and grumbling. During the second dog watch, from six to eight in the evening, a banjo was often heard accompanying the forecastle songs on the foredeck. There were other songs, too, that spoke of hope and disillusionment in the gold fields. The storms they encountered were few and flickering, and as they sailed through the green Philippine Sea into the yellow waters of the South China Sea, no pirates came out from the islands to molest them.

Clyde Rawlings recovered quickly from his wounds and was able to return to duty their second week out. With three mates to enforce discipline, the ship worked smoothly and well.

Once they reached Hong Kong, there were two desertions. The men whom the police had put aboard in San Francisco disappeared over the side one night, but they were easily replaced by better sailors. Most of the men just wanted to go home, and they would get there faster aboard the *Crystal Star* than by any other means.

Trouble finally came after they had cleared the Cape of Good Hope and were in the lower latitudes of the South Atlantic, where the Clouds of Magellan blazed across the night sky and the Southern Cross pointed out their path. After taking the noon sights that day, Julia and Stephen had gone below in a jubilant mood to enter a splendid day's run of two hundred and fifty miles.

Suddenly two shots rang out. Almost instantly a man began screaming. His voice was quickly drowned out by a roar of other voices from the usually quiet deck. Stephen immediately dashed to the weapons cupboard and unlocked it, then tossed the keys to Julia.

"Lock up the charts, sextants, and chronometers," he said as he took a rifle and two pistols from the cabinet and loaded them. "Arm yourself and stay here. Hand out weapons to the officers or the cook if they come below, but shoot anyone else who tries to get in."

The unexpected shock, the swiftness of it, left her feeling numb. She couldn't believe that after so long a period of peace, the men had decided to mutiny. And how in heaven's name had they managed to smuggle a gun aboard and keep it hidden?

"What do you think's happened?" she asked.

"God knows. It was calm enough fifteen minutes ago." He kissed her lightly on the cheek as he passed her. "Take care of yourself, Julia."

"I will," she said to his retreating back. The vision of what he might be walking out to meet suddenly terrified her. She clutched the keys so tightly, they bit deep into her hand. She half said, half whispered, "And God go with you."

The moment the door closed behind him, she spun into action. After locking the door, she secured the navigational instruments and the charts. She checked the gun cabinet. Then there was nothing more to do.

The tumult on deck grew continuously louder, but no one came. She held her breath and tried to still the beating of her heart as she strained to interpret the sounds. Was that another shot? Stephen! If only she could see what was going on. If only someone would come. Anyone.

I have to know! I can't stay here. If the mates won't or can't come, I'll take weapons to them.

Is that Stephen's voice? It's so hard to tell over that horrible din. Or have the men overpowered him? Have they *killed* him?

Oh, my God!

She quickly gathered up a selection of guns, then locked the cabinet and hid the keys in the bodice of her dress.

At the bottom of the steps to the companionway, she stopped. How stupid to even consider taking weapons on deck! If the men were in control of the deck, they would jump her and take them from her the minute she appeared.

She started back towards the safety of the saloon, but after only two steps, she swung about and faced the ladder. Stephen needed her! She knew he did!

She desperately looked around for a hiding place. Then she jammed the guns into a dark corner underneath the ladder. With one pistol in her pocket and another in her hand, she stealthily crept up the steps.

At first glance, she couldn't comprehend what was happening on the main deck. Most of the crew were clustered near the foremast. Others were trying to squirm behind anything that would hide even a portion of their bodies. Two men lay sprawled on the deck. As she watched, frozen on the steps, she could see the second mate edging his way around the cook house, and the third mate was on his hands and knees behind the pig pens.

Stephen! Thank God he was alive and unharmed. He stood not far away with his weapons at his feet. Why at his feet? He was staring up at the quarterdeck.

"Come down, Mister Evans," he shouted in a voice that made most men quail. "This is the last time I'm going to tell you."

"I'll not come down for the devil himself!" Homer Evans shouted back. He was invisible to her, but Julia could almost envisage his twisted face from the snarl in his voice. "I've got my orders, and those are the ones I follow."

"I'm master of this ship, Mister Evans, and my orders are for you to put that gun away and come down here."

"Hell no!" the mate screeched. "You're not master of this ship anymore. There's another more powerful than you, and she says there's more business to be finished."

Another shot was fired, and Julia watched in horror as a man fell out of the rigging and landed on the deck with a thump that sounded very final.

"Now your business is finished," Stephen said without turning to look at the fallen man. He walked very slowly but very purposefully towards the steps to the quarterdeck.

"Stay where you damned well are. I'm warning you, Captain," Evans snarled.

Stephen said nothing, but with his eyes fixed upon a spot above him, he started up the steps. He vanished from her range of vision, but Julia could almost count the three steps he had taken before she heard the two shots. Her heart stopped when she heard the crash as Stephen hit the steps. When he rolled onto the deck practically in front of her, she lost all caution. Complete uncontrollable fury, the savage need to avenge, gave her cold-strength and dispelled every other emotion.

Without showing herself long enough even to check on Stephen, she slid out of the companionway and hugged the bulkhead until she was near the foot of the quarterdeck steps. She was aware that all the crew were watching and she hoped that none of them would give her away. With both pistols in her hands, she prepared to mount the steps. She pointed the guns in the direction in which Stephen had been looking and rushed up the steps.

Just as she saw the mate, he turned away from her and fired at the cook house, where Clyde Rawlings had shown himself only long enough to distract the madman. Quickly she emptied both pistols at Evans and ducked down the steps. A shot went over her head, and then there was a thud. Instantly the two junior mates and some of the crew swept by her up the steps, and she raised her head to see if Evans had really fallen.

He was lying on the deck with his eyes on a level with hers and he was staring at her in absolute horror.

"Mary," he croaked, and then although his eyes were still fixed upon her, they no longer saw her.

She wasted no time on him, but rushed down the steps and knelt on the deck beside Stephen. He was breathing, but there was blood on the white shirt that covered his chest and more was soaking his right leg.

His life's blood! No! I have to stop it!

Although she had seen her share of blood over the years, the realization that this was Stephen's completely unnerved her.

"Mister Rawlings," she screamed at the quarterdeck. "Come here! Come quick!"

"Ma'am." A slender sailor with a short black beard approached. She recognized him as being one of the Californians who had come to them in discouragement. "Let me help. I apprenticed to a doctor once."

"Oh, thank God. Do something for him. Quick! Hurry!" she urged even as he knelt on the deck beside the fallen captain.

She watched, biting her lips, as the man efficiently sliced away the cloth covering the wound on Stephen's chest. As it came away, she could see that blood was still pumping up from a jagged hole.

"He's going to be all right, isn't he? He has to be all right!" She was almost incoherent as she unconsciously wiped her damp hands again and again over her skirt.

"I don't know." The young man frowned as he concentrated on his work. "We have to move fast. I need the medical chest, sharp knives, clean cloth, boiling water, alcohol, whatever else you can think of." He glanced at her for a second. "Can you get it? You're not going to faint, are you?"

"No. I won't faint." She stood up, swaying with dizziness, but then she straightened her shoulders and sent the cook and the steward to fetch the necessary articles.

Then she dropped to her knees beside Stephen again. Even as she gazed at him, the color seemed to be draining from his face. She took his hand and felt for his pulse. Though his wrist felt cold, but she thought she could feel a flutter. She looked with pleading desperation at the young sailor.

"Take a swig of that brandy," he said, nodding at the bottle the cook was putting on the desk beside them.

"No." She uncorked the bottle and handed it across to the sailor.

"I said take some of it and then get out of the way," the man said harshly as he thrust the bottle back at her. He seemed angry. "You're pale as a ghost and you're going to faint if you don't do as I tell you."

She shook her head. "I couldn't swallow it and I won't leave him."

"Then move back a little. You can't help me, but a couple of these can." He nodded at the sailors who were gathering in a respectfully distant ring around their fallen captain, and gestured for a couple of them to come forward.

"The other men . . ."

"We'll take care of them, ma'am," Mister Smithers said as he came up behind her and pulled her to her feet. "You come along with me now. You can watch from the quarterdeck."

"Mister Evans . . ." she said.

"He's dead," Smithers answered.

"Then I killed him."

"He killed himself, Mrs. Logan," the tall, raw-boned third mate said firmly as he led her to the quarterdeck steps. For a man who had started the voyage as a young able-bodied seaman, he was becoming very forceful.

"He shot himself?" she asked numbly, not really caring or thinking about her words. If the man was dead, it was enough.

"No, ma'am. It was your guns, but when he started on that rampage, he must have known he was committing suicide. Or would have if he hadn't been mad."

Then as they reached the top of the steps, she could see the mate was still lying where he had fallen. In his outstretched hand, he held one of the few repeaters they had aboard.

"Mister Smithers. The guns! We've got to lock them up."

"There's not much time for that." He glanced down at the main deck where small groups were gathered around the four fallen men. Then he nodded at the horizon. A mass of clouds was boiling up and the sea beneath them was tormented. "I think we're in for some heavy weather."

Julia looked aft at the helmsman, who had stolidly stayed by the wheel during all the excitement. Then it struck her. With the first mate dead and the captain seriously injured, there were only two very junior officers left to run the *Crystal Star*. And a storm making up!

Why, whenever there was an emergency aboard, must the wind always bring additional violence?

The axiom she had heard all her life struck her with a new impact. The ship comes first. It didn't matter who was ill, who was dying, who was dead. Feelings didn't matter, grief didn't matter, nothing else mattered. The ship comes first.

"There's no time for anything, Mister Smithers." She heard the words come crisply from her mouth. It was as though another had spoken. "Gather up the guns, get Mister Rawlings, and come below immediately."

"That'll leave no officer on deck." As if reminded of his duty, he glanced up at the sails and then went aft to check the compass. Satisfied, he returned to Julia. "And the men . . . they have to be tended to."

"I'm well aware of that, Mister Smithers, but I think we'll have to make do without a deck officer for five minutes. As for the men, without the ship, none of us is going to survive."

Smithers was taken aback. Where a moment before, the captain's wife had looked as though she were going to faint, the color had now surged back into her face, her shoulders were held very straight, and her chin was tilted at an angle that brooked no argument.

"Yes, ma'am," he said quietly so that the helmsman would not hear him. "Are you taking over for the captain?"

"That's precisely what we're going to discuss. Let's not lose any more time. The guns, Mister Smithers." She nodded at him and swept off the quarterdeck.

However, when she gained the main deck and saw the doctor's apprentice and the two men he had called upon to assist him kneeling beside Stephen's body, all of her resolution failed. Nothing else mattered. Not the ship, not the men. Nothing but Stephen.

She stopped beside him and clenched her jaw to keep from crying out, to keep back the storm of tears that threatened to engulf her. His face was a dirty grey-brown and so still, so deathly still. Out of the corner of her eye, she was aware of blood. Blood on flesh, blood on bandages, blood in the bowl of water. She dared not look at it directly, but only continued to stare at his face.

"How . . . how is he?" she asked.

"Mrs. Logan," the young bearded sailor said from between his teeth. "Go away."

The tone of his voice shocked her back to a realization of her surroundings. Several of the men were watching her, some with commiseration, some with fear, some with curiosity. Joe Smithers had approached Clyde Rawlings over near the galley house, and they were looking at her. Was it with skepticism?

She took one last look at Stephen's face. Was it *the* last look?

It took all of her strength to turn away from him and go to the companionway with her head held high. No one was aware that she nearly fell by tripping on her skirts when she descended the steps.

By the time the two mates followed her, she had regained control, and they found her returning the guns she had cached to the weapons locker. She nodded at them and then at the locker.

"Each of you keep a pistol or two. We may need them."

While they were stowing the guns, Julia unlocked a drawer and drew out the chart. She spread it across the table and then looked up at the two men.

"I know neither of you can navigate, at least not according to the sights you took at noon today."

"Still learning, ma'am," Mister Rawlings said with his square face held impassive. His brown eyes offered no apology.

"Yes, I'm aware of that, but it doesn't help us at the moment. Therefore, I'm the only one aboard who can. As such, I'll be the one who will give the ultimate orders aboard this ship till Captain Logan is well enough to take over. Is that clear?"

The two mates looked at each other. Joe Smithers ran a hand over his sandy hair and the color mounted in Clyde Rawlings' cheeks, but neither man spoke.

Finally Mister Rawlings looked back at her and said, "I don't know that the men are going to like taking orders from a woman."

"They don't have to take orders from me. *You* will take your orders from me, and you will be the ones to convey them to the men."

She looked at them intently for a moment. When neither man replied, she pointed with the tip of one finger at a penciled mark on the chart.

"This was our position at noon. We should now be steering northwest by north. How are the men, Mister Rawlings?"

"One dead. The other two . . ." He shrugged his shoulders.

"They're incapable of performing their duties?" she asked stonily. She was beginning to feel a resistance from the man who was now the senior officer of the *Crystal Star*.

"Yes, ma'am. Incapable and may never be capable again."

"Well, have the injured men brought below. The steward, the sailmaker, and the carpenter can see to them if that doctor's apprentice . . . What's his name? Jenkins?"

"Yes, ma'am. Jenkins," Mister Smithers said quickly. He had felt the tensions rising between Mister Rawlings and Mrs. Logan, and he had immediately realized that those tensions could endanger the ship. These two were the most knowledgeable persons aboard, and they would have to work together if any of them were ever to see their homes again.

"If Jenkins doesn't need them to help with the captain, they can take care of the others," Julia continued. "Stow the dead man somewhere till we have time to give him a decent burial. You might as well throw Mister Evans in with him, too. You are now first mate, Mister Rawlings, and you are second, Mister Smithers. You've both carried out those duties before, so you have the advantage of experience."

Stephen! The thought of him suddenly seared her with pain and she instinctively glanced towards the door to the passageway. How long would it be before they could bring him down? No. She had to concentrate on the matters at hand. What had she been saying? She hoped that they hadn't noticed her lapse. Oh, yes. She had to set them straight for once and for all.

"Once the captain has been brought below, no one is to see him except the three of us, the cook, and Jenkins," she continued in an even stronger voice. "No matter what his actual condition, we will say he is recuperating and is giving the orders. Do you understand? Captain Logan is still master of this ship."

"Yes, ma'am," Joe Smithers said without hesitation. He could see no other solution, and he'd lived in the forecastle too recently himself to have forgotten the danger of mutiny that was always present, especially when the crew felt that there was weakness in the officers.

Clyde Rawlings paused for a moment before he answered, but when he did, he nodded.

"Yes, ma'am." He spoke with reluctance and yet he had been too long at sea not to know the voice of command when he heard it.

After they had gone, Julia sat down and buried her face in her hands for a moment. Then she forced herself to get up and reload her guns. It was only when the weapons cabinet had been secured and the chart tucked safely away in its locked drawer that she allowed herself to pour the glass of brandy the doctor had ordered for her earlier. She sat down to sip it and closed her eyes as she tried to think things out.

Thank God for her experience in running the shipyard. If she had to run a ship, she just thought she could do it, but it was going to be a difficult line to walk. The crew would have to be kept in ignorance and the two mates would have to be dealt with by a firm hand. Any show of weakness on her part, and she would lose control.

Oh, Stephen! A pain slashed through her chest. No. I can't think about you yet. There's too much else. Men dying, dead, a short-handed crew. I should appoint another mate, but with so few men left, how can I? And if I did, who would I choose? The man who was on the helm just now? It took a cool head to stay in such close range of a madman while the shooting was going on. I'd need Rawlings and Smithers to advise me on that. That weakens my position. Or does it? Maybe not. One thing certain. I'm not going to show the charts to anyone again, not even the mates. I'll keep the drawer locked and the key well hidden. As long as they don't know where we are, no one will dare rebel.

And there may be a storm coming. We'll have to shorten sail soon. Mister Rawlings can handle that. They've got to get those men below. They've got to get *Stephen* below.

She swallowed the last of her brandy and firmly set her glass back in the rack. No matter what Jenkins had to say, she was going on deck. If her husband was dying, she had to be with him.

The next morning, after the burial services had been held and the mate and his victim had been sent in their weighted tarpaulin shrouds to lie forever under the waters upon which they had sailed, Mister Rawlings found Julia in the saloon. She had ordered breakfast, for she knew she must eat to keep up her strength, but at the moment she was staring at the cold meat and hard ship's bread with revulsion.

"Ma'am," Rawlings said, taking off his cap and revealing his curling chestnut hair as he entered the room. "Are we going to tack ship?"

"Tack ship? Why should we tack ship? The wind's from the right quarter, and we're making good speed." She picked up her fork resolutely. She *would* eat.

"Yes, ma'am, but we're making it in the wrong direction."

"Wrong direction!" She put her fork down again and stared at him. "I gave you orders to head northwest by north. What do you mean we're heading in the wrong direction?"

"I've been thinking, ma'am. We should turn back. We're not that far from Cape Town. If we turn back now, we can put the captain ashore. Jenkins says he thinks we'd best do that."

"So now you're taking the advice of a sailor and passing it along to me?" In her anger, she threw her napkin down and stood up to face him. She wanted to slap that square, phlegmatic face that was bisected one way by a long thin nose and a deep cleft in his chin and the other by the dark brows that slashed in a straight line across his forehead. She clutched her hands together to control her passion.

"Have you seen the captain this morning?" Rawlings asked without taking his eyes from her.

"Yes, I've seen him! I spent most of the night with him."

"Then you know he's losing strength."

"How do you know he's losing strength? He hasn't regained consciousness since he was shot. He was seriously wounded, Mister Rawlings. Do you expect him to leap out of bed a few hours after he's been wounded?"

"No, ma'am, but we ought to get him to a good doctor as soon as we can."

"Yes, we will. Do you know of a good doctor in Cape Town?"

"No, ma'am, but . . ."

"Do you even know if there *is* a doctor in Cape Town?"

"No, ma'am, but we've got to take the chance. We can't go on like this, with no master, not enough crew. What if the captain . . . dies?"

"I can tell you one thing, Mister Rawlings, and that is that Captain Logan *will* die if he wakes up to find himself in Cape Town. He'll die of apoplexy. We're going on. If it's necessary when we get to St. Helena, we'll put in there."

"St. Helena?" Finally she had startled an expression into that placid face.

"Yes, Mister Rawlings. I thought you were well qualified as a second mate."

"I am."

"Well, then you should realize that we have hit the southeast trades." She smiled, but her eyes were coldly mocking. "If we tried to return to Cape Town, we'd have to battle headwinds practically all the way. I can't think of a condition more suited to killing off the wounded men than having a ship bucking and heaving under them for days and nights on end. Furthermore, if the winds hold up, we can make it to St. Helena a lot faster than we can make it to the Cape of Good Hope. Now do you have any more questions, Mister Rawlings?"

"No, ma'am." His eyes finally left hers and he looked down at the cap he held in his hands.

"Then I have one," she snapped. "How many voyages have you sailed as second mate?"

"This is my second, ma'am." He looked at her again with unwavering eyes, sure now of his position. "Captain Thompson on the ship *Annabelle* appointed me second mate on my last voyage."

"You were second mate for the entire voyage?" she asked suspiciously.

"Well, no, ma'am. The second was sent forward for insubordination, and Captain Thompson brought me aft."

"When? How long before you docked did that happen?"

"About two months, ma'am." He looked down again, this time at his feet.

Dear God! Julia thought. It was far worse than she had realized.

"So now you're suddenly a first mate with less than a year's experience as an officer?"

"Yes, ma'am."

"Well, Mister Rawlings, you're not qualified for a master's berth yet, so I'll thank you not to question my decisions in the future." When she saw that he was still dubious, she felt like pleading with him, explaining to him. She needed his loyalty. But any show of softness on her part would only weaken her position, so she continued relentlessly. "Furthermore, this ship does have a master. Me. I have seven years more experience than you have. If you can't believe in me, then you'll just have to go forward."

As she watched him with narrowed eyes, she hoped her bluff would work. He must know as well as she did that there was no way she could force him forward, and even if she could, she knew there wasn't anyone with even his quarterdeck experience aboard. Smithers certainly didn't have it.

Finally he looked up at her. "Seven years, ma'am?"

"Yes. I've been sailing with Captain Logan since eighteen forty-two, and *all* of my time has been spent on the quarterdeck."

He thought about it for a moment and then nodded. "Yes, ma'am. Northwest by north."

After he had gone Julia gave up all attempts to eat and went into their cabin, where Stephen lay unconscious. His breath came in short, ragged rasps. Sometimes it seemed to stop altogether. Although she had spent hours by the dim light of a sperm oil lamp listening to the sound, it still lacerated her. During the night, she had found herself inhaling and exhaling more deeply than usual, as though the effort she made would ease his strain. She caught herself doing it now, and purposefully turned to the doctor's apprentice.

He had taken time to administer to the other wounded men and had snatched an occasional nap on the settee in the saloon, but for the most part, he had remained at Stephen's side. The hours of sleepless tension showed on his face. When Julia had first entered the cabin, he had glanced up at her, but now all of his attention was centered on Stephen.

"Jenkins? That is your name, isn't it?"

"Yes, ma'am," he answered quietly.

"Can you leave the captain for a moment? I'd like to have a word with you."

He nodded and stood up. After pausing for a second to check on Stephen once more, he followed Julia into the main cabin.

"The mate tells me you've advised him to put back to Cape Town," she said abruptly as soon as he was well away from Stephen's cabin.

"No, ma'am." Jenkins looked at her calmly. "Mister Rawlings asked me if the captain would be better off ashore. I just said yes. I didn't say anything about Cape Town."

"You overheard some of our conversation, I gather."

"Yes, ma'am. I think you're right to go on to St. Helena. We've got to

97

avoid headwinds as much as possible. If any of the wounded get tossed out of their bunks . . ." He pressed his lips together and shook his head. "I'm afraid it'll be the end for a couple of them."

"You're talking about the captain, aren't you?" She blinked her eyes to keep back the tears.

"Yes, ma'am, I am. I'm sorry."

"Do you think he overheard any of my conversation with Mister Rawlings?" she asked and nodded her head towards the cabin.

He hesitated as he examined Julia's face to see how much of the truth she could take. Then he shook his head again. "I don't think he can hear anything at all, ma'am. I don't think he's going to hear anything for quite some time to come."

"If ever," Julia added to see what his reaction would be. The words sliced her like a rusty knife, but she had to make herself face whatever possibilities the future might hold. To deny them would only sap her strength.

The man made no response, but there was compassion in his light brown eyes.

"I think you'd have made a good doctor, Jenkins. How long were you apprenticed?"

"Three years."

"Why did you give it up?"

"Gold," he said wryly and twisted his lips. "Gold and a girl. Thought I'd make a fortune in a few months and be able to set up my own practice and have enough left over to marry her. But I didn't find enough gold to even buy food, and every tenth man out there claims he's a doctor."

"All right. As far as I'm concerned, you are a doctor, and you know your qualifications. Do you think I'm apt to find a better doctor on St. Helena?"

He stroked his short black beard as he thought about it.

"I really can't say, ma'am. I've never been there. What's it like?"

"It's a rock sitting all by itself out in the middle of the South Atlantic. They have a fairly decent settlement, and a lot of vessels put in there for fresh supplies."

"A large settlement?"

"Not too large."

"I really can't say, ma'am. The British must have *some* doctor there if it's not near a mainland."

"Well, I'm sure they did when Napoleon was alive, but now who knows?"

"How long before we sight it, ma'am?"

"A week, maybe less. If the weather goes against us, it could be longer."

"Then why don't you postpone your decision until we get there, ma'am? We'll know more about the captain's condition then."

"*My* decision." She looked at him quizzically. "You overheard a lot, didn't you, Jenkins?"

"It would have been difficult not to." He smiled at her with sympathy and yet there was a certain admiration in his eyes. "I have no feelings about a woman acting as master, ma'am. My father died when I was very young, and my mother had to hold our family together until we were grown. As long as she lived, she saw to it we all got the schooling we wanted. Six children. I don't know of many men who could have done as well under the circumstances. If you say you can run a ship, well, then, ma'am, I believe you can run a ship."

"So I have one man loyal to me." Julia sighed and went to the doorway to look in at Stephen. He groaned and flung his arm across his face.

Jenkins came up behind her, and as he entered the cabin, he touched her lightly on the shoulder. "There'll be others, ma'am. I don't think you have to worry about Mister Smithers."

"Thank you, Jenkins." She took one more look at Stephen as Jenkins gently moved his arm away from his face. Then she turned away. It would soon be time to take the noon sights, and this time their course would depend completely upon her findings.

As she wound the chronometers and gathered up her instruments, Julia thought apprehensively about St. Helena. When she had told Jenkins that it was a rock in the middle of the sea, it was because that was the first impression it had given her the one time they had put in there for supplies. Upon landing, they had found that there was a valley of sorts between two towering mountains. The town, which was scarcely a quarter of a mile wide, consisted of small houses built of mud and stone. There were well-kept gardens with tropical fruit trees set all around, and the constantly changing vistas of crags and ravines were breathtaking.

But in the midst of all that beauty, what kind of medical help would be available? Would they find anyone better than Jenkins? In the short time Julia had been able to observe him, she had gained a great deal of confidence in him and his abilities. Perhaps it was misplaced. She had been wrong before. Yet she felt that she could trust him. And what of medical supplies? Everything on the island must be shipped in. Would they have anything that wasn't aboard the *Crystal Star*?

There was danger there, too. If the men suspected the real situation, if somehow they discovered how incapacitated Stephen was, there were bound to be desertions. She was almost certain that she would not be able to find a shipmaster there to take temporary command of the *Crystal Star*, and they would not be able to lay there long.

There was a good anchorage in the lee of the land, but there was no protected harbor. Without a crew capable of sailing her away from the land, a gale from the wrong direction would mean the end of the ship and her cargo of perishable tea. If they lost the ship under those circumstances, would the insurance cover her? Most likely not. Then Stephen, as major shareholder in the *Crystal Star*, would be responsible to the agents who had consigned the cargo to her. It could well wipe him out. He would never forgive her.

But his *life* was at stake!

She glanced at the chronometers and saw that there was almost half an hour before she would have to go up on deck. She wandered to the stern windows that had been unboarded after they had rounded the Cape of Good Hope. The clouds of yesterday had only accompanied a passing squall and now the sun shone through the tall, white-crested waves as though they were made of opaque green glass. The sleek graceful bodies of three or four porpoises flashed black as they played their game with waves and wake. They met the world so joyously, those creatures of the sea. What did they know of the griefs of men, of the lonely burden of responsibility for other lives?

What did the sea know that it should sing so harmoniously along the hull, proclaiming the perfection of wind, water, and ship? The long song was deep and rich and strangely hypnotic, and for a few moments Julia fell under its spell. It soothed her, caressed her, and gave her of its strength.

She longed to go in to St. Helena, to lay down the burden of the ship, of her husband, to find other, stronger hands, but now she knew that she couldn't do it. There was no real help, no real hope on that sea-moated island. Only death and desertion awaited them there. The sea would carry them safely on to England. The decision was made . . . or had been made for her.

She straightened up and took a deep breath. Yes. They would go on. And if she were to keep control, she would have to see to it that they didn't go close enough to the island to sight it. Once they were near land, Rawlings and the rest of them could take the ship away from her, but as long as they were in midocean, there was nothing they could do. The Scilly Islands would be their first landfall.

Unless Stephen died. She gasped as the thought, which she had been trying to keep buried, blazed into the open. What would she do then?

No! She would not think it. She would not believe it. Not so long as there was one shred of hope.

She picked up her sextant, called to the steward, and fled up on to the deck.

* * *

Yet that resolution did not still her doubts. Each day, when she heard Stephen's moans or when she watched his awful stillness that more nearly resembled death than it did sleep, she changed her mind only to change it back again. Each time she heard the cry "Sail ho!" from the lookouts, she hurried on deck always with the hope that the vessel sighted would be under the command of a friend.

If only the tall raking masts of *Neptune's Dragon* would appear on the horizon. Julia would think longingly of the clipper with her low freeboard and her figurehead of an enormous golden dragon, its tail trailing down the long hollow bow. Cousin William, bluff and hearty, would be standing on the quarterdeck with the sun sparkling on the gold that still shone in his white beard. He had come to her rescue so often before. Why couldn't he appear now?

She remembered the first time. She had just turned sixteen when she and William's eldest son, Jason Thacher, had discovered their love for each other. When they had decided to elope, it had been Cousin William who had seen that they were safely wed and that she was cared for until her father had relented and brought her home. When her friend Megan had needed passage home from China, it had been William who had provided it. When Julia had been determined that her child would be born at sea, it was William who had somehow convinced Stephen to let her have her way. And when the *Crystal Star* had been attacked by pirates on the China coast, William and David Baxter had come to their rescue.

David. The friend of her childhood who had always been on her side, right or wrong. Why couldn't the *Free Wind* suddenly appear? She could see him so clearly. Too large a man to fit in any cabin but his own, he gave the impression of clumsiness. The wide lips that always seemed on the verge of a smile contrasted sharply with the sorrow she had sometimes glimpsed in his grey-green eyes. Yet there was a steady, quiet kind of strength that ran consistently beneath his gentle surface. He would know what to do.

Either one of them would help her. She knew they would. Somehow they would find a solution, and in their faster ships, they would get Stephen to England much sooner than she could.

But no matter how often she searched the sea, theirs were not the sails that appeared. Nor did she know any of the other masters they encountered. It was a sea of strangers.

The person she yearned for most was her father. He had taught her first to row and then to sail on the waters of Cape Cod Bay. Later he had instructed her in the lore of ships. Her earliest lessons in the art of command had been learned at his side. After the many years he had spent at sea, he would be able to advise her. Her wish for him was so strong that at times she felt his presence, usually when she was at her lowest ebb. Then she would hear him saying, "You can do it, Julie. You can do anything you set your mind to." Even though she knew it was only wishful thinking, the sound of his voice comforted her and renewed her strength.

Often it was Jason who haunted her thoughts. She remembered only too well what his death had done to her. Tall and lean, as quick with his laughter as he was with his love, he had been just twenty-one when an August hurricane had ended all his prospects for a future. The grief that had sent her beyond the edge of madness was something she had never been able to completely forget just as she had never been able to completely forget him. She carried him always in a secret part of her soul that she kept well hidden from all others.

But now in her fear for Stephen's life, Jason rose to the surface. If she could lose one husband, she could lose another. How could she survive it? She would rather die herself. And she would remember the words of an old Tahitian woman. Many years ago, Omemema had told her, "You will live a long, long life, but you will die many small deaths before the big one."

And Julia knew she would not die. If Stephen didn't survive, a part of her would die, a vital, important part. It would be a major amputation, but she would be condemned to go on living that long, long life.

It was a bitter battle. There were joyful days when Stephen seemed to be improving, and there were the dark ones when he lost the ground he had gained. At times he was conscious enough for Jenkins to spoon a little water and broth into him, but once in his tossings, he reopened the wound in his chest. Stephen finally became aware of his surroundings on a day when they were a hundred miles east of St. Helena.

Jenkins had been sitting with him for a few hours while Julia charted their course and wrote up the log. She had been pleased during the past few days to see that neither Rawlings nor Smithers had come close in their observations. She had told them so, but she had given them false bearings and had kept the charts and log book carefully locked away. The keys she always kept on a chain around her neck, and they were well hidden in her dress. Since either she or Jenkins was awake at all times, she had entrusted the secret to him. By sleeping on the settee in the saloon as Stephen had so many times in the past, she made it difficult for the mate or the second to pry open the drawers without awakening her or alerting the doctor.

She was dusting sand over the last entry in the log to blot it when she heard Stephen call, "Julia!" He had often done that in his stupor, but even so she was quick to gather up the book and secure it. His eyes were closed when she entered the cabin, but he reached out a hand to her when she sat down beside him.

102

"Yes, Stephen. I'm here, love," she said soothingly.

He opened his eyes and this time he really seemed to see her. However, the short burst of elation she felt was quickly spent. She was too aware of the pallor of his face, the lines of strain impressed into his forehead, and the pain in his eyes. Although it was difficult, she tried to smile.

"Julia?" His voice was no more than a hoarse whisper.

"Yes, Stephen," she said, leaning forward to hear him better.

"The ship . . . Evans . . . how long . . ." Each word was an effort.

"Don't try to talk, sir," Jenkins said quickly.

"Who's . . ."

"He's a doctor, Stephen," Julia answered rapidly to save him from completing the sentence.

"Where . . ." His eyes became foggy with confusion.

"We're still at sea. He just happened to be in the crew. The ship's all right. Evans is dead. And we're just passing St. Helena."

"Have to get up." He tried to disengage her hand, but she held his firmly. He was so weak, it wasn't hard to do.

"No, everything's fine. It really is, Stephen." She looked deep into his eyes as she tried to convince him of the truth. "I appointed Rawlings first mate and Smithers second. The men are working better for them than they ever did for Evans."

"_You_ appointed?" The ghost of a smile appeared on his lips and then was gone.

"Yes. Someone had to."

He closed his eyes for a moment, and she thought he was going back to sleep, but he managed to rouse himself from his lethargy. "You running the ship?"

"Yes, Stephen. There was no one else," she explained. She didn't know what effect the news would have on him, but she had to tell him the truth. "The men don't know it, though. They think you are."

"Good." He closed his eyes and repeated almost as a sigh, "Good."

She waited for a while. Thinking he had gone to sleep, she began to pull her hand away.

"Don't go," he murmured. "Been thinking. You going in . . . to St. Helena?"

"No. We're way east of it."

"Good. Take the ship home, Julia."

"Home? Our cargo's for England."

"Meant England. Not thinking . . . clearly."

"Don't try to, Stephen. You'll be feeling stronger tomorrow. You can think then."

"Yes. Take . . . her . . . home . . . Julia."

This time when he lapsed into silence, he did sleep, and when Julia rose to leave him, she felt greatly relieved. He was going to make it. *He was!* And now she could tell Rawlings that the captain approved her course of action, and Jenkins was witness to the fact.

She needed that assurance, for the next day, Stephen's temperature rose. Jenkins looked as concerned as he had in the beginning, although he said that it was what he'd expected and that it was nothing to worry about. She did worry about it, though.

A few days later when Mister Rawlings finally realized that they must have passed St. Helena and confronted her with it, she was able to tell him that it had been on the day when Stephen was lucid and that he had ordered them to go on. The mate had simply nodded and gone on deck to relieve Mister Smithers of the watch. Julia dismissed him from her mind. With Stephen's explicit orders to back her up, she believed she had finally won Rawlings to her side.

Chapter Seven

1851

Two days later, as they entered the outer fringe of the doldrums, they sighted a barkentine tacking her sails through the light equatorial airs and were soon up with her. An American vessel, the *Frederick Gunston* of Baltimore, she was bound from Rio de Janeiro to Pernambuco. After exchanging greetings with her, Clyde Rawlings requested permission from her captain to go aboard. As the boat swung out, the mate kept himself surrounded by sailors and well away from Julia, so there was no opportunity for her to question him.

Her fingers were white with strain as she clutched the forward rail of the quarterdeck and watched him go over the side. Then she swung around and called to Joe Smithers, who had been standing nearby.

"Yes, ma'am?" He touched his cap as he came towards her.

"Mister Smithers, what's he up to?" Her whispered words hissed in the breeze.

"I don't know, ma'am," he answered, his light blue eyes concerned as he watched the boat riding the long waves of the foam-speckled azure sea. "Mister Rawlings never was one to talk much, and since the captain's been ailing, he hardly opens his mouth."

"I don't like it." She narrowed her eyes in anger and then raised her hand to shade them against the sun that flashed from every ripple in that vast circle of ocean. "He's up to something."

"Maybe he just went to see if he could get some fresh provisions, ma'am," Smithers suggested, hoping to calm her.

"Well, he's costing us time. He had no right to leave this ship without the captain's permission."

When the second mate raised his sandy eyebrows at her, she felt almost betrayed. She was certain the mate was plotting something, and she'd hoped that she could rely on Smithers to stand by her. Now she wondered.

She dismissed him to return to his duties but she remained by the rail, staring at the *Gunston* for over an hour as if she could penetrate through the wooden hull to the meeting that was taking place.

Finally Rawlings returned, bringing bananas and pineapples with him as well as some onions. However, his closed face looked smug to Julia. There was no way she could talk to him on deck without arousing some suspicions in the crew, so she went below to check on Stephen while she waited for the mate to appear. No matter how much he might want to avoid her, he would have to come down sometime.

He surprised her by following almost immediately. She'd had a chance to do no more than look in at Stephen, who was drenched with sweat, when Rawlings came into the saloon.

"Mrs. Logan," he said immediately, even before he had removed the cap that sat squarely on his head. "We're going to put in at Pernambuco. I wanted to tell you before I gave the order to change course."

"We are not going to put in at Pernambuco," she said and her indigo eyes glittered dangerously. "We are going to Liverpool."

"No, ma'am." His voice was firm and his eyes never left her face. He refused to let her anger intimidate him. "I'm sorry to disagree with you, but I'm not going to be responsible for losing the captain's life and maybe the ship, too. Captain Train says we can follow him in, and he gave me the proper course as well."

"Oh, Captain Train did, did he? Well, he's not master of this ship, and Captain Logan has not given orders to put in there."

"Ma'am, I'm afraid Captain Logan's not able to give any orders, and I'm not asking anyone's permission. As senior officer aboard, I'm telling you what I'm going to do. I explained our situation to Captain Train, and he advised that we should put in to the nearest port or I might be held responsible if the ship is lost."

"And just who are you going to be responsible to?" She stared at him imperiously, her chin held high. He was no taller than she, and when she stretched herself to her full height, she gave the impression of looking down at him.

"To the owners . . . and the courts."

"Well, Mister Rawlings, Captain Logan just happens to be the major shareholder of this ship, and in his absence I am empowered to handle all of his business affairs. Therefore, I am, in essence, the owner. As for the courts, I'll bring you into them if you dare take this ship anywhere but Liverpool."

"Yes, ma'am. Now if you'll excuse me, I'm going on deck and give orders to change course."

"*I will not excuse you*," she blazed at him, but he never turned to glance at her as he left the room.

When Joe Smithers came below a few hours later, he found the captain's wife sitting and staring blankly at the stern windows. She appeared to be trying to shred a wet linen handkerchief to pieces.

"Excuse me, ma'am," he said as he went to stand before her. "I wouldn't bother you right now, but I want to get some sleep while I can. Did you order Mister Rawlings to change course and follow the *Gunston* in to Pernambuco?"

"No, Mister Smithers, I did not!" Her words were cold and evenly spaced as she raised her head to look at him.

"I didn't think so, ma'am." He paused for a moment as he studied her face. Although it was obvious she had been crying, her dark-shadowed eyes were now heavy and lackluster. She seemed to be looking through him rather than at him. "What are you going to do about it, ma'am?"

"Do about it? There's not much I can do, is there?" she said bitterly.

"Maybe not just now, but later . . ."

"Later?" For the first time since he had come in, she really saw him. "Please sit down, Mister Smithers."

He dropped his lanky frame into a chair opposite hers, and leaning his elbows on the arms, he laced his long fingers together as he considered the problem.

"Well, ma'am, Mister Rawlings can't stay on deck twenty-four hours a day, and when he sleeps, he goes deep into it. If we wait till he gets to sleep and then tack ship, we might lose the *Gunston*."

"Yes, we might, mightn't we?" Julia brightened and her lips curved into an almost malicious smile. But then she shook her head. "I don't know how easy that'll be to do in these light airs."

"They won't stay light," he said earnestly, "and we have the faster vessel."

"But if we don't manage to lose the *Gunston*, and Mister Rawlings goes on deck and finds you've changed course? What'll happen then, Mister Smithers?"

"If we don't manage to lose the *Gunston*, I'll change course back again before it's time for him to relieve me. If he suspects anything, I'll just lay it to a change of air."

"And the crew? You think there isn't someone who'll be glad to inform him?"

"Most of them won't know the difference, and the helmsmen on my watch are loyal to me."

She bit her thumb as she thought about it, and then said, "Well, it's worth a try, Mister Smithers. You'll do it tonight?"

"Yes, ma'am, and every night hereafter. It's a long way to Pernambuco, isn't it?"

"Yes. A good long way . . . especially in light airs."

Joe Smithers carried out his plans for two nights, but dawn of each succeeding day found the *Gunston* still within sight. From morning until evening, whenever she wasn't below with Stephen or charting their course, Julia stayed on deck and watched the barkentine as she would an enemy. If she could have made it disappear suddenly below the horizon by sheer will power, she could not have concentrated upon it more closely.

On the third night, Mister Rawlings went up on deck well before it was his watch. Even before he had checked the compass, he knew that something was wrong, and after questioning the helmsman, he told the man to change course. Then he rounded on the second mate.

"I'll see you below immediately, Mister Smithers," he said in a tight, ugly voice.

"Aye, aye, sir," the second mate replied calmly.

Rawlings led the way down the dark passageway, but he didn't wait until they reached the saloon. As they passed the open door of his own cabin, he rounded on the second mate, and with one blow, knocked him through the doorway.

Smithers was up in a second, and grabbing the mate by his collarless shirt with one hand, he punched him soundly on the chin with the other.

Julia, who had been sleeping on the settee in the saloon, woke to the sounds of their scuffle, and with a pistol in one hand, ran up the passageway. In the dark, she couldn't see who the brawlers were, so she stood well away from the door and raised her gun.

"Stop it!" she commanded. "Stop it this instant or I'll shoot."

The two men broke away from each other, and Smithers said, panting, "Don't, Mrs. Logan. It's the mate and me."

"What in the lower levels of damnation do you think you're doing?"

"He changed course on me," Rawlings snarled. "How long's this been going on?"

"It was done by my orders, Mister Rawlings," Julia said coldly. "I told you we were not going to Pernambuco, and we are not."

"By all that's holy, we are. I don't want any more interference from a woman or her lackeys. If you don't give this up, I'm going to tell the crew about the captain's condition."

"You wouldn't dare!" Julia said with contempt ringing in her voice.

"Aye. I would. They'd be happy enough to go in if they knew the truth. They're already complaining about the fact that there's too much work and not enough men to do it."

"All right, Mister Rawlings." Julia slipped the pistol back into her skirt pocket. "You win. Go to Pernambuco if you want, though there's a hotter place I think better suited for you. But don't think I'm going to tell you how to get to Pernambuco."

"I know how to get there. Even if we lose sight of the *Gunston*, Captain Train traced his chart for me."

"Good. Now if you learn how to handle your sextant and are able to calculate your findings, you won't need any advice from me. I presume you do have your own chronometer. Now hadn't one of you better get on deck?"

She turned and walked proudly back into the saloon. Somehow she would best him. It just took a little more thinking on.

Fortunately, Joe Smithers didn't give up. The next night in the middle of his watch, a storm, which had been flickering on the horizon for several hours, struck. By the time the mate came on deck, it was too late to alter their course, and when morning came, the *Frederick Gunston* was nowhere to be seen.

"Well, Mister Rawlings?" Julia said, smiling sweetly at him when he came below for some breakfast. "It seems you've lost your friend."

"We're still going on for Pernambuco," he said stolidly as he sat down at the table.

"And how do you plan to get there?" she asked innocently. She was beginning to enjoy the idea of taunting him. He had put her through enough fear and frustration during the past few days.

"By dead reckoning." He looked at her steadily with no admission of defeat on his square, solid face. "You may have the chronometers locked up somewhere, but my watch keeps very good time."

"Does it? That's very interesting. Have you ever been to Pernambuco before?"

"No. But I will be soon."

"Well, I'm glad it's you and not me that's responsible. I'd hate to be running towards the coast of Brazil and not know where I was, especially when we get heavy weather. Captain Train did tell you about the rocks, didn't he?"

"What rocks?"

108

"Oh, you'll find them, I'm sure." She gave him a dazzling smile and went into her husband's cabin.

When she got there and saw Stephen's grey, glistening face, she stopped smiling. Perhaps she should give in and plot a course for Pernambuco. Anything that would help Stephen. Time seemed to be running out for him.

Then she reminded herself of the diseases that land held. Many of the people she'd known had died there or not long after they'd left it as a result of yellow jack, malaria, and other terrible diseases. It was no place to take a man in Stephen's weakened condition.

She sank down on the chair Jenkins had silently vacated for her and put her face in her hands. No matter what she did now, there seemed no hope. She should have put in at St. Helena.

Jenkins touched her lightly on the shoulder.

"I think he's better," he said quietly.

She just shook her head without lifting her face. Jenkins was kind, but she knew he was only trying to cheer her up.

"Really he is, Mrs. Logan. He woke up a little earlier and I was able to get some food in him."

"Was he lucid?" she asked as she finally looked up at the dark-bearded young man.

"I don't think so. He spoke about a place." He looked puzzled as he tried to remember the name. "Ombedia, I think he said it was. Do you know where it is?"

"Yes." Suddenly everything gave way. Unable to control the sobs that broke from her chest or the tears that poured down her face, she remembered the tenderness of their wedding night. Then at the beginning of this voyage, there had been the mirage of that golden city. It had seemed to be a promise that at last they would find Ombedia, their kingdom, where all their dreams would come true. And now Stephen lay here senseless, perhaps on the very brink of death.

"Come, Mrs. Logan." Jenkins pulled her up out of the chair and led her into the saloon. "You're exhausted. Lie down for a while."

Rawlings had gone, but the thought of him finding her in her weakness dried her tears as quickly as they had begun.

"I'll be all right," she said as she wiped her face with her handkerchief. She realized that what Jenkins had said was true. She was exhausted. "Go back to him. I'll lie down for a while."

Only two days later the mate came to her. During that time, they had not exchanged a word, not even a look. Now, after she had taken the bearings on the evening star, he followed her below.

"Are you going to tell me where we are?" he demanded.

"No." She glanced at the sextant he held in his hand and pretended grave concern. "Are you lost, Mister Rawlings?"

"I'm not the only one who's lost. *We're* lost."

"I'm not," she said coolly as she fitted her sextant into its velvet-lined case. "I know exactly where I am, and I know where *you're* going to be when we get home." She snapped the case shut and then turned on him in a fury she could no longer conceal. "You're going to be in prison. And I'm going to put you there for trying to murder my husband."

"Now, that's something you can't lay at my feet!" Exasperation sheared the normally impassive expression from his face, and in the lamplight, his dark brown eyes glittered with an anger that overlay fear. "I'm trying to get him ashore as fast as possible. You're the one who's murdering him by insisting that we go on."

"You want to take him to some filthy, flea-ridden town, where he's sure to die before a week is out. Meanwhile, you get lost in the Atlantic Ocean, and you've cost us precious time. Time that might make the difference in his life."

"Are you going to tell me where we are?" He put his hand to the pistol at his belt.

"You wouldn't dare," she said witheringly, disdaining to even glance down at his hand.

He challenged her in silence for a moment and then he slowly moved his hand away from his weapon. But he was determined not to give ground completely.

"Then maybe it's time for me to tell the men about him."

"Suit yourself, Mister Rawlings." She pretended indifference as she reached up to raise the wick in the gimbaled lamp that was swinging above their heads. "It won't have any effect on me or the captain, though I think they'd be a mite put out with you for deceiving them."

"They'll force you to get us on a proper course."

"I don't see how."

He took a step towards her with his fists clenched by his sides. "If I tell them you're withholding it . . ."

"I really don't think they'd touch a woman in anger any more than you would, Mister Rawlings, but if they were to kill me, I could hardly give you any course at all, could I?"

They stared defiantly at each other for a moment. Then he took off his cap, which he had not bothered to remove before, and slapped it against the palm of his hand.

"All right, Mrs. Logan. What's the course for Liverpool?"

"You might begin by sailing north. I'll give you a correction in about an hour."

"Due north." His face was drawn with angry defeat. "Aye, aye, *ma'am*."

110

Julia locked the saloon door behind him before she took out the chart and log. Whatever triumph she might have felt was stifled by a groan that came from the cabin. She worked slowly and precisely, and when she had finished, she studied the chart carefully. Thanks to the usual light airs of the doldrums, they really hadn't come very far out of their way. Now if they would just get a good, strong favoring wind, they might be in Liverpool in a month. If only Stephen could hold out that long.

They finally crossed the equator, and as they broke free from the doldrums, they picked up the northeast trades. It would have been a welcome wind if they had been going to Boston or New York, but as it was, it fought them and pushed them towards the wrong side of the Atlantic.

Headwinds always irritated her, but now as the ship pounded and slammed against the gathering waves, Julia worried about the effect it would have on Stephen. His wounds had been healing fairly well, despite the ravages the fever was wreaking upon him, and Jenkins felt that the action of the ship would no longer open them. Yet he wasn't able to calm her fears completely.

Often she would order a change of course to give him a couple of hours' ease, but she never dared to hold it too long. If she waited for a kinder wind, they might never get Stephen to England in time to save his life.

And now there was another danger, she thought as she watched the hands aloft to make sure they were properly scanning the horizon.

Saying that she expected more traffic in this area, she'd had Mister Rawlings double the lookouts, but she knew he was suspicious of her, especially since they had not sighted another vessel for two days. As she took the telescope from her eye, she was aware that he was watching her and she made a pretense of looking west as well as east. All morning she had been torn between the cabin where Stephen lay and the deck where she was afraid she would find the Cape Verde Islands looming on their starboard bow. The islands should lie well to the east of them if her calculations were correct . . . and yet . . .

There was nothing to be seen except spume flying from the crests of waves that rose higher than their lower yards when the ship hit the trough. The men aloft were quiet. Holding onto the rigging with one hand, Julia was just about to hand the glass back to the mate when a sailor who could have been Fair Henry's cousin, although he was an American with dirty blond hair named Link, came screaming up onto the deck.

"He's dead!" the man howled. "The captain's dead!"

She stared at him for a moment of incomprehension.

No!

The next thing she knew, Rawlings was supporting her, though when

111

she had turned to give him the glass, he had been a few steps away. His tan had turned sallow, and he was looking at her with anger that was edged with fear.

"Looked like you were going to faint," he said as he moved carefully away from her.

"No." She stared at him. Then the impact of Link's words returned. Stephen! It couldn't be true. She picked up her skirts and stumbled across the heaving deck as she tried to run to the steps.

Stephen! The word screamed through her head, echoing and echoing without ceasing. Stephen! Stephen! Stephen!

She didn't notice the men who reached out to help her as she fought her way across the pitching deck. Nor did she notice those on the main deck who had ceased in their work to stare aft with shocked incredulity. It was only the sight of Jenkins emerging from the companionway door that stopped her.

"He's not dead, Mrs. Logan," Jenkins said quickly. "He's still the same. There's been absolutely no change."

"But Link said . . ."

"Link's wrong," he said firmly.

"Go tell Mister Rawlings and have him announce it." She pushed past him and then she sank down on the topmost step. She was trembling so violently, she didn't trust herself to continue down the steps unaided.

Joe Smithers came out of his cabin and saw her there. His sandy hair stood on end and his shirt hung loosely outside of his denim pants. He had obviously been startled out of a deep sleep.

"Is it true?" he asked, staring at her with startled disbelief.

She shook her head, but when she tried to speak, her throat was too clenched to release the words.

"You look awful," he said and hauled himself up the steps until he could reach her. "Here. Hold onto me. I'll get you into the saloon."

Her legs felt as though they would never hold her up again, but when they reached the saloon and he tried to steer her to the settee, she said, "The captain. I have to see Captain Logan."

"No, ma'am," Joe Smithers said with kindness as he pushed her down onto the settee. "You stay put. I'll go check on the captain."

He did no more than glance into the cabin at Stephen, and then he returned to her and held out his hand.

"He's sleeping right peacefully, ma'am. Do you have the key to the liquor locker?"

"Yes." She fumbled with the chain around her neck as she tried to pull out the keys. Her hands were shaking so badly, she couldn't detach the one he wanted. When she tried to lift the chain over her head, the links caught in her hair.

"Take it easy, Mrs. Logan." He reached out and gently untangled the chain and then lifted it free. "I'll fix you something to settle you down. Do you prefer rum or brandy?"

"There's . . . there's some sherry." She still found it difficult to speak.

The first few sips had no effect, and she was shivering so badly she spilled some of the sherry from the half-filled glass before Jenkins returned.

"What's it all about, Jenkins?" Smithers growled the minute the man walked in.

"I was in the steward's galley for a minute, heating up some broth, when Link went by me shouting that the captain was dead."

"That man had no business down here in the first place. He needs a taste of discipline." Smithers strode towards the door with a purposeful glint in his light blue eyes.

"Wait!" Julia said. At least the sherry had given her back her voice even if occasional tremors still shook her body, but she was too late. The second mate had already gone.

She turned to look at the doctor's apprentice, who stood at the door between the cabin and the saloon so that he could keep an eye on both Julia and his patient.

"All, right, Jenkins. It's time to be absolutely truthful with me. How is he really?"

"I don't know, ma'am." He took a step into the cabin to feel Stephen's forehead and to listen to the sound of his breathing. When he returned to the saloon, where Julia had remained watching him, he sat down at a respectful distance from her, yet close enough to speak without shouting over the roaring of the wind and the crash of the waves. His light brown eyes were full of candor when he spoke.

"Every time I think I've got his fever under control, it shoots up again. I don't know how much longer he can take it."

"Will he last another three weeks?" Holding her breath, she watched him without blinking.

"I can't say. I wish I could."

"We're not far from the Cape Verde Islands." She stared at the glass she had unconsciously been twirling between her two hands. Then coming to a decision, she picked it up and swiftly drained it. "We could put in there. What do you think?"

"The only thing I know about them is that salt comes from there," he said. "What about doctors, medicines?"

"I don't know much more than you do about them, Jenkins. I've only seen them in the distance, but I wish to God I did."

"They don't sound likely. I think it would be best for us to go on. What's ahead?"

"At the moment, the Atlantic Ocean and not much else," she said as she saw the chart in her mind. "The Azores, but they'll be hard to reach. Once we get into the westerlies, we could head for Portugal. Maybe France."

"Well, why don't you start thinking about Portugal," he said gently. "I don't think he'll make it to England."

Julia stared at him. She had asked for the truth and she had gotten it. But it wasn't the truth! It couldn't be. Stephen wasn't going to die. He would never die. Not so long as she lived! He couldn't go off and leave her like that.

And if he did, how much of it would be her fault? If only they had put in at St. Helena, or Pernambuco. If he died, it *would* be her fault. For the rest of her life, she would have to carry the guilty grief around with her. Stephen! No! I'll never let you go.

She jumped to her feet, but before she was able to get to the cabin, the ship shot down the side of a wave, and she nearly fell when she reached the door. Propping herself against the frame, she looked in at Stephen. He was alive. Right now, right this moment, he was alive.

Braced boards made a barrier at the foot and on the nearer side of the bed, and the bulkhead enclosed him from the head and the far side, but Jenkins had also woven a cat's cradle over him to insure that he would not be tossed by the action of the waves. Fever had brightened his cheeks to a semblance of their normal windburned color, but his skin was stretched tautly across the bones of his face, and sweat glistened on his forehead and soaked his hair.

Jenkins followed her into the room and picked up some sheets from the bureau, where he kept his supplies. "It's time for me to sponge him off and change these," he said.

"I'll help you." Oh, Stephen, how I want to help you, to do something for you.

"No, ma'am," Jenkins said firmly. "I'm used to doing it alone. You go get some rest."

"Don't you see?" She looked at him, bewildered. How could he not see? "He's my husband. He's part of me. I *have* to help him."

"I'm sorry, Mrs. Logan," he said as he began to loosen the lacings that held Stephen in the bed. "I think I can understand, but then you're part of him, too. The only part that's functioning just now. I can't have you getting sick. Someone's got to navigate, someone who's had enough experience to know exactly what to expect from the winds in the different latitudes. From what I've overheard, neither of the mates has."

"I guess you're right," she said reluctantly. She could feel waves of weariness washing over her body, and she suddenly felt as though she had no will of her own. She was actually glad to have someone responsible to tell her what to do, even in so small a matter.

Still she lingered and watched Stephen's quiet breathing. He was alive. He was still alive, and yet who knew how long he would be. She tried to remember the exact color of his eyes, but all she could think was that they were slate grey, and that wasn't really true. They were other colors in them. Weren't there? Would he ever open them again? Would she ever have the chance to see them, to memorize them again? Oh, God, she thought, at least let me have my memories. Let them be true.

"Mrs. Logan?" Jenkins paused as an especially rough wave struck, and he looked at her with concern.

"Yes. I'm going."

She was just about to lie down on the settee when Clyde Rawlings came into the saloon.

"We've got a real mess on our hands now," he said angrily. "Who let that man down here?"

"I really don't know, Mister Rawlings," she said wearily. "That's your department."

"And Jenkins?" He looked malevolently towards the open cabin door. "What the hell was he doing?"

"Tending the captain," she shot back at him. "What the hell do you think he was doing?"

"Well, that man Link swears he saw the captain dead, and the men won't believe me." He held onto the table to brace himself, but preferring to look down at her, he remained standing. "They've asked to see him, just to prove I'm not lying. What do you think of that, Mrs. Logan?"

"Don't you have any control over the men, Mister Rawlings?"

"Yes, ma'am, I think I have a lot of control considering we're in the middle of the ocean with no captain, practically no crew, and for all I know, we're lost. I didn't ask for this job, ma'am. I signed on as second mate, and Captain Logan knew my background."

"All right, Mister Rawlings. You're doing a fine job, a splendid job. Now will you go away and leave me alone?"

"And what am I supposed to do with the men?" He would give no ground as he glared down at her. "They're panicking."

"The men, yes." She rubbed her forehead as she tried to think. Despite Rawlings' attitude, he was right. Something would have to be done. "We'll just have to let them see him. There's not much else we can do to reassure them. Tell them to appoint one . . . no, make it two men they trust, and then say that those men may see him tomorrow."

The forcefulness seeped from Rawlings' face as he considered her words. Suddenly Julia could see him for what he really was. A very frightened young man.

"But when they see the shape he's in," he said, "they'll know . . ."

"They won't know anything." She tried to remain calm as she thought it out. "We'll have Jenkins say that he's taken a powder to ease the pain and that he's asleep, but we'll let them take a short look. All they have to see is that he's breathing." If he still is, she added to herself.

"It's not going to work, ma'am."

"Do you have anything else to suggest, Mister Rawlings?" she snapped.

"No, ma'am."

"Well, if I come up with something new, I'll let you know." Then she realized how long she had been absent from the deck, but she also realized that she didn't have the strength to go up. Not now. "You haven't sighted any vessels, have you?"

"No. I think it's a waste of time." His face closed against her once more.

"Well, I don't, so keep the lookouts doubled. Now I'd like to get some rest before noon."

"Yes, ma'am." He glanced at the overhead doubtfully. "I'll go talk to the men and see how they take to the idea."

"For God's sake, Mister Rawlings. You don't talk to them. You tell them. And if there are any protests, you know how to conduct a flogging as well as any man."

While Jenkins slept that afternoon, it seemed to Julia that her husband's temperature continued to rise, and in his delirium he continually called out to her and spoke of things from their past. Some of them she had forgotten.

Clouds covered the sky by late afternoon, and there were no stars to be seen that evening. Rawlings reported that the crew had agreed to her idea and had already appointed the two men. There was nothing left for her to do but sit by her husband that night.

The *Crystal Star* bounced and pounded on the waves in the unrelenting wind. When Stephen groaned and muttered, she sent word to change course so that the ship would ride more easily. Even as she did so, she regretted having to do it, for the change would drive them farther away from Portugal. But she had to see that her husband lived through the night. With morning, things would look better. They had to.

She heard the watch change at midnight, but she must have fallen asleep shortly after that. When she woke up, she was lying on the settee, and she was sure that she had been sitting in the chair beside Stephen's bed. The first dim light of morning gave substance to the furniture, and she knew that she had slept for hours. When she sat up, her body was cramped and stiff as it so often was these days, but she slowly got to her feet. Each time she wakened, she dreaded what she might find. When she reached the doorway of the cabin, she saw that Jenkins was holding Stephen's hand.

"How is he?" she asked.

Jenkins' smile was glowing as he looked up at her. "The fever's broken," he said.

"Do you think it will come up again?"

"I don't know, but he hasn't been this cool since it first came on. It's a good sign."

Julia wanted to believe it, but she couldn't. Her hopes had been raised too many times before. She couldn't take another disappointment. She went in and looked down at Stephen. He did look more comfortable. Some of the lines had smoothed out of his face. She gently laid her hand on his forehead. It was dry and cool. Despite herself, she began to hope.

When the men came below to see Stephen, he was still sleeping peacefully. Rawlings had tried to put them off until the dog watch, but when he saw them muttering to each other as they went desultorily about their work, he decided that it would be best to get it over with that morning. Upon consulting with Julia, she agreed with him. Stephen looked better now, but who knew what might happen by late afternoon.

The two men came below respectfully enough. One was a disappointed young miner named Tim, who carried his slouch hat in his hands. The other, whose clothes were patched with flour sacking, was a few years older. Julia recognized him as Malone, the leader of the malcontents. The first mate as well as Jenkins and the burly cook were on hand in case there was trouble. Julia watched them from the foot of the bed as they entered the room preceded by Jenkins. There was scarcely space for so many people to stand in the small cabin.

"He is dead!" the man with the slouch hat said and began to back towards the door.

"No! Only sleeping," Jenkins said in a rougher voice than Julia had ever heard him use. "He took some sedation a while ago."

"Feel 'im, Tim," the tattered man said. "Looks colder than a mackerel to me."

As Tim reached out fearfully to touch Stephen, Jenkins grabbed his wrist. "None of that. Get your filthy hands away. You can see he's breathing."

"It's a trick," Malone said. "It's like when they put rats in the clothes of dead men to make 'em look alive so's they can palm them off on ship captains."

"What's a trick?" Stephen opened his eyes and looked at them. "What are you men doing in my cabin?"

"It's the captain!" Tim said, stumbling back into the other man.

"Who the hell'd you expect it to be?" Rawlings barked, and hauling them out of the room by their collars, he threw them across the saloon. "Now get back on deck and get to work before I have you both flogged."

"Stephen, you're awake!" Julia pushed her way past the gaping, rotund cook to reach the head of the bed.

"Of course I'm awake, and damned hungry," he tried to growl, but his voice was hollow with weakness.

117

"Good!" She smiled at him, still not believing, not trusting. "Jenkins and the cook will go round up something for you to eat."

As she looked up to see the two men leave, she noticed that the mate was still standing near the door, staring in at them. "Don't you have something to do on deck, Mister Rawlings?" she asked.

"Yes, ma'am." Clyde Rawlings hesitated for a moment. "It's good to see you feeling better, sir."

When Stephen only looked at him without replying, the mate left quickly.

"It feels cold for these latitudes this time of year," he said to Julia after Rawlings had gone. "Shouldn't be having headwinds this bad. Are you sure you've got her on the right course, Julie?"

"Yes. We're on course." She looked at him puzzled. "The North Atlantic's always cold in April."

"North Atlantic? April? Where are we? How long have I been out of it?"

"It's been a while. Too long, Stephen." Tears stung her eyelids. He was going to make it! Already he seemed to be gathering strength. "We were at a latitude of sixteen degrees north at noon yesterday."

"And the longitude?"

"Thirty-six."

"And it's April?"

"Yes."

He squeezed her hand, and his smile was the first she had seen from him in months. Then he closed his eyes and concentrated on his breathing. There was pain there. He could feel it inside him. When he opened his eyes again, he saw that Julia was looking at him with love and concern.

"I gather you didn't hit anything," he said.

"Not yet." She had to smile at the smoky glimmer of blue in his eyes. "But I've kept well clear of land."

"Rawlings, Smithers, they any good to you?"

"They've done a lot of growing up." She leaned over and kissed him on his cracked lips. "As a matter of fact, so have I."

"I don't see any grey hairs." But he could see the lines that had appeared in her face and the weariness written into the slump of her shoulders.

"If you go and get yourself shot just one more time, I'm going to turn pure white," she mockingly threatened him.

"Evans is dead, you said?"

"Yes. Thank God, he's dead."

"Have you been at it again?"

"At what?" She wondered if his mind had begun to wander again, and yet it had seemed remarkably clear till now.

"Shooting people."

She half smiled and shook her head. "Well, Mister Rawlings distracted him long enough for me to get a good aim, so he's partly responsible."

118

"Oh, Julia Logan, you're going to have a lot to answer for when you die," he said with a grin.

"As long as Mary isn't there to meet me, I'm not too worried."

"Mary?" He wondered how much his illness had affected his mind. He couldn't recall any Mary who was important enough to mention in that connection.

"Remember?" Julia took his hand and held it up to her cheek. "I told you about Evans' Mary."

"Oh, yes. Was that what did it?"

"I think so."

"She's not still aboard?"

"No. I think she went over the side with him. Here's Jenkins with something for you, and you listen to what he says. He's in charge of the health department aboard this ship."

Stephen grinned at her weakly. "Yes, ma'am. Where are you going?"

"It's nearly noon. Seems I have to go take the sights as long as the captain's so lazy he lies in bed all day."

"Do that. Then come back and tell me where we are."

"Aye, aye, Captain." She smiled, but in her hurry to leave, she nearly knocked Jenkins over. She didn't want Stephen to see her tears.

Chapter Eight

1851

From that day, Stephen's health rapidly improved, and as he put on weight, he gained strength. By the time they had reached the latitude of the Azores, he decided that he was going on deck, and no one could dissuade him. With the help of two of the strongest men in the crew, he half walked and was half carried up into the sunshine where a lashed-down armchair awaited him. He was still terribly thin, and he had a decided limp whenever he put weight on his right leg. The carpenter carved a cane for him, and with its help, he was able to get around.

No one minded Stephen's carpings and his criticism. Even Clyde Rawlings smiled when the captain snapped at him about the set of the foresails. Both the mates and Julia were relieved to have him back in command. And he was. From the moment he set foot on the quarterdeck, there was no doubt as to who was master of the *Crystal Star*.

He was still weak when they approached their destination, but he was on deck to greet the pilot when they picked him up twenty-seven miles out from the Scilly Islands.

That night when he was alone with Julia, Stephen broached the subject that had been on his mind for some days. It was after supper, but he didn't want to sleep while they were entering the Irish Channel. He sat now with his leg propped up on a chair. The exertions of the day had left him pale and strained.

"I'm going to sell the *Crystal Star* in Liverpool, Julie," he said abruptly.

"You don't think you'd get a better price for her back home?" Julia asked as she thought of the demand there had been for any kind of vessels, especially one of the *Crystal Star*'s reputation, before they had left home.

"I don't know. Since the British repealed the Navigation Laws, their shipowners have been hurting. You saw what happened when we were in Hong Kong. The Americans are taking all their business away from them. Remember, British agents consigned their teas to us while their own countrymen were sitting in the harbor begging for a cargo. I imagine we'll find some shipowners in Liverpool who'll bid high for the *Crystal Star*. She may be nine years old, but she's still better than the arks they're using."

"How will we get home?"

"By packet." When he saw the look on her face, he laughed. "Why not? It'll be a vacation for us. Nothing to do all day but see the sights. No worries. No work."

"It would drive you crazy. You'd spend all day and half the night, too, criticizing everything the captain did."

"No. The White Diamond Line has some of the world's crack masters." He took a sip from the glass in front of him and thought deep and long. He hadn't wanted to tell her, but now he knew that he must. Finally he said, "Julie, I'm not up to taking a ship across the Atlantic. Not yet."

"Well, you will be," she said cheerfully. "For a vacation, why don't we spend a couple of months in England? We can put the *Crystal Star* in dry dock and have her overhauled. We'll just relax and have a lovely time."

"More likely I'll be spending my time with the doctors."

"But you're so much better now!" She looked at him with concern. What was he trying to say? "You are, aren't you?"

"There's something wrong inside my chest, Julie," he said quietly. "I don't think Jenkins got everything out."

"But you haven't mentioned it before!" The color drained from her face as she stared at him. After the months of worry, she had begun to relax, to feel once more that she would never lose him. Now the leading edge of those nightmare clouds seemed to press in on them again.

"There was no point in mentioning it until something could be done." He reached across the table and patted her hand. "There are some fine doctors in London, and I'd like them to take a look before we go home."

"He said the shot went straight through." She tried to cling to the belief that Stephen was only imagining it, that all would be well.

"Most likely it did go straight through, but something happened in its passage." He smiled at her reassuringly. He knew the toll his illness had taken of her, and he didn't want to put her through more. "Don't worry about it until we know what it is. Meanwhile, you can begin making lists of all the things you want to see and buy in London."

"Have you told the mates about selling the *Crystal Star*?" she asked as she tried to avoid thinking about his health. It was better to think of anything else until she could absorb what he had told her.

"No." He shook his head, grateful that she had turned to another topic. He didn't want to dwell upon the mysteries of his body. The fear was already too great. "I wouldn't mention it to anyone until I discussed it with you."

"They'll have to find new berths or we'll have to pay their way home," she warned. " 'Twill mean further expense."

"I realize that. I'll try to find a good berth for each of them. They've earned the highest recommendations I can give them."

When he saw her frown, he said, "What's the matter? Don't you approve?"

"Yes, yes." She rose to go to the door and looked out into the passage-way. It was empty. The only sounds came from the pilot issuing orders on deck, the creaking of the masts and spars, the taut song of the rigging, and the ever-present singing of the sea upon the hull.

"Well, what is it?" He eased himself into a more comfortable position as he watched her. "Did you have some sort of trouble with them that you haven't mentioned to me?"

"Well . . . not with Mister Smithers," she said hesitantly as she looked back at him sitting in the swinging circle of light. "But I did have some problems with Mister Rawlings. I think he was afraid. He kept wanting to put in every chance we got."

He was silent for a moment while he tried to imagine the situation that had existed during those weeks that would be forever lost to him. If there had been a difference of opinion between Rawlings and Julia, there was no question in his mind as to who had the soundest judgment. He was sure that it was only due to her efforts that the cargo would be delivered in good time and that he himself would shortly receive the best medical attention. Yet without a good mate, it wouldn't have been possible for her to have brought the ship as far as she had.

"I can understand his fears, Julie," he said gently. "I've had them myself. The responsibility for another man's life, especially the captain's life, can be crushing at times."

"I know." She returned and put her hand on his solid shoulder. After having so nearly lost him, she found herself constantly wanting the reassurance of his body. "It was just that he made things so much more difficult than they had to be. I reckon it's hard to forgive and forget, but he *has* done a good job. The decisions about the amount of sail to carry, keeping the men under control and disciplined, it all fell on his shoulders. He's even learned to navigate pretty well, though I didn't dare tell him till you were better."

"Well, his fixes in the past couple of weeks have been all right." When he looked up to smile at her, his grey eyes were intensified by the tan he was regaining. He looped his arm around her waist and pulled her down until she was sitting on the arm of his chair. "You can't let your personal feelings stand in the man's way, Julie, but if you can think of any legitimate reason why I shouldn't recommend him as fully qualified to serve as first mate, I'd like to hear it."

She leaned her head against his as she thought about it. After all, what had the mate done that was so wrong? Throughout the long ordeal, they'd only had one basic difference of opinion, and if things had gone differently, it might have been she that was wrong. Aside from that, he had stood long, arduous watches, gotten very little sleep for weeks on end, and had brought the ship through rough weather with the loss of only two sails.

"No. I can't think of any reason not to recommend him. He held up his end. In fact, I hope you are able to get him on some vessel as mate." Then she smiled. "I doubt he's qualified to serve as master yet, though, much as he might believe he is."

"No. He'll need a little more seasoning for that." Stephen laughed, then gasped as he put his free hand up to his chest. He tried to cover it up with another laugh. "I remember when my uncle used to tell me the same thing."

Julia jumped up and stared at him. "Stephen! You *are* in pain."

"No, it's nothing. Just something a little loose in there."

"Come on," she said and took his hand. "Mister Rawlings is on deck with the pilot, and since you think so highly of him, I reckon you can leave it safe with them. Time for you to lie down."

"I think I will." He took a few shallow breaths and then a sip from his glass. "Let me just rest here for a few more minutes.

A sooty yellow haze hung over the city of Liverpool as the steam tug towed them into the wharf, but it was one of the most beautiful sights Julia had ever seen. The ship, her cargo, and her captain would all soon be safely docked. It was only now that she fully realized how many doubts she'd had that this moment would ever come.

A crowd of people was waiting to meet them. They couldn't be just boardinghouse crimps, for those parasites were already aboard, tempting the haphazard crew with their wretched whiskey and offers of friendship. Before they had come swarming out in Whitehall boats to meet them, Stephen had warned the men what would happen if they were taken in.

Yet he'd had no choice but to let the crimps come aboard his ship.

As soon as the lines were made fast, people of all conditions and walks of life started to pour aboard, and Stephen retired with Julia to the saloon. There they would await the agents for the cargo and any other persons whom the mates considered had legitimate business with the captain. Many of the people had come only to see the ship, for even now the *Crystal Star* was a beautiful thing.

The first person to come through the door seemed to fill it, and he had to bend his head, covered with dark blond curls, in order to clear the lintel.

"David Baxter!" Julia jumped up and threw her arms around him as far as they would go. "How did you get here so fast? You hadn't even arrived in China when we left."

"Julia." He gave her a light kiss on the cheek, but the wide lips that usually seemed to verge on a smile were tight, and there was no particular joy in his grey-green eyes, not even when he said, "Eighty-seven days from Shanghai. They tell me it's some kind of record, but then you always could build a fast ship."

"So the *Free Wind*'s still as good as new?" She smiled at him and tried to make him smile back while she wondered what was wrong. He should be on top of the world with a record like that.

"Better than new," he said tersely and looked at Stephen over her shoulder. "Julia, I'd like a word alone with your husband."

She laughed. "Why surely you two can't have any secrets from me."

"Captain Thacher asked me to deliver a message to him privately," David said quietly, never taking his eyes from Stephen's.

Then she saw the tension and anguish that were written on his face. And suddenly the realization of what such a message from Cousin William could mean overwhelmed her. Stephen understood it, too.

"You'd better do as he suggests," Stephen said to her quickly. "Leave us alone for a moment."

"It's Clara, isn't it?" she gasped as her hand flew to her throat. "What's happened to her? Or . . . or is it Papa?"

"It's your father, Julia," David said as he looked into her dark blue eyes with sadness and sympathy. Afraid of what effect the news would have on her, he put a large, square hand on each of her arms.

"Another stroke?" She stared up at him and held her breath, praying that he would say yes. The alternative was too awful.

"I'm afraid that's not all, Julie."

"Then he's dead. Oh, dear God! Oh, no . . ." she wailed, and bent with the anguish of it as David propelled her into a chair. "Papa! Papa!"

She hardly felt David's hands as they gripped her shoulders from behind or noticed the glass that Stephen folded into her hand. All that she could think of was the tall man with his laughter, his love of the sea, his love of her. Who would ever believe in her so completely again? Who would ever now say, "You can do it, Julia. You can do anything you set your mind to"?

Then Stephen was kneeling beside her and she was folded in his arms. Over the painful blur of memories, she heard him say to David, "Will you go out and explain? The agents will be coming. The pilot. He has to be paid off. The men . . ."

"I'll take care of it," David agreed.

"The key to the money box . . ." Stephen said.

"I brought some cash along. We can settle accounts later. I'll tell the agents to return in three hours?"

"Yes. Three hours."

The door closed, and then there was just Stephen holding her so close and letting her cry.

After a while, he said gently, "You knew it might happen, love."

"I know," she sobbed, "but that doesn't make it any easier. Oh, Papa, Papa. Please don't be dead, Papa. Please don't be dead."

"Hush, sweetheart," Stephen said as he kissed her wet cheek.

"He taught me everything I ever knew."

"I know."

"I shouldn't have left him," she whimpered.

"Hush, Julie, hush. He wanted you to go to sea."

"If I'd been there, I wouldn't have let him die."

"Oh, Julie." He stroked her hair and held her even closer. He could feel her heart breaking within his own chest. "No one can stop death when it comes."

"But he died alone."

"We don't know that. Oh, Julie, your mother was probably with him . . . and your sisters."

"But *I* wasn't with him."

"I know, love, I know. Come on, sweetheart." He pulled a large linen handkerchief out of his pocket and wiped her face with it, though the tears were coming faster than he could blot them dry. "Try to get hold of yourself."

"I can't, I can't. I don't want to. I want Papa."

"You have him, Julie. You're a lot like him, and as long as you're alive, he can't really die. After all, I don't know of any woman except your father's daughter who could have brought a ship safely through the way you did."

"He would have been so proud of me. I wanted to tell him." She sniffed and then took the handkerchief from him to blow her nose.

"Julie, if there's any justice in heaven, he knows all about it."

"Do you think so?"

"I'm sure of it."

"Sometimes . . ." She twisted the handkerchief in her hands as she looked at him with the bewilderment of loss. "Sometimes when I was so tired and when I was so scared you weren't going to live, I felt as though he were there, sort of watching me, wanting to help."

"Then he probably was."

"I have to go home."

"I know. We'll take passage on the next packet."

"But you have to see the doctors!" The fear of a double loss splintered the control she had been gaining, and she threw her arms around him. "Oh, Stephen!"

"I'll see some in the States," he assured her as he held her close.

"No." Her words were muffled by his black broadcloth jacket. "You said there were good ones in London. You've got to consult them long as you're here. Clara needs her papa, too."

"All right." He was willing to agree to anything that would comfort her. The real decisions could be made later. "We'll stay until I've had a chance to see them. I'll see if I can't get through it quickly."

"Yes, but the shipyard?" While still clutching at his arms, she pulled a little way back so that she could look at his face. "How long has Papa been . . . gone? What's happening at home? You know how Sarah and Uncle Josiah were last time. And Mama? What's happened to her? Her whole life was built around Papa."

"Julie." He stroked her face with warm and gentle fingers. "You'd better go on home. You won't be able to rest until you get there. I'll stay here and see about selling the *Crystal Star*. Then I'll go over to London and consult with the doctors. It won't take long. I'll be home before you know it."

"No!" Her fingers pressed fiercely into his arms. She was close to panic. "I can't leave you, Stephen. If anything should happen to you . . ."

"Nothing's going to happen," he said firmly. He was afraid that she was getting close to hysteria and he had to stop it. "You've done everything you could for me. Now it's up to the medical profession."

"No. I'm going to stay with you. I can't help Papa now, but I can at least be with you. Besides, I . . ." Her face crumpled and she fought to hold back the fresh onslaught of tears that threatened. "I don't think I can face crossing the Atlantic alone on a packet full of strangers. Not now."

"Well, we'll see." He rose from his knees. His bad leg was becoming more painful with each moment. Then he pulled her up from the chair so that he could hold her against the length of his body. He pushed the disheveled black curls away from her face. "Are you feeling any better?"

"I don't think I'll ever feel any better, but I reckon I won't disgrace you by bursting into tears again."

"You can burst into tears any time you want, sweetheart," he said as he looked at her with a sad smile. "You've earned the right to them."

"Stephen, I need you," she said earnestly. "I need you more than I ever have before."

"You do know how much I love you, don't you, my lady?" He tilted her chin and looked deep into her moist sapphire eyes.

"Yes. I think so."

"I do." He held her very close. "I do with all my heart."

When David Baxter returned, he found the saloon empty and the door between it and the master's cabin closed. He looked at it contemplatively for a few moments and then went into the passageway and shut the door behind him. Standing guard there, he refused to let anyone by and dealt with the problems as they came up. When he finally heard a noise from the saloon, he knocked on the door, and Stephen opened it for him

"Julia's lying down," her husband said. "She was . . . very attached to her father."

"Yes, I know," David said quietly. "Your mate just told me the story of your voyage. How are you feeling?"

"Not well, really. I'd planned to go to London to see about it, but now I think I'd better take Julia home. She's been through a lot, and I don't know how much more she can take." Stephen sat down in the nearest chair, and his face was white. "You've known the family a long time. Do you know anything about the time when . . ."

"When Jason Thacher died?" David asked and thought of those long past times when Julia's first husband had gone down with his ship during a hurricane.

"Yes," Stephen said abruptly. He abhorred even the thought of the man who had preceded him, but now it was necessary to speak of him.

"Aye. I know about it," David said quietly.

"I think she'd be better off at home right now . . . in familiar surroundings. Her father's death . . ." Stephen shook his head.

"She's not wandering, is she?" David sat down and leaned tensely forward. "In her mind?"

"No. Not yet."

"She's stronger now than she was then," David reassured him. "She was right young at the time. Doubt it will happen again."

"I hope not. I sincerely hope not." Stephen stared at the closed cabin door.

David watched him and wondered if the anguish that showed in the lines around his eyes wasn't caused by physical as well as mental pain. He pulled several sealed letters from the pocket of his coat and laid them on the table.

"Soon as he heard the news, Will Thacher sailed for Boston. Felt he could be more use there than here, but he asked me to wait for you. He left these letters." As Stephen pulled them wearily towards himself, David added, "I've got a house here in Liverpool. Least it's my wife's house. There's a room waiting for you and Julia."

"We couldn't," Stephen said, passing his hand over his face. "It would be an imposition."

" 'Twon't be any imposition, and I doubt it's a good time to take Julia to a strange hotel. Captain Howard did a lot for me. Meant a lot to me, too. I'm asking a favor of you. Let me do what I can."

Stephen rubbed his chin as he looked steadily at the big, rugged man who seemed cramped in the confines of the saloon. With his low forehead and oversized jaw, David Baxter certainly wouldn't be called handsome, but he had been Julia's friend since childhood. There had always been an affection between the two of them that Stephen had never cared for, but there was no one else.

"Will you take her home with you?" he asked. "To the States?"

"Yes, of course," David said quietly.

"I really think it would be best if I stayed. If she sailed with you, she'd be with someone who understood her, someone who . . . cared for her."

David glanced sharply at him, but Stephen was leafing through the unopened letters on the table.

"I'll do my best."

"But you don't own the *Free Wind*, do you?" Stephen asked casually. "Does Captain Richardson approve of your carrying passengers?"

"I don't think he'd object to my taking Julia under the circumstances. He's a great admirer of hers. She can have my cabin."

"Yes. Well, that's good of you. We'll accept your other invitation, too. I'm going to have to get Julia off this ship, and I don't want her left alone when I go out to settle my affairs. When do you sail?"

"Within the week."

"Good." Stephen straightened up. "Would you mind bringing that decanter and a couple of glasses over here? Then we can get down to business. I'm afraid you've had a lot of mine to handle today."

She would have preferred to stay in her room, Julia thought as she sat in the parlor that always seemed dusty. The furniture had been elegant, but the once brilliant colors had faded, and the sun shone through dirt-streaked windows. As she watched Cynthia Baxter and her friends gathered around the piano, Julia longed to be home away from their discordant laughter

127

and their even worse singing. They never seemed to stop except to eat and drink.

It wasn't so bad when Stephen or David was here, but each had gone out to attend his ship's business. She hadn't even wanted to come here, hadn't wanted to meet David's wife, but her husband and her friend had insisted, so here she was.

The front door shook with a series of loud knocks, and more friends of Cynthia's came flocking in. Julia wondered how the small house could hold them all.

"Julia," Cynthia said as she brought the new arrivals over to her, "I want you to meet Jessamyn Foster, James Foster, and Fenton Parkinson. This is our houseguest, Julia Logan." Cynthia's hands, which were never still, fluttered her fan as Julia stood up to meet the newcomers.

While they were shaking hands, Cynthia went on in her lilting, laughing voice. "You won't believe it, but Julia is one of David's *oldest* and *dearest* friends. They used to play together when they were children in that *barbaric* country of his. When we heard she and her husband were in Liverpool, we absolutely *insisted* that they stay with us. In fact, she's going to sail back to America with David. Can you *imagine* that?" Cynthia tossed her brown curls and laughed up at James Forster over her fan.

Cynthia's exaggerations were becoming more irritating with each passing hour. David was fully six years older than Julia, and they had never played together, but she had looked up to him as a replacement for the older brother she had lost and only dimly remembered. While David was growing up at sea, he had always sought her out and been kind to her during his short visits home.

"I hope your departure won't be for a long time, ma'am," Fenton Parkinson said, as he stroked his pencil-thin blond mustache with the back of his index finger. Julia thought his pale blue suit clung much too tightly to his slender body, and she disliked the smile that was entirely too knowing and familiar to come from a stranger.

"We sail very shortly, I believe," she said tersely.

"What a pity! You should find some excuse to stay here . . . pretend you're ill or something of that sort . . . and let your husband sail off with Captain Baxter. I'm sure you'd find our little group here in Liverpool quite compatible." His small brown eyes danced with conspiratorial delight.

"I'm afraid that's impossible, Mr. Parkinson," Julia said quietly and tried to think of some way of escaping from the room.

"Oh, her husband isn't going with them," Cynthia trilled. "Julia and David are going alone. That's what's so absolutely *hysterical*. I'm afraid you'll have a dull time of it, though, Julia. I don't believe David's ever said two *consecutive* words together in his life."

"I'm afraid you'll have to excuse me," Julia said. "I'm not feeling well. I think I'd best get a breath of fresh air." She started towards the door, but Fenton Parkinson was ahead of her.

"If you're feeling ill, you shouldn't go by yourself. Permit me to accompany you," he said, picking up his silk hat and his slender cane.

"No. Please. I'd rather be alone."

"But I insist."

"Well, I insist that you don't!" Julia flashed at him. She had had just about all of these people that she could stand.

Cynthia looked at her in surprise. "Why, Julia! Fenton was just being polite."

"I know." Julia tried to control her temper, but she found it impossible to smile. "I'm sorry, Mr. Parkinson, but I don't think my husband would understand if he heard I'd been out walking alone with a gentleman I'd just been introduced to."

"Ah, but I do understand." Fenton Parkinson beamed at her. "If I had a wife half so beautiful, I rather imagine I'd be jealous, too."

Julia nodded and caught up her shawl. She didn't care whether it was cold out or not. She wasn't going to stay here long enough to get her coat. She swept swiftly out of the house and into the street.

She walked blindly and rapidly. She wasn't aware of the roughness of the brick sidewalks or the excrement and filth of the cobblestone streets. Nor did she notice, as she had earlier, the soot that stained the mortar and the woodwork of the tired brick buildings a uniform smudged black. She brushed by hawkers selling muffins, ragged women who thrust flowers and ribbons in her face with never a glance at them.

The docks weren't far away. If only she could get there, she would go on board the *Crystal Star* and sit in her own quiet saloon. Her eyes were fixed on the hundreds of masts that lined the waterfront. When she turned the corner, she could see the bowsprits that rose high above the street. She had been so dazed when they'd left the *Crystal Star*, she wasn't completely sure where they were berthed, so she searched for the sweet lines of her ship and the golden-haired figurehead clad in white robes who held a star aloft in her hand. She was concentrating so sharply upon her search, she wasn't aware of the faces around her when she bumped into someone.

"Julia, what are you doing here?" Stephen asked as he took her arm.

"Oh, Stephen!" It was so good to see him, to feel the security of his presence in this dirty city full of dirty strangers. "I had to get away from them. They're the most unbearable lot of people I've ever met. Every time that Cynthia opens her mouth, I think I'm going to scream."

"You really are upset, aren't you?" Stephen said as he studied her face intently. With no hat, her hair trailing down beside her face, and her shawl thrown haphazardly around her shoulders, she might have been one of the sailors' women. He was glad he had found her before anyone had mistaken her for one.

"Yes. Cynthia's full of insinuations all the time, and her friends . . ." She clung tightly to his arm and her eyes were damp with despair. "Her friends aren't very nice people."

Despite his concern for her, Stephen gave a short bark of laughter. "Is that the best adjective you can come up with? I'd say it's an understatement. They're a wretched lot."

"Stephen, please take me somewhere else. I don't want to go back to that house."

"Of course." He put his arm around her shoulders and guided her back towards the street. "I'll take you to a hotel, but aren't you afraid of offending Baxter?"

"No. He'll understand." She pressed her lips together as she tried to think of David, but all she could see were Cynthia and her friends in all their tawdry, unwashed finery, and the sound of their taunting laughter echoed in her ears. "Even if he doesn't, I don't care. I won't go back there."

"You don't have to, sweetheart." He signaled for a hansom cab. "I'll take you to a hotel. Then I'll go back to the Baxters' and pack up our things."

"Oh, Stephen," she said as he helped her in. "I can't put all this on you. You're not feeling that well yourself."

"I'm well enough to do that," he said as he settled himself down beside her after he had given instructions to the driver. "I promised your father I'd look after you, and I shall. Besides I'd just as soon move out of there myself. With that infernal racket going on half the night, I'm not getting much sleep."

With Stephen's arm securely around her, Julia relaxed and thought how little time she had left to feel that familiar pressure. "How did things go today?" she asked.

He sighed and she could see that he was tired.

"We finished unloading. The ship will be shown beginning tomorrow and the auction's to be held next week."

"Oh, no!" A pain lanced through and startled her. She jerked upright.

"It had to come someday, Julie," he said as he watched her. Until now, she had shown none of the sorrow he'd had whenever he had thought about selling the *Crystal Star*.

"I know, but she was your first command. Our home for so many years." Her lips quivered as she spoke. "Remember when we were building her . . . you and I?"

"I remember, Julie," he said quietly and pulled her back to lean against him, "but you know there's a time for everything. That time is over for us. After all, you're the one who kept trying to build a beautiful new clipper for me. Now when we get home, the *Star of Gold* will be waiting for us in Boston."

"Yes." Her eyes misted with tears as she remembered going over the model of the new ship with her father. She'd designed it and he'd built it for them in their absence, but now he wouldn't be there to see them take possession of it. And then there was Stephen. Before they'd arrived in Liverpool, he had gained strength with each new day, but now he seemed to be slipping backwards if anything. A sense of loss overwhelmed her, and she felt as though her world were flying into scattered pieces that could never be rejoined. First her father. Then the *Crystal Star*. What next?

"Stephen, I've decided I'm going to stay here with you."

"We've been over that before, Julie." He smiled at her, hoping that he looked cheerful. It wouldn't do for her to guess how much he wanted her to be by his side during the ordeal that lay ahead. However, if anything happened to him, she would be alone in a strange city with no friends to comfort her. He wasn't sure that she could cope with the double loss of a father and a husband. "I want you to go home with Baxter. It'll make it easier on me if I don't have to worry about you."

Julia sighed and looked out the window at the hansom cabs and carriages, the peddlers and grimy urchins who packed the seething streets. If only she weren't so worried about the shipyard, she would insist upon staying with Stephen no matter what he said.

Clara would be all right for a few more weeks, but the yard was another matter. She had no idea what was happening there. Would Daniel Sears, the head foreman, be able to keep things going or had all work stopped with her father's death? Her mother would need the profits from the yard to live on, but equally important were the men. With large families to support, they had to have the work. Many families in the township depended upon the Howard Shipyard, and now she was the only Howard left capable of running it.

"I mean it, Julie," Stephen said, his arm tightening around her shoulders. "I want you to go home."

"Are you sure?"

"Quite sure."

"And you'll go to London immediately?"

"As soon as the *Crystal Star* is sold."

It seemed that the day of departure almost immediately followed their removal to the hotel, and bags that had been briefly opened were quickly repacked. Later when Julia tried to think about Liverpool, she couldn't remember the cobblestoned narrow streets, the shops, the warehouses. All that she could remember was the anguish she felt every time she saw her husband wince or tighten his jaw with pain or give any of the other signs he tried so very hard to conceal from her.

There were crowds everywhere that day. The sailing of the *Free Wind* was an event that emptied the population of Liverpool onto the waterfront and even into the Mersey River, where smaller craft darted about as they tried for the best position. Ever since she had made her record run of eighty-one days from New York to China and her subsequent voyage from Shanghai to Liverpool in eighy-seven days, the *Free Wind* had become the most famous ship in England. The excitement caused when the Admiralty surveyors took off her lines while she was in dry dock had inflamed the public's imagination.

Now as the small steamer approached the ship with her long sleek black hull, her tall raking masts, and her crossed skysail yards, the party on board the steamer paid for the publicity. Despite frequent warnings, sloops and cutters, rowboats and sidewheelers darted into their path. When Captain David Baxter was recognized on their boat, the water between them and the *Free Wind* became almost impassable.

Eventually, however, Julia and Stephen as well as Cynthia and her group of friends were swung in a chair up over the stern and onto the deck to join David, who ushered them to the poop deck, where they would stay until the time came for the pilot to leave them in the Irish Channel. Then all those who were not to cross the Western Ocean would depart with him.

For Cynthia and her friends, it was an occasion for celebration and soon wine was flowing freely from bottles they had brought aboard. It was difficult to find a corner where a glass was not thrust into their hands, but at last the others left Julia and Stephen alone in the chart house.

"Baxter's quite the hero of the day," Stephen said as he sipped from the glass someone had handed him.

"Well, that's normal, isn't it?" Julia reminded him. "After all, there've been times when I've seen just as much fuss made about you."

"Yes. I suppose so. It all seems far in the past now."

"And the future." She smiled at him, trying to cheer him up, though it was difficult for either of them to feel cheerful in the face of their imminent separation. "Wait till you take command of the *Star of Gold*. You'll break all the records, no matter who set them."

"I wonder."

"You will. Don't be low, Stephen."

"It's rather difficult not to be, isn't it, my lady?" He took her hand and held it tenderly up to his lips.

"Yes. It's difficult." She looked deep into his eyes and saw her own sadness reflected there. "I wish you'd let me stay."

"No." He shook his head and squeezed her hand. "If you stayed, you'd spend the entire time fretting about what was going on at home. Besides, you'll see Clara soon now."

"Suddenly that doesn't seem so important." She turned her head to look out through the plate-glass windows at the people milling about the poop and some who had leaked onto the main deck, where they were in the way of the sailors who were trying to ready the ship for sailing. But she wasn't really watching them. It just hurt too much to continue looking at Stephen. "You don't think I'm going to be fretting about what's going on in London?"

"There's less to fret about," he said gruffly.

"Is there? Tell me the truth, Stephen." She whirled to look directly into his eyes. "You haven't been completely honest with me so far. You didn't tell me about seeing that doctor in Liverpool."

This time it was he who averted his eyes, and the muscles in his jaw tightened.

"How did you find out?"

"You left his address lying on the table . . . together with the names of some doctors in London."

"Careless of me."

"What did he say?"

"He just recommended the men in London."

"Did he examine you?"

"Yes."

"Well, for heaven's sake, what did he say?" Pressing her fingers into his arm, she compelled him to look at her.

"He couldn't tell me anything, Julie," Stephen said with as much candor as he could muster. "My leg will be all right. I may have a limp for the rest of my life, but it will be so slight, it probably won't be noticeable."

"You're still not being honest with me about your chest." She bit her lip. The shipyard and Clara no longer seemed important. Only Stephen was. "Stephen, I won't hear anything from you for weeks. Please tell me everything you know."

"I've just told you. There's nothing more to discuss, Julia." He stroked her cheek lightly, then tucked some escaping tendrils of hair beneath her black bonnet. "You'll see Captain Asa for me? Tell him he can have as many shares in the *Star of Gold* as he wants?"

"Yes," she said dully. "I'll see Captain Asa."

"It's no good, is it? This saying good-bye."

"It's better than not saying good-bye."

They heard the anchor chain rattle aboard accompanied by a song led by the chantyman. Glancing aloft, they saw the sails were popping out of their gaskets.

"Damn fool," Stephen grumbled. "He intends to sail out of here. Why doesn't he use the tugs?"

"Well, he has a favoring wind and tide."

"But with all those spectators out there? He's bound to hit some of them."

"I reckon they'll just have to get out of the way."

"I shouldn't trust you with him." He glared out the window at David, who towered above all the others on deck. Not knowing what was to come, Julia caught her breath, but he continued. "All that man cares about is speed. He'll drive this ship without giving a thought to your safety."

Relieved, Julia smiled. "Reminds me of someone else I know."

"I cared about your safety."

"I know you did, Stephen. Didn't keep you from breaking a few records though, I notice."

"No. I had those, didn't I?"

Julia pressed her lips together. If he wasn't going to tell her what his condition really was, there was no way for her to force him.

"You could have had a ship like this if you'd come home from California earlier. Or even if you'd written me. I built one for you."

"And then I'd have had a chance at Baxter's records?"

"Yes."

"I'll come home this time, Julie," he said as he pressed her hand. "I promise you that."

But when he left the *Free Wind* with the pilot, Julia wondered if he were going to come home. Cynthia and her friends were loud and gay with wine, but Stephen was a lonely figure in black. Even while she and David were watching the water open up between the ship and the steamer, they could see Cynthia loop her arm around Stephen. They also saw Stephen's rejection as he shook her off to go forward.

Chapter Nine

1851

Even after the steamer had become a smoke-trailing speck that was finally lost in the haze, Julia stood at the taffrail and continued to stare after it. She wasn't aware that David had come up behind her. He startled her when he spoke.

"Well, that's the last we'll see of England for a good long while."

She turned slightly to look up at him and saw that he had changed from his frock coat and silk hat into a pea jacket and a visored cap. The cap was pulled low over his eyes, but even in the shadow cast by the visor, she could tell that he was staring towards the empty horizon.

"Yes," she agreed sadly. "The last of England and the last of Stephen. Cynthia, too."

"Aye," he said morosely.

She realized that she hadn't seen him smile since she had moved out of the house. Even during the excitement of this day when he was being acclaimed a hero by the public, he had remained silent and aloof. She wondered if she had hurt him. It was something she had never wanted to do, and she decided it was best to bring it out into the open.

"David, there's been no chance to apologize before. I'm sorry about moving out of your house so abruptly."

"It's not my house, and I don't blame you," he said brusquely. " 'Twas a mistake to think Cynthia would behave better in your presence. Seems she knows only one way to behave, though. I'm the one who should apologize for taking you there."

"No. 'Tisn't your fault, either. Let's just forget about it."

"I only wish I could." He leaned on the rail beside her with his hands clasped out in front of him and continued to look across the water at the invisible land.

"Cynthia's very pretty," Julia said softly. She had rarely seen him in a lower mood, and she tried to cheer him up.

"Pretty?" He glanced at her with surprise and then stared back at the sea. "Is she? I hadn't noticed. Not for many a day. Not since she finally made it clear that she would never make her home with me in East Dennis. And the little she lets me see of her bed, there's no hope I'll ever have a son."

Julia pulled off her hat so that the fresh, clean sea breeze could wash the stink of Liverpool from her hair, and she thought about this strange marriage of David's that had hardly been a marriage at all. How had it all begun? Out of loneliness? Because he had mistakenly thought that she herself had rejected him?

Over the years, David had told Julia quite a lot about his wife. He had felt sorry for the orphaned daughter of a British sea captain and one night his sympathy had taken too ardent a form. When Cynthia announced that she was carrying his baby, he married her. A few months later he received a letter from her saying that she had miscarried. He had once expressed his doubts to Julia that there ever had been a child. Two years ago he had discovered that another man was living in Cynthia's house, but even then he had refused to consider divorce.

"David," Julia said finally. "Now that I've met Cynthia, I know that she'd never have fit in on the Cape. 'Tis best to leave her where she is. With the British Navigation Laws repealed, you'll be able to get over to England and see her more often."

"No. I doubt I'll be seeing her again. Ever."

"David!" Julia was shocked by the bitter finality in his voice. "Take time to think it over. After all, it's going to be pretty hard to avoid seeing her when you're carrying tea to England. Even if you find cargoes for London instead of Liverpool, she'll still know you're there. It'll be in all the papers. You're right famous, you know."

"I don't have to see her," he said quietly and ambled across the deck to watch the crew at work for a few minutes. When he was satisfied that all was going well, he returned. "The day after you left the house, I went to talk to a lawyer. Seems as long as I continue to support her, nothing more is necessary. I've arranged to send payments to him and he'll see to it that she gets them."

"You make me feel . . . rather guilty. If my leaving had something to do with it . . ." she faltered.

"No. Nothing to do with it," he said firmly. "I've been through this nonsense of hers before. You know that. I'd make up my mind to end it. Then after a few months at sea, I'd convince myself that it wasn't as bad as I thought or that maybe she'd have changed."

"People do change," she said softly.

"Maybe some." His eyes automatically swept over the ship. With just the right westerly breeze, all the sails were set and bellied out taut against the lift lines. The wind hummed through the rigging and the bow cut cleanly through the water. He nodded and then looked at Julia as if for approval.

Even while thinking about his words, she too had been contemplating the powerful vessel that sang beneath her feet and under her hand as she held onto the rail. She saw the pride of his ship in his eyes.

"Pretty," she said with an understanding smile.

"Aye. We work well together, don't we, Julie? You build a fine ship." But there was another question in his triangular eyes which she didn't completely understand. She really didn't want to understand.

"Takes a first-rate master to sail a ship like this, though," she said. "Breaking records all over the place."

" 'Twas what I meant. Takes both of us to do the job." His lips curved slightly upwards, but it was difficult to tell whether he was really smiling or not. "I've got a confession to make, Julie. I realize now that, when I asked you to be our guest, I was being downright selfish. Somehow I thought that, when Cynthia saw you, saw what a real lady was like, she'd imitate you. I reckon I was hoping you might become friends."

She gave a short, wry laugh. "Doubt that would *ever* be possible. There never were two people more unlike."

"No. I see that now," he said as he studied her face. She had changed as she had grown older. Her features were more finely drawn than those of the picture he'd carried hidden in his heart for all these years, but the delicate arch of brows over her sapphire eyes was the same. The firm rounded chin and the blue-black tendrils of hair that clustered so sweetly around her clear forehead had never altered. "What's the saying about a sow's ear and a silk purse?"

"I don't think it applies," she said sharply as she turned away from him to study the hopeful gulls that followed in their wake. She had read too much in his eyes and she felt jeopardized. They could be heading for dangerous waters, especially now when the voyage stretched out ahead of them. She changed the course of their conversation quickly. "How soon do you think we'll reach home?"

"I'll get you there fast as I can," he promised.

"At six pounds a ton, you'd best be thinking about getting your *cargo* there fast as you can," she said tartly.

"Aye." He laughed down at her. She sounded more like herself than she had since he'd had to give her the awful news of her father's death. "Captain Richardson will be right disturbed if I make a slow passage. I couldn't care two straws what he thinks, though. Doubt I'll be taking the *Free Wind* out on her next voyage."

Julia looked at him in surprise. "After the records you've set in her, you'd let another man take her out? I don't believe it."

"Well, I'll tell you how it is," he said lazily. "I've spent nearly all my days at sea since I was a boy, and I'm thirty-six now. Be thirty-seven pretty soon. Time for me to spend a little of my life ashore. See more of my folks. They're getting on."

"The more you talk, the less I believe you," she said skeptically. "I've watched you looking at the *Free Wind*. Seen you run your hands over her. You can't deny you love this ship."

"Aye. I love her." He glanced at Julia and then his eyes wandered over the decks, the men, the tall masts, and the billowing sails. His color was high when he added, "There's things I love more, though."

"And just how long do you propose to stay ashore?" she asked with mounting suspicion.

"Depends," he said tersely and quickly went forward to speak to the mate.

Julia was left alone with a confusion of thoughts for a quarter of an hour. She had just decided to go below and unpack a warmer dress from her sea chest when David returned.

"How long before you expect Stephen home?" he asked abruptly.

She sighed and felt very tired. As she looked at the clean wake that rolled out behind them, she was reminded that the knots were reeling off a widening gap between herself and her husband.

"I don't know how long it'll be. You know as much about that as I do. I'm certain he was hiding things from me." She hazarded a guess. "He told you more, didn't he?"

"I doubt it." He frowned as he thought over his last private conversation with Stephen. "He just said his wound was bothering him. Mostly he was concerned about you. Asked me to look after you."

"Does that have anything to do with you planning to stay home?" she asked with narrowed eyes.

"No, no," he said with bland innocence. "I told you. There's lots of reasons."

"And I'm one of them," she persisted.

"You always have been." And always will be, he thought.

"Well, you're welcome to look after me so long as I'm aboard your ship," she said tartly. "But once I'm home, I'll do very well for myself."

He looked down at her and saw her back was straight as a ramrod. With her chin lifted and her eyes flashing, she looked as though she was preparing for a fight. He'd known her for too many years not to read all the signals.

His smile was more tender than he knew when he said, "Will you? You plan on handling all your problems, taking on the world, alone?"

"Of course, I will." She was not going to be taken in by that smile. Not this time. "There aren't going to be any problems, and if there are, there's always Cousin William. In one of the letters he left for me, he said he'd be there as long as I need him."

"Then you'll be in good hands," he said quietly to calm her. But one pair's going to be mine, he added to himself.

The voyage took eighteen days, and at first they seemed endless. Although Julia enjoyed the luxury of the chart house, where she was able to observe the beauty of the ship and sea without having to brave the elements, her thoughts and her heart were divided between two shores. The past and the future, she often thought. But which was the past and which was the future?

Despite the comfort of the large feather bed in the captain's cabin, it was a lonely bed. During those endlessly long nights, she couldn't avoid the desolation of grief and only the exhaustion of tears had the power to give her sleep. But awake or asleep, her mind dwelt on her father. She could see him striding into the dining room, crisp and fresh-shaven, joyfully ready to tackle a new day. She could see him fuming over a piece of poor craftsmanship and hear him roar out orders for its replacement. And she could see those dark blue eyes join their sorrow to her own or see them dance with laughter over a good joke or a great happiness.

And then she would awake from her grief into fear. She would think of Stephen, white and drawn, as she had last seen him, and she would wonder what was happening to him. Had those faceless doctors found it necessary to cut into him, lay open his flesh, and bring pain by their probing? Was he even now lying in some strange bed needing her, wanting her? Or was it possible that, through their clumsiness, he was no longer able to feel pain, to feel anything?

She would rise as the first shadows of grey tinged the black waves of night and dress quickly to go on deck, where the men had begun their ritual morning chores of washing and holystoning. More often than not, she found David there before her, and his welcoming smile would put things in a more proper perspective.

He was her greatest comfort, greater than she dared let him guess. Their common past formed a bond she had with few people. The years of childhood, the years of her grief after Jason's death, the years of meeting in foreign ports, all these were part of their friendship. Sometimes when they were talking, she would think of Cynthia's belittling remarks about David and she would feel sorry for the woman. Cynthia didn't know what she'd had. She had obviously never realized or valued his gentleness and his strength, his warmth and his humor. Had she ever really looked at him?

For herself, Julia was grateful for his presence. Speech was not necessary between them, and often they walked the deck together and watched the stars, or they would sit below in the elegant saloon and play cards when the light became too dim for her to sew or for him carve. She found it impossible to read even by daylight, for her thoughts would not focus on the printed page but would wander to England or to East Dennis. Whenever David saw anxiety fill her eyes or pain wrinkle her forehead, he would create a diversion, and sometimes he could even make her laugh.

When they sighted Provincetown in the distance, Julia was almost sorry. The sea and David had soothed her and made her more tranquil. Now the land with its problems was fast approaching. Decisions would be asked of her, responsibilities would land on her shoulders, and although there would be those who would be willing to help, the ultimate answers would have to be hers alone. Her father wouldn't be there to advise her. He would never, never again be there, but it was a fact she could not readily accept. There was a part of her that still expected him to be waiting for her when the packet bearing her home docked in Sesuit Creek.

Julia was putting the final touches to her black silk shore-going dress when they sailed into Boston Harbor. She had just closed her final bag when David sent the steward below to fetch her with the message that there was a sight she must see.

When she had climbed the steps that led to the chart house, she found him standing just outside the door. He was pointing excitedly to starboard.

"Julie, you can't miss this," he said as he reached for her hand to draw her out on deck. " 'Tis the largest merchant ship I've ever seen. Looks like she's just been launched and rigged."

Julia followed the direction of his finger. She caught her breath when she saw the enormous ship that looked as if she were about to leap forward even though there were no sails on her towering masts and immensely wide yards. She had seen that bow that swooped five feet above the stern before. She had imagined the golden-haired figurehead who held a large nugget of gold in her cupped hands and who was made more beautiful by the stark simplicity of ornamental work only around the hawse holes and on the ends of the cat heads. Into the model, Julia herself had carved that breadth of midships beam and contoured it until it narrowed sweetly at the stern. Yet even she had not truly visualized the immensity or the sweeping wonder of her creation.

"The *Star of Gold!*" she gasped.

"Is it really?" He raised his telescope to his eye, and when he handed it to Julia, he looked at her with new respect. "And you designed her?"

"Yes," she said with pride. "Of course, it was Papa who built her. Most likely modified her a bit."

And then she remembered with sudden pain that it was on those very decks her father had died. He had lived long enough to see her launched. He had ridden down the ways on her but the strain had evidently been too much. She pushed away the telescope that David tried to hand her. She didn't want to inspect the *Star of Gold* any further. Not now.

As she turned her back on the ship, David caught her arm. "What is it, Julie?"

"It's Papa." The words were too difficult to say. They were impossible. "The launching . . ."

"I'd forgotten." He looked at her rigid back with commiseration and then put his arm lightly around her as he helped her over the coaming into the chart house. "I'm sorry, Julie."

"It's all right, David," she said in a muffled voice.

"No, it's not all right." He guided her to the tall swivel chair that was bolted to the deck. "I doubt you'll want to go aboard her for a while. Want me to look her over before we start for home?"

"No." She turned her head and looked resolutely through the plate-glass windows at the *Star of Gold* once more. "I've got to face her someday. Might as well be tomorrow."

"Not tomorrow, Julie," he said gently. As he watched, her dark blue eyes seemed to grow ever larger in her pale face. "There's no need to rush things."

"Yes. Tomorrow. If the packet still has the same schedule, it won't be sailing for home for a few more days. I have to fill in the time somehow. Besides, I'd best go over the ship before we leave Boston. I'll have to write a report to Stephen."

"Hold on, Julie. Give me time to talk to Captain Richardson. I'll find out when he can spare me. I can't let you go out there alone."

She finally took her eyes away from the *Star of Gold* to look at David.

His rugged, honest face was filled with compassion and she knew that his presence would make it easier. David always did make things more bearable, and she was sure he would not fail her on board the *Star of Gold*.

"All right, David," she said in a low voice. "If you don't mind."

"Mind?" He carefully leaned back against the chart table and folded his arms. What he really wanted to do was to hold her, to protect her against any further anguish the world might deal her. But the crew was on deck, and furthermore, it was not his right. "Of course I don't mind. There's nothing I'd rather do. After the *Free Wind* was built, I reckoned there was nothing more could be done to perfect a ship. Seems I was wrong."

"I hope you are. But that's something no one will know till she sails." Under the right master's command, she added to herself. Her true master. Stephen.

This time there was no one waiting for her with a schooner as there had been when she had returned home after her father's first stroke. David engaged rooms for her at the Tremont Hotel, where they had quiet meals together. Captain Hiram Richardson insisted that they dine with him on the second night, and Julia was too numb to refuse in the face of his persistent invitations. Besides, she *had* come home on his ship, and he had only laughed when she offered to pay for her passage. She was indebted to the man and disliked the feeling of obligation although there was nothing she could do about it at the moment. However, she was resolved to discharge that duty as soon as she possibly could.

Richardson's five-story brick house on Louisburg Square had changed very little. The same giant black butler met them at the fan-windowed door, and inside the long, high-ceilinged rooms, some treasures had replaced others. Because of the warmth of the June day, no fires burned in the great fireplaces, and the doors stood open to green lawns and trees. Despite the lingering sunlight, the crystal chandeliers sparkled with candles. The effect was very much the same as it had been when she had dined here nine years earlier.

No matter how comfortable the house, however, she found it depressing, for she remembered that on that occasion, her father had sat close to her and Stephen had been young and exuberantly healthy as he looked forward to his first voyage as master of his own ship. Her mother and Captain Asa had been there, too. Now there were only David and herself.

Strangely, Hiram Richardson's attitude towards her had changed. Where before he had overplayed the role of gallant in front of her husband, he now treated her as though she were one of the fragile ivories or porcelains he displayed in teak cabinets that lined the walls.

As she sat sipping sherry in his drawing room, he concentrated most of his conversation on David. Although the two men had spent the day together, his interest in and questions about the entire voyage seemed inexhaustible. From time to time, he tried to include her in the conversation by inquiring about her own voyage in the *Crystal Star*, but for the most part, he allowed her the silence she preferred.

It was only after they had sat down to dinner around the linen-draped table that the suave, chestnut-haired merchant said to her in his rich, deep voice, "So you're luring my most able shipmaster away from the sea."

"Oh, no!" She looked at him, horrified. That he should even think such a thing! And heaven knew what connotations he would put on it. "I'm not the reason."

"Aren't you, my dear?" Seeing her dismay, he added kindly, "Well, if you aren't, you should be. From what I hear, you're going to need all the help you can get."

"What have you heard?" she asked with frozen lips. She couldn't avoid the suspicions he aroused in her. Somehow, she had the feeling that he had fresh bad news, perhaps some of his own making.

"Not that much really. I do know you have a new ship sitting idle in the harbor." He managed to inject both wisdom and sadness into his light blue eyes as he shook his head. "That's a waste. A terrible waste. Do you realize how much money you're losing?"

"My husband will be home soon," she said tersely. "It's his ship."

"But he's not here now. She's one of the largest, sharpest merchant ships ever launched. You can charge the highest freight rates, say a dollar-forty a cubic foot to California, and you'll have shippers standing in line to pay it. Mrs. Logan, you simply can't let that ship sit idle." His distress seemed quite genuine.

"*One* of the largest ships?" David, sensing Julia's growing discomfort, quickly came to her rescue. "I'd say she's the largest."

"No." Hiram Richardson's assured smile was one of pure pleasure. "Not since Donald McKay launched *Flying Cloud* in April. She's almost two hundred fifty tons bigger than the *Star of Gold*, fourteen feet longer overall and a foot more beam."

"Really?" For the first time that evening, Julia's interest was awakened. Despite her sorrow, nothing could dampen her fascination with ships, big fast ships. "Where is she? I want to see her."

"She's in New York," Hiram Richardson said casually, nodding at the butler to pour more wine. "Enoch Train sold her to Grinnell and Minturn for their Swallow-Tail Line. Much as he wanted that ship, they made him an offer he couldn't refuse. I wanted to buy her myself, but I didn't think it necessary to go as high as ninety thousand dollars."

"Ninety thousand dollars!" Julia looked at him in amazement. "I've never heard of such a thing."

"No?" He paused as she helped herself from the platter of lamb the footman held for her. When he was sure that he had her full attention, he continued. "Well, the *Star of Gold*'s a bit smaller, as I've said, but I'll make you an offer of eighty-five thousand for her."

It was such a tempting figure, it would have been difficult to resist, but all she could think of was Stephen. "No. She belongs to my husband. And I have to discover what the situation is at home before I could consider anything."

"Which means that you might consider it?"

"No, Captain Richardson, I don't mean anything of the sort." Then as she remembered her first meeting with the merchant prince, a subtle smile curved her lips. At that time, she and Stephen had wanted something from Hiram Richardson. Now the situation was reversed. "Besides, as I recall, you don't approve of discussing business in the evening."

Smiling back, he showed his improbably perfect white teeth. "You're quite correct, although it disturbs me every time I see your ship sitting out there in the harbor. She'll begin to deteriorate soon if you don't do something about her." As he helped himself to more peas from the platter the footman held out for him, he asked casually, "Tell me, have you heard anything recently about your friend Mrs. Fairfield and her bonny son?"

"Yes. They're well."

"And still living with your family?" Even with his apparent nonchalance, Hiram Richardson couldn't completely conceal a deep underlying interest.

"As far as I know," Julia answered tersely. She wasn't about to tell him any more about her friend than was absolutely necessary. Megan was too vulnerable.

"I'm glad to hear that. I've been planning a trip up to the Cape for some time. I'd like to look in and see how the youngster is doing. After having seen him when he was less than an hour old, I've taken a special interest in him."

"I hardly think that's called for," Julia said sharply as she tried to end the discussion. A newborn child was one thing, but how much of his father's Polynesian blood would show in Robert now that he was two years old? The secret of his parentage might no longer be a secret, and yet in her letters, Megan never mentioned it. She only spoke with a mother's pride of how quick, how strong and handsome he was.

"I have some friends who might be interested in purchasing the Howard Shipyard if the price is right," Hiram Richardson broke into her thoughts. "When I'm up on the Cape, I'd be happy to advise you concerning its disposition. In fact, if there's any way I can be of service to you, I'd be delighted."

"Thank you," Julia said firmly, "but the shipyard *is not* for sale."

143

"Oh, surely you can't be serious." Hiram Richardson's light blue eyes were filled with commiseration. "I could understand your filling the breach while your father was ill, but now . . ."

"It is the *Howard* Shipyard, and I promised my father that it would remain in the hands of a Howard."

"Strange." Hiram Richardson gestured for the footman to pour more wine. He looked thoughtfully for a moment at the rich red liquid that sparkled in his crystal goblet and then sipped it with equal care before he turned again to Julia. "I've heard rumors that your family is planning to sell it. Your uncle *is* Josiah Howard, isn't he?"

"Yes." Julia stiffened at the mention of her uncle's name. The effects of the wine, which had been making Julia feel more mellow, immediately vanished. She glanced quickly at David and saw that he, too, had become more alert.

"Well, when your uncle was in Boston recently, I know for a fact that he was talking to several people about its sale." Hiram Richardson almost purred as he saw the reaction his words had produced, yet his smile was most sympathetic. "However, I don't believe that he'll be able to arrange for the best price. When I spoke to him, he didn't strike me as a man with a very strong sense of business."

"*You* spoke to Uncle Josiah?"

"Yes. He came to my counting house one day completely unannounced. Walked in and asked how much I'd give for the yard."

"Captain Richardson, he had no right to do that," Julia said indignantly. "Uncle Josiah has absolutely no interest in the business. My father bought him out years ago."

"Well, he didn't say outright that he did," the merchant said in a soothing voice. "I must say, from his attitude, you wouldn't blame anyone for coming to that conclusion. He said he represented the family."

"Well, he doesn't represent anyone but himself." In her anger, the color rose so high in Julia's cheeks, she appeared feverish. "I'd appreciate it if you'd see that word of *that* is circulated. If anyone wants to discuss business connected with the yard and the vessels we produce, they can apply to me."

Hiram Richardson looked grave. "My dear, I'm not sure you fully appreciate what you'll have to contend with. Whenever there is divisiveness amongst the members of a family after a death . . . and there usually is, especially if the deceased has been the head of the family . . . the entanglements can become incredible."

"Not in my family."

"He showed me a paper signed by your mother and one of your sisters, a Mrs. Martin."

"I don't believe it," she said with finality. "Sarah, yes, but not Mama."

"I wouldn't lie to you, my dear." He appeared to be completely and compassionately sympathetic. "I saw it with my own eyes. I'm not trying to distress you, but I think you should know what's been taking place in your absence. Also, if there's anything I can do to help you, whether financially or with advice, I want you to know that I'm always at your service."

She dropped her eyes to her gold-rimmed plate. She didn't trust the man. She would never trust him. He had to have an ulterior motive in offering to help her. The question was what did he have to gain?

"It's kind of you," she said, trying to be polite. "But it won't be necessary. Captain William Thacher will be there."

"Your first husband's father?" His eyebrows shot up in mocking amusement. "I must say that's an odd relationship."

"There's nothing odd about it," Julia said and looked at him levelly, all pretense of politeness now gone. "He's still as close to me as he was when I was married to his son. Furthermore, he's my mother's cousin and one of my father's oldest friends. And even if he wasn't, he's a good, kind man who would never desert me when I needed him."

"You seem to have a lot of good friends," the merchant said as he glanced at David. "Captain Thacher, Baxter here . . . and me."

"You forget my husband, Captain Richardson. He'll be home soon."

"But going to sea again equally soon." He reached into an inner pocket of his black velvet coat. "You'll forgive me for not giving this to you earlier, but I thought it best to wait until we had finished dinner. You'll probably prefer to read it in privacy. I'll have coffee served in the drawing room, and Captain Baxter and I will join you after we've sampled the port."

She took the letter he handed her. The red wax on the back bore the imprint of Stephen's ring, and the front was written in his flourishing hand. She looked questioningly at the merchant.

"It was in the sealed mail bag that Captain Baxter handed to me yesterday," Hiram Richardson explained.

"David, did you know about this?" Julia was shocked that he could have kept it from her all these days. Worse than shocked. It was almost a betrayal.

"Aye, but I couldn't tell you before." He looked miserable. "Your husband swore me to secrecy."

"Do you know what it says?" She tapped the letter against her fingers.

"No. I'm sorry, Julia."

"It's not your fault." She sighed. Things were mounting up so fast. Too fast. "Not if you gave your word."

His lips didn't move, but his eyes spoke of many things.

She nodded and laid her napkin on the table. "If you'll excuse me?"

The two men stood as she left the room, and it was a relief when the butler closed the double doors behind her. Drawing a chair up to the brightest lamp, she quickly broke the seal and opened the letter.

My dearest wife, my Julia,

Please don't blame me for delaying your receipt of this letter. I wanted to be sure that you were at home amongst your family when you read it.

I want you to find a master for the *Star of Gold* and send her to London. I am certain you may rely upon Captain Thacher or some of our other friends to handle the matter of offering cargo space. Don't attempt to send any goods on our own account.

When I spoke with the doctor in Liverpool, he indicated that the doctors in London would probably detain me for some time, and there is no reason that the *Star of Gold* shouldn't be put to work. I hope that, when she arrives here, I will be ready to return home in her. However, you may tell the master you retain that he is to be in command during the return voyage as well as on the eastward passage.

I am sorry to place this additional burden upon you when I am aware that you have so many others, but after much consideration, I realize it would distress you far more if I attempted to place the matter in other hands.

Believe me when I say that never a day will pass that I don't think of you and long to be with you.

With my greatest affection,
Stephen Logan

After she had read the last word, Julia sat completely immobilized by the shock of the letter. For a few minutes, the myriad thoughts that jostled on the outer fringes found no way to break into the vacuum of her mind. Eventually she held the letter up again and read it through once more.

She shivered and walked over to the fire that had been lit while they were at dinner. The room had felt close when she had first entered it, but now it seemed deadly cold . . . just as the letter had. Stiff and cold. It might just as well have been a letter to a business associate. It was not the loving letter of a husband to his wife. Why?

His chest? Was he trying to conceal from her the fact that he wasn't going to recover from the wound?

No. He wouldn't order the *Star of Gold* to London if that were the case. He would have sent the ship around the Horn to California or to China, where she could likely make the most profit.

Or would he?

Maybe he just wanted to see his ship before . . . No!

146

He was coming home in her, and the sooner she herself found a master and a cargo, the sooner he'd be home.

But he had said the other master would be in command on the way home. Then . . .

The doors between the rooms opened and David Baxter and Hiram Richardson strolled in.

"My dear, you haven't had your coffee," the merchant said, his chestnut eyebrows rising.

"No." She glanced at the silver service on the gate-legged table on the other side of the fire. She hadn't even been aware that it had been brought in. "I was thinking."

"About the letter?" David looked down at the piece of paper she held clasped between her fingers, its whiteness stark against the blackness of her silk dress.

"Yes." She looked at him, but didn't seem to focus upon him. "It . . . it changes a lot of my plans."

"Not bad news, I trust?" Captain Richardson said smoothly as he busied himself with cups and saucers.

"No. I don't know." She turned to look at him in bewilderment. Then she squared her shoulders with resolution. "I'm going to load the *Star of Gold* and take her to England."

"Yourself? My dear Mrs. Logan!" The merchant looked at her carefully. He had always admired her spirit, but what she was suggesting was sheer madness. He must stop her . . . if he could. "Captain Baxter has told me about your prodigious feat in helping to bring the *Crystal Star* safely to Liverpool, but I really don't think you should consider . . ."

"No! Of course not," Julia said impatiently. "I'll hire a master for her."

"Julie, I don't think you should go." David moved protectively closer to her. "Remember your Uncle Josiah. And if Stephen wanted you over there, he'd never have sent you home."

"I have to go, David."

"Take a few days to think it over before you go jumping into anything. He must have had a reason for writing instead of telling you in person whatever is in that letter."

"Here. You can see it." She handed the letter to David. "There's nothing personal in it."

She watched his face as he scanned the page and she could see her own concern reflected in his expression. When he handed it back to her, Hiram Richardson held out his hand.

"May I?"

Julia's first reaction was to refuse, but since she had already shown it to David, it would have been pointedly rude. Besides there was nothing there that she hadn't already told him. She shrugged.

"If you wish."

"Well," he said as he returned the letter to her, "I think I can solve your difficulties. If you won't sell the *Star of Gold* to me, I'll charter her. Young Baxter here can take her over and bring your husband home."

David shook his head. "I'm sorry, sir, but I'm staying home. I'm quite set on that."

"You wouldn't even go for Mrs. Logan?"

"I don't want him to go for me," she said quickly, surprised to find herself hurt by David's refusal. Furthermore, she didn't like the way Hiram Richardson seemed to be trying to insinuate himself into her affairs. "There are other masters, and I doubt my husband had it in mind for me to charter the ship. His wishes are quite explicit. *I'm* to hire the master and arrange for the cargo."

"Well, not exactly." Captain Richardson looked at the silver service and then gave it up. There was no point in considering coffee until the matter was settled. "Your husband says that you should look for help in the matter of cargo. As to the master, the man I hire will be subject to your approval."

"And to your orders."

Hiram Richardson smiled sadly and shook his head. Then he went to the tapestry bell pull and rang for the butler to serve the coffee. It would be far better if they sat down and discussed this in a civilized manner. Perhaps in a matter of time, she would calm down enough to discuss the situation reasonably.

After they were seated around the fire with their cups in their hands, he made another attempt.

"My dear, I don't know what I've ever done to warrant your disapproval, but I've been aware from almost the first that you didn't quite trust me. Why?"

"There's no reason, Captain Richardson," she said coolly. Except for all those stories I've been hearing about you for years and the way you treated Stephen when you had him in a bind, she added to herself. She intensely disliked the way he was pushing her, but she reminded herself once again that she was his guest. She tried to smile as she continued. "It's not a matter of distrusting you, but I'd rather handle my own affairs, and you have a way of taking over."

"Oh, it isn't a matter of taking over, Mrs. Logan, and I assure you my intentions are most honest." He was glad to see her sketchy smile even though he realized that it was forced. "There are some goods I'd like to ship to London by the fastest means possible, and I'll pay the highest going rates. On the other hand, you have a ship and would like to take on freight. What could be more clear cut than that? It's a simple business proposition."

"I don't know." She looked down at the delicate porcelain cup and saucer and realized that her hands were shaking. All she wanted was to be gone from here. Why wouldn't he leave her alone? "I'll have to think about it."

"By chartering," he persisted, "I'm simply guaranteeing that you'll sell every inch of space and you won't have the burden of provisioning the ship."

"Will Mrs. Logan have approval of the goods shipped, Captain Richardson?" David had been lounging back in his chair watching with concern. He had been determined not to get involved in such a way that Julia would feel that he was pressuring her, but now he had to interrupt.

"Well, that's most irregular, but I think it can be arranged," the merchant said with a condescending smile.

"I don't think it's irregular at all," Julia said tersely. Maybe that would discourage him.

"Then, of course, you'll have approval."

Julia stood up and put her cup on a small ebony table. "I'm very tired, Captain Richardson. It's been a lovely evening, but I think I'd best return to the hotel. If you'd have someone fetch a cab for me, I'll leave you and Captain Baxter to discuss your business."

"I can't allow that," Hiram Richardson said, springing to his feet. "My carriage is available whenever you wish it, but I don't want to send you out into the night alone. It would best if Captain Baxter accompanied you."

"Thank you," she said simply. She really was tired and she wanted to be alone so that she could study Stephen's letter again.

"You'll at least consider the charter?" the merchant said as he placed her shawl around her shoulders.

"Yes. I'll consider it, but I can't promise anything."

"Then I'd suggest you come to a decision within the next few days."

"I intend to, Captain Richardson. I intend to."

In the privacy of the carriage, David stretched his long legs out in front of him and said, "What *is* it you have against Captain Richardson? When I first went to work for him, you tried to warn me off. Every time you get near the man, you act spleeny."

She looked over at him, but except when they passed under an occasional street lamp, he was just a large shadow on the horsehair seat beside her. Even when the glow of a lamp momentarily lightened the shadows in the carriage, it was impossible to read the expression on his face. As she thought of his question and wondered how best to answer it, the green filigree of trees shone in the haloed light beyond him, and the rich scents of burgeoning summer overpowered the usual rancid city smell.

149

"Oh, I don't know, David," she said finally with a sigh. "I reckon it's a lot of things."

"What things?" He spoke quietly, his voice low and warm. He obviously was going to persist until he got the answer she had always refused before.

"You've heard the tales," she said a little impatiently. She didn't want to discuss Hiram Richardson. She wanted to be left alone with her thoughts. "Slaving, smuggling, barratry. He was a privateer once."

"Well, I've yet to hear any proof of the first three, and remember, your father was a privateer, too," he said firmly. "A lot of captains carried a letter of marque back in the war."

"Yes, but it seems there's always been more than a bit of doubt that he confined his efforts to the enemy. Besides, look at the way he treats his shipmasters. Strone, Emory, Pratt. Let them make one mistake and he sees to it they never get another command."

"He's always been fair with me," he said stolidly.

"He would be." Julia had to wait until they had passed a string of high-laden carts, whose wheels rumbling over the stones made it impossible to be heard. "But you haven't made that mistake yet, have you, David? All you've done is add to his glory."

"Well, I doubt he has it in mind to take advantage of you. He's . . . very fond of you."

Julia laughed sharply. "That man would take advantage of the devil's tail if he had it to hang onto."

"Julie!" David straightened up and his voice had the force she had only heard before when he'd issued orders aboard his ship. "Stop acting so hard and suspicious. 'Tisn't like you. The man's never had aught but good to say about you, and his concern is an honest one. Ever since we've been in Boston, you've been constantly in his thoughts. Keeps asking about you, worrying how you're going to handle things once you get home. Thinks someone's going to cheat you out of your inheritance. I was expecting him to be downright upset when I told him I wasn't taking the *Free Wind* out again, but he just said he thought it best if I went on home and kept an eye on you."

"Everyone wants to run my life, don't they?" she said bitterly.

"Not run it, Julie." He reached over and took her hand in his large one. "Just be there in case you need us."

She let her hand lie in his. Despite herself, she found it warm and comforting.

"Maybe you do, David, though I wish you wouldn't, but I still don't trust that man. He has a reason for everything he does, and I'd like to know his real reasons for offering to charter the *Star of Gold* the minute he heard she was available."

150

"Most likely just what he said. He has goods to ship and you have a vessel."

"Maybe."

Chapter Ten

1851

When they boarded the *Star of Gold* the next day, a grizzled shipkeeper came out of the topgallant forecastle and met them.

"I'm sorry, folks, but you'll have to leave. No one's allowed aboard. Owner's orders."

"Well, I'm the owner," Julia said stiffly, looking down at the short, potbellied old man who reeked of alcoholic fumes. "And I gave no such orders."

"No, ma'am." He stood his ground on the bleached deck and glared at her. "You ain't the owner. He's down below this very minute, and if he finds you here, it'll be worth my job."

"Now, just a minute, mister," David said in a quiet voice that carried a threat. "This is Mrs. Logan, and she and her husband do own this ship. Whoever you've got down below is an impostor. Where is he?"

"No, sir. You ain't puttin' nothing over on me. I happen to know the Howards built this ship, and that's Mr. Howard who's give me the orders."

"Mr. Howard?" David looked at Julia.

She nodded grimly. "Uncle Josiah. Let's go down and see what Uncle Josiah is up to now."

"I've got my orders!" The shipkeeper planted himself in front of them.

"You've just gotten new ones." David picked the man up by the elbows and put him to one side as lightly as he would a child. Then he took Julia by the arm and led her amidships to the square portico that formed an entrance to the cabins beneath the long poop deck.

Despite her forebodings about Uncle Josiah, Julia had to smile at David when they arrived below. He had stopped at the foot of the short companionway ladder and was looking about him with obvious bemusement.

"Do you like it?" There was a touch of pride in her voice as she watched him admire the carved mahogany panels, which were divided by elegantly enameled columns and cornices and were topped with gilded moldings.

"Like it? I've never seen anything to match it, not even aboard the Liverpool packets." He took off his silk hat, then put his hand on top of his dark blond curls and raised it to the overhead to measure the distance. "Why, I can even stand up straight in here with inches to spare."

"That's only the beginning." She reached her hand out to him and pulled him aft into the large saloon, where crystal and silver fittings competed with the red velvet semicircular settee and the highly polished mahogany furniture. "Look how bright it is in here."

"Aye. That's a good-sized skylight," he said, looking up. "Right airy, too."

"Isn't it!" The excitement of a dream come true took possession of her and her dark blue eyes sparkled. "There's plenty of ventilators and every single cabin has a decklight as well as a sidelight. Look!" She began pulling open doors to reveal the staterooms and the two water closets.

The plate glass of portholes and beveled mirrors gleamed as though they had been recently polished. Brass lamps and fittings glowed against walls the color of pearls. Bright Brussels carpets and red velvet curtains added to their warmth. As she had wished, no expense had been spared in furnishing the *Star of Gold.*

When they returned forward to the officers' quarters, the aft starboard door, which led to the captain's cabin, quietly opened and her sister Sarah, her crinolines pushing her black skirts wide and her light brown curls swinging forward from her black straw bonnet, stood dainty and perfectly poised before them.

"Well, Julia," she said, her first greeting in almost a year. "We didn't expect to find you here."

"That's obvious. What did you expect, Sarah?" Julia fought to keep her voice calm and to conquer the irritation Sarah always provoked in her. "She *is* my husband's ship, you know. Isn't it natural that I'd visit her?"

"Your husband's ship?" Sarah's black eyebrows shot up and her grey eyes opened wide. "This ship belongs to the Howard Shipyard. At least it does till it's paid for."

"Paid for! This ship was paid for before she was built." Julia's control snapped and she advanced on her sister, who, stepping back into the cabin, revealed the lanky frame of Josiah Howard and the portly one of Aaron Martin, Sarah's husband.

"There's no record of the money, Julia," Sarah said sweetly. "Do you have a receipt?"

"It's no business of yours whether I have a receipt or not. What I want to know is what *you're* doing here."

"Looking over our property." Sarah shot a conspiratorial smile at her uncle, who was dressed in a light grey suit of cheap broadcloth. The dandy's cut was far too young for his years. "Uncle Josiah and I thought it best to see what kind of assets Papa left so we'd be able to dispose of them to our greatest advantage."

"Looks like that's not all you're trying to dispose of." Julia glanced around the cabin. Cabinet doors had been pulled open and drawers were stacked on the rich carpet. "What are you looking for?"

"Papers," Josiah said in his harsh cracked voice. "Seems your pa mislaid them afore he died. Left things a mess, and now we got to tidy up after him."

"Papa never mislaid anything in his life, Uncle Josiah, nor did he ever leave things in a mess, though I don't doubt there's been many a time when you wished he had." Julia glared at him and then looked at her sister's husband, who had tried to withdraw from the whole scene by staring out the port that overlooked the main deck. "And you, Aaron? You're party to this nonsense? I wouldn't have thought it of you."

"Well, Julia." He turned towards her and ran his hand over his thinning auburn hair, but he didn't directly meet her eyes. "I've got to look after my wife's property."

"And Lydia's, too," Josiah hastily cut in. "We got to look after your ma since it's sure you won't."

"You are all really . . . despicable. Couldn't even wait for me to get home before you started trying to take over, could you? I might have expected it, though. Well, let me tell you something Uncle Josiah, Sarah . . . you, too, Aaron . . . I'm home now, and I'm not going to put up with any of your tomfoolery."

"Seems as how you might have to, being your pa died without leaving a will." Josiah leaned his scrawny body against the built-in mahogany bureau, and his smile revealed his few remaining yellow teeth.

"He had a will," Julia said.

"You seen it?"

"Yes, I have."

"Then you're the only one as has, and I doubt the courts are goin' to take the word of a woman as to its contents, specially when that woman's the most interested party."

"You seem to know a lot about its contents, Uncle Josiah. Have *you* seen it?"

"Me? Not likely I'd be wastin' my time searchin' for it if I had."

"You know as well as I do he wouldn't put his will aboard a ship that was leaving. Could be you're searching for something else . . . say, the ship's documents . . . to dispose of."

"Now you watch what you say!" Josiah straightened up and, gathering his sparse brows together, frowned at her threateningly. "You go round insinuatin' things, we can take you to court."

153

"You seem right fond of the courts, Uncle Josiah, though I can't imagine why. I recollect your taking Papa to court once and losing. Now Sarah wouldn't be so witless as to try a thing like that, would you, Sarah?"

"Don't be too sure, Julia." Sarah narrowed her eyes at her sister and then looked towards the door. "I see you brought a bodyguard along."

"You know David Baxter, Sarah," Julia said quietly.

"What are you doing here, Baxter?" Aaron was suddenly interested.

David half bowed to Sarah and then directed his attention to Aaron. "It's just as your wife said. I'm the bodyguard."

"I'm sure Steve would like to know about that," Aaron said thoughtfully.

"He does know." David, lumbering into the cabin, left little room for the rest of them. "He asked me to look after Julia till he got home."

"And Stephen didn't come with you, Julia?" Sarah raised her delicate eyebrows once again. "Seems strange."

"He had business to attend to and I wanted to get home fast," Julia said firmly. She had no intention of telling Sarah about Stephen's wounds. "I thought there might be things I'd have to attend to. Seems I was right."

"Ah, Julia, you always did think the world couldn't run without you, didn't you?" Sarah said coolly. "And of course, you're always right. No one could ever misdoubt that."

"Where's Cousin William?" Julia asked, suddenly remembering that he had come on ahead of her just so he could take care of such eventualities.

"How would I know?" Sarah said. "He hasn't seen fit to inform me."

"Must be gettin' old, though." Josiah cackled. "Hear tell he hired another shipmaster to take the *Neptune's Dragon* on her next voyage."

"He's up on the Cape, Julia." Although Aaron spoke placatingly, he cast an apologetic glance at his wife. "We took the packet out immediately he arrived."

"Aaron, we're leaving now." Sarah's narrowed eyes when she looked at him were threat enough. "If you'll be so kind." She attempted to sweep past Julia and David.

Julia caught her by the arm. "Sarah, what are your plans?"

"Plans?" Sarah looked with contempt at Julia's hand, then lifted her head arrogantly. "I have no plans. The next step is up to you. Now, if you would release me . . ."

Julia dropped her hand and stood aside. "Go ahead, Sarah, but just remember I'm home now."

"How could I forget?" Sarah tossed her head and waltzed through the door.

"Be better off if you went back to sea," Josiah muttered as he followed his favorite niece. " 'Tis where you belong. Preferably at the bottom along with the rest of them sea witches."

"Dear Uncle Josiah." Julia was able to smile at him. "I'd forgotten how charming you could be."

Aaron passed her without a word or a glance, but his face was almost as red as his auburn hair.

Julia shook her head as she watched the trio ascend the companionway steps. "What a family I do have," she said softly to David, who had begun to pick up the discarded drawers.

"No better nor worse than any other," he said as he fitted a drawer into place. "The only trouble with you Howards is you stir up a commotion wherever you go."

"You're not going to include me with *that* lot!"

"Aye. Different sides of the same coin." He studied the interior of a cabinet over the bureau. "Life would be right dull without you, though."

As the packet sailed on the flood tide into the mouth of Sesuit Creek with a flock of hungry gulls soaring, dipping, and keening in her wake, Julia forgot Sarah and Uncle Josiah in her eagerness to see the shipyard, which lay on the bank opposite the landing. For a long time, she had been dreading this moment. There had been nights when she had dreamed of an idle yard emptied of men with half-finished or barely begun vessels on the ways.

But there on the largest ways, the summer sun shone bright on a new ship with her exterior planking nearing completion. Julia caught her breath when she saw how the ways had been extended to hold her. Larger than the *Star of Gold*! And the men were there, too, swarming around her hull and scattered all over the scaffolding.

Papa's last design. The one he wrote me about, she thought.

For a moment, her eyes misted, but then as the packet nosed into the wharf, Julia saw the small group of men who stood on the shore directly across from her. They were waving wildly. Even above the noise of the crowd that stood on the wharf and watched the lines being looped around the pilings, she could hear the voices shouting, "Julia! Miss Julia!"

There was no mistaking Cousin William's bulk and golden white hair as he beat the air with his top hat. Nor could she ignore Daniel and Philip Sears, who stood side by side and swung both arms above their heads as they called out to her. Then she saw a small figure in a stark black dress running from the office to the bank. Megan hadn't even taken time to cover her silver-blond hair with a bonnet.

155

Julia, in a rush of exhilaration, waved back at them. She was home, really home, and even if Papa wasn't there to meet her, she was rich in her friends. With tears coming fast to her eyes, she glanced impatiently over her shoulder to see if the gangway had been lowered.

Interpreting her look correctly, David touched her elbow. "Come along. I'll see you're the first off, and I'll tend to your baggage. I notice they're sending a boat for you."

Julia waved once more at the far shore, from which one of the yard's workboats was already pushing off, and followed David to the larboard side. There he elbowed people gently out of the way with a murmured explanation of why Julia must disembark immediately, and they, respecting her grief, allowed her to be the first to step upon the gangway.

After greeting the men in the boat, it took only a few swift strokes of the oars, and they were on the other side. It was swarthy Daniel Sears, the chief foreman of the shipyard, who first offered his hand to help her out of the boat. Although his dark brown eyes were shadowed by the brim of his cap, Julia could read the joy of his welcome mixed with gentle sympathy at the sadness of this homecoming. However, she barely had time to greet him before she was swept up into William Thacher's burly arms.

"Well, Julie, you're a sight for sore eyes," he said as he set her back down on the sand. "And it's high time, too, miss. You're sorely needed here."

"Am I?" Julia was startled by the emphasis he put upon his words. It wasn't like him. "What's happened?"

"Oh, Julie, everything," Megan said as she reached up to hug Julia and plant a kiss on her cheek. "Sarah and your uncle started stirring up trouble the minute your father died, and they haven't stopped to take a breath since. Oh, Julie!" Her hand flew to her mouth. "I'm sorry. I haven't even told you yet how I feel about . . ."

"It's all right, Megan. I know how much you loved him." Julia leaned over and returned her kiss. "I've already had a run-in with those two. Aaron as well."

"So that explains it," Cousin William said. "Thought it had been a mite too peaceful around here the last few days. Where are they? Boston?"

"Aye," Julia said with a long sigh and shook her head. "That's where they were when last I saw them, and since they didn't come up on the packet with us, it's my guess they're still there. Did you know they're trying to sell the shipyard as well as the *Star of Gold*?"

"But they can't!" Megan's delicate hand fluttered to her throat. "They have no right."

"That's what I told them, but it seems there are some papers missing. Important papers. I called on Papa's lawyer while I was in Boston, and he doesn't have them, though he knows their intent." She looked around at her friends. "Do any of you know anything about them? You're the people Papa trusted most."

"I . . . I'm afraid I'm to blame, Julie," Megan said, her black eyes troubled. "I was there when . . . I was at the launching, and as soon as I realized . . . Well, I remembered what happened when your father had that stroke. I went straight to the office and . . . secured a few things. I gave them to Amelia later."

"Thank heavens you were here," Julia said as she gave Megan another hug. "Lord knows what would have happened if you hadn't been."

"I can tell you the answer to that!" Megan's eyes flashed with remembered anger. "Not ten minutes after I'd taken care of the most vital records, Sarah and your uncle came into the office and started ransacking the chests. I had to call Daniel and Philip in to stop them, and even then it wasn't easy. They looked like . . . like vultures." Megan shivered. "I've never seen anything like it. You wouldn't have believed it, Julie."

"Oh, I'd believe it," Julia said grimly.

"But I'm not sure the papers you're looking for are there," Megan added, obviously troubled. "Not if they're the ones those two have been demanding from everyone."

"You mean the will and . . ."

"Let's go over to the office and discuss this," Cousin William said gruffly. "No point broadcasting your private affairs to the world."

"Yes." Julia glanced at the men who had been gradually drifting up from all over the yard. They were standing a little apart as they waited to greet her, but she could see the impatience in their faces. "I want to say hello to everyone first, but I'll join you in the office directly."

Julia tried hard not to slight any of the men as she spoke to them. These men, young and old, were the backbone of the yard, and they would have to take orders from her from now on. It would make a poor start if there were any hurt feelings, she thought as she smiled and then patted their hands when they offered their condolences. Later she would have to call them together and thank them for going on when neither she nor her father was there. Later she would have to tell them that she knew that they felt his loss almost as keenly as she herself did. But that was later. Now there were other matters that must come first.

Yet even as she walked to the office, men hurried to catch up with her. With each step, she had to pause, remember a name, and shake a hand. Finally she was able to escape into the small, one-story wooden building. After shutting the door, she leaned against it with her hand still on the knob while she caught her breath.

"Julie, are you all right?" Megan asked anxiously.

"Yes, I'm fine." Julia straightened up and untied her bonnet ribbons. "I'm just trying to think of what comes next. Everything seems so important. Somehow I hadn't pictured homecoming as being this hectic. Mostly

157

I'd been thinking about Papa. I'd planned to go direct to his grave before I even set foot in the yard or the house." Her laugh was shaky. "It doesn't matter, though. I reckon there's more of him here than there is up on the hill. At least what's left of him that's alive is here. His ships, his men . . . his friends." She smiled a little crookedly at Cousin William and Megan.

"It was his life, Julie." William Thacher stroked his short, gold-flecked white beard thoughtfully. "May not have been his choice of the way he wanted to live it, but when it came to doing it, no man could have done better. He took this yard and built it into one of the most respected in the country. What he did, he did well."

"Yes." Julia pressed her lips together, then straightened her shoulders and tossed her bonnet on the tall desk near the door. "He did and now it's my turn."

"Do you want some coffee, Julie?" Megan gestured at the potbellied stove that was pouring forth its heat despite the warmth of the day. The years of living near the equator as the wife of a missionary had left their mark on Megan. She often felt cold in this northern land.

The sight of the old battered coffee pot did what neither the vessels, the men, Josiah and Sarah, Megan, nor even Cousin William had been able to do. Tears flooded down Julia's face as she remembered the many cups of coffee she and her father had shared. She could see the two of them sitting comfortably together, discussing the business of the yard beside that stove in winter when the wind howled around the corners of the building and pried icy fingers through the cracks of the door. There they had sat lining up the work schedule on summer mornings before the heat of day became oppressive.

She fumbled for her handkerchief, but before Megan or Cousin William could approach her, she held up her hand, warning them off. "Please don't. I can't stand any sympathy. I don't want any coffee. I just want to find out about the papers you . . . secured. What are they and does Amelia still have them?"

"I've got 'em," William Thacher said. "They're over at my house in Brewster. Seemed a safer place than anywheres round here, and Samuel's keepin' a sharp eye on them. Doubt Sarah or Josiah want to tangle with him."

Julia nodded. As she fought for control and gained it, she thought of her father-in-law's second son, Samuel. He had been a cheerful and gay young man when she had first met him, but with the years, he had grown morose. It was something she had never been able to understand, though William had hinted at a broken engagement.

"I don't doubt but what you're right," she said. "There's not many would tangle with Samuel, but what's he doing home? I thought he never left the sea."

158

William Thacher pulled a much-battered black pipe out of an inner pocket of his frock coat and searched until he found a worn leather tobacco pouch. When he spoke, it was almost too casually. "Won't be here much longer. Just while *Neptune's Dragon*'s gettin' patched up at Jack Blade's shipyard in Boston. Then he'll take her to sea."

"Your ship?" Julia stared at the weathered face, which had been carved by the winds and suns of tens of thousands of sea miles. "You're really going to let someone else sail as master of your ship? Uncle Josiah said you'd taken on someone, but I didn't believe him."

"Aye." He concentrated upon filling his pipe, thereby avoiding her eyes. "Might as well give the boy his chance. Been master of smaller vessels for eight years now. He's gettin' on. Thirty-one now. Same as you. About time he had something worth braggin' on."

"And what are you going to do?" Julia folded her arms and looked at him skeptically. "Get yourself another ship?"

"Nope." He scraped a match against the stove and then touched it against the bowl of his pipe. After he was satisfied that the tobacco was drawing well, he finally looked at her and his emerald green eyes were full of candor. "I'm goin' to retire, Julie. I've had enough of the sea."

"That I don't believe. You'll never have enough of the sea."

"Have, though." He spoke around the pipe he held in his mouth. "That's the truth of it. I've got a touch of rheumatism. Not much. Just enough to tell me it's time to slow down."

"Do your plans for retirement have anything to do with Papa's death?" she asked, never taking her eyes from him as she searched his face for the truth. "You figure I'm going to need you to help me run the yard?"

"No, Julie. Once you get things set straight, you won't need any help from me." He broke away from her gaze and strolled to a small, multi-paned window that looked out over the yard. "But it does have something to do with Ben's death. I may be right fond of the sea, and I may love that ship, but I'm fonder of life. Once you slow down, you put everyone in jeopardy. Your ship, your crew, yourself."

He puffed on his pipe for a moment while he looked at the great ship rising on the ways and thought of the days when the *Belle of Canton* had been born on that very spot. Later it had been *Neptune's Dragon*. And Ben had built them for him. He turned to Julia, who was still standing near the stove and studying him with those dark blue eyes, so like her father's, that seemed to see beyond his lies.

"Thought you wanted to talk about papers," he said gruffly.

"I do. What do you have over in Brewster?"

"Just the yard records, Julie," Megan quickly said, breaking the tension rising between these two people who were so dear to her. "Who owes us money. The banking papers. Insurance."

"Anything on the *Star of Gold*?" Julia asked, thankful for the day when

159

she had asked Megan to act as clerk for the yard. Fortunately, her father had realized Megan's worth and had kept her on, unorthodox as it was for a woman to act in that position.

"Yes. All the records of her cost. I had a feeling they might be important."

"They are. But isn't there anything else?" Julia frowned as she looked at the brass-bound chests that lined one wall. They were filled with papers that went back to the days when her grandfather had founded the yard. "Something proving that we paid Papa for her?"

"No." Megan shook her head as she followed the direction of Julia's eyes. "I've been through all those. Your father must have kept the receipt somewhere else. Perhaps amongst his personal papers. Amelia would now more about that than I would."

"Amelia?"

"Yes. Aunt Martha gathered up all the papers she could find before Sarah and Josiah could get to the house. She gave them to Amelia. I think Captain Thacher has those, too."

"Cousin William?"

"Aye. I've got them." He drew on his pipe while he thought about it. "Haven't had much of a chance to go through them, though. I've been stayin' here in East Dennis, keepin' an eye on things, whilst the papers are in Brewster. Can't say I recollect seein' anything like that. Mainly I was lookin' for the will."

"And it's not there."

"Nope. Matter of fact, there's nary a sign of a heap of papers I'd call important. Must be one whole batch, the most important of all, hidden away somewheres. Less Josiah and Sarah have found them."

"I doubt it." Julia began to pace the close confines of the office. Looking at each familiar picture, each plane model that traced the growing beauty of the ships they had built, she saw only Josiah, Sarah, and Aaron in the midst of their created chaos on the *Star of Gold*. "They wouldn't be searching for them in Boston if they'd laid their hands on them. What about Mama? Does she have any idea where he might have put them?"

Megan and William looked gravely at one another. Then William drew his pipe from his lips and clenched its burning warmth in his hand.

"Julie, you've got to be prepared for what you're goin' to find at the house. Lydia hasn't been . . . right since your father died."

"Not right?" Julia stopped her pacing to stare at them. "What do you mean by not right?"

William looked at Megan while she, in turn, looked down at the hands she had folded in front of her. Each was waiting for the other to speak.

"Well?" Julia demanded.

William slowly looked over at her, and in his distress, he had to force the words to come. "Half the time, she thinks your father's still alive. The other half . . . Well, she's hysterical. Even blames you for his death."

"Me?" Julia stared at him, aghast. Mama? No. She couldn't. And suddenly she realized how much she had been looking forward to being with her mother, of finding comfort in their common sorrow. "That's horrible!"

"Aye. 'Tis a terrible thing."

Julia was still staring at him incredulously when there was a rap on the door and Daniel Sears limped in.

"I got to talk to you, Miss Julia," he said as he whipped his cap off, revealing a thatch of straight, dark brown hair. His other hand he kept tucked in his trousers pocket.

"Not now, man," William Thacher said impatiently. "Can't you see we're goin' over important matters?"

"That's what I want to discuss with Miss Julia." Daniel stood his ground with an obstinacy born of long years of dealing with the Howards. Every line of his wiry body proclaimed he was going to stay until he decided to go.

"Daniel, I really don't think I can cope with yard problems right now. I'll be down first thing in the morning, and we can go over anything you want. I have to get home and see my mother."

"It's not about the yard, ma'am." The determination in Daniel's brown eyes softened as he looked at Julia. "Captain Howard told me to talk to you private soon as you got home."

"Well . . ." Julia was feeling the weight of the day, of too much emotion, of the long trip from Boston on the packet. The vision of a tub of cool fresh water and a bed with clean sheets in her own darkened room beckoned her across the green marsh and the hills that lay between the shipyard and home. Her daughter waited for her there, too. How much had Clara grown? Had she filled out in the long months of their separation? But Daniel was obviously not going to leave until he had his say, and she owed him that much. "If it's really that important, go ahead, Daniel."

"Captain Howard said *privately,* Miss Julia." Daniel glanced at William and Megan.

"Do you mind?" Julia asked her cousin and her friend.

"Not at all, not at all." William clapped Daniel on the shoulder but his eyes were troubled. He offered his arm to Megan. "We'll take a stroll around the yard. Megan can tell me all about her youngster's latest accomplishments. Seems he's elected me grandfather."

As soon as they had gone, Daniel pulled his hand out of his pocket and extended it towards Julia. On his open palm was the small amber Buddha her father had so treasured. She could remember him holding it in his hands and stroking it as he told her about his early days in China when he had been a boy sailing before the mast. He had held it at other times, too, whenever the wistful longing for the sea had stolen across his face. Of all the beautiful things he had brought home from his voyages, it seemed to be the one he had treasured the most. Perhaps because it had been the first.

"He had this with him that day, Miss Julia. When he knew he was goin', he gave it to me and asked me to keep it safe for you."

"You were with him, Daniel?"

"Aye. I was with him."

She took a deep breath as the pain of that day hit her. That Daniel had been there, strangers had been there, but she had not been with him to say good-bye. It wasn't fair.

She sat down in the nearest armchair while she waited for the pain to subside. Then she looked up at Daniel and gestured towards a nearby chair.

"Can you tell me about it?" she asked in a voice tight with tears.

" 'Tain't really that much to tell," Daniel said gravely as he sat down. "He insisted on goin' down the ways on your ship. Said he was goin' to take her to Boston. Your ma, a lot of people tried to talk him out of it, but he wouldn't listen. He hadn't seemed too well for a few days. Seemed to be listenin' to voices no one else could hear and he spent a lot of time up on the dunes just watchin' the water. Well, I determined that if he was goin', I was goin', too."

"Go on," she said numbly as she stroked the warm amber. She could imagine the scene with the crowds, the flags whipping in the wind, the mounting excitement.

"The launching was fine. She stayed stubborn on the ways for a minute. Then she shot down into the water. It was then it happened. Just as we hit the water, Captain Howard staggered back. I wouldn't have thought nothin' of it except he clutched at his left shoulder and turned pure white. I grabbed for his other arm, and he like to knocked me over when he fell to the deck. Told me to look in his pocket, and I found that." He nodded at the small figure in Julia's fingers. "I asked him if it was what he wanted, and he said yes. Then he said, 'Keep it safe. Give it to Julie. Take care of her, Daniel.' "

He pressed his lips together and stared at the floor.

"Is that all?" Julia asked him.

"Yes, ma'am. He didn't have time to say nothin' else."

"Thank you, Daniel. I'll treasure it . . . always."

He raised his head and looked at her for a long moment, and in his eyes she could see the love he'd had for her father and the loss he too felt. Julia realized what an effort it had taken for him to tell her of that final scene, to live through it once more.

"But that's not all, Miss Julia," he continued. "I'm certain he knew what was goin' to happen. Almost directly after you left last year, he

162

started givin' me things to keep safe for you. Said I was the only one he could trust. A couple of days before the launching, he come over to my house and went over all the papers I had hidden there."

"Papers!" Julia clutched the Buddha and took a deep breath. "What papers?"

"Reckon they're the ones everybody's been huntin' for. His will's there. Lot of other things."

"And you didn't tell anyone?"

"No, ma'am. Captain Howard swore me to secrecy. Said I wasn't to let anyone get wind of them. That I was to put them in your hands and yours alone."

"Are they still at your house, Daniel?"

"Yes, Miss Julia. It's good you've come home. Been a burden with only me knowin'."

"Yes. I imagine it has been. Do you know if there are any papers on the ownership of the *Star of Gold*?"

"Aye. They're there. Want me to go fetch them for you now?"

Julia thought a moment. "No, Daniel. You keep them for the time being. I want to see which way the wind's blowing before I bring them to light. I'll let you know when I want them."

"It better be soon, Miss Julia."

"Why? Aren't they safe with you?"

" 'Tisn't that, ma'am, but we're runnin' out of money again."

"Money." She sighed. Why was it always money? She should have had the foresight to have dealt with it while she was in Boston. Now it would take days, maybe weeks, before she knew what her own private financial standing was. "I'll get it somewhere. Even if I have to borrow it, I'll get it."

"I got a bit saved up, Miss Julia, if that'll help." Daniel made the offer quickly without pausing for thought. Having reached the age of forty-five with no wife and no children, his entire life and loyalty revolved around the shipyard and the Howard family. Although he had a brother and sister as well as numerous nieces and nephews, it had always seemed the Howards needed him more than his own kin did. What he had was theirs.

"Oh, no, Daniel!" Then she saw that she had somehow hurt him, and she continued more gently. "It's good of you to offer, but I couldn't take your savings."

" 'Twouldn't be any savings if it wasn't for the shipyard and Captain Howard, Miss Julia. Your pa had a lot of faith in me when I was right young. Brought me along fast and paid me more than I deserved," he said earnestly. "If the shipyard needs help, if you need help, then that's where that money belongs."

"Oh, Daniel, you earned every penny and more, but I'll remember your offer," she agreed. She could see how much it meant to him. "That

163

reminds me. I've got letters and a lump of gold for you. They're in my sea chest. Paul gave them to me in San Francisco and asked me to bring them home to the family."

"Paul?" Daniel's swarthy face lit up with pleasure at the mention of his nephew's name. "You saw Paul? His ma frets about him. How did he look?"

"He looked grand, Daniel. All grown up. Without his help, we might never have made it out of San Francisco, but I'll tell you about that later. At any rate, you'd be very proud of him. Tell his mother not to fret. He said he was going to come home with enough to give her a life of ease, and knowing that young man, I don't doubt it. Not in the least."

"I'll tell her." He wanted to ask more about the nephew he had watched over after the death of the boy's own father, but he could see the lines of strain on Julia's face. She needed to rest. Yet there was one more thing he must discuss with her. "About the yard, Miss Julia. There've been rumors it's for sale. Even had a couple of people lookin' it over. The men are gettin' a mite nervy. A lot of talk about lookin' for work elsewhere."

"And you've held them together." She smiled at him and then said firmly, "Well, you can tell the men it's the Howard Shipyard and that it's going to stay the Howard Shipyard. And if any more people come around looking at it, you tell them the same thing."

"I will, Miss Julia." He rose to his feet and looked down at her. Captain Howard had put a heavy burden on those slender shoulders. He would have to help carry that load as much as she would let him. "I never had any doubts but that you would keep the yard goin'. I must admit, though, 'tis good to hear it from your own lips."

She reached out and took his hard, calloused hand.

"Thank you, Daniel."

Chapter Eleven

1851

While Julia had been talking to Daniel, William Thacher had sent for the Howards' buggy. When it arrived, Julia was more than ready to go home. It had been a long emotional day and she was tired. The ride between sun-scented summer fields, where delicate yellow butterflies fluttered above purple clover, was soothing. The white of Queen Anne's lace mingled with the golds of tall dandelions and daisies along the side of the road, and wild roses climbed the grey stone walls.

A robin sang in one of the elm trees beside a stately captain's house, and in the yard of a modest grey-shingled cottage, Julia heard the lilting song of a cardinal only a moment before she saw the flash of his red wings through the foliage of a cherry tree. When she heard the young crickets, she sighed. The sounds of home.

There was the grace of shade from tall trees that arched over the road as they left the hot sunlight, the smell of bayberry and pine, and then the lush green of grass in the open marsh. Julia straightened up when they turned onto the main road. There was no sign of life when they passed by Amelia's small cottage, and then they rounded the last bend in the road.

The sight of the large white house with its black shutters brought tears to Julia's eyes as it always did when she returned home from a voyage. However, this time they did not spring from joy. She didn't notice the chestnuts, spruces, and elms that surrounded the house or the trumpet vines flowering on the lattices as she usually did. It was her father's empty window she saw first.

The doors were standing open as though in welcome, but there was no one sitting on the wide porches. No children were playing in the yard. Not even a leaf on the trees was stirring. Silence seemed to enwrap the house and its grounds.

"Where are Clara and Robert?" Julia asked as she stepped out of the carriage onto the oyster-shell drive.

"I imagine Becky took them over to Amelia's house," Megan said as she tripped out of the buggy behind Julia. "They often spend the day with her and her children. Amelia says that with her brood, two more don't make any difference." She lowered her voice. "It's better for the children to spend some time away from your mother."

Julia paused and raised her parasol, although she hardly needed it for the short distance to the house.

"Is she really that bad, Megan?" she whispered from behind its cover.

"You'll see," Megan said sadly.

Not knowing what to expect, Julia almost tiptoed into the hallway when they entered the front door, but there was no need for it. Her mother, who was sitting quietly in the parlor with Aunt Martha, showed neither surprise nor excitement at her appearance, but smiled at her sweetly.

"Hello, dear. Glad to see you've come home early. 'Tis far too hot to stay at the shipyard today. I wish you'd brought your papa along with you, though. I keep telling him he works too hard. He's not getting any younger and it's about time he realized it. Do you think he'll be home soon?"

Julia started at her mother. Beneath the white hair that now only hinted at its once-golden color, her face was more placid and unlined than it had been for years and her green eyes were serene. No one had prepared Julia for this. How was she to handle this delusion? The ghost of Homer Evans

165

flitted through her mind, but she banished it quickly. It wasn't the same. It couldn't be the same.

"He isn't at the yard and he's not coming home, Lydia," William Thacher said gruffly from behind Julia.

"Oh, I recollect now. I declare I don't know where my mind is. He was going to take the *Star of Gold* to Boston. Well, I hope he'll be home soon. Somehow I thought he'd be on the packet today."

Julia went to her mother and leaned over to kiss her. "How are you, Mama?"

"Why, I'm fine, child," Lydia said with surprise as she looked up from her embroidery. "No different than I was when you saw me this morning."

"No headaches?"

"Just a light one earlier, but Martha rubbed my forehead and it's gone now. Why don't you get washed up, child, and then we can have some tea. You'll stay, won't you, William?"

"Yes, Lydia, I'll be here." He sat down on the sofa beside her and picked up the needlework that was lying on her lap. "Now tell me what it is you're making."

As soon as William had Lydia's attention engaged, Martha Chambers hoisted her ample body out of her chair. Going to Julia, she took her by the hand and pulled her into the hall. "We'll talk upstairs," she whispered.

Julia followed Aunt Martha, whose steps had grown slower just as her bulk had grown larger during the years that had passed since she had first appeared to nurse Julia through her illness. Now it was inconceivable to any of the family that they could ever have lived without her steadying strength and able supervision of this household and family with which she had no connections other than love.

Once they had gained the upper hallway, Martha led the way to her own room, which was over the kitchen in the ell of the building away from the main house. It was smaller and lower-ceilinged than the other rooms, but it was cozy with the clutter of Martha's accumulated years.

"Miss Lydia can't hear us in here," Martha said as she closed the door.

"Oh, Aunt Martha!" Julia flung herself into the older woman's plump arms.

"There, there, child," Martha said as she pulled Julia's head to her shoulder and patted her back. " 'Tisn't a thing that's easy to come home to."

"But, Aunt Martha, I didn't know what to say to her, how to act. My own mother!"

"This is a good day for her, Julie," Martha said as she held Julia away and searched her face with her own candid blue eyes. "Best not to upset her."

"But I can't lie to her. I can't go around pretending Papa's alive. I can't believe he's dead myself, but . . ."

"You don't have to lie to her, Julie, but you got to understand. 'Tis easier for her to believe he's here. She won't ask many questions about him, though she'll talk about him a bit. May make you uncomfortable, but you've got to realize it makes her comfortable. 'Tis when it comes over her he's truly gone that the bad times come. You'll see them and then you'll be thankful for days like this."

"But what do I say to her? How can I even talk to her?"

"Talk about anything, long as it's not him."

"And when she asks me about him?"

"Do just what Captain Thacher did. Tell her the truth. She'd remember a lie. But you don't have to go into any detail. She'll make up something to account for his absence."

"The way she did just now."

"Aye."

As Julia tried to understand just what this change in her mother involved, she wandered around the small, neat room, touching first one familiar object, then another.

"What about the children, Aunt Martha?" she asked as she picked up a silver-plated button hook. "Clara was so attached to Mama. Is it safe to have them in the same house with her?"

"Oh, your mother'd not harm a hair on either of those children's heads. She fair dotes on them both. Besides I don't let Miss Lydia out of my sight without there's someone there to keep an eye on her."

"Yes, but Clara . . . Oh, my God!" Julia sank down on the feather bed. "I haven't even asked how my own child is."

"She's fine." Martha sat down on the bed next to Julia and put an arm around her. "Gettin' plump and rosy and hasn't had a sick day since you left. Not even when some of the others was comin' down with colds last winter."

"Then it's a good thing I left her home." Julia's shoulders sagged and she stared down at her hands. "At least, I've done something right."

"You've done a lot of things right, Julie." Martha gave her a squeeze against her own warm, firmly plump body.

"The thing is I'm not all that sure that Clara should be exposed to Mama's . . . delusions." Julia began to rub the palms of her hands against each other as her mind rocked back and forth. "The child must understand that her grandfather's dead."

"She's been told, but whether she took it in or not, I don't know. She and your mother talk about him sometimes." Martha, putting her free hand across Julia's, stopped the rubbing motion. "May be that Clara can't understand the difference between life and death. May be that she's wise enough and kind enough to humor your mother. They're right fond of each

167

other. I don't know as it makes any difference what she believes. Can't see as how it's goin' to harm her."

"But to live a lie?" Julia shook her head vehemently. "No. Clara must be taught to live with the truth."

"Come now, Julie. Clara understands the difference between right and wrong. Isn't that enough at her age? She is only six."

"Old enough, and I'm going to have to see what's going on for myself. If it gets too bad, we'll be forced to move."

"Move!" Martha clutched Julia's hands with alarm. "Don't you even think such a thing, Julie. Hasn't your poor mother lost enough without losing her favorite grandchild, too?"

"Aunt Martha, Stephen's ill." Julia tried to keep her voice calm as she spoke. "I don't want anyone else to know it yet, but he's seeing doctors in London. I don't know what shape he'll be in when he comes home. If it's serious, I'm not all that sure that this is the place for him, either."

"You have a load on you, don't you, child?" Martha said sympathetically.

"Yes, I do." Julia gave a long sigh. "Just now it seems too much. Maybe if these things had come one by one . . . Do you know, I feel all tensed up, waiting for the next blow. It seems as if it could come from anywhere . . . anyone."

"You know I'll stand by you, Julie. Anytime you have the need to talk things out, come to me. 'Twill make you feel better."

"I always do, don't I?" Julia said ruefully. "And you've always had some good advice. Thanks for getting Papa's papers out of harm's way."

"Oh, harm came round fast enough, but they got nothing for their pains. They searched the house. Didn't think to look under my mattress, though." She chuckled.

"You're holding us all together now, aren't you, Aunt Martha? Papa gone, Mama not really here. That leaves you."

"And you, Julia." Martha's smile was confident. She dropped her arm from around Julia and stood up. "Are you goin' to be able to keep the house out of Sarah's and Josiah's clutches?"

"Yes. I'm pretty sure. I've got to look over the will first before I'll know for certain."

"You know where it is?" It was one of the rare times that surprise ever showed in Martha's tranquil blue eyes.

"I know. It's hidden in an even safer spot than your mattress."

"Well, land's sake, don't tell me. Then I won't have to lie about it the next time those two come around. I've got enough on my conscience as it is. I'd best rouse up Janet and see to that tea Miss Lydia wants," she said as she started towards the door. "You'll come down, won't you?"

"Yes." Julia hesitated for a moment and looked out the low window across the road at warm summer sunlight on the foliage that screened the marsh. "I still don't know how to handle Mama, though."

"Just do your best, Julie. No one can ask any more of you than that." She pulled out her gold watch and inspected it. "The children should be coming home soon. Clara will distract her."

Julia was just descending the stairs when she heard children's voices on the lawn and she rushed out of the open door. At first it was difficult to believe that the rosy-cheeked child with her pale blond hair in long braids was Clara. Bangs now covered her too high, slightly bulging forehead, and as she romped with her cousins, her grey eyes sparkled. She displayed none of her former timidity.

"Clara," Amelia, who was following the children across the lawn, called to her. "Your mother's here."

"Mama?" Clara suddenly stood very still and looked warily at the tall woman, who was striding towards her, as though she were a stranger.

"Yes, sweetheart, I'm home." Julia swooped her daughter up and kissed her before she noticed how rigid the child's body was. "What is it, sweetheart? Aren't you glad to see me?"

"Are you going to take me away?" Clara asked while she stared at her mother accusingly.

"No." Julia laughed with relief. So that was all it was. "I'm going to stay here with you."

Clara dubiously searched her mother's face as though she would find the truth written there. Then reassured, she began to wriggle. "Want to see Grandma," she said.

Julia reluctantly set her down and watched her run up the steps of the porch followed by her cousins. Freckle-faced Becky, who had originally been Clara's nurse, was carrying Megan's Robert. She curtsied as well as she was able and said, "I'm glad to see you home, ma'am."

"Thank you, Becky. I'm glad to be home. You'd best keep an eye on those wild Indians." Julia nodded at the house. Then she turned to her flaxen-curled sister and held out her arms. "Amelia!"

"Oh, Julie!" Although there were dark smudges of sorrow under them, Amelia's cornflower-blue eyes sparkled with delight. "I'm so glad to see you home . . . even if I can't get as close to you as I'd like." She laid her hand ruefully upon her stomach.

"Oh, Amelia, not again!" Julia laughed as their arms twined around one another. "You do better being separated from your husband most of the time than I do spending all my time with mine."

"Well, Michael and I have to make the most of what time we do have, and after that one trip to California, he's been making short voyages just so he can get home more often." Amelia rained kisses on Julia's face. "I *am* glad you're home."

"It's nice to get a proper welcome from somebody," Julia said as she gave her sister a final squeeze. "What between Clara, Mama, and Sarah, I was beginning to think no one missed me."

"Sarah's been here already?" Amelia's fair eyebrows flew up. "*I* didn't even know you were home till you walked out of that door."

"Sarah's in Boston," Julia said grimly. She took Amelia's hand, and together they strolled under the tall elms and oaks that were scattered across the spacious side lawn, which the sheep kept neatly sheared. While they walked, she described all that had taken place since she had landed.

When she had finished, Amelia looked at her thoughtfully and said, "So you know where the will is."

"Yes. I didn't till today. I was right worried about it."

"I can believe that. We all were. Julie, do you know what's in it?"

"More or less. I've never seen it, but Papa told me about it after he had it drawn up."

"Can you tell me?"

"Amelia . . ." Julia hesitated for a moment and then went on. "If it's the same will, he left most everything to me."

"Oh." Amelia's face looked suddenly pinched.

"But you see, 'Melia," Julia added hastily, "it's not really for me. It's for all of us. It was just that he didn't want to split things up so much we'd have to sell the yard or the house. He said I was to make sure Mama could live the way she always has. The house is for all of us whenever we need it. After Mama's taken care of, the excess profits from the yard and his other investments are to be split up amongst you and Sarah and me. Do you need money, 'Melia?"

"No. Not now." The color quickly returned to her normally rosy face. "We're doing well. Michael owns the *Laughing Lady*, thanks to my dowry, and we have the cottage. It was just that I was hoping Papa would leave something to the children. And . . ." She looked down at her well-filled dress. "Michael and I've been talking about adding onto the house. We have almost enough, but I was going to ask Papa for a loan."

"Well, it's certain you're going to need more room," Julia said, smiling. "We'll have to see how the will reads. Papa may have left you enough outright to take care of it. If not, can you wait till I've had a chance to go over the finances? I don't know exactly what I've got, much less how Papa's business stands. But I'm sure that, one way or another, I'll be able to find something for you."

"Oh, Julie, there's no rush about anything." Amelia bit her lip. "I hope you don't think I'm mercenary-like . . ."

"Oh, no, Amelia, no." Julia put her arm around her sister. "I could never think such a thing. It's only natural you should wonder about it. You know how much Papa loved you. I think you were always his favorite."

"No, Julie. You were."

"I wonder." Julia smiled at memories that were happy. "I remember how his face used to light up every time you came in the door, every time he heard your voice. When he talked to me, he was very insistent that you should never want for anything. He said you'd gone without your dowry far longer than you should have, and he never wanted to see you go without anything you wanted ever again."

"Did he really, Julie?" Amelia's cornflower eyes begged to be told that it was true. "Did he really say that about me?"

"Yes, he did," Julia said emphatically. "So you see, if you want an addition for your house, you'll have an addition for your house. One way or another. Meanwhile, you've got to help me with Mama. It's . . . it's difficult for me to know how to talk to her."

"Is she calm today?" Amelia asked.

"Yes, but she's certainly not in this world."

"Maybe she's had as much of this world as she wants," Amelia said softly. "She wouldn't go to the funeral, you know. Just sat there holding tight to the arms of her chair and saying, 'He's not dead. He's not dead.' It went on and on. We had to leave her home with Aunt Martha. Julie, don't take it personally when she gets upset. She's not responsible for what she says."

"I'll try not to, Amelia."

"Remember, you went through a pretty hard time once, too, Julie. I hoped it would make you understand her more than the rest of us do."

"No. I don't really remember that much about it," Julia said and found that it was true. "The important thing I do remember is that you were always there. You and Papa. Later, Aunt Martha. You've had more experience with this sort of thing than I have."

"It's different with Mama. Doctor Willett always believed that you'd recover." Amelia frowned as she glanced at the tall parlor windows that led onto the porch. "He's not so sure about Mama."

"I'll do my best, Amelia, even if I don't have your patience." She took her sister's hand. "But I shouldn't be keeping you standing out here. Come on in the house and sit down."

The next day set the pattern of many that would follow. Julia's night had been a restless one, filled with unrelenting thoughts of the responsibilities that were now hers. Unable to make any decisions, she had filled the hours of darkness by assigning priorities to the problems that beset her.

When the birds announced that dawn would soon be coming, she thankfully rose from her bed. However, when she entered the dining room, she was surprised to find that she was not the first. Cousin William was sitting at a table already spread for breakfast in the dimly lighted room.

"Mornin', Julie." He rose with his napkin in hand as she entered. "Figured you'd be up early today."

"Looks like I'm not the only one," Julia said as she sat down at her place. "Who got the servants up?"

"I did." Martha Chambers bustled through the door from the kitchen with a tray. "I'm not lettin' you out of this house till you've put down enough food to hold you a few hours."

"More like a few days," Julia said as she watched Martha and auburn-haired Janet, who followed her, place large platters of fried fish, boiled eggs, ham, and various breads and preserves on the table. Then she turned to William. "What are you doing up so early?"

"The older I get the less I need to sleep. Figured I'd ride on over to Brewster and pick up those items I've been keepin' for you. Sooner you get them, the sooner you can make a start on them."

"I'm not all that sure that I'm in a rush for them. The day's barely begun and I'm tired out already."

"That's because you've been thinking of what's to be done and not doing it. You'll pep up once you get to work."

"Cousin William," Julia said as she helped herself to fish and eggs. "Are you really serious about leaving the sea?"

"Oh, I might take a trip now and then, but not as master. Those days are over. Why?"

"I've been thinking about the *Star of Gold*. Stephen wants me to send her over to England for him. I thought that maybe either you or Samuel could do it."

"Well, one more voyage . . ." He looked at the window, where light was just beginning to filter through the fog. Then he shook himself. "No. I said I was retirin' and I'm retirin'. I'll help you find a master for her, though."

" 'Tisn't really necessary," Julia said slowly as she heaped blueberry preserves on a hot buttered muffin. She was reluctant to take the step, and yet it was the one that seemed most logical. "Hiram Richardson offered to charter her from me. I can have David Baxter go down to Boston. He'll make certain the master and cargo are acceptable."

"Baxter works for Richardson, don't he?" William said tersely.

"Yes, he does. What does that have to do with it? I may have a few doubts about Captain Richardson, but David's an honorable man. He'd never let his employment stand in his way."

"You're puttin' him in a bad position, Julie." He put down his fork and leaned both arms on the table as he looked intently at her. "Between the net and the hook. Let him go down and negotiate with Richardson for you, but leave the final word up to me. I have a feeling you're goin' to want some errands run in Boston right soon, and I may as well tend to them for you."

"Yes. Well, that was one reason I asked you." She toyed with her fish, flaking it idly with her fork. It had always been difficult for her to ask favors of anyone on her own behalf. But if there was one person she could ask, it was William Thacher. "If you really plan on being here, then David might as well go on back to sea."

"What's my bein' here got to do with it?"

"He gave up his command as soon as we arrived in Boston. I suspect I'm the reason. If we can assure him that you'll be here to back me up, he'll most likely still be able to take the *Free Wind* on her next voyage. I doubt Captain Richardson has had time to hire his replacement yet."

"Be just as well." William wiped his hands on the napkin he had tucked over his cravat and then stroked his short beard. "Put a stop to idle tongues, too."

"What are you talking about?" Julia stopped flaking her fish and looked at him suspiciously.

"Here he is a married man with his wife on the other side of the Atlantic, and you, a married woman whose husband is in the same place. People round here see you spendin' a lot of time together might start puttin' two and two together . . . or one and one, as the case might be."

"Cousin William!" Julia's indigo eyes flashed indignantly. "How can you even think such a thing? David and I've been friends ever since I was a little girl."

"I've heard he was sweet on you once."

"Never."

"No? Well, that may be," William said placidly, but he remembered times when he'd caught Baxter watching Julia with something that was a little more than friendship in his eye. "That may well be, but there's a lot of folks who enjoy seein' what isn't there . . . like Josiah and Sarah."

"And Aaron," Julia agreed reluctantly, as she remembered Aaron's remarks on board the *Star of Gold*. "I don't care what people say about me, but I don't want David or Stephen to be hurt. You're right. He'd best go back to sea."

"There's your daughter to think of, too, you know."

"Yes." Julia picked up her fork and tried to eat again, but thoughts of Clara weighed heavily on her. Last evening, the child had been polite but distant. Then when it came time for bed, she had caused such a scene that there had been nothing to do but allow her to sleep with her grandmother. Julia felt as though she had lost Clara, too.

"Oh, Cousin William," she burst out. "I don't know how I'm going to

173

win Clara back. I don't believe she even thinks of me as her mother anymore. She's closer to Mama and Megan and Aunt Martha than she is to me . . . and I've missed her so much."

"Well, that's only natural considerin' you've been gone for a year," he said soothingly. "She'll come round. Just give her a little time."

"I hope so. If only I could stay home with her for a while till she gets used to me again." She sighed as she rolled her napkin and put it back in its silver ring. "But I can't, and I'd best be on my way if I'm to accomplish anything today."

William nodded. "I'll bring your things over to the yard later this morning. Or do you want me to bring them to the house?"

"No. The office. I think they'll be safer there."

"I wouldn't count on it. Josiah's been known to pick locks before."

"Well, I'll find someplace, but not here. Did you know Sarah talked Mama into signing a paper offering the yard for sale?"

"Seems unlikely. Maybe Sarah signed it for her?"

"Could be, but it's not important. The yard isn't going to be sold." She pushed back her chair and walked briskly into the hall.

As soon as Julia arrived at the yard, she sent Daniel for the will and the other papers he had hidden. Her hesitancy of yesterday had vanished with her impatience to solve everything as quickly as possible.

The will was a shock. Signed only three months before her father's death, there was no mention of either the house or the shipyard in it.

A thousand dollars had been left to Martha Chambers as well as suitable amounts to the other servants. There was a bequest of his shares in one vessel to Amelia, his shares in another to Sarah, while the household furnishings were left to Julia with the reservation that they were for her mother's use during her lifetime. Also he willed to Julia whatever cash was left in the bank after the bequests had been paid. The remainder, of which he mentioned some railway stock but left other things unnamed, was to be divided among his three daughters.

Julia was aghast. This will did not in any way resemble the one he had discussed with her or the one his lawyer in Boston had described. She looked the document over carefully. It had been drawn up by a lawyer in Yarmouth.

After only a quick glance the rest of the papers, she returned them to Daniel for safekeeping and mounted her horse. There had to be something else. Papa would never have left the house and the yard to be divided up three ways. But that's what would happen unless she got to the bottom of his unexplained behavior.

174

* * *

It was a long ride and it took her even longer to find the lawyer whose name the will bore. She finally tracked him down in a small whitewashed wooden building on Church Street. As she entered the large empty front room, she looked around suspiciously. The leather chairs were old and cracked in places, as were the bindings of the books that lined the walls. It seemed very unlike her father to choose such a lawyer. Upon closer inspection of the room, she was relieved to see that his degree was from Harvard.

"It's genuine," a man's voice came from behind her.

She turned to find a slender, sharp-faced man in his thirties standing in the doorway on the far side of the desk. His small brown eyes sparkled with amusement behind his gold-rimmed spectacles.

"Mr. Dewing?" she asked, not in the least embarrassed at being caught.

"Yes, I'm Chester Dewing, and I rather suspect you're Mrs. Logan. Julia Logan."

"Why, yes, I am." This time she was not able to conceal her surprise. "How did you know?"

"You look very much like your father . . . and I've been expecting you."

"Well, I hope you have some explanation for this," she said imperatively and handed him the folded copy of her father's will.

"Yes." The lawyer was grave as he glanced at it and then at her. "This will take a little time. Won't you sit down?"

He planted himself behind a large polished desk that made him seem very official, and with his fingers formed into a steeple, he waited for her to speak.

"You'd best read it over," Julia said bluntly. "It *can't* be his last will. There must be another one, and I want to know where it is."

"I only drew up one for him, and I'm familiar with its contents." He seemed quite uninterested in the will which lay before him as he continued to examine Julia's face.

"But he doesn't make any mention of the shipyard!" Julia fairly exploded. Chester Dewing's calm, uncommunicative manner was beginning to irritate her. "That yard was the most important thing in his life. He wanted it to go on, and if it's split three ways, it won't. Then there's the house. Where's my mother to live if it's sold?"

"I wouldn't worry on either of those accounts, Mrs. Logan." Chester Dewing got up and went to an iron safe that was let into the wall next to the stone fireplace. When he returned, he had a sheaf of papers in his

175

hand. "Look through these. Before your father died, he had almost all of his assets transferred to your name. You own the shipyard, the house, and a good many other things outright."

Julia riffled through the papers, but she was too bewildered to study them at the moment. This was the last thing she had expected. "But why would he have done that? From what I know of his previous will, he was going to leave them to me, anyway."

"Your father was concerned . . . more than concerned . . . about what would happen after his death. He said that there were interested parties who might contest a will such as he had, and after I had gone over it, I agreed with him. He commenced transferring the property, piece by piece, almost immediately after you left the country. We both felt that your absence would remove any suggestion of coercion on your part." He removed his spectacles and his small brown eyes looked suddenly piercing. "You realize you *do* have a moral obligation to the others? Your father trusted you implicitly, Mrs. Logan. I hope he wasn't mistaken."

"Mr. Dewing," she said as she sat up very straight and lifted her chin at him. "I don't need you to lecture me on my morals. I'm quite capable of taking care of them myself."

"Of course, of course." He replaced his glasses and his eyes once again assumed their former mildness. "My part in the matter is solely of a legal nature. If I've overstepped the boundaries, it's only because he was such a fine man. One of the finest it's ever been my privilege to know."

"I didn't mean to snap at you, Mr. Dewing. I *know* he was one of the finest men who ever lived, and I fully intend to take care of my mother and the others."

"I'm relieved to hear it," he said and smiled for the first time. "Never having had the pleasure of meeting you, I wasn't entirely in favor of his passing almost everything on to one person. I can see now that I was mistaken. You'll find a letter from him in there. It's not a legal document and is not binding. It's a private letter to you, but in it, he communicates his wishes and suggestions as to how to handle things."

Julia nodded and toyed with the papers. "Tell me, Mr. Dewing, why didn't you come forth with this information before? Everyone's been searching for the will."

"Your father's instructions were not to contact anyone until you got in touch with me. I did make a few discreet inquiries and found that you were still at sea." He spread his open hands and shrugged. "There was nothing for me to do but wait."

"Well, you'd best take care of the will now. It'll save a lot of people the trouble of searching any further for it. I suppose it will have to be read and filed?"

"That's the usual procedure."

"Then go ahead and put things in motion," Julia said. Despite his dry, dispassionate manner, she was beginning to like Chester Dewing. She sensed an unbiased honesty in him and felt that he was a man she could trust. "You needn't say where the will was, though."

"I doubt anyone will ask, but if they do, I'll simply say that I drew it up. As for the delay, I'll take the blame for it."

"I appreciate that. And if anyone does contest either the will or the transfer of property, you'll handle the defense?"

"I wouldn't miss it for the world." He smiled with absolute relish. "I understand one of your sisters would make an interesting opponent."

"*That* she would . . . if you enjoy a battle."

"It's part of my profession. There's a certain amount of enjoyment when you have a keen mind on which to sharpen your own."

"I'll leave her to you, then. I don't have either the time or the energy to waste on Sarah . . . Mrs. Martin." She picked up the papers he had handed her. "Would you mind if I looked these over here? I'd rather leave them with you than take them home."

"Not at all." He rose from behind his desk. "I'll have tea sent in. Or would you prefer coffee?"

"Coffee, please. I need all my wits about me, and tea's not strong enough."

"If you like, I can have copies made and send them to you."

Julia looked at the thickness of the pile of papers that were covered with fine copperplate writing. It would save time if she could examine them later. Then she changed her mind. "No. I think not. The fewer people see these, the better I'll like it."

Julia returned to the shipyard more slowly than she had left it. With the horse's hooves pounding a steady cadence to her thoughts, she was able to comtemplate the magnitude of her inheritance. Several years ago, her father had begun speculating in cotton mills and railroads, a fact she had not known since their accounts were kept completely separate from the shipyard's. There were bonds and notes as well as shares in several vessels. Another surprise was the amount of money he had funneled into her own private accounts during the last few months.

The financial holdings were not her greatest inheritance, however. In his letter, her father had made it clear that he held her responsible for her mother's and her sisters' welfare. He also mentioned Megan Fairfield and Martha Chambers as well as his various grandchildren. He had been quite specific in how far she was to go in helping each one.

Amelia was to receive help only when she asked for it or when Julia thought she needed it, so that Michael would not depend upon her as a source of income. Sarah was not to be allowed to starve or go homeless if

177

her husband's fortune vanished. Megan was to be considered part of the family as long as she lived or until she remarried, as was Martha. Daniel and Philip Sears and several of the men in the yard were to retain their jobs until they were no longer able to work, and then they were to receive healthy pensions.

She pulled out the letter, the one item she had decided to bring home with her, and read again his greatest legacy to her. The concluding words were ones she would never forget.

Many people have taken great pleasure in pointing out to me over the years that I did wrong to bring you up as I did, and yet I don't believe I was. Knowing that you are here and esteem honor as highly as I do and that you have the strength to follow its dictates, I feel I can leave this place. I don't know what lies on the other side of the curtain, but I believe that God is just and that we will be reunited someday. My life on earth would have been a sadder thing without you. Therefore, it remains that I must be granted the joy of your presence in Paradise. If you ever have a son, Julia, will you name him for me so that you will have some memory of the happiness we once shared together? Perhaps he will bring you as much delight as you have brought me. It is hard to leave you, my darling Julia, but I know I must soon go.

> Your loving father,
> Benjamin Howard.

As her vision blurred, she quickly tucked the letter away to save it from water spots. His own dear hand, which would never hold a pen again, had written those words, and as the ink flowed strong and vibrant across the page, she could hear the rich, low voice. No. He wasn't dead. Not so long as the letters, the log books of his voyages, the ship models shaped and created by his fingers continued to exist. Not so long as she continued to exist. He would ride beside her, he would work beside her, and he would lend her his strength.

She tapped the horse lightly with a switch, which sent him into an ambling trot. There was still a lot to be done before the sun went down, and with her father's help, she would accomplish what she set out to do.

At the yard, she discovered that Cousin William had returned from Brewster with a staggering armload of records and papers. He was sitting alone in the office with his arms crossed upon his chest and he looked like a formidable dragon guarding his treasure.

"Where's Megan?" Julia asked as she entered the coolness of the building. "Did you banish her?"

"Not I. It's that son of mine. He lured her over the dunes to take a look at the water."

"Samuel?" Julia asked incredulously. "Samuel and Megan?"

"They seemed right interested in one another," he said noncommittally.

"And you don't approve?"

"Don't know whether I do or not. Now, don't look at me that way, Julie. Has nothing to do with her son, at least not directly."

"What do you mean by not directly?" Standing over him with one hand on her hip, she challenged him. She was not going to allow any aspersions to be cast on Megan, not even by Cousin William.

"Well, when Samuel first come home, he seemed to take a shine to that young lady, and she was too embarrassed to tell him that Robert was the product of her liaison with a Tahitian gentleman, that though the truth is known to only a few of us, in actual fact the poor boy's a bastard. Megan couldn't bring herself to tell Samuel, but she thought he ought to know about it. Asked me to break it to him."

"And you told him." When he nodded, she asked, "How did he take it?"

"Didn't seem too pleased at the beginning." William stroked his short beard and his green eyes were thoughtful as he looked towards the open door. "Matter of fact, this is the first time they've been together since we discussed the situation."

"Well, they're old enough to know their own minds," Julia said briskly and put her hat on the shelf above the clothes pegs. "I don't see that it's any concern of ours."

"Just don't want to see them hurt. Samuel, he's right touchy. If he gets too interested and Megan turns him down, he's bound to take it hard. If he can't reconcile his feelings about Robert, he'll make her miserable."

"So you think it's serious?"

"Could be. I'm not sayin' it is, but it could be. You take a look at them and then make up your own mind."

"I will." Julia went to the table beside William and idly began to flip through the papers on the stack he had laid there. "I'm not so sure she should have asked you to tell him, though. With his black eyes just like Megan's and that carrot-red hair of his, his heritage isn't all that noticeable."

"He looks different, Julie," William said with much gentleness. "And he could look even more different when he gets older. I'm not sayin' there's any need for the girl to broadcast her shame, but she'd have no right concealin' the truth from a man she intended to marry."

"I suppose you're right." Julia couldn't bear the thought that Megan, who had suffered so much, might be in for yet more pain. Hadn't it been enough for her to see her little boy die in agony after being poisoned by a stone fish? Hadn't it been enough for her to find her husband's body swinging from the rafters of her bedroom? She had suffered rejection by the other missionaries, and later, rejection by her own family. There should be no more rejection of Megan by anyone. Not if Julia could prevent it. She said bluntly, "If Samuel's taking it so much to heart, then he's not the man for her."

"Could be it was the shock of it more than aught else," William said thoughtfully. "Megan is so delicate and . . . spotless, it comes as a bit of a surprise to find she's not a saint, but human like everyone else."

"Well, I don't think Megan ever billed herself out as being a saint," Julia bristled at him. "She's a good person, though, and one of the best friends I ever had. If Samuel's the one that does the hurting, he's going to have to answer for it to me."

William chuckled. "Doubt he'd want to tangle with you. You're sounding more like your old self. Must have had good news."

"Good news?" Julia glanced at the papers in her hands and then flung them back onto the table and sat down. "If anything under the circumstances could be called good news, I reckon it is."

Julia had just finished telling William about her visit to Chester Dewing when Megan floated up the steps and into the office followed by Samuel Thacher. She looked more like the young missionary's wife Julia had first met under the coconut palms beside the rippling waters of the lagoon in Tahiti than she had since George Fairfield's death. Despite her black dress, she seemed to bring the summer sunlight with her.

Julia smiled at her and held out her hand to her brother-in-law. "Hello, Samuel. Thank you for taking care of the records for me."

" 'Twas nothing," he said tersely, his dark eyes examining her face. His expression wasn't exactly hostile, but it wasn't very friendly, either. But then Julia had never seen Samuel betray his feelings. He was the most tightly controlled person she had ever known.

"I hear you're taking command of *Neptune's Dragon*," she said.

"Aye. I'll be sailing soon." He was constantly watchful to see what effect his words would have on others, although he took much care to conceal his own emotions. It made Julia very uncomfortable. Then, as though he had read her thoughts, he added with some warmth, "I'm sorry about your father, Julia. It must have come as a shock to you."

"Yes. Yes, it did. Thank you."

"Do you need me for a while, Julie?" Megan asked. "If not, Samuel and I thought we'd walk over to the house and see how Robert's getting along."

"No. Go ahead," Julia said, but there was a small part of her that resented Megan's defection. She had counted on her help in going through the reams of paperwork that weighed down the table. Still, if Megan *was* serious about Samuel, Julia knew how precious those days before a sailing could be.

Chapter Twelve

1851

A week later Julia was once again at the wharf, but this time, she and Megan had come to say farewell to Samuel Thacher and David Baxter, who were off to Boston to take command of their respective ships. David would be sailing for California aboard the *Free Wind* in a few days while Samuel would be following shortly in *Neptune's Dragon*. They wouldn't return for nearly a year, for they both planned to continue on to China and England before they were homeward bound.

William Thacher was also on board the packet. While in Boston, he planned to combine the tasks he had assumed on Julia's behalf with the rather dubious pleasure of watching his son and his ship sail away without him.

Once the schooner had crossed the bar and disappeared from sight, the crowd quickly dispersed and the only ones left on the wharf besides the men working at the fish house were a few boys with baited lines, who swung their bare legs over the side, and some white-bearded gentlemen, who sat in the sun with their chairs tilted against the salt-grey walls of wooden buildings and sheds while they reminisced about the days of their youth and storms and adventures that had long since passed.

"Well, they're gone," Julia said as she turned to Megan, whose black eyes still rested on the mouth of Sesuit Creek. "Time for us to get back to work."

"Yes." Megan's smile beneath the black lace of her parasol was touched with sadness. "There's a lot to be done."

But neither of them hurried as they strolled toward Toct Bridge, which crossed the creek to the shipyard, nor did they speak. There was an emptiness to the sunlight, an emptiness to the fleece clouds that sailed the summer sky, an emptiness broken only by the occasional harsh laughter of a gull. Although the village was well populated, a sense of desertion and desolation always hung over it when men left for the sea.

For the first time, Julia realized how much she was going to miss David. From the moment she had received news of her father's death, he had been nearby. Until now, she hadn't understood how much she had counted on his quiet strength. She was almost sorry she had encouraged him to leave, but she knew it was for the best.

When they reached the middle of the bridge, Megan paused and leaned on the wooden rail to stare across the sandy curve of the creek. The wind touseled the long silver-blond curls that cascaded from beneath her black hat as she gazed in the direction the packet had taken.

The water gurgled as it raced around rocks and boulders and stranded islands of salt grass to return to the ebbing sea. The smell of freshly exposed marl rose ripe around them and the church bell high on the hill struck the hour.

"He promised to write," Megan said in her soft, slow drawl as the last note died away.

"After seeing him around the shipyard and the house from morning till night, I'd have thought he'd have more than that to say for himself," Julia remarked rather sharply, trying to shake off her own melancholy.

"No. I didn't really want him to say more," Megan said dreamily. "It's nice to have an admirer, but I'll never rush into a marriage again. I made that mistake with George. We never truly knew each other until after we'd arrived in Tahiti, and then it was too late to repair the matter."

Julia nodded soberly as she thought of the tragedies that marriage had produced, of the tragedy of the marriage itself. Then she smiled to herself.

"Well, I do tend to rush into marriages myself. Least I did when I was young. Yet I can't say either of them was a mistake."

"Weren't they, Julie?" Megan looked at Julia around the corner of her straw hat.

"No," Julia said definitely. "You never knew Jason, but he was a good man. We didn't have much time together. Yet if we hadn't married, I'd have regretted it all my life."

"I'm sure he was wonderful if he was anything like his father, but I've spent a lot of time with you and Stephen." With one finger, Megan traced a pair of initials that were carved deep into the rough timber of the rail. "I know your life with him hasn't always been easy."

"Maybe not easy, but I doubt anyone's is," Julia said as she thought of the times she had loved him beyond passion and the times she had wanted nothing more than to be far away from him. Through it all, one thread bonded them together. "He's a part of me, Megan. Can you understand that?"

"No. Not really. George and I were always too far apart. Perhaps someday I'll understand, but I'm not sure that the person will be Samuel. Is he at all like Jason?"

"No." Julia thought back, and despite the fact that it had been almost fifteen years, she could see that tall and slender young man laughing in the sunlight as they sailed her dory together down the creek and out into the waters of the Bay. That had been before they had married, but it was one of the most vivid pictures she carried in her heart. It was on that day she had first understood what it meant to love a man.

"Julie?" Megan put her hand on Julia's sleeve.

"What? Oh, no, Megan. You might have guessed they were brothers, but it would have been more from an occasional expression than anything else. The way Samuel lifts his left eyebrow. That was Jason's. The color of their hair, but Jason's was darker and thicker. You've seen his portrait."

"Yes. He was a handsome man."

"He was, but now he's gone." But was he really? Was anyone ever truly gone? "Sometimes I dream about him, and when I wake up, it's as though I'd lost him all over again."

"And now you're worried about Stephen," Megan said sympathetically.

"Oh, Megan." Julia sighed and shook her head. "You don't know how very much. I've tried not to let on. I don't want Clara to guess. But at night, I lie there and wonder if I'll ever see him again." She watched a tern flash black and white in the sun as it soared down the creek on its way to the Bay. "We've had a lot of happy times together. I remember when the *Crystal Star* was launched and we sailed off on her together. We were very happy then."

"And later?"

"Yes. Later, too. Times without number. Stephen respects me, Megan. He respects what I can do, and that's important. And I respect him. There's no captain afloat who's any better than he is. He deserves the *Star of Gold.* I hope they're able to get her off to England quickly."

"If Captain Richardson's chartering her, I imagine she'll sail soon. He impresses me as a man of action." Megan paused for a fraction of a moment and then asked, "You said you saw him in Boston, didn't you, Julie?"

"Yes. I saw him." Julia looked over at the shipyard. The sight of boys stirring the steaming cauldrons of tar, the top sawyers at the saw pits wielding their long-handled saws, the men loading hackmatack knees onto the wagon while the shipyard ox stood patiently in his shafts, all served to make her feel guilty for idling while everyone else was busy. "We'd best get on back to the yard. We won't get any work done loitering here."

"Julie." Megan put out her hand to restrain her friend, who had begun to turn away. "Did he say anything about me?"

Julia stopped and looked at her in amazement. "Hiram Richardson? Yes. As I recollect, he asked to be remembered to you."

"Why didn't you tell me?"

"I didn't think you'd be interested." Julia looked at Megan intently. "Are you?"

Megan's eyes danced as she said, "Did you know that while you were away, he wrote and invited Robert and me to come to Boston?"

"Lord, no!" Julia raised her voice in surprise. A couple of housewives, who were passing with market baskets on their arms, stopped their gossip long enough to stare at her, and the patch-eyed shoemaker nudged his companion while his good eye sparkled. Julia lowered her voice, but none of the vehemence was lost. "What an insulting thing to do!"

"Why?" Megan twirled her parasol and looked innocent. "I don't see anything insulting about it."

"*You don't?* Megan, he's a widower and you're a widow and he's asking you to visit him alone in Boston. If that's not the most improper thing I ever heard of, I don't know what is."

"Julie," Megan said, laughing, "you really are a Puritan sometimes. He didn't ask me to stay at his house. He said he'd make arrangements for me to stay at a hotel or with friends of his, whichever I preferred. Furthermore, he suggested I bring along a friend to act as chaperone."

"Well, don't you even consider it. I don't trust that man."

"You're going to charter your husband's ship to him."

"That's different."

"I don't see what's so different about it. Besides, David Baxter likes him. Seems to me, he'd know more about Captain Richardson than you would."

"David Baxter would get along with the devil himself. Everyone likes David, so he likes them. You take my advice, Megan, and have nothing to do with that man. You'd best stick to Samuel."

"And if I do have anything to do with him, you'll disown me?" Megan's laughter was full of impish gaiety.

"No, Megan, but it would make me unhappy."

"Julie, you can't run my life. I realize what you've done for me, and I truly appreciate it. I owe everything to you. A home, the food Robert and I eat, our clothes, even the chance to do something where I feel I'm earning my keep. But I'm only thirty, and there's a lot of life ahead of me. I'm going to dispose of it as I see fit."

"Has Hiram Richardson proposed to you?" Julia's blue eyes grew darker as she studied her friend.

"Good heavens, no, Julie. I've hardly ever seen the man," Megan said impatiently. She knew that Julia truly cared about her, but there were times when she thought that things were a lot calmer when Julia was away at sea. Not better, but calmer. "I promise you I'd no more rush the fences with him than I would with Samuel, but there aren't that many chances for a widow of my age, and I think I should explore each one just a little. I know he admires me, and I liked him the few times I've ever seen him. That's enough for now."

"I should think it was. He's far too old for you to consider, anyway," Julia said tartly. "Do you know, I think those teeth of his are all false . . . and I sometimes do wonder if he doesn't dye that chestnut hair of his. Seems right suspicious there's not a strand of grey in it. As I recollect, there was quite a bit showing when I first met him almost ten years ago. Probably wears a corset, too."

"Julie, I think you're right." Megan paled as she resolutely turned and started to walk over the wooden boards of the bridge. "We'd do well to go back to work."

"All right," Julia said, easily catching up with short and dainty Megan. "I'll say nothing more against him, but just think over what I've said."

The reading of Benjamin Howard's will was held before William Thacher was able to return to the Cape. Julia had wanted to wait for him, to have his bluff support in the face of the gale she suspected would rage. However, Sarah returned with Josiah and Aaron by stagecoach, and when she learned that the will had been found, she became shrill in her insistence that the terms be made known immediately.

To quiet Sarah's sharp tongue, Julia arranged with Chester Dewing to have the reading held at the house on the following Monday. She had told Amelia almost immediately of the provisions of the will and about the transfer of property. They had agreed that it was a needless ordeal to put their mother through. Since the servants were mentioned in the will, Megan had volunteered to take Lydia and the children for a drive in the carriage.

The day was hot as only a day in August can be, and the crickets had been singing since shortly after sunrise. Although a good breeze blew through the tall windows that led onto the porch as well as through the side windows that looked towards the curve of the road, Aunt Martha sat patting her face with an embroidered white handkerchief and Amelia plied her fan vigorously. Chester Dewing was content to sit in front of the empty fireplace, quietly checking through his papers, but Julia paced the silent room as they waited for Sarah.

When a half hour beyond the appointed time had passed, Julia considered postponing the meeting. There was too much to be done at the shipyard for her to waste her time waiting upon Sarah's whims. Just then, however, Maryanne, who had been waiting with the other servants in the dining room, came in to announce that the Martins' carriage was coming.

Julia quickly seated herself on the blue brocade sofa beside Amelia and tried to appear composed. She was determined not to give Sarah the satisfaction of knowing that she had succeeded in irritating her.

But when Sarah swept into the room with Josiah, her son, and her husband in tow, it was difficult for Julia to remain calm. She decided it would be a waste of energy to protest Josiah's presence, but an eight-year-old child was another matter.

"Why don't you let Thomas Benjamin go out and play in the garden," she suggested as diplomatically as she could. "He'll only be bored by all this."

"My son is Papa's grandson and his only namesake," Sarah said loftily as she ensconced herself in a chair with a tall, rounded back. "He has every right to be here."

"But none of the other children are here," Julia pointed out. "They're just as much Papa's grandchildren as Thomas Benjamin is."

"Just because you and Amelia have no interest in educating your children properly is no reason why I shouldn't." Sarah, who had never let go· of her son's hand, pulled him to her side and proudly put an arm around his slender shoulders. The smile in his black-fringed grey eyes was as catlike as his mother's.

"All right, Sarah. As you wish." And it's going to be quite an education for him if he understands it, Julia thought as she smiled back at her nephew. "I think we're all here, Mr. Dewing, if you want to begin."

Halfway through the reading of the bequests to the servants, who were clustered just inside the door that led to the dining room, Clara's large, fluffy white cat strolled through one of the tall windows, whose ledges rested very nearly level with the deck of the front porch. Thomas Benjamin let out a whoop and dashed for the startled animal, who quickly ran outside again with the boy behind him. Almost immediately they reappeared through the other window, and while they dashed to the first one, a small pie-crust table, which held a tall Chinese vase with a bouquet of summer flowers, overturned with a crash.

Chester Dewing gave up all attempts to make himself heard over the racket while Janet rushed to get a cloth to blot the water from the flowered carpet and Maryanne dropped to both knees to gather up the shards of china.

"Thomas Benjamin, come here!" Aaron shouted irately as he tried to capture his son, but the boy slithered out the window.

"When I tell you to come here, you will come here!" Aaron exploded as he bent his bulk with difficulty to pass under the upper panes of the window in pursuit of Thomas Benjamin.

As soon as his father straightened up on the porch, the boy ran through the other window and straight for his mother's arms. Sarah held him protectively while she watched, completely unperturbed by the whole scene. This time Aaron did not attempt another passage through the window, but entered the front door and then the one into the parlor. He immediately made for his son, but Sarah clutched the child closer to her.

"Don't you dare lay a hand on him, Aaron Martin," she said with ice in her voice. Then she stroked her son's light auburn hair as he laid his head on her lap and began to cry. "There, there, love. Mother knows you didn't mean to do any harm. 'Twas just an accident because of that wretched cat. Did he scratch my pretty boy?"

Julia and Amelia, who had remained sitting on the sofa during the entire episode, looked at each other and shook their heads. Then as the maids returned to the room after disposing of the wreckage caused by the pretty boy, Chester Dewing cleared his throat and looked around at the group. His eyes lingered on Thomas Benjamin, whose sobs were muffled in his mother's skirts, before he turned to Julia.

"Do you think it's safe to proceed now?"

"I think we'd *best* proceed before another cat takes it into its head to walk into the room. I hope you can make yourself heard over Thomas Benjamin."

"I'll manage," he said wryly and then picked up his papers again.

The servants' bequests were soon finished, and as the lawyer entered into the family's affairs, Julia unobtrusively took the small amber Buddha out of her pocket and began to rub it between her fingers while she watched Sarah's face. When mention was made of the three-way division of the remainder of the estate, Sarah flashed a look of triumph at Julia, but at the conclusion, she pushed her son away from her lap and rose in anger.

"There must be a mistake, Mister Dewing. You omitted my son, and I know my father would have left something to his namesake," she said haughtily.

"He didn't ask you to name Thomas Benjamin after him," Amelia said with uncharacteristic sharpness. Although she believed in giving all the love she could to her children, Sarah's complete lack of discipline and her dithering over her son rubbed Amelia raw. She was uncomfortable enough carrying her fourth child around in this heat. "No reason why he should single him out from his other grandchildren."

"No reason!" Sarah stared daintily down her nose at her sister.

"I'm afraid there's no mention of your son, Mrs. Martin," Chester Dewing said mildly.

"Well, at least, you'll have to give us a full accounting of the shipyard *now*, Julia," Sarah said, triumphantly switching her eyes from her younger to her older sister. "If you'll be good enough to send the details up to our house, we'll decide whether we want to sell my share or not. I rather think we will."

"No, Sarah. I won't," Julia said quietly but firmly. "There's no mention of the shipyard in the will."

187

"It's included under the remainder of Papa's property, though I'd hardly have thought it necessary to point that out to you."

"But you see, Sarah . . ." Julia paused to smile almost lovingly at her sister. "It's not mentioned in the will nor is it included with the remainder of the property because the shipyard belongs to me."

"What kind of swindle are you tryin' to pull now?" Josiah, who had remained quietly behind Sarah's chair throughout the proceedings, spluttered, pushing himself forward with his skinny neck protruding from above his full-fashioned cravat. He placed himself between Julia and Sarah as though he were defending his favorite niece from attack.

"She's just being ridiculous as usual, Uncle Josiah," Sarah said airily. "Don't get steamed up about it. Our lawyers will see to it that she submits the material we require. Or they'll get it for us themselves."

"Mrs. Martin," Chester Dewing said blandly, "Mrs. Logan is correct. She does own the shipyard. These are only copies of the original documents, but if you'll look them over, I believe you'll find they're in order."

Sarah snatched the papers from his hands. She glanced through them hurriedly and handed them to her husband as she finished with each sheet. There weren't many, for Chester Dewing had brought only those which he thought might contain a property that would be a matter of common knowledge. When she reached the last one, Sarah exploded.

"The house, too! He had no right to do this. You're trying to rob us all of our inheritance. Amelia!" She turned to her younger sister, who was still sitting calmly on the couch beside Julia. "You're not going to let her get away with this, are you?"

Amelia shrugged. "It doesn't seem to me Julia's done anything. 'Twas all Papa's doing, and he had the right to dispose of his property any way he wished. As long as Julia's got it, we know Mama will be well taken care of, and that's what we should all be thinking about now."

"Oh, you're always so saintly, Amelia. Don't tell me you don't care whether your children are left without their rightful inheritance. You're just siding with Julia because you think you can get something out of her. Well, let me tell you, she's not going to get away with it. I fight for what's mine."

"So do I, but I never considered Julia's property mine. If the shipyard was sold, Mama might suffer. Besides, it's something Papa built up with his own two hands, and he wanted it kept together. You've just said that you'd have sold any share you might have gotten in it. Most likely you'd have charged Mama rent on the house, too, if you hadn't decided to blackmail Julia and me into buying you out." Amelia's fan was building up speed as she spoke. "You're no worse off than you were before Papa died, Sarah. In fact, you're better off. You've got shares in a ship and there's other things to be divided."

"Well, I want a full accounting of everything concerned, and I want it tomorrow." Sarah swung on the lawyer with renewed venom. "I'm not so certain that you aren't responsible for all this. My sister probably persuaded you to convince my father to do this before she went to sea. I'll have my lawyers look into the matter."

"I never met Mrs. Logan until recently," Chester Dewing said sternly, his eyes flashing behind their gold spectacles. He was not about to be cowed by Sarah. "I can assure you of that. In fact, that was one reason why your father chose me to represent him. He suspected you would attempt to circumvent his wishes in any way you could. As for an accounting of his estate, you may have the papers on it now. I had a copy drawn up for each of you."

Sarah took the papers from him, then pointed to the papers of Julia's ownership, which Aaron was still holding. "And those?"

"You may keep them. They're only copies."

"I will, and you'll hear from our lawyers. So will you, Julia. Until then, don't try to contact me."

"I had no intention of it, Sarah," Julia said calmly.

"Come, Aaron," Sarah said commandingly and held her hand out to her son, whose face was streaked with the dry paths of tears. "Thomas. I don't think we need call you Benjamin anymore."

After Sarah had swept out of the room, Amelia said softly to Julia, "Well, at least the afternoon did something good for that little boy. He doesn't have to carry two names around with him any longer. Might even improve his nature. He always did have too much to live up to."

Julia laughed. "I think you're right, Amelia. Stay for a few minutes after the others go. I want to talk to you about that addition to your house."

When the servants had cleared away and the lawyer had made his departure, Amelia said, "The shares Papa left me in the ship and the railway should be more than enough to cover the most expensive addition I could ever dream up."

"No, Amelia. Papa wanted you to have that addition without disposing of anything you have. I'll see that the money is transferred to you whenever you need it. All you have to do is let me know the amount."

"Julie, I can't take your money."

"That's just the point, Amelia. It isn't really my money. Papa left it to me so that I could administer it without any interference. It's your money, too."

"And Sarah's?"

"I don't know about Sarah. Papa felt she's rich enough as it is. After all, Aaron's an only child, and his parents are quite wealthy." When she saw a cloud pass over Amelia's cornflower-blue eyes, she patted her hand. "Don't worry, Amelia. Sarah will never go in want."

189

* * *

The trees were just beginning to flicker color on the September hills when Stephen came home. He had written to tell Julia he was coming, but he asked her not to meet him in Boston. She was to wait at home until he arrived. Julia felt that she should be standing on the wharf to welcome him home when the *Star of Gold* sailed into Boston harbor, but the pressures of the forthcoming launching seemed to weigh more heavily. She had to be content to watch the ship sail past the Cape for Boston. Wearing a red cloak over her black dress, she hoped that he would at least see the spot of color on the dunes and guess that it was she who stood there.

When news came that the packet would soon arrive, Julia was on the wharf long before the crowd had begun to gather. As the schooner swung into the creek, she scanned the figures on board. Although Stephen stood at the port rail, she overlooked him until the vessel was near enough to recognize the faces, and then, with a pang, she knew why. The electricity that so often radiated from him seemed to have ebbed away, and he looked tired and haggard. Instead of being the first to disembark, he stood aside and let the other passengers precede him. It was almost as though he feared the crush of the crowd. When he did come ashore, Julia was standing at the foot of the gangplank to greet him.

"Oh, Stephen, how I've missed you," she said as she threw her arms around him, but he held her slightly away as his lips barely grazed hers.

"No more than I've missed you, my lady," he said quietly as his grey eyes solemnly searched her face.

His black suit emphasized his pallor and deepened the lines of weariness that creased his forehead and bracketed his mouth.

"How are you feeling?" She tried to keep her voice steady so that she would not betray her rising concern that was approaching panic.

"I'd rather not discuss it now, Julia," he said formally as he glanced around at the crowd that was milling on the wharf.

"No. Of course not." But she did want to discuss it. She had to get him alone as quickly as she could. "I brought the buggy in case you wanted to ride home."

"Yes. That's best." He looked across at the wooden rail that ran along the far side of the road, and when he recognized the family horse and buggy, he took her arm and steered her towards it. "How's Clara? I'd hoped she would be here to meet me."

"She's fine, but you know how children are. She'd have been bored with the waiting." There was no point in telling him that when she had suggested that Clara accompany her, the child had raised such a fuss about being taken away from her play that Julia had given in. "We can pick her up at Amelia's house on the way home if you like."

"Yes. I'd like to see her," he said as he handed Julia up into the buggy. He paused for a moment after he had unhitched the horse from the rail and looked up at the autumn hills and then across the marsh that was turning golden. Home. There had been times when he had despaired of ever again seeing this mellow land that lay in close embrace with the sea. When he pulled himself up to sit beside Julia, he was careful not to awaken the pain. "I'd hoped to see you in Boston, Julie," he said quietly.

"But, Stephen!" Her eyes widened with amazement as she stared at him. "You expressly told me not to."

"I know, but still somehow I expected that . . ." When he saw the mixture of bewilderment and guilt in her eyes, he patted her hand. "Well, it doesn't matter, my lady. It was just that you so rarely do as you're told. You designed a beautiful ship, Julia."

"You like the *Star of Gold?*" she asked, eager for the approval of the man who was not only her husband, but one whose opinion she respected above all others.

"Who could help but fall in love with her?" He started the horse off at an ambling walk. As he thought of his ship, a glimmer of his old enthusiastic smile appeared. "You'll love her, too, when we take her to sea. She rides the waves as though they'd given her birth."

"I'm glad." She glanced nervously towards the edge of the marsh where the windmills that belonged to Aaron's father were turning briskly in the breeze as they pumped salt water into wooden vats.

This wasn't the time to tell Stephen that she wouldn't be sailing with him, that perhaps she would never go to sea again. It was a thought too painful to be borne. Somehow she *would* return to sea. If only Clara had been a boy, she would have been able to look forward to a future when she could have turned the business over to a son. Then she herself would have been free to return to that world that beckoned to her with every ebbing wave. But Clara hated the shipyard. And Stephen?

"You still haven't told me how you are. There's no one to overhear us now."

"I wrote that they had to reopen the wound," he said gravely and his eyes never left the road.

"I know, but your letters were so cheerful. You don't look very cheerful."

"It's just the strain of the trip," he said patiently. "I'll be all right after I've had a few weeks rest. I've chartered the *Star of Gold* to Richardson for one more voyage across the Atlantic. It should give you time to get your affairs in order."

"I don't know, Stephen," she said slowly. Even if she couldn't tell him

191

the truth, she couldn't entirely mislead him. "Sarah's trying to take me to court. I'll have to be here to defend myself."

"Can't the lawyers handle that?"

"No. I wish they could, but it'll be necessary for me to appear in person."

"Dear, sweet sister Sarah," Stephen said grimly and his mouth settled into harsher lines. "Perhaps I'll have to straighten out sister Sarah while I'm home."

"If you could straighten out Sarah, you could walk on water, too."

"I suppose I knew that you weren't going to come with me."

"Stephen, it's not for lack of wanting to be with you."

"I know it isn't." He really smiled at her for the first time since he had stepped ashore. "It's all right, Julie. I understand. There'll be other voyages."

The equanimity with which he accepted this worried Julia more than his pale face or the way he slumped back against the seat. "Do you think you're going to be up to sailing that soon, Stephen?"

"I think so. If not, I can always charter the ship to someone. There's no lack of interest in the *Star of Gold*."

"I'm glad you're not going to rush things." As they rounded a stand of pine trees, she said, "There's Amelia's house. You can see the addition she's having built."

"Yes." He looked down the road at the framing that was just rising new and raw along one side of the Adams house. "It's about time we built something for ourselves. It would be pleasant to have our own home."

"But the house is mine now. I wrote you."

"I know, but it's also heavily populated. Julia, I've never had a home that was completely mine. At least, not one I can remember." As they drew to a stop in front of the grey-shingled cottage, he said, "Would you mind going in and getting Clara? I don't feel up to facing that mob of children."

"I'd be glad to," Julia said lightly, but as she went up the rose-lined path to the front door, she allowed herself to worry. Despite Stephen's denials, she couldn't believe that he wasn't seriously ill. Everything else he said and did pointed in that direction.

At first, Julia had trouble convincing Clara that she should come with her. She certainly didn't want the child to greet her father with tears on her face. When she and Amelia finally coaxed Clara into leaving her friends just long enough to welcome her father home, she came reluctantly, but she came. When she was lifted up into the buggy and saw that it was Stephen, she went into ecstasies.

"Papa! Papa!" she cried, clambering up on the seat beside him. When he put his arms around her, she assaulted him so enthusiastically she knocked off his hat.

Amelia smiled and shook her head when Julia tried to pull her forward to speak to Stephen, and then she returned to the house. Stephen never realized that his sister-in-law had been there. All of his attention was concentrated on the bundle of squirming energy Clara had suddenly become.

After Julia had stepped up into the buggy to sit beside them, Stephen smiled at her over their daughter's fair head. Julia was surprised and somewhat shocked to see there were tears in his eyes. It was so unlike Stephen, it gave her something else to brood about.

It was only a short distance to the house, and as the buggy crunched up the oyster-shell driveway to the door of the carriage house, Stephen said, "I'd like to go directly upstairs."

"But Stephen, everyone's waiting for you. They'll be disappointed . . ."

"Julia," he interrupted her. "I'm very tired, and I want to lie down."

"Of course. I'm sorry. Let me go in first and warn them away."

"Take Clara with you and hand her over to someone. Then follow me up."

"All right, Stephen," Julia said quietly and let young Ezra, who had replaced his father as the general man of all work around the house and grounds, hand her down from the buggy. Then she reached her arms up. "Come along, Clara."

"No," Clara said and her grey eyes narrowed in defiance. "I'll stay with Papa."

"Go with your mother, Clara," Stephen said sharply and pulled her roughly off the seat. "Children must obey their parents."

"Yes, Papa." Clara looked at him with an expression akin to awe. Then she held her arms out to her mother to be lifted down.

After Stephen had slipped quietly into the house and up the stairs, Julia followed him to their room. She found that he had already removed his coat and waistcoat and was lying on the bed. He was staring at the ceiling and continued to do so when she entered. She hesitated and then sat down beside him.

"Clara was so happy to see you," she offered tentatively.

"Yes, she was," he said and finally looked at her.

"Is there anything I can get you?"

"Yes. Some rum. It eases the pain."

"Oh, Stephen! Are you still in pain?"

"A little. Please get it for me, Julia."

"I will. Right away."

When Julia returned with the decanter and a glass, he had propped himself up on the many pillows that she allowed herself as a luxury whenever she was home without him.

He glanced at the silver tray she carried and said, "Good. Pour it half full of rum and top it off with water."

"Don't you want anything to eat?" she asked as she followed his instructions.

"No. Not now. All I want is that and to have you lying here beside me. It's been a long time, my Julia."

"Too long," she agreed as she leaned over to brush the hair away from his pale forehead. "You look so tired. Oh, Stephen, I wish there were something I could do to help you."

He grasped her wrist and pulled her down beside him. "You are helping . . . just by being here. It was hot in London. Hot and dirty. When I was recovering from the operation, I would lie in bed and try to picture you. I would see you flying around the shipyard with sawdust on your skirt and a smear of tar on your cheek, straightening out one problem after another. Or I would see you perched on your stool in the office, your brow puckered and your chin in your hand, going over plans for some new vessel. I would think about the way you walk barefoot along the beach with your skirts gathered up, just daring the waves to touch you."

"Did you see me worrying about you? Pacing the floor at night, feeling helpless, wondering if I would ever see you again?"

He put his glass on the bedside table and eased himself around on the pillows so that he could see her more clearly. "You knew I'd come back to you this time, didn't you?"

"I knew you would if you could." Her eyes clouded as she thought of her past fears. "Stephen, I was so afraid and there was nothing I could do about it. An entire ocean separated us."

His smile was a little crooked as he kissed her lightly on the tip of her nose. "Well, I'm here now and you're going to have a hard time getting rid of me."

"Get rid of you!" She laughed and planted a kiss on his lips with mock ferocity. "I'm not even going to let you out of my sight! Not for a long time."

In the days that followed, Stephen placed an added burden on the household. After a supper with the family on his first day at home, he declined to eat with them again. Lydia's refusal to accept Benjamin's death and her constant referrals to him in conversation irritated Stephen beyond measure. Now, all of his meals were served in their bedroom. Since he wanted Julia beside him, she dined with him there.

He slept late, retired early, and rested much of the day. When the weather was good, he would ride over to the shipyard and sit outside in the sun or in the office beside the stove, depending upon where Julia was working. Although he always had an open book in his hands, his eyes more often rested upon her than upon the pages. His continued lethargy alarmed Julia, but he refused to let Doctor Willett see him nor would he discuss the state of his health with her. On rainy days, which he spent at home, he would often call Clara to him and tell her stories to while away the long hours. The decanter of rum was always near at hand.

It was late October when he first showed any sign of returning energy. Anxious about Stephen's future, Julia found it difficult to concentrate on her work and returned home early that stormy day to find the house in an uproar.

The minute she opened the door, she could hear her mother's hysterical screams mixed with laughter echoing down the stairs to where Stephen and Sarah stood confronting each other in the hall. Stephen had one hand clamped tightly on Sarah's wrist and seemed to be trying to pull her towards the front door while, with the other hand, he held some crumpled papers. For her part, Sarah had just delivered a resounding slap to Stephen's cheek.

"You bitch!" Stephen shouted at her. "Get out of this house and stop tormenting your mother."

"It's you who're tormenting her, you with your interfering ways," Sarah spat at him. "Give me those papers and let me go. *I'll* calm her down."

"Calm her down! You'll more likely kill her. She was fine until you came in to devil her with your maleficent papers. Now get out of here!"

"What's going on?" Julia asked as she hurried up to them. "Do you need any help, Stephen?"

"No. I can take care of this creature. Go see to your mother."

"But what happened?"

"Can't you hear what's happened?" He jerked his head towards the top of the stairs. "Get up there and make her stop that noise."

Julia took one final glance at her husband and her sister, then picked up her skirts and ran up the stairs. In her mother's room, she found Martha Chambers holding her mother in her strong arms as she attempted to restrain her.

"Mama!" Julia put one arm around her mother's back. "Calm down, Mama, and tell me what's happened."

Despite Martha's strength, Lydia whirled out of her arms and faced Julia. Her heavy white hair had tumbled all around her face and down her back. Her face was puffy and her eyes red with weeping.

"You took him from me!" she screamed at Julia. "You and your sea! You murderess. Murdered your own father. You always wanted to take him away from me."

195

"Now, Miss Lydia." Martha grabbed her by the shoulders and forced her to sit down on the bed. "You know that's not true."

Lydia didn't fight Martha off but continued to stare at Julia with malevolence. "Now you've done it. You've got him. Ever since you were a little girl, it was always, 'Papa, take me to sea.' You can't deny it."

"Mama." Julia dropped to her knees beside her mother and tried to catch her hand. "Oh, my dear Mama. Don't you think I grieve for him, too?"

"Grieve for him? You took him! Get away from me." She struck out at Julia with her hand.

Martha Chambers shook her charge. "Now, stop that. Julia wasn't even here. She was at sea."

"She took him. If she was at sea, then she had something to do with it. You don't know about her yet, do you, Martha? She's a witch. A sea witch."

"You know better than that, Miss Lydia. She's your own child."

"No. Not mine. She's the sea's child. The sea took my child from my womb and put that one in. A sea witch, that's what she is. Ask Josiah. Ask Sarah. They know. They'll tell you."

"Now, you just calm down, dear," Martha said, and looking at Julia, gestured at the door with a nod of her head. "Julia's going. Don't upset yourself."

Julia slowly went to the door and turned once to look back. Her mother was sobbing with her head resting on Martha's ample shoulder.

"Keep her out of my sight, Martha. Keep her away from me."

Julia shut the door upon the scene and weakly leaned back against it. This was the first time she had seen her mother during one of her bad spells, as Martha called them. Although both she and Amelia as well as Megan had tried to warn Julia about them, she hadn't realized how awful they were. That her mother should accuse her in such a demented fashion! Especially when she was sure that she herself had loved her father more than any of them. Thank God the children weren't in the house.

Chapter Thirteen

1851–1854

Low-flying black clouds swept the sky and the long hall had grown into dusk when Julia finally pushed herself away from her mother's door. She went to the banister and peered into the hall below, but there was no one to be seen. All seemed quiet. Evidently Stephen had gotten rid of Sarah or had moved her to some other part of the house.

As she started down the stairs, the impact of her mother's words and demented anger struck Julia, and her legs suddenly refused to support her. Clutching the banister, she sank down upon one of the carpeted steps. The storm struck with new fury. Hail mixed with rain battered the windows accompanying the harsh sobs that came from behind the closed door. When thunder crashed so near it drowned out all other noises and lightning flared its ghostly whiteness through the windows, Julia buried her head in her lap.

It was too much. Too much.

She stayed there for a few moments, but then she heard the many voices of duty clamoring. Unable to still them, she rose and continued down the steps.

First she went to the kitchen, where she found the servants clustered together near the black cast-iron stove while they watched the unseasonable rage of the elements. Julia hated to send them out into the storm, but it was necessary. She gave instructions to Ezra to fetch Doctor Willett. As soon as there was any letup, Janet was to go directly to Amelia's and warn Megan not to bring the children home. They nodded rather mournfully at the prospect, but they were loyal and would do as she requested.

Then she went in search of Stephen and found him alone in the darkened parlor, where only firelight flickered in a small circle surrounding the hearth. He was sitting in the shadows with his head against the back of the chair and his hands lying listlessly on the arms. He opened his eyes when Julia came to stand in front of him and spoke his name.

"She is a bitch," he said in a tightly controlled voice. "Your sister is a real bitch."

"That's been obvious for some time," she said and sat down in a chair on the opposite side of the fire. "What is it now?"

"Some papers her lawyers drew up for her." Stephen passed a hand over his face and straightened up. "She was trying to push your mother into signing them. Part of Sarah's assault on your property. When I came in, she was trying to convince your mother that your father was dead. She told her that she couldn't hide from the fact forever. Said it was immoral."

"Well, Mama seems convinced now."

"Oh, yes. Dear Sarah hammered away at your mother until she snapped. She kept waving those papers in front of her face even then, until I grabbed them away from her."

"Where are the papers?"

"In there." He nodded at the fire.

"That's a shame," Julia said thoughtfully as she looked at the charred blackness that still retained the shape of crumpled paper. "Mr. Dewing might have been able to make some use of them."

"I'll tell you what they said." Energy spurred by anger gave renewed vigor to his voice. "I just didn't want that filth lying around."

"Was it that bad?"

"Yes. Sarah's either getting very stupid or she's getting very bad advice from her lawyers. I doubt they had anything to do with it, though. It was in her handwriting."

"And to think of upsetting Mama with such greed! 'Tis no wonder she's taking on like that."

"She seems quieter now." Stephen looked up at the ceiling near the door.

"I hope Doctor Willett can get her calmed down when he gets here."

As the storm rumbled off to sea, the room grew quieter and the pelting of raindrops drumming against the windows brought a kind of peace. No sounds could be heard from the rest of the house. They sat together in an exhausted silence for a few minutes. When the ormolu clock on the mantel struck four, Stephen roused himself once more.

"Julia, we have to move. I don't want my daughter in this house, and I don't think I can put up with much more of it myself."

"I can't leave Mama, Stephen," Julia said in a voice not much louder than a whisper.

Stephen gave an abrupt laugh. "From what she had to say just now, she'd just as soon see you out of here."

"You heard?"

"She was loud enough. It would have been impossible not to."

"Well, that was just brought on by Sarah. Mama will be all right tomorrow."

"All right? You call her behavior, even when she's calm, all right?" He shook his head. "No. We'll find something. Even the smallest cottage would be preferable to this."

"If I leave, Sarah will be over here every day with some new trick. I daren't leave. What if you hadn't been here today?"

"It wouldn't really have made any difference. Martha wasn't far, and when your mother went into hysterics, it was possible to hear her all over the house anyway. I doubt Martha would have let her sign the papers. Even if she had, we could prove your mother was insane when she signed them."

"No!" Julia sat up straight and clutched the padded arms of her chair. "I'm not going to let anyone go to court and prove that my mother's insane. Never."

"Well, I'm going to start looking for a house tomorrow, and when I find one, I'm going to move into it, and so is Clara. You may come or not as you please."

"Stephen, don't do this to me."

"It's you who're doing it, Julia. All I want is quiet and sanity around me. I'm very tired. Can't you understand that?"

198

Suddenly the front door shut with a bang. Julia and Stephen barely had time to glance questioningly at each other before Aaron Martin burst into the room. Water streamed onto the carpet from his caped coat and the hat he held in his hand.

"All right, Logan," Aaron said. "I've found you."

"I hadn't been aware that I was missing, Aaron," Stephen said quietly. Then he looked at Julia. "You see what I mean about this house?"

"You've insulted my wife." Aaron marched over to the fire. Standing with his back to Julia, he confronted Stephen. "She came home in tears and showed me her wrist. She could barely bring herself to repeat the names you called her and the language you used."

"Oh, Aaron, go away," Stephen said. He leaned his head against the back of the chair and closed his eyes.

"You can have your choice of weapons."

Stephen opened his eyes and laughed in delighted astonishment. "You don't even know how to challenge someone to a duel properly, much less handle any weapon I know of except your fork. And with a fork and a few heaping platters of food, it wouldn't be a fair challenge. You could absolutely destroy my reputation as a trencherman." He looked pointedly at Aaron's paunch.

"I will not have this treated as a joke, Steve." Aaron clenched his fists and his face grew redder. "Either you apologize publicly to Sarah or you'll answer to me."

"Aaron, stop it," Julia said. "There's never been a duel fought on the Cape and there never will be. Only idiots go around spilling blood needlessly."

"I was speaking to your husband, Julia." Aaron never turned to look at her but continued to stare down at Stephen. "This is not a matter for ladies."

"You'd better watch how you speak to Julia," Stephen said, still smiling. "She's a better shot than I am. A couple of men could testify to that if they weren't dead."

"If you won't fight, I'll spread the word that you're a coward."

"For some strange reason, that threat fails to terrify me, Aaron. Go ahead and spread the word. I won't even bother to deny it. We'll see what people believe."

"Stephen doesn't *have* to prove that he's not a coward, Aaron," Julia said in a strong clear voice aimed at Aaron's back. "Not like some people I know. Some men can't even stand up to their own wives. Have you seen the papers Sarah brought over here?"

"No." Aaron swung around and glared at her. "And I'll thank you to return them. We went to great expense to have them drawn up."

"Certainly, Aaron. They're right there." She pointed to the fire, where the charred papers rested on top of the coals.

Aaron looked over his shoulder and then turned back on her with a new

199

vengeance. "Destruction of property. That's another charge against you, Julia."

"What about defamation of character?" Stephen asked. "You really should read the things your wife and your lawyers dream up before you let her run around loose with them."

"Defamation of character?" Confusion and doubt appeared in his soft brown eyes and he slowly unclenched his fists.

"You might try locking Sarah up for a few days. In fact, I'd highly recommend it." Stephen's smile was mocking and his eyes smoked with enjoyment. "It seems that her delusions are worse than her mother's, and she's far more dangerous. Look at what she's trying to do to you. She sent you over here to get yourself killed. You're just fortunate I didn't take you up on that challenge. And now, why don't you go away . . . quietly? We've had enough excitement around here for one day."

"I'll have a talk with Sarah." Aaron's voice was subdued with just a hint of shame. "Not that she isn't right. You did steal her property, but she can't resort to slander."

"No she can't," Julia said dryly. "Good-bye, Aaron. Give our love to Sarah."

The sedation Doctor Willett prescribed eventually calmed Lydia. When she awakened from a drugged sleep the next afternoon, she had returned to the land of placid delusions. However, Stephen could not forget the episode. When the weather cleared two days later, he began the search for a home for his family. It occupied the long hours of his convalescence and gave him something to plan for, but there was nothing available in the village. Even the meanest dwellings were occupied.

Then on a sun-filled day in November, when the coming winter paused in its assault, Stephen arrived at the shipyard at midday to find Julia warming herself near a forge in the blacksmith's shop. The coals were smoldering with a tinge of red, but the giant bellows above the two forges were still. The apprentices and the journeymen had gone to their dinners. Only Julia and Blackie remained in the soot-raftered room.

For several days, the master blacksmith had wanted to talk to her. This was the first time she had been able to break away from the pressure of her many duties for what she knew would be a long conversation. When Stephen arrived, she was deep in discussion with the towheaded man, whose fair skin was smudged with soot. He was a tall man, his wiry muscles formed by years spent bending and shaping iron into many of the tools as well as the intricately wrought fittings that held the vessels together.

Julia looked up when Stephen entered the shop, but she only gave him a fleeting smile before she turned back to the blacksmith. Blackie rarely

200

spoke, but when he did, it was difficult to stem his deluge of words. Now he was complaining about the high carbon content of the iron they had received from two of their suppliers. Julia respected his judgment in matters relating to his profession, but when he lengthened his list of complaints to include some of the other workers, she was not so certain as to the veracity of his account. While she had never thought of him as a trouble-maker, trouble seemed to center itself around him. However, she listened patiently, for the master blacksmith was one of the most valuable men in the yard, and she couldn't afford to lose him.

Yet even as she listened, an awareness of Stephen's impatience grew and clouded her concentration. Finally, with a promise to Blackie that she would take up the matter of carbon content with the suppliers, she left the shop with her husband.

"Well, Stephen?" she asked curiously once they were outside. There was more color in his face than there had been for months, and suppressed excitement deepened the blue in his grey eyes. "What is it?"

"Land," he said as he took her elbow and steered her rapidly towards the horse and buggy, which were hitched at the rail near the office. "I've found some land, and I've decided to build a new house. A place where no one has ever lived before. One that will be completely ours with no memories and no ghosts."

"Where is it?" There was a catch of laughter in her voice when she spoke. Although each day she had dreaded coming home to discover that he had found a house, she had tried to hide it from him. She knew that, if they moved, her days would become even more complicated. Now seeing Stephen take an interest in life once more made her completely forget her reservations. Watching enthusiasm infuse his face and lengthen his stride, she was joyfully ready to fall in with any plans he might have.

"Next to the Whaling Grounds and on top of a bluff! The air will be clean and fresh up there, and there are no near neighbors." He handed her into the buggy and sprang in behind her.

No road had ever been built to the parcel of land which interested Stephen. Instead they drove to Nobscussett Point and hitched the horse to a weathered pine tree. Then they climbed over the dunes to the beach where Julia had so often played when she was a child. On this long stretch of sand, she and Jason had laid plans for their elopement. A few years later, it had been Stephen who had courted her here. As they neared the edge of the high-tide mark, Julia glanced eastward in the opposite direction from the point. Although wind and waves gradually changed their contours, each dune held memories.

"Do you remember the first time you tried to tell me a sea story?" she asked as she saw between two dunes a young man dressed in his best tailcoat.

Stephen followed her glance, then looked at her and smiled fondly. "On Sarah's wedding day? I remember."

"It was about a princess in a narrow, water-bound kingdom who was under a spell."

"You were sad that day. When you ran away from the wedding feast, I was afraid you regretted the fact that it was Sarah and not you who had become Aaron's wife. It shows how little I knew you then."

"I just wanted to be alone. But you followed me. I remember earlier how you stared at me all through the marriage service."

"Did you know what I was thinking?"

"I suspect it wasn't anything proper." She gave him a roguish smile.

"On the contrary. It was most proper. I was considering how I was going to get you up at that altar beside me. I was convinced that someday I'd have you there, but I didn't know how long it would take. Then you wouldn't even let me finish my sea story."

"Oh, you finished it." Julia laughed. "Maybe not that day, but the handsome captain finally did break the spell and land me at the altar."

"You're not sorry, are you, my lady?" His eyes softened and he looked at her with yearning.

"Oh, no, Stephen. Never." She smiled gaily as she linked her arm through his. "Now let's go see this land of yours."

They followed the westward path. It ran along the top of a low dune that was bounded on one side with giant rocks and on the other by two salt ponds. The ebbing tide exposed solitary boulders that were just awash on the flats, and the air was rich with the scent of newly exposed sand. A black-backed gull cruised above the water's edge, where sanderlings skittered busily in rhythm with the lapping waves. A few plovers piping their sweet high notes flew overhead. As they clambered down a fold of the dunes to the far beach, Julia listened to Stephen's excited account of the land, but she was constantly aware of the joyful voice of the sea.

Walking through the soft sand of the upper beach, they followed the base of the tall bluffs until they reached a point where three boulders rose above the pastel pebbles that surrounded them. Here Stephen stopped and looked up.

"It's quite a climb and there's no path," he warned.

"That's all right," Julia said. "I remember exploring here when I was young. David Baxter brought me. As I recollect, I went home with my clothes covered with cockleburs and came down with poison ivy the next day. I thought I'd never hear the end of it from Mama."

Stephen's face clouded at the mention of David's name. So even here, Baxter had been before him. But when he saw Julia's rueful expression as she scratched her hand in memory of that poison ivy, he had to smile.

"Well, I can assure you that there's still plenty of poison ivy and enough cockleburs to exceed your fondest memories. I'll lead the way."

Beach heather and poverty grass growing thickly here helped anchor the sand and clay of the land. By holding onto bushes that were rooted deep into the bluff, they managed to pull themselves up, but at almost every step wild roses and bramble bushes tore at their clothing. In his eagerness, Stephen tore free of their embrace without a thought, but Julia was forced to stop frequently to clear the briers that caught at her full skirts and held her fast. It hadn't seemed such an arduous task when she had been a child.

At the top, Stephen held out his hand and pulled her up the last few steps. The view that appeared when she was finally able to stand upright was breathtaking. The curve of the Cape was clearly visible to their right and in the distance they could see the break in the horizon that was Provincetown. Directly in front of them, the Bay became part of the Atlantic. There were sails on the dark blue-green waters, and Julia wished that they had brought a telescope.

Turning her back on the sea, Julia looked inland. Beyond the dying vines, there was a filigree of silver-grey and black branched trees. Here and there golden leaves clung to their autumn colors and the greying green of a fir was visible. In their forefront, bayberry bushes competed with snake berries, blueberries, and beach plums.

There was a quiet here, too, a loneliness broken only by the rush of the south wind in the treetops and the call of crows. The solitude reminded her of the quarterdeck of a ship at sea. She understood why Stephen had chosen this spot. Turning to share the beauty of it with him, she found that he was looking at her with hopeful anticipation.

"Do you like it?" he asked and his voice was husky with tension.

"Oh, yes, yes. I do like it, Stephen." And her smile was brighter than the autumn sunshine, her eyes deeper than the blue of the robin's-egg sky.

"We'll build a tall house with two stories and an attic. On top of it, like a crown, we'll put a railed walk, and in fine weather we can sit up there and watch the vessels come and go." His eyes were lit by the dream, and he looked at the woods as though they had already been cleared with the house standing solid and rooted in the earth. He reminded Julia of the young man she had first seen standing in the shipyard, staring up at the unfinished *Crystal Star* as she sat on the ways.

"You'd be content here, Stephen? Content to live on the land?" she asked curiously. It was the first time in all their years together she had seen any indication that he would consider any life but that of the sea.

"Content? Yes. Between voyages." He put his arm around her waist and pulled her close to his side. "When we sail by the Cape, we'll be able to see our own house sitting proudly on this bluff, waiting for us to return. And when the news is telegraphed that we've been sighted, someone can bring Clara up here. It would be good to know that she's watching and waiting for us."

"Yes. It would be good to know," she said and hoped that she sounded as enthusiastic as he did. He was dreaming a lovely dream, and she would do nothing to shatter it. She only wished that she could dream it with him, that reality did not impinge so harshly upon her sight.

"Once we've taken down a few trees, we'll have a good breeze all summer," he continued.

"It's really a beautiful location, Stephen," Julia said, even as she thought of the cruelty with which winter gales would sweep it. She would somehow have to insure that they built well enough so that they would be snug in winter, and it *would* be pleasant in summer. At any rate, she didn't intend to live here unless Stephen was home. "We shouldn't get as many mosquitoes up here, either."

"No." He swung her around until she faced him and traced the line of her lips with one finger. "And on warm summer nights, we can take a couple of quilts up to the roof. We'll watch the moon and stars wheel across the heavens while we lie together. It'll be like the deck of a ship."

"You never would let me sleep on deck," she reminded him as she slid her hands up his chest and around his neck.

"No, but you'll sleep on this deck," he promised. "I'll see that you sleep very soundly. Perhaps one summer night, we'll conceive a son."

"A son? I didn't know you wanted a son. I thought you were content with Clara."

"Your son, my lady. The one you've been waiting for all these years. The one you're determined to save the shipyard for. The one you've been saving your love for."

"Saving my love?" She looked at him perplexed. "I'm not saving my love. Do you think I could love anyone more than I love you? I do, Stephen. I do so very much. I carry you around like an ache inside me."

"And a joy?"

"Yes. And a joy."

He ran his tongue across his lips and then grazed them across hers. Looking into her eyes, he saw the rich desire he could still arouse. She was his. There was no mistaking that, he thought with some satisfaction.

"I know you love me, Julie, but I was talking about the love you're hoarding for your son, the love you don't give Clara."

"Clara?" Her fingers dug into the shoulders of his thick peacoat. "But I do love Clara!"

"She doesn't know it. She asked me the other day why I loved her more than you did. You don't spend enough time with her, Julie."

Tears sprang into her eyes and anger sprang with them. She tore away from his arms and turned her back on him. How dare he accuse her of such a thing when it was he who insisted that she follow him to sea, even at the expense of their daughter! It was he who had estranged her from her own child. But she couldn't confront him with it. Not on this day of his dream.

204

Rubbing her eyes with the back of her hand, she smeared the salty water into a cold dampness across her cheeks and turned again to look at him.

"Stephen," she said with too patient an edge to her voice. "I would spend more time with her if I could. You should know that. But you should also realize how impossible it is for me to do it. I've only been home a few months, and I'm still trying to get the yard under control, to say nothing about Papa's affairs."

"I know, Julie," he said gently when he saw how upset she was. He hadn't wanted to spoil this day, either. He reached out for her hand. "I'm sorry I mentioned it. I spoke without thinking. I suppose it was just that it's been on my mind ever since she asked the question. Forgive me."

"There's nothing to forgive." She managed a weak smile. "I've tried to come closer to Clara. Maybe I haven't tried hard enough. Or maybe it's · just that little girls are more drawn to their fathers than they are to their mothers."

"Some are." He smiled back at her and then looked at the view all the way from Provincetown to the hills on their left. The panorama was already embedded in his heart. "The days are growing short and the sun sets early. We'd better start now or we'll still be fighting our way through the underbrush in the dark."

"Yes. It's getting colder, too." She shivered inside her rough black wool cloak and pulled the hood up over her tousled black curls.

"Aye," he said as he pulled a sapling away from their path and held it until she had passed. "But when we get home, I've devised a plan I think you'll like. Then we'll both be warm."

It took very little time for Stephen to purchase the property, but it wasn't as simple to find workmen willing to spend the short winter days on top of a windswept bluff. One day in early December, he went to talk to the contractor who had almost completed the wing of Amelia's house. He hadn't been there long when the mail arrived. While Stephen was still trying to convince the man to build for him, he heard an unearthly scream from inside the house.

His seaman's instincts galvanized him into immediate action and he sprinted for the front door. Just as he arrived, it burst open and Becky tore out into the winter cold.

"Come quick, sir," the round-faced nursemaid panted. Her pale blue eyes were wide with fright and the freckles seemed to jump from her pale skin. "Miss Amelia's fainted and it's near on her time."

"Send someone for Doctor Willett," Stephen crisply ordered as he brushed past her into the small parlor. "And send someone else to the shipyard for Mrs. Logan and Mrs. Fairfield."

Amelia lay crumpled near the fireplace with a scattering of letters around her while her three children stood in various stages of shock. Six-year-old Hattie was wailing with her eyes screwed tightly shut. Lucy, who was ten, felt she should do something and knelt by her mother, but her hands fluttered helplessly in the air. Levi, a year younger, was standing apart with his hands jammed deep in his pockets and his light blue eyes filled with fear.

"Lucy," Stephen said as he gently pulled the child to her feet. "Take the children out into the kitchen to Minna."

"Mama, she's . . ." The girl was white and trembling.

"She's just fainted," he said firmly as he pushed the girl towards her brother and sister. "She'll be all right in a minute. Now go."

When he saw that Lucy had Hattie by the hand and that Levi was prepared to follow his sisters, Stephen dropped down on one knee beside his sister-in-law. As he took her hand to feel her pulse, she opened her china blue eyes and gazed groggily at him.

"Michael . . ." she murmured.

"No. It's Stephen."

"Michael's dead!" The words tore themselves from her in a shriek, and as she struggled to sit up, what little color there was left in her face drained away from it.

"No, Amelia," he reassured her as he put an arm around her back to support her. "Michael's not dead."

"He is." Her lips were trembling so, it was difficult for her to speak. She pointed to the open letter that lay near her feet. "Yellow fever."

"Oh, no, Amelia, no." He felt her anguish as he pulled her against his chest and held her tightly to him, but Amelia didn't cry.

"The children," she whispered.

"They're in the kitchen with Minna," he assured her.

"They're orphans! Oh, my poor children." And then she did break down, but only for a moment before she was shaken by a spasm and her breath was forced from her in a stifled scream. "The baby!"

"Doctor Willett's on his way," Stephen told her. "So are Julia and Megan. Can you hold out for a little while?"

"Just hold me, Stephen. Please hold me."

"I will."

When Julia burst into the house followed by Megan, she found Stephen still kneeling on the floor beside her sister with his arms around her in a tight embrace.

"Oh, Stephen, thank God you were here," Julia said as she knelt on Amelia's other side. "Amelia, can you get up? We'll help you into the borning room."

"No!" Amelia gasped. "The children are in the kitchen."

"I'll take care of them," Megan said. Then she looked doubtfully at Julia. "Should I send them over to the house?"

"You'll have to, but don't let Mama know why they're there," Julia cautioned.

"Don't tell them!" Amelia looked up at Stephen, her plea shining through the tears in her eyes.

"Don't tell them what?" Julia looked at her husband in puzzlement. "About the baby?"

Stephen shook his head in warning. "We'd better get Amelia comfortable before the doctor arrives. Help me get her up, Julia."

Together they managed to half lead, half carry her into the small room beside the kitchen that had been used for generations of Adamses for just such a purpose. Once they had laid her on the bed, Stephen went into the kitchen to give orders to the young maid, who stood helplessly staring at them, while Julia loosened her sister's clothes.

It wasn't long, but it seemed hours, before Megan returned. Almost immediately she was followed by the midwife, Annie Fuller.

When Stephen saw the midwife, he said harshly, "I told Becky we wanted the doctor. Where is he?"

"He sent me," the tall, gaunt, dour-faced midwife said. "He's not needed here. I delivered three of Mrs. Adams' children and I'm capable of fetchin' the fourth one into the world."

"I said I want the doctor," Stephen said grimly. "And I'm going to find him. Where is he?"

When the woman didn't answer, he took a step closer to her. "I asked you a question. Is he at home?"

The midwife nodded sourly and then said, "Well, looks as if I'm not wanted." She began to retie her bonnet strings.

"You're wanted, Mrs. Fuller," Stephen said impatiently. "I'll pay you twice your normal fee, but I want the doctor, too."

Julia caught up with him as he strode through the parlor towards the door. "Stephen, what is it? Amelia's good and healthy. She's never had any trouble bearing."

"Julia." He turned to face her as he swung his greatcoat around his shoulders. "Michael's dead. There's no telling what kind of reaction Amelia's going to have."

"But he *can't* be. Not now."

"But he is. That's what brought Amelia on." He pointed at the letters that were still strewn on the floor. "Read that, but for God's sake, let me go."

When Stephen returned with the doctor, Amelia's son had already been born. The midwife looked up at them in triumph when they entered.

"See," she said. "The truth's what I told. This one never has no trouble. A fine boy we've brought into the world."

"Yes, yes, Mrs. Fuller." The doctor smiled at her soothingly through his spectacles. "I've always said you deliver only the bonniest babies. 'Tis Mrs. Adams I should see to."

"Nothin' wrong with her," the woman sniffed. "A strong, strappin' young woman like that."

Doctor Willett smiled and nodded, but as soon as he had divested himself of his coat and washed his hands, he went directly to Amelia. After he had examined her, he turned to Julia. "She'll be all right, but I'll stay with her awhile. Amelia's always been one of my favorite nurses. Can't let anything happen to her."

Seeing that her sister was in the capable hands of the doctor and Mrs. Fuller and that Megan already had the baby wrapped up and was crooning to it, Julia went into the parlor and closed the door behind her. Stephen had lit the lamps and was sitting close to the fire with Amelia's letters on the small table beside him. When Julia entered, he looked up, a terrible sorrow etched on his face.

"Another good man gone, leaving a young family behind," he said. "Damn the sea. Damn the pestilential holes we're forced to put into. Just for a cargo of ivory and coffee he loaded at Prince's Island, Michael's dead. Damn!"

Julia drew a deep breath and then picked up the sheet of paper that was lying on top of the letters. "Is this the letter?"

"Yes. It's all there. The mate's written the details. Too many details. The bark's lying in quarantine off the Battery at New York. God knows how he got the letter off, but the fever's still raging aboard. Michael didn't seem to be ill when they sailed from the Gulf of Guinea, but he was dead by the time they were halfway home. The poor devils on that ship. They can see the land, but how many of them will ever live to walk it again? Perhaps Michael was fortunate."

"How can you say that!" Julia looked up from the letter with a frown. It was impossible to believe that blond, black-browed Michael with his big bones and his easy smile was gone, that he would never come whistling up the walk in search of Amelia again.

"No. I can't say that. It's better to be alive with hope than it is to be at he bottom of the Atlantic." He rubbed his forehead and then stared into the fire. The tongues of flame that flickered over the coals gave him no comfort. His eyes were weary when he looked up at her. "I'm going back to sea, Julia. The *Star of Gold* is due in Boston in two or three weeks. I'll take her on her next voyage."

"But, Stephen, you're not strong enough yet!" She clasped the letter tight against her breast and stared at him in astonishment. "And what about the house?"

"I can't find anyone to *build* the damned house!" He struck the arm of the chair with his fist. Then he lowered his voice as he continued. "I have to get back to sea before I lose my nerve. If I leave soon, I'll be able to round the Horn during the winter when it's summer there. It'll be easier than waiting."

"You'd never lose your nerve." She sank down on the floor next to his chair, and leaning her head against the arm, she reached up for his hand. "Wait till spring and take a few shorter voyages to begin with."

"Like one to Prince's Island?" He stroked her black curls back from her forehead with his free hand and his smile was filled with a tender sadness. "No. The Western Ocean's not for me. I'm for the East Indies. I know every rock and current from here to China and back again."

"Stephen, please don't." She brushed her lips across the hand she held and then looked up at him. "You know I can't go with you, and I'll not rest easy knowing you're at sea in your condition."

"I'll gain strength as I go along. The sea's a healthier place than the land. You've always said so yourself."

"Not for a master rounding the Horn, it isn't," she said adamantly. "You know you never sleep till you fetch up in the Pacific."

"I don't sleep all that well in that house, either." He saw the consternation in her eyes turn to fear, and he made an effort to smile in his old light-hearted way. "I have to go, my lady. You know the old saying. Only the best and prettiest girls are good enough to marry an East India captain. That's what you married, and it wouldn't do to let your reputation slide. I have to go back to work. Besides," he added more soberly, "there's Amelia and her children to be taken care of now that she's a widow. We'll need all the money we can make to support her brood as well as all the others."

"There's the shipyard, Stephen, as well as Papa's other investments," she said earnestly as she gazed up into his shadowed face. "They'll take care of Amelia. Mama and everyone else, too."

"Everyone but you and me and Clara. I won't have your father's money paying for my family's support. Or your money, either, for that matter," he continued more quickly when she opened her mouth to protest. "I still want to build that house someday, and I haven't made enough to retire on yet. When I do, I'll leave the sea and dabble in something else, but in the meantime, there's money to be made. The opportunities we have at our command now may not last forever. Someday the gold will all be dug, the British will be building ships as fast as ours, or steam will take over the trade. When any or all of that happens, I want to be ready for it. I want to be so rich that none of us will ever have to worry again."

"The shipyard should provide for us all, Stephen. If you could take over the management of it . . ."

"*Your* shipyard?" Even while he gripped her hand, he shook his head. "No, Julia. We've been over that before. Besides unless you start thinking in terms of steam, that shipyard isn't going to continue to provide."

"It'll continue," she said and pressed her lips together. She was not going to get into another argument with Stephen about steam-powered vessels. She hated the filthy things and she was *not* going to build them. Besides, she knew that steamships would never be able to compete in round-the-world runs. They were too clumsy to negotiate either the Cape of Good Hope or Cape Horn with the swiftness of a clipper.

"You won't listen to me, my lady, but someday you'll remember. I only hope you won't regret it when you do."

Although Julia pleaded with Stephen during the weeks that followed, his determination to return to sea became an obsession. He insisted it was the only place he would recover, but Julia privately thought that it was because he could no longer tolerate a house filled with women and children.

When the time came, she turned the management of the shipyard over to Daniel and accompanied Stephen to Boston. Standing in the biting wind on that winter wharf, she watched him sail away on the most beautiful ship in the world knowing it would be almost a year before she saw him again. When the words *if ever* threatened to surface, she quickly slammed the door upon them.

Once she was home, problems again inundated her, and Amelia and her family were now added to them. Even though her sister rapidly recovered her health, her bubbling gaiety had disappeared. Amelia insisted that they had enough to carry them for a long time, but Julia worried about their future. The day would come when Amelia would run out of money.

Although Julia tried not to dwell upon him, the shadow of Stephen's pale face colored all her days and nights. Without his presence, her own energy seemed to have dwindled. It was only with Cousin William's help that she was able to go from the shipyard to lawsuits to the daily management of providing for so many lives. Sometimes when she fell into bed at night, she felt as though she were fragmented into so many pieces, there was nothing left of herself, only an empty shell.

The following two years passed quickly although they seemed static in their constancy. Stephen would return from a voyage and would spend a few weeks at home only to return to the sea without her. He had never regained his youthful vigor and his health was a constant worry to Julia. Sarah continued to devise lawsuits against her. Neither the lack of success in bringing about Julia's downfall in court nor the death of Uncle Josiah, who strangled on a piece of meat, deterred her in her contrivances.

By slow degrees, Amelia recovered her natural buoyancy and centered her interests on the entire family's children and on the Church, where she played the organ. Her giggles and dimples, combined with Megan's silvery laughter, served to lighten all their days. Megan never spoke of marriage again. Often Julia glanced at her friend when they worked together and wondered, but there was never the time for them to talk as they once had. On his infrequent visits home, Samuel rarely called upon them, and he and Megan no longer exchanged letters.

The shipyard continued to prosper as the ever more beautiful ships descended the ways, and Julia felt justified in her refusal to experiment with steam. Trade with California and Australia dropped off as gold in those places became harder to mine and as those territories became more self-sufficient. Ignominious cargoes of guano were being dumped into the holds of some of the loveliest clippers. Yet these factors failed to diminish the demand for vessels built by the Howard Shipyard.

Aside from the few moments she stole from the demands of her life to walk alone beside the sea, the only joys Julia really felt any longer were the ones she found in the creation of her ships, for they were hers until they sailed away. All else seemed flat. Even Clara still clung to Lydia or Amelia and remained quiet, almost secretive, around her own mother. While Julia loved her and longed for her love in return, she couldn't blame the child she so rarely saw.

She yearned for the son her father had wished her to name for him, but he had never come, and now Julia doubted that Stephen would ever be capable of giving her one. When he was home, he held her in his arms at night and whispered of how he loved her, but little else passed between them.

Often when she walked the sands, she felt her father's presence beside her, and she knew that he had walked the same path before her. But he hadn't been so alone—he had had *her!*

Into this never-ending succession of days the news that was to change her life exploded. During a snowstorm on New Year's Day of 1854, the *Star of Gold* struck a rock off Cape Sable while returning home from Liverpool. Although many lives were saved, many others were lost with the ship.

Chapter Fourteen

1854

On a bitterly cold day in early January, Julia first heard the news. When the sound of stamping feet sounded on the steps outside the office, she looked up in surprise and more than a little irritation. Since it had been snowing for two days, and the wind had come up in the early afternoon, she had sent the men home so they wouldn't be caught by drifts. Once they had gone, she had poured herself a last cup of coffee and settled down beside the stove to savor a few moments of rare privacy before making her own way home. Now even this brief interval of stolen time was to be taken from her, she thought impatiently as the door opened.

A whirl of white entered with the large man who removed his snow-encrusted hat and shook it outside before he closed the door. His greatcoat made his bulk loom almost menacingly in the shadows cast by the stove. Yet when he came forward and the low lamplight revealed grey-green eyes and dark blond curls clinging to a low forehead, the peace of the afternoon was restored.

"I've come to take you home, Julia," David Baxter said, and it was as though only a day had separated them rather than two years.

"Not yet, David." She didn't rise to greet him nor did she feel any surprise at his sudden appearance. It was as though they had lived through this time before in some other place where the wind flicked snow off window panes and cold crept from the far corners of a room. Somehow, she felt, without even being conscious of it, she had been waiting for him to come, to give her new strength with his calm presence. She smiled up at him. "It's so quiet here and restful. Take off your coat and have a cup of coffee."

"You should go now, Julia," he said, but it was difficult to tell in the play of light and shadow whether he was smiling or not. He began to unbutton his coat. "I've just walked most of the way from Yarmouth, and the roads are well on impassable. Soon as they told me at your house that you were still at the yard, I had them hitch up the sleigh and drove over to carry you home."

"You walked from Yarmouth! You must be frozen." She quickly poured a cup of steaming coffee for him. "What ever were you doing in Yarmouth, and why in heaven's name would you try to walk that distance in this weather?"

He didn't answer as he took off his wet coat and draped it carefully across a chair where the heat from the stove would reach it. Although he took the cup from her, he set it down on the table without tasting it. stead he came up behind her chair and put his hands lightly on her shoulders.

"The packet from Boston wasn't going to sail for several days, if then, so I took the railroad to Sandwich and from there the stage to Yarmouth, but the driver refused to come any further. I had to be with you, Julia."

She twisted around to look up at him, but he was staring at the opposite wall. Above his large chin, his face looked unusually somber.

"Well, it's good to have you here, David. I always miss you when you're gone, but I don't understand why you were in such an all-fired hurry. You should have waited till the storm had passed."

"No, I couldn't, Julie," he said gently as he glanced down at her. "I didn't want you to hear it from anyone else."

"Hear what, for heaven's sake?" Now he really had her alarmed. The peace he had brought with him was shattered.

She pulled at his hand to bring him around to where she could see him. With a litheness that always surprised people accustomed to his usual ambling gait, he was instantly half kneeling, half squatting on the floor beside her. While one arm rested on her shoulders, he kept the hand she had raised to him in his own. His eyes were on a level with hers as he looked seriously into them.

"Julia, Stephen is safe, but the *Star of Gold* has been lost." He spoke quickly as though the rapidity with which he said the words would ease the pain they would cause.

She stared at him numbly, frozen into immobility. For Stephen to lose a ship! No! It was impossible. Never. It could never happen. And the *Star of Gold* with her soaring bows and sweetly narrowed stern, her crystal and silver fittings, her magnificent carvings. That living, lovely creature who swept around the world of waves with a swiftness that had won her a place in men's hearts as well as fame in the newspapers. How could she lie shattered on some bleak shore? How could she lie lonely beneath the storm-tossed waters of winter?

And Stephen. Dear God! He had lost his ship.

"Where is he?" she demanded as she clutched at David's huge hand. "Where's Stephen? Why isn't he here? Why you?"

"He asked me to come, Julie." He watched her anxiously and remembered times when he had brought her bad news in the past. Once she had fainted, but that had been long ago. Her father's death had been more tragic, and yet she had taken it relatively well. "There's sure to be an inquiry, and he wants to stay in Boston till it's over. And . . . he's exhausted. Ten hours in an open boat with heavy winds and snow off Sable Island."

"You saw him? You're sure he's all right? Was he in pain? Did you notice?"

"He said he was all right. Tired when I saw him, miserable about losing the *Star of Gold,* but he didn't seem to be feeling any pain. Said he'd suffered some frostbite, but with no lasting effects."

"And he's in Boston now?" Although her eyes rested on David, she was looking beyond him, trying to understand, trying to plan.

"Aye. Fishermen and their wives took him in on Sable Island. He went from there to Barrington, then on to Halifax and St. John's. From St. John's, he took the stage to Waterville and the railway to Boston."

"I have to go to him!"

She pushed herself up from the chair, but David's arm tightened around her and pulled her back down.

213

"You wouldn't be able to get there for days," he tried to reason with her. Then he knew he would have to give her the whole message, no matter how brutal it sounded. "Julie, there's something else Stephen asked me to tell you. He doesn't want you there."

"Doesn't want me there?" She looked at him in confusion and anger. "Of course, he wants me there!"

"No, Julie. He doesn't."

"But he does! He said the same thing once before. Then he was put out when I didn't meet him. I'm going!" She tried to get up once more, but David held her firmly in place.

"Julia, don't!" he said sharply in an authoritative voice. "He meant what he said. For the love of God, leave the poor man alone."

"He's my husband. He wants me," she said steadily, and her eyes challenged him to just try to stop her. When David silently and sorrowfully shook his head, she had to believe him. But there was something else. Something he wasn't telling her. "What do you mean? Why doesn't he want me? And what do you mean by *poor man?*"

"He . . . well, he thinks the inquiry will go against him."

"You mean negligence?" Her eyes grew wider until they completely dominated her pale face.

"Aye." He paused for a moment to gauge her strength. How much could he tell her now? Couldn't the rest wait till later? No. It had to be now. "Over one hundred lives were lost, Julia. Immigrants from Liverpool."

"Oh, my God . . . no!" She stared at him in horror with the unspoken thought between them. Negligence. And the captain had saved himself while his passengers were lost. "But it couldn't have been through any fault of his. Not with his experience. I've sailed with him. I know. There must be some other explanation."

"I hope there is. I most truly hope there is." He loosened his grip on her shoulders although he still held her hand clasped firmly in his own. Looking at the table where the cup of coffee was growing cold, he said, "But you know Stephen's been drinking a lot in the past few years. Everyone knows it."

"They can't use hearsay against him!" she snapped as she prepared to defend her husband against the world.

"It may be more than that." David wished that this hour and this conversation were over and in the past. The things that must be said. Why was it he who had to say them? Why had he been the one chosen to hurt her when all he wanted to do was to protect her? But between Julia and himself, there could be nothing but the truth. "Stephen said nothing about it outright, but . . ."

"But what?"

"He asked me to be a character witness for him, Julie." He dropped his eyes to the hand he held because, in his shame, he could no longer look into hers. "I said I couldn't. I've seen him in his cups too often, and I know he has trouble gettin' first-rate officers anymore because of his reputation amongst the mates."

"David, how could you!" she accused him. Then she lifted her chin and looked proudly towards the door. "Well, if there's no one else, *I'll* go and swear to his good character."

"No, Julie." His arm once more tightened around her shoulders. "I had to refuse him the first thing he asked of me, but I intend to carry through with the promises I made him. He asked me to leave Boston so I wouldn't be at hand to testify against him. And he asked me to keep you here."

"Oh, David . . ."

Suddenly all her resolution, all her pride, collapsed in pain and bewilderment. She knew it was true. Stephen *didn't* want her there. How awful it was that he would share his joys with her, but never his sorrow or his shame. If she went to Boston, she knew he would be formal and distant across that barrier she had never yet been able to penetrate. David was right. She must leave Stephen alone if he wished it.

"What . . . what can I do for him?" Her voice broke, and then both his arms were around her, holding her with gentle strength.

"Nothing," he whispered into her hair. "Leave him alone. It's what he wants."

"Lawyers. I'll hire lawyers for him."

"He has the best. Come, Julie, I'll take you home now."

"No. I don't want to go home." She moved a little away from him, but not out of his arms completely. She rubbed at her eyes, which felt dry and gritty as though she had not slept for a very long time. "I want to think, and I can't think there. Mama's been raving the last couple of days, and everyone's nervy. Oh, if only Stephen had been able to build our own house."

"I'll take you home with me, then," he said as he looked at her with grave concern.

She looked back at him and thought about it for a moment, then shook her head. "No. Your parents have always been good to me, but I can't."

"They'd welcome you, especially my mother." The corners of his wide lips tilted upwards in a self-mocking smile. "Even if you are a grave disappointment to her. When we were young, she was always half expectin' us to wed."

"That was a long time ago," she said with a sigh. So much had happened since then. So much joy, so much sorrow. She felt the weight of all those years. "I'll be thirty-four come July. How old does that make you?"

"Forty come May and still as foolish as I was when I was twenty," he said as he tried to lift her spirits.

"And Stephen's a couple of years older than you." It was true. The years were passing so swiftly, and there seemed no happiness left. Now this calamity of Stephen's . . . and his rejection of any comfort she might give him. Was life just going to get worse and worse till the end? "We're all getting old, David."

"Are we? I hadn't noticed it." His arms tightened around her until her head lay against the bulk of his shoulder. He ran his hand over her loosened curls. "No white hairs yet."

"It's a wonder." She sighed.

"Aye. That it is. I have to take you home," he said, but he held her still closer. "One home or t'other."

"I'd rather stay here with you," she surprised herself by saying. "It's terrible. I feel so awful about Stephen. The *Star of Gold*. I can't face anyone else. With you, I'm . . ."

"I know." He looked into her eyes, which had always startled him with the depth of their blue. Now he felt himself disappearing into them.

Neither of them meant it to happen, neither of them wanted it to happen, but when their lips met, it was with a sweetness that was surprising and yet as familiar as an early, recurring memory. His lips never left hers as he drew her from the chair and sat down in it himself with her still in his arms. When they drew apart, it was only so they could come closer.

"You're right, David," she said softly. "You should take me home."

"Aye. In a little while. This is all we have. This much and no more out of all the years of the past and all the years to come. I wonder what life would have been like if things had gone as my mother expected."

"We'll never know that now," she said as she lifted her lips to brush them across his wide jaw. " 'Twould have been different. Very different."

"Aye. And better." The band of blue that rimmed the grey-green of his irises grew wider as he looked at her with love and sadness. "Why was it that 'twas never right for both of us at the same time? You married so young, before I'd even realized you'd grown up. Then I was fool enough to marry Cynthia, but even the times in between were wrong."

"And now we're both married." She reluctantly withdrew her arm from around his neck and sat up. "It's something we have to remember, David."

"It's not something we're likely to forget. I didn't mean this to happen."

"I know." She slipped out of his arms, and rising, she placed a short distance between them. "Nor did I."

"Makes it a little more difficult to ask you something I've been thinking on for a long time now," he said as he looked over at her. He made no attempt to follow her, but remained where he was.

"You know you can ask anything of me, David. Almost anything."

"Who do you lay the next keel for?"

"Hiram Richardson." She chose a chair on the other side of the stove and sat down. She felt safer here in the shadows, where she could see him well in the lamplight without being closely observed in return. "Hiram Richardson!" He looked at her curiously. "I thought you didn't like the man." "I don't, but I didn't have much choice in the matter. Business has been falling off. I don't know why. The other shipyards are doing well enough, from what I hear. At any rate, he's the only customer in the market for a large vessel who's come along in several months. I'd thought about building one for our own account, but somehow I've been afraid to take risks lately."

"Strange Richardson didn't mention anything about it to me," David mused as he stretched his long legs towards the stove. "The reason I asked is that I'd hoped you'd build a ship for me."

"So you've finally saved up enough money," she said as she thought of the years of frugal living that money would represent. At least Cynthia hadn't taken it all.

"Aye. Will you build one for me?"

"If you can wait. We lay the keel for his ship this spring. Then we can make a start on yours come fall."

"I can wait."

The wind blew a fresh gust of snow that rattled the panes, and Julia looked at the near window. The snow was building up on the ledge. She thought of Stephen alone in Boston on this winter evening, and then she tried not to think of him. She ached to fly to him, to hold him and comfort him in his pain, but he didn't want her. She had to think of something else.

"David, why should it have been difficult for you to ask me to build a ship for you?"

" 'Twasn't the question that was difficult." He couldn't see her expression clearly in the dusk, and he wondered if she was hiding in the shadows because she was ashamed of what had taken place between them. "But if you build my ship, we'd be seeing each other every day, working together on her design, on her construction. After this afternoon . . ."

"This afternoon won't happen again," she said sharply.

"I know."

"I didn't mean to snap at you, David. I'd like seeing you every day, working with you. We were friends long before this afternoon."

"And always will be." He smiled his reassurance at her, then rose and stretched until his arms nearly touched the ceiling. "The snow's drifting. If we wait much longer, we won't be able to leave here before morning. Then it won't matter how much innocence there is between us, there's bound to be speculation on the part of others. I'm afraid 'twould only be confirmed in some unguarded moment when I look at you."

217

He went to stand in front of her and held out his hand. She gazed up at him in silence. Then she took his hand and stood up.

"Yes. You're right. And when Stephen comes home . . . we have to protect him. The torment he'll be living through will be all that a man should be asked to bear."

"More," David agreed. He had seen masters who had been scarred for life by much less. "Do you want to come home with me or shall I take you to your own house?"

"There's really no choice, is there?" she asked as she looked up at the big, comfortable man whose life had been so intertwined with her own. "I'll have to stay close by my family."

The inquiry and the trial that followed lasted for three months. During that time, Stephen remained adamant in his determination that Julia should not come to Boston. The best that she could do was send Cousin William there in her stead. Through his reports as well as through the terse notes from Stephen and the too-wordy descriptions in the newspapers, she was able to keep up with her husband's ordeal.

Even the story of the seven days that led to the loss of the *Star of Gold* was a grim one. A winter storm such as only the North Atlantic could produce had overtaken the ship. Gale winds had twisted the rudder head, leaving the tiller useless. A temporary tiller was rigged, but it worked only until winds and waves smashed everything forward, including the bowsprit, fore-topmast, and foreyard. These were swept into the sea, and their wreckage carried away the temporary rig. During a tempestuous night and day, the crew worked steadily to raise a new foreyard aloft and to rig yet another tiller in the cabin. They managed to hold their own until eight o'clock on the following night when northwest winds came sweeping down on them in hurricane force.

The newspapers reported that Stephen had laid a course without taking into account the fierce current that was running. Then, even while he knew that they were in the vicinity of Seal Island, he had gone to sleep for four vital hours. The mate had awakened him at ten minutes before midnight to report that Seal Island light had been sighted.

He was on deck when they wore the ship around, but it was too late. The *Star of Gold* struck a rock. The waves lifted her and she struck twice more before she fell off into deep water. The sea came rushing into the holds at the rate of almost five inches every minute. The pumps were useless and Stephen tried to beach her, but the wheel ropes parted, leaving the ship unmanageable. Just when all hands were desperately needed, the fourth mate panicked. He lowered a boat and took nine sailors and a woman with him.

Stephen then knew that all was lost. He ordered his crew and passengers to abandon ship. He managed to maintain order while frightened women and crying children were put into the boats, but he couldn't keep many of the passengers from jumping overboard. Even while he helplessly watched boats being smashed and swamped in the launching, dumping their contents into the sea, he ordered the men into the remaining boats. When he left the ship, there was no one aboard, but the icy waters were filled with bodies.

The men and women in the few unwrecked boats had to bail continuously while they searched for survivors. They pulled many aboard only to find them dead. These they returned to the sea in order to make room for the living.

For twenty minutes after the final boat was launched, the exhausted men, women, and children watched the lights of the *Star of Gold*. Then they were extinguished and there was only darkness. The search for survivors continued throughout the night, but when dawn came, it revealed an empty sea.

Although there were many who came forward to testify in his behalf, there were equally many who spoke against Stephen. The mate's testimony finally doomed him. The man swore that Stephen had been drinking for days. The second mate confirmed his testimony. He was fined thousands of dollars, but in view of his ill health, he escaped serving a jail sentence.

In late April, after the keel had been laid for Hiram Richardson's ship, Stephen finally came home. And then he came not by the sea that he loved, but by rail and coach, where he would not be subjected to observation by knowledgeable fellow seamen. When Julie saw him stepping stiffly down from the coach, it was a lovely spring evening. She was glad that she had warned the rest of the family away from the front lawn. His face was whiter and more haggard than Julia had ever seen it, even during his illness, and he had aged beyond his years. The sea had finally broken him.

Instinctively, Julia moved forward to help him, but then she thought of his pride and checked herself. She waited for him to take the few steps that lay between them. She scarcely noticed Cousin William counting the baggage that was thrown down from the roof of the coach, for her eyes never left her husband's.

As he approached, she held out both hands and whispered, "Stephen."

"Well, Julia," he said. He took her hands in his but came no closer. "Here I am if you want me."

"Of course, I want you. Oh, Stephen!" She stepped forward, but when she kissed him, she found his cheek was cold.

It was only then that he allowed himself to relax and to slip an arm around her waist. "I've lost everything, Julia. The ship, the cargo, most of the money I have in this world, my good name. I hope I haven't lost you, too."

"Never, Stephen," she said and stared directly into his tired grey eyes as she tried to give him some of her own strength and determination. "You can begin again."

"It's too late for that now."

"Nonsense." She pressed the hand she still held. "You're not even forty-two yet. Won't be for months. There's still time for you to make a fortune."

He smiled at her with amused pity as though she were a child. "You never give up, do you, Julia? I'd like to go into the house. I feel rather . . . exposed here."

"Of course. Everything's ready for you. There's a fire in our room and you can rest."

"Yes," he said as they walked up the path together with their arms around each other. "I want to rest. There's something else I want, Julia. I never want to speak of the past few months. Not the wreck, not the inquiry, not the trial. I never want any mention of it to be made in my presence as long as I live."

"There's no need for any mention to be made," she said quietly, but she knew that, unless he sealed himself up in a room for the rest of his life, it would be impossible for him to avoid it. There were many who thought he had been treated too harshly, and many others who believed he was not at fault. His defenders said it was something that could have happened to any master in the gales of a wintry North Atlantic. They would speak their sympathy to him, even if none stepped forth to taunt him.

That night when they went to bed, Stephen clung to her as would a child, and she soothed him to sleep with caresses she had learned with Clara. Long after his breathing had deepened into sleep, she lay with her eyes open and stared into the darkness. It was not only the *Star of Gold* whose rudder had been smashed. The same gale had taken from Stephen his ability to steer his own life. But how could she replace it or at least rig a temporary one that would see him through until the storm had passed?

For him to return to sea was obviously impossible, at least for the present. After the trial, no company would insure any vessel he might command, even if such a vessel were available, which was highly unlikely. Who would entrust one to him? And with his financial losses, he would not be able to buy or build one.

He had always refused to take an interest in the shipyard, but perhaps now he would see it differently. Yet even that was not possible immediately. There was no way she could keep the men from watching him, waiting for a slip, and whispering behind his back. The newspapers had done their job all too well. Where once his name had been famous as one of the glamorous breed of top clipper captains, it was now notorious.

There was the house he had wanted to build for so long. The windswept bluff he had purchased still stood waiting for him. That would mean working with the men who would build it, and he showed all signs of wanting to live the life of a recluse, completely withdrawn from the world. How would he react to that view of the sea and distant sails, none of them now his?

There was Clara, of course. While his daughter could give him joy, she could not give his life a purpose. A man like Stephen had to have a goal, an end for which the work was worthwhile. Somehow she had to give him back his pride, but how?

With these thoughts marching tediously through her mind, she finally fell asleep. It seemed only a few minutes before she was awakened by the noise she would hear intermittently at night for many months to come.

At first, she thought Stephen was choking. The way he thrashed around the bed and the strangled sounds that came from his throat were frightening.

"Stephen!" she said as she sat up and tried to find his face in the darkness. "Stephen, what is it?"

Then the sounds turned into words as he came up from the depths of sleep. "No! No! Make them stop screaming! Make them stop!"

"Stephen, it's all right. You're home. You're safe. Everything's all right," she said as she shook him gently and tried to break through the dream to him.

"Julia," he muttered as he emerged. Then he grabbed her and laid his head on her breast as great ragged sobs were torn from his throat. "Oh, Julia . . . Julia. They won't leave me alone. I keep seeing them. Women and children, their faces in the sea, white faces screaming, and I can't help them. I can't get to them. They jumped overboard. They jumped and now they won't leave me alone. They screamed all night, and I can never wash the sounds from my head. Sometimes you and Clara are there. I see you there in that black sea with all the other white faces."

"Hush, Stephen, it's over. It's all over. Everything is all right now."

"No. It'll never be over. Never. They'll keep drowning as long as I live."

"Oh, love, it is over." She held his head tight against her breast and stroked his face, which was wet with tears. "Hush, my love. I'm here now. They won't hurt you."

"No. They can't hurt anyone. I murdered them."

"Oh, Stephen, you didn't murder them. You saved quite a few. You couldn't save them all."

"Yes. All. I took them on board my ship and promised them a safe passage. And then I killed them. It was my job to keep them safe."

"It isn't your fault. So many men we know have lost their ships. And their lives. At least you didn't lose your life."

"I should have." He drew away from her, and sitting up, clutched his head. "I should have. Then maybe they would have lived."

"No, Stephen, no. If you'd died, how would you have saved the ones you did?"

"It's my fault. All my fault." He threw back the covers and staggered out of the bed.

"Stephen! What are you going to do?"

"Don't worry," he said with a laugh that sobbed. "I'm not going to kill myself. I'm too much of a coward for that. I'm just going to fix myself a drink."

"Do you have to, Stephen?"

"Yes. I have to."

"Then I'll build up the fire," she said as she got up.

"Don't bother. I don't mind the cold. Think how cold they were."

"And so were you out in that boat all night," she said as she poured some coals onto the grate. "Stop punishing yourself. I think others have done enough of that to you."

"They could have put me in jail. It might have been easier then. But they won't even let me expiate my crime."

After she had the fire going, Julia slipped into her robe and sat down on a chair near the warm glow. "You said you didn't want to talk about it, Stephen. Don't you think it would help now? Sit down and tell me about it, and then perhaps you can get some sleep."

"Didn't you read the accounts of it?" he said as he sank down into a chair next to hers. "Isn't that enough?"

"I read them, but I'd like to hear it from you. There was something else. There had to be something else. I've never known you to sleep through a situation like that."

"I've never been in a situation like that." He took a long swallow from his glass.

"You have. The typhoons you've encountered, the hurricanes, your many roundings of the Horn."

"No. Nothing like that, Julia." His voice was steadier now. "Nothing like that. But you're right. There is one thing you don't know."

"What?"

"Do you remember the account of how we lost the temporary tiller as well as everything forward?"

"Yes." She leaned forward tensely as she listened to his words.

"Well, we had no steerage way, and as soon as it was light, I went aloft to see if we could rig another foreyard. Everything was coated with ice, and

222

as I was coming down, I slipped and fell to the deck. I was in pain, Julia, a lot of pain. It went on and would never stop."

"But why didn't that come out at the inquiry or the trial?"

"It was no excuse for what followed. I killed those people and I deserved to be punished."

"That's terrible, Stephen! It would have been considered a mitigating circumstance. You should have a new trial. Who else knows about your injuries?"

"Most of the crew knew I'd been hurt, but not how seriously. I didn't want the men to panic. The doctor in Boston knows, but I swore him to secrecy." He shut his eyes for a moment and took a deep breath that made him wince, but when she started to rise to go to him, he held up his hand. "That's why I couldn't let you come to Boston, Julia. I knew you'd insist that my injuries be brought into it. And I don't want a new trial. I've had my trial and now it's over. If another trial would bring those poor people back to life, I'd go through with it, but for no other reason."

"Oh, Stephen, maybe not now, but later."

"Later will be too late. Now is too late. I've finished with trials. I've finished with the sea. I've finished . . ." He leaned back and rubbed his face with one hand.

"What exactly were your injuries?" Julia stared at the front of his brocaded dressing gown as though she could see through it to the body underneath. "David said you'd only had light frostbite."

"David said exactly what I told him to say. He didn't even know about the other." He took another swallow of brandy while she watched him expectantly. "I did something to my back and shoulder and broke a few ribs on the same side as that old wound of mine. Somehow it affected it, too."

"But they're better now?"

"Better, yes. The ribs are healed. The back and shoulder still give me pain occasionally. It's nothing to worry about. They'll heal, too. It's just a matter of time."

"Then what will you do?"

"Julia, it's all I can do to get through each day as it comes. I'm not thinking about a future . . . if there ever is one."

"*If?* But you said you would heal."

"My body will heal. That's all I know about the future, my lady. If you still have that crystal ball of yours handy, I'd sure as hell like to know what it says, because all I can see is a cloud. A very black cloud."

"Well, it's a little early to be looking into crystal balls, but I'm certain things will work out. Why don't you come back to bed now?"

"Bed." He shook his head. "Shakespeare knew about sleep and dreams. I wonder if he ever had any as bad as mine. You go on. You need your sleep. I'll just sit up awhile."

223

"I'll sit with you, Stephen."

"If you wish. Will you join me in a drink? I'm going to have another," he said as he pushed himself up out of his chair.

"No, I think not. Do you think you should?"

"Don't try to get between me and that bottle, my lady. I need it more than you could ever understand."

She tried not to watch how much he poured into his glass before he added the water. It felt too much like spying, but she couldn't avoid listening to the splash of the liquid. She wasn't aware that she was frowning when he returned to his chair by the fire.

"Julia, if you don't want to watch me drink, go to bed. My nights have turned into days and sometimes the days into nights, but you have your work. You're not going to be able to do it if you sit up with me night after night, so you might as well become accustomed to sleeping alone."

"I've been accustomed to that for too long a time."

"Well, don't blame me for it."

"I'm not, Stephen," she said quietly and rose from her chair. "You're right. I have to sleep."

But once she was in bed, she lay awake for hours and watched him through lowered lids as he sat drinking the night and evil dreams away.

Having Stephen safely at home was even worse than the lonely years when he had left her to follow the sea and the tragic months that had followed the wreck of the *Star of Gold*. She wasn't even sure that he was safe, for he seemed to have embarked upon some inner voyage where none could follow him. The black cloud of which he had spoken seemed almost palpable to Julia when she was with him. He spent his days in their room or in her father's study, from which he barred the household by locking the doors. After dark, he had taken to roaming the roads he shunned by sunlight. He refused all company on those lonely excursions, and Julia could only stay at home and hope that he would eventually exorcise the demons that drove him.

David Baxter, whom Hiram Richardson had employed to represent him during the construction of his ship, reported that he had seen Stephen on the beaches. Her husband had stood motionless, staring at the starlit sea on the two occasions David had observed him. He had been tempted to go down onto the sand to talk to Stephen, but Stephen seemed to have draped himself in a rejecting despondency that David felt he could not shatter.

Although they rarely spoke of anything but the work on the new ship, Julia found it comforting to have David in the yard. That snowy afternoon when he had brought her the news of the *Star of Gold* had not marred their friendship, but had strengthened its bonds. By unspoken agreement, they refrained from touching one another, but there were no new tensions in their relationship. Often Julia would look up from her work to see him intent upon his own project across the yard, and she would feel calmer and less tired.

With each passing day, she found herself greeting the rising sun with greater enthusiasm, for she could escape the house and immerse herself in the life of the shipyard, where people laughed and sometimes sang, where there were smiles and affectionate respect.

One fair July morning, when summer clouds were drifting low on a light southern breeze, Julia and Megan closeted themselves in the office to go over the week's correspondence. Julia was often difficult to corner, and now that she had her, Megan was determined not to let her go until everything had been examined and signed. Although the windows were open to admit the strident melody of the shipyard in full swing, Megan had firmly closed the door as soon as Julia had entered.

As Julia studied a letter, Megan shuffled through the papers once more to be sure that those with the highest priority would be seen first. Megan responded with some alarm when she heard her five-year-old son talking to someone outside the office window.

Robert, who loved the shipyard, had recently been allowed to accompany his mother. At first, his curiosity had led him into straying away from the office, but after he had fallen into the sawpit and been threatened with absolute exile, he stayed carefully within the prescribed boundaries. There he played with wood chips and shavings and the small, rough boats the men occasionally fashioned for him. The only problem that remained was his uncontrollable desire to engage everyone who came near him in conversation. Though the men were under orders to stay away from him, there were few who could resist his magic smile and sparkling black eyes.

As Megan stole softly to the window so that she wouldn't disturb Julia's concentration, she frowned. If Robert persisted, Julia might banish him from the shipyard permanently, and Megan enjoyed having him near her. She leaned out the window, ready to reprimand her son and send the man on his way, when she looked into a pair of twinkling light blue eyes set in a tan face.

"Good morning, Mrs. Fairfield," Hiram Richardson said, sweeping off his top hat to expose his chestnut curls to the sun.

"Good morning, Captain Richardson," Megan replied and looked nervously over her shoulder at her employer. Julia glanced up from the document she was perusing and shook her head.

"Mrs. Logan can't see you at the moment," Megan told the merchant as she stuck her head back out the window; "but she'll be with you in a little while. Would you care to take a look at your ship while you're waiting?"

"Yes, I'd enjoy that. Will you be my guide?"

"I'd like to, but I'm afraid Mrs. Logan can't spare me just now." Megan's lightning smile was gone almost as soon as it had appeared. "I think Captain Baxter is aboard, though."

"Well, if you won't come, would you mind if I abducted this young man?" He smiled down at Robert.

"Oh, yes, Mama, please." Robert's hair, the color of fresh young carrots, flashed in the sun as he tilted back his head to look up at her.

"Oh, all right." She tried to hide the smile that always appeared when Robert widened his dark eyes with that intense pleading. "Don't let him talk your ears off, though, Captain Richardson. I've never been able to convince him that little boys are meant to be seen and not heard."

"I want to hear every word he has to say." The merchant put his hat on and held his hand out to Robert. "Now, young man, I want you to tell me all about this shipyard."

When Megan turned back into the room, she found Julia studying her expressionlessly.

"You don't mind, do you, Julia? As long as Captain Richardson's with him, I don't think Robert can get into any trouble."

"I don't mind about Robert," Julia said and went back to examining the papers in front of her.

"Well, what is it you do mind then?" As Megan smoothed her lemon voile dress, she felt uneasy, sensing that a rift was about to open between herself and the friend who had done so much for her.

"Megan, 'tis no affair of mine, and you made it very clear once before that I'm not to meddle in your life." Julia continued to study the page without raising her eyes.

"It's Captain Richardson then."

"I didn't say that." Julia finally looked up from the papers. "Megan, I think it's best not to discuss it. I'm concerned for your happiness, but I'm not going to let that come between us. We've gone through too much together to let harsh words set us apart now."

"I'm going to marry him, Julia, if he asks me, and I'm going to try my darnedest to see that he does." Megan's black eyes danced with defiance as she looked up at Julia. "I've already made up my mind to that."

"And Samuel, Megan?" Julia asked softly. "He was asking for you the other day when he came to the yard with Cousin William. I told you about it."

"If he'd wanted to see me, he knew where the house was." Megan turned back to look out the window. Sunlight flickered on her neat silver blond chignon as she watched the slow progress of the man and boy across the cluttered, sandy yard.

"You could have made some effort." Julia lowered the papers she had been studying and watched her friend with concern.

"No. I won't chase after him. Besides, I don't care for the way he looks at Robert." The hurt that touched her eyes was matched by the tightening of her lips. "Do you know why we stopped corresponding, Julia?"

"I didn't like to ask."

"It was because of Robert. Samuel was very generous." Megan's voice was tinged with bitterness. "He said that if I married him, he would support Robert but he could never consider him his own son."

"Maybe he's changed his mind," Julia said with cheerful enthusiasm. She'd often thought how wonderful it would be to have Megan a true part of the family she'd adopted. "He really did seem anxious about you."

"Well, I don't care anymore. Have you seen Captain Richardson with Robert?" As she turned her thoughts from Samuel to Hiram Richardson, Megan's face was lighted by a soft, dreamy smile. "He already has Robert calling him Uncle Hiram. He's also told me he reminds him of the son who died so young."

"Megan, he never saw that son," Julia said flatly and slapped the papers she held down on the desk in front of Megan. Somehow she had to bring Megan back to reality. Right now, she was heading for pure disaster. "The child died at birth and Captain Richardson was at sea at the time. Has it ever occurred to you that Captain Richardson is flattering Robert just to get on your good side? If you *do* marry him, how will he treat Robert then? He's an old man. Way too old for you."

"I don't think so, Julia. In many ways, he's a lot younger than dour Samuel. How many times have you ever seen Samuel smile, let alone laugh? And perhaps I want an older man, someone who'll protect and love me. I never had it with George."

Julia sighed and paced to the door. She put her hand on the handle, but changed her mind and returned to stand near the desk.

"You're a rather passionate person, Megan," Julia said slowly as she struggled to find the right words, ones that would not offend her friend with any references to the past. "They say passion fades with age. Don't you think you should marry someone closer to your own?"

"Captain Richardson never struck me as a passionless man." Suddenly Megan burst into a peal of laughter that evoked visions of hidden pools in tropical glades. "I'd be willing to bet he's as vigorous in bed as he is out of it, if that's what you're referring to."

"It's exactly what I'm referring to. You don't know what it's like to lie beside the man you care about and know that nothing is going to happen, that it may never happen again."

"You forget I was married to dear, cold George. No, Julia. I *like* Captain Richardson. I like him very much. He enjoys life, every minute of it, and I think I'd enjoy living it with him."

"But for how long?" Julia impatiently brushed the curls back from her forehead. "He's at least as old as my father would have been."

"How long is anyone going to live?" Megan flashed back at her. "Can you guarantee Samuel's longevity? Shipmasters aren't exactly famous for their long lives. And who else am I going to marry, Julia? Who else is going to treat Robert like a son? Robert's very bright. Who's going to pay for his education?"

"And you think Captain Richardson will?"

"He's made a good start." When she saw that Julia was still looking at her dubiously, she added, "All right. I'll make certain. Before I marry him, I'll ask him to adopt Robert."

"That'll stop him."

"We'll see, Julia. Now are you going to go through these?" She tapped the pile of papers in front of her. "If you don't hurry, someone else is sure to come along, and some of these have to be mailed by tomorrow at the latest."

"All right, Megan." Julia smiled reluctantly. "But if you do go off and get married, what am I going to do without you to bully me?"

"Oh, you'll find someone, and they'll probably be able to do it better than I."

When Julia caught up with Hiram Richardson an hour later, she found him coming down the path from the dunes with Robert riding on his shoulder. The boy was crowing with delight, and Julia couldn't suppress a smile.

"Well, how do you like your ship?" she asked.

"I haven't been aboard yet," he said with a grin far younger than his years. "Robert and I thought we'd take a look and see if we could sight any vessels out there. I wanted him to picture how the *Western World* will look once she's launched."

"So you've decided on a name for her?" Julia said as she glanced up at the boldly raking stem and flaring bow of the ship that was growing on the ways.

"Yes. It seems appropriate." His eyes caressed the lines of his new vessel. When Julia had first described her plans and then shown him the plane model, he had felt that he was taking one of the greatest gambles in his life by allowing her to build it for him. The long, hollow bow was the sharpest that had ever been built to his knowledge. Now that he could see it taking form, he had to admit to its beauty. Then, too, her relatively full run and flat floor should give her an enormous amount of power and stability. His eyes sparkled as he thought of the speeds she might attain. "You know, the British are boasting that they can match anything we build, but I've yet to see them come up with it. This ship will prove to them that the Western world still produces the best."

"Well, I thank you for your confidence," Julia said warmly. It was difficult to dislike a man who saw beauty in her creation. "I only hope she'll live up to it."

"Oh, I don't have any fears on that score," he said as he swung Robert down from his shoulder to the sand. "I've been hearing some rumors, though. I rather imagine she'll squelch those, too."

"What rumors?" Julia stood very still for she had a feeling that she knew what they were.

"Well . . ." He watched the brawny men on the scaffolding swinging their caulking hammers with a grace that matched the tinkling music they produced. "There seems to be some doubt in shipping circles that a woman can design a ship."

"That's nonsense! I've been turning them out ever since my father died, and I've never had a complaint about any of my vessels. Some of them have even set new records. I don't see how anyone can doubt my ability."

"*I* don't. Obviously. But how many orders have you received lately?"

"Not many," she admitted.

"Robert!" he said and held out his hand as the child started to wander away from them. Robert returned to his side, and taking the man's hand, he looked up at him adoringly. Hiram smiled at the boy and then turned his attention back to Julia.

"The story that's been going around," he said, "is that you've been building to your father's designs. No one says that this shipyard can't build a good, seaworthy ship, but what everyone wants is speed. They don't think you'll be able to keep up with the latest developments and create your own designs."

"You know that's not true!" she protested hotly. "It's been three years since my father died, and every ship that's come off the ways of this yard has been an advance on the last one."

"I know that." He glanced up at the *Western World* and then grinned at her reassuringly. "I intend to see that other people know it, too. In fact, I've got a real driver lined up to be her master. You've heard of Nat Catterton?"

"Yes, of course. Everyone has."

"Well, since Baxter's leaving my service, Catterton's going to sail that ship, and he's going to sail her hard. If there are any records broken, I'm going to see to it that your name is one of the first things mentioned. And I don't mean the Howard Shipyard. I mean Julia Howard . . . Logan."

"That's kind of you, Captain Richardson." She studied this man whom

229

she had disliked for so long and wondered if he had really mended his ways or if she had once again fallen victim to his charm. Yet he seemed to be in earnest. "You've changed a lot, you know."

"Nonsense," he said gruffly. "I'm still the same man I've always been."

"Oh, I can remember your smile when I was building the *Free Wind*. It wasn't exactly one of confidence. And your incredulity over the years whenever I've said that I intended to carry on alone."

"Well, Miss Julia, I'm a man who needs convincing, but once I see that a person is capable or better than capable, I hope I'm not so bigoted that I can't change my mind." He looked down at Robert, who had a tight grip on his fingers, and added softly, "I hope I'm not bigoted at all."

"I don't think you are, Captain Richardson," Julia said gravely. "Seems I'm the bigoted one around here."

"You probably had good reason." The merchant's smile forgave her. Then he tugged at Robert's hand. "I'd better take you back to your mother, young man. Your Aunt Julia and I have business to discuss, and I'm sure it will bore you."

"I want to stay with you." Robert's black eyes sparkled impishly.

"You may for a while. I want to talk to your mother for a few minutes." He looked at Julia. "I hope you don't mind?"

"No," Julia said and knew that she was being asked for more than a delay. "Take your time. There are a few things on the *Western World* I want to check out before we go over them together. I think you'll be pleasantly surprised in more than one way today."

"Really? Then come along, Robert," he said and swung the boy up on his shoulders again.

Julia watched him stride away. Despite the boy's weight, there was the spring of youth in his step. After seeing the smile that had lit up Hiram Richardson's face, she was assured that Megan knew what she was about.

If only I did, Julia thought, as she climbed the scaffolding ladder to the *Western World*.

Chapter Fifteen

1854–1855

Almost immediately after the launching of the *Western World* on the high autumn tide, Megan married Hiram Richardson in a small, private ceremony in the same church in which Julia and Stephen had been wed. Stephen refused to attend either the service or the quiet wedding breakfast that followed. Cousin William escorted the bride to the altar, for Megan's parents, who lived in Maryland, had not replied to her letter just as they had never replied to the many letters she had sent over the years. Despite her family's concern about Lydia, she was quiet throughout the ceremony and seemed to be under the impression that Megan was one of her own daughters.

The next day Megan and Robert sailed with Hiram Richardson to Boston, where they would take up residence in his house on Louisburg Square. Their departure left a hole in Julia's life, for no longer did Megan's silver laughter float through the house nor was she at the shipyard with names, dates, and figures at her fingertips. The young man Julia had hired prior to Megan's departure was willing and anxious to learn, but he couldn't truly replace her.

Meals were often a dreary affair now with only Clara, Aunt Martha, and Julia present. Stephen, who rarely joined them, preferred solitary meals taken at odd hours. On her good days, Lydia dined with them. Strangely enough these were often the happier times, for although Lydia still lived in a world that had vanished with Benjamin's death, it was a gayer world than the present reality.

As they began work on David's ship, his presence was a sustaining force to Julia, though she was careful not to depend upon it. Come spring, his ship would be launched, and then he, too, would be gone.

Cousin William often drove over from Brewster to spend the day both at the shipyard and the house, but he was becoming increasingly involved with his own investments. He was steadily funneling his funds into railways and factories, as though, in leaving his life at sea, he had turned his back upon it.

That fall, when Julia heard that there were over seven hundred and seventy ships, many of them clippers, lying idle in New York and that Boston was almost as overstocked, she wondered if Cousin William wasn't right. Perhaps too many ships had been built, and the future no longer belonged to the sea. She worried when she received no inquiries from merchants and shipowners about building a vessel. It would be disastrous if, after David's ship left the ways in the spring, there was nothing to take its place.

However, with the coming of winter and with England and France focusing their attentions and their fleets upon the Russians on the Crimean Peninsula, French and British merchants began to flood American vessels with charters. Every day saw two, three, or more vessels set sail for all points of the world, and with their departure came renewed interest in building more ships. In one week alone, Julia received five inquiries as to when she could build a ship.

She knew that a lot of the interest was due to Hiram Richardson, who never hesitated to proclaim that Julia Logan had designed and built the fastest ship to ever cross an ocean. His was not an idle boast. During her maiden voyage, the *Western World* arrived in Liverpool exactly thirteen days and twenty hours after leaving Boston Light. When it became known that in one twenty-four-hour period she had a run of four hundred and thirty-six miles, there was no doubt in anyone's mind about the ship's capabilities. Julia was thankful to him for including her personally in the publicity.

She hadn't dared confide her anxiety to Stephen, who suffered from a permanent depression. With the future assured, she came triumphantly home with the letters in her hand.

She found him cloistered in her father's study. When she entered the room, he was sprawled in a large leather chair with a book in his lap, but his attention was not on the open pages. Instead he was idly tracing a path across the large globe that stood beside his chair. She felt a pang as she wondered if he were reliving some of his past glories. Hoping that it would cheer him, she showed him the letters, but he merely glanced at them and shook his head.

"It'll happen again, Julia. You won't listen to me when I tell you to start exploring steam, but unless you do, you're going to run out of orders permanently."

Julia had been waiting for months for him to mention the word, and now she pounced on it. Much as she hated the thought of steam-driven vessels, she would do anything to yank Stephen out of the morass that sucked him down.

"All right, Stephen," she said calmly as she sat down in the carved ebony chair that had been her father's. "If you know so much about steam, why don't you do something about it? I don't have the time to explore anything that complicated. It's all I can do to keep up with wind-driven vessels while I try to maintain our livelihood. Why don't *you* explore the steam-powered ships? We might start on something small, like a river steamer or a ferryboat. We could work up from there."

"And how do you propose I go about it?" he asked wearily. "You know I don't have the money to build anything like that. Just last week, I had to write to Paul Kelley and instruct him to send all monies due me. He's doing well and I hated to withdraw my investment, but even that isn't going to pay for a steamer."

"You have an entire shipyard at your disposal," she said with an impatience she couldn't master. "What more do you want?"

"You're offering me the shipyard so that I can run my little experiment. Is that it?" he said with the bitterness that had tinged so much of his conversation since he had lost the *Star of Gold*. "Well, I don't need any charity from you, my lady."

"Stephen," she said slowly as she tried to control her rising temper. "It is not charity. You yourself are always pointing out that the shipyard won't survive without steam. All right. Maybe I agree with you now. You know very well we can't build a larger steamship right off. We don't have the equipment for it. The men aren't trained for it, but they can learn. However, it won't work unless you do something about it. Don't you think it's time you turned your hand to something except a bottle?"

"So that's it." He set the globe spinning so wildly, it rocked in its stand. "You're trying to reform me."

"I'm trying to do nothing of the sort, but you're no good to anyone, not even yourself, now."

"I'm a shipmaster without a ship, my lady. Are you going to give me one?"

"Yes. A steam ship."

"A ferryboat." He laughed sourly. "But even you don't trust me with a clipper anymore, do you? That ship you're building for Baxter. That should by rights be mine."

"I don't know how you've come to that conclusion." She gripped the arms of the chair with both hands.

"When you heard I'd lost the *Star of Gold,* why didn't you start making plans for my new ship?"

"Because I didn't know where the money was to come from to pay for it."

"Money!" he exploded. "It's always a matter of money with you, isn't it, Julia? What about all that money you inherited from your father? There must be enough there to build a fleet of ships."

"Stephen, that money isn't mine. You know that. What would happen to Mama and Amelia if I used it for our own interests?"

"You *could* consider it an investment. After all, I *have* turned a fair profit over the years." He picked up a glass from a nearby table and looked at her shrewdly over its rim. "But you've lost faith in me, haven't you, Julia?"

"I have faith enough to believe that you're capable of doing more than you're doing now," she snapped at him.

"But not command a ship?"

"No. Since you're forcing the issue, I'll tell you. I don't think you're capable of commanding a ship. As long as you keep on drinking, you'll keep on losing your commands, and no company is going to either insure or pay for your losses. What do you want? More nightmares, Stephen?"

He tossed off the remains of his drink, and picking up the decanter from the table, poured another one.

"Have you ever paused long enough to consider why I drink, Julia?"

"Yes, I have. Many times. And I try to understand, but you won't discuss things with me. If your injuries are still bothering you, you should see

Doctor Willett, but you won't let him anywhere near you. If it's the nightmares, you should do something to take your mind off them instead of sitting around brooding all day. Then maybe they'd go away."

"You have an answer for everything, don't you, Julia? The black-and-white world of Julia Logan."

"No." An overpowering melancholy swept through her. "There's no black and white anymore. The whole world is shades of grey, mostly the color of ashes."

"And the taste of them. So you do understand a little."

"That bottle is not the answer, Stephen."

"Then what is?"

She pushed herself out of her chair and went to the window at the far end of the long room, where she looked out at the dusk that illuminated the few leaves that still clung to the elms. She pulled the curtains closed to shut out the sadness of evening and turned to find that Stephen was watching her.

"I've just given you the answer. Come down to the yard and start looking into what modifications we'll have to make to go into steam. You've got a good brain. Use it."

"To make more money for the Howards. Well, I might just take you up on that, Julia, but I'd have thought you and Baxter might find it a little inconvenient having me around."

"You know there's nothing between us," she said in a voice that was rimmed with ice.

"Isn't there?" He cocked an eyebrow at her and tried to look wise, but she realized that he was on the verge of drunkenness.

"No, there's not, and if you'd ever thought there was, you'd never have sent me home with him when Papa died."

"Perhaps I was just giving you some rope."

"There's no point in trying to talk to you." She went to the door, and with her hand on the knob, looked down at him. "When you sober up, maybe we can have a rational conversation. Meantime, I have too much to do to play games with you."

"Send Clara in. At least she cares about me."

"I'll do nothing of the kind. She's too young to spend her time with a sot," Julia shot at him and swept out of the room.

Much to her surprise a few days later, Julia found that their conversation had some effect. The first intimation she had of it was when she returned home from the shipyard and found him packing.

"Where are you going?" she asked in alarm when she saw his clothes neatly folded next to his valise. She had visions of his leaving for some unknown part of the world from which she would never hear from him again.

"To Boston," he said casually as he put one of his dress shirts into the bag.

"What for?"

"To look into steam. That's what you want, isn't it?"

"Yes, I do," she said and sat down on the bed with relief, but she was still not convinced. "You'll come back, won't you?"

"You won't get rid of me very easily, Julia, but I may go to Baltimore, perhaps over to England before I come home again. If I'm going to learn about it, I might as well do it right."

" 'Twill be Christmas soon."

"All the more reason for me to be gone."

"But Clara . . ."

"You don't want Clara spending time with a sot," he said caustically.

"Stephen, I'm sorry. I didn't mean to say that. It just slipped out somehow."

"Well, perhaps you're right. I'm not so certain I want my daughter spending her time with a drunkard, either."

Stephen didn't go to Baltimore or to England. He stayed in Boston less than two weeks and returned with a trunkful of plans and books. When she knew that he now spent his days poring over them in the study at home, Julia became more optimistic and cheerful than she had been for a long time.

On an early-December evening she returned home eager to discuss the future with him and found him sprawled across some papers on the desk. An overturned glass was soaking the open book beside him. The reek of brandy and the heavy snores issuing from his loose lips told her the cause.

As she looked at him, the plunging disappointment became physical, and she had to fight nausea. Her hopes for him, the joyful anticipation she had felt whenever she had thought of him working with her in the shipyard, all vanished in those few seconds.

She swiftly left the room and closed the door behind her. After a quick word with Martha Chambers, she rushed to the hall and snatched up her warmest coat. The smell of supper drifting from the kitchen was repellent to her. She only wanted to escape from the scene of her failure.

It took just a few minutes to saddle her horse. As she rode to the shipyard, she didn't notice the cold wind blowing in from the sea. All she could think of was Stephen and she yearned for the haven of the snug office, where she would find a tranquillity that no longer existed at home. She knew the only relief she could find from the terrible despair that overwhelmed her was in her work.

As Christmas approached, Amelia tried to make it a festive occasion. After school, she took the children out to cut greens, with which they decorated the large white house as well as her own cottage. Aunt Martha put the maids to work in the kitchen. Delicious aromas filled the house for days. Everyone tried to make it a cheerful season. However, Julia found gaiety difficult to attain.

She never confronted Stephen with the state in which she had found him that night, but she lost the little confidence she had gained in him. When he talked to her about his plans for a small passenger steamer, she tried to show enthusiasm. Yet, when he repeated the same details from day to day, she felt that those plans would never attain reality. If anything, he seemed to be drinking more heavily than ever, and he swung between wild elation and deep depression.

He still locked himself into the bedroom or the study, but he began to join them for meals occasionally. When he appeared, Julia found herself guiltily wishing he wouldn't. His slurred speech and sudden attacks on others were an embarrassment, especially when infrequent guests were present.

Stephen had been drinking steadily on Christmas morning. When the rest of the family returned from church, they found him singing Christmas carols in front of the parlor fire. Julia felt that the best tactic would be to ignore him, but he insisted that the others join in. The children, understanding only that he was enthusiastic, were quick to gather around him and began to sing, but Amelia cast an anxious look at Julia.

It was a relief when Cousin William, looking like the Spirit of Christmas, his pockets bulging with presents, arrived with Samuel. There was no resisting his delighted grin or the kisses he bestowed on everyone as he gave out his presents. Even Samuel, for once, was smiling. When they had settled down around the dinner table, they quickly found out why.

As soon as everyone had been served and the children had begun to assault their heaping plates, Cousin William rose, and tapping his crystal goblet with a bone-handled knife, called for silence.

"I want to make an announcement, and then I intend to propose a toast, which I want all of you to drink to." He paused and smiled as they watched him with curiosity. "I want to announce the engagement of my young cousin, Amelia Adams, to my son, Samuel Thacher. They managed to keep things a secret, even from me, for quite a spell now, but since they plan to get married right soon, I thought it best to have it out in the open."

236

"Amelia! How could you?" Julia stared in astonishment across the table at her sister. "You never said a word of it to me."

"You never slow down long enough for anyone to *have* a word with you," Amelia said, but the dimples deepened in her flushed face and her cornflower-blue eyes were sparkling. "Aren't you going to congratulate Samuel?"

"I most certainly am," Julia said to her cousin. "You're a very lucky man, Samuel. Congratulations."

However, while the others all spoke at once and forgot their dinners long enough to kiss Amelia, Julia thought of Megan and of Samuel's interest in her. Had he only asked Amelia because Megan wouldn't have him?

"I don't think Julia approves of marriage." Stephen, who was sitting at the head of the table, had been watching her reaction. Julia glared at him, but he continued. "Wasn't it Montaigne who said, 'Marriage happens as with cages; the birds without despair to get in, and those within despair of getting out'? You see, it's all a matter of perspective."

"Stephen, I do not disapprove of marriage," Julia said sharply. "Especially of Amelia's and Samuel's. I'm delighted."

"After all," Lydia said with the innocent glow of happiness the announcement had created, "Julia's been married twice. Wouldn't have married you, Stephen, if she'd disapproved of it."

Julia caught her breath, but she forgave her mother. Mama just didn't understand the extent of Stephen's jealousy.

"That's right. Thank you for reminding me I wasn't the first," Stephen said with his eyes narrowed. Then he looked at Samuel. "Your brother, wasn't he, Samuel?"

"Yes." Samuel had withdrawn behind his habitual mask as he watched Stephen.

"Well, I hope you have better luck than your brother did after marrying a Howard." Stephen slapped the table with the flat of his hand and roared as though his words were hilarious.

"Wonder if you'd carve me a little more of that bird," Cousin William said and picked up his plate to create a diversion.

"Carve it yourself, old man," Stephen said as he rose from the table and threw his napkin down on it. "I may sit at the head of the table, but I'm not master of this house. You fill the role better. Or perhaps it's my dear wife who fills the role best of all."

Julia watched in frozen silence as he stalked out of the room and slammed the door behind him, but she made no move to follow. All the sorrow and pity she had for him were swept away by an overpowering hatred. That he should do this on an occasion that should have been so joyful!

"I'm sorry," she said quietly into the shocked vacuum. "I hope this hasn't spoiled your day, Amelia."

"No, Julia," Amelia said gently. "It hasn't spoiled anything, but I wish there was something I could do to help."

"So do I." Julia forced a smile which she hoped was gay. "Well, tell us about your plans. When are you going to be married?"

"As soon as possible," Samuel said and there was pride in his eyes as he looked at Amelia. "Won't be long before I sail, and there's no reason for delay."

As Julia drove the buggy home from the shipyard on an evening in early March, she thought about the strange pairing of her sister and Samuel, who was her brother-in-law twice over now. They had waited only long enough for the banns to be published, and then were married in a ceremony which was supposed to be quiet, but which Amelia's children had made joyous. Julia had worried that Amelia would move away to the Thacher house in Brewster, but her sister and Samuel had decided to remain on in Amelia's cottage onto which they planned to build another wing come spring.

As Julia drew up before it now, she looked at the cottage appreciatively. Although nothing could be heard from within and only cracks of light escaped the heavy draperies, warmth and happiness seemed to radiate from the house into the frozen darkness. When the young maid opened the door for her, laughter spilled from within. She saw Clara's grey eyes filled with that laughter in the instant before she was aware that Julia was there. Then she put down the rag doll she had been holding out to little Michael and became once again the silent child who inhabited the house of adults.

Amelia, who came bustling in from the kitchen, didn't notice the change, however, and greeted Julia with delight.

"I've come to carry Clara home," Julia said after she had hugged her sister.

"Can't you and Clara stay for supper?" Amelia asked.

"Yes, Mama," Clara chimed in.

"I'm afraid not," Julia said reluctantly. "Clara practically lives here now, and I think I'd best get home and see how things are. I left early this morning, and Mama was acting restless. I'm afraid she's building up for a bad spell."

"I should go over there more often," Amelia said with her fair eyebrows puckered. "Time just gets away from me."

"No, Amelia. You have enough on your hands, and you do an awful lot just by having Clara over here. I don't worry about her so much when I know she's with you."

238

"There's no need to worry about Clara." Amelia smiled at her niece. "She's a big help to me."

Julia looked doubtfully at her daughter, and Clara looked doubtfully back. It was the first time she'd heard that Clara was a help to anyone. Still, at ten, Clara was likely changing. She'd have to pay more attention to her, she resolved.

"Can you spare a few minutes, Julia?" Amelia laid a hand on the sleeve of Julia's coat. "I'd like to have a word with you."

"I shouldn't stay too long. I left the horse hitched out front, and it's coming on cold."

"This won't take long." Amelia gave her a secret, almost shy smile and led the way across the small hall to her bedroom. As soon as she had closed the door behind them, she whirled about gaily and then threw her arms around Julia. "I have to tell somebody. If I don't I'm going to burst. But I want to keep it a secret from everyone else a while longer till I'm positive."

"What on earth is it, Amelia?" Julia said, laughing at her sister's unrestrained merriment.

"You know, Samuel wanted a child so much. Now I'm pretty certain I'm going to give him one."

"Oh, I'm glad, Amelia." Julia hugged her sister. "So glad. And it'll make Cousin William happy, too. The Thachers will go on now. I certainly wasn't much use to them."

"But you were so young, Julia. What would you have done with a child?"

"I don't know, but I do know this one's going to be spoiled to death."

"That'll be pretty hard to do in a family the size of mine." Amelia laughed. Then she grew more serious. "You know, Samuel and I talked about the possibility of it happening before he left. We agreed that if it's a boy, we want to name him Jason."

Julia felt the tears come to her eyes, and she had to press her lips together to keep from crying. She turned her back quickly so that Amelia wouldn't see while she fumbled under her coat for a handkerchief.

"Jason Thacher," she said shakily. "I'm afraid he really will be spoiled. By me, if no one else."

"We didn't mean it to hurt you, Julie. If it does, we'll name him something else."

"No. Name him Jason," Julia said quickly.

"You still can't forget, can you, Julie? After all these years."

"No. I'll never forget Jason. There's a young girl still somewhere inside of me who'll never stop loving him. I usually keep her out of sight. There are too many other parts of life that are more important." Julia wiped her eyes hard and blew her nose. She tried to smile when she turned to face

Amelia. "Most likely the man I remember never existed. I've probably idealized him. Memory does strange things. The girl I remember most likely never existed, either."

"They existed, Julie," Amelia said gently. "I remember them well. I think I was half in love with Jason myself."

"Weren't you a little young for that, Amelia?" Julia laughed. "You couldn't have been much more than thirteen when he died."

"Fourteen, and I was only in love with him the way a young girl is with some dashing hero. I guess I was really in love with you both and your happiness. I used to pray I'd find it, too, and I did with Michael."

"And now Samuel."

"Yes. Now with Samuel, but neither one of us is so young anymore. I'll make him happy, though."

"I'm sure you will, Amelia. If anyone can make a person happy, you can. It's a special gift you have."

"Not so much a gift. I just like to see other people smile. If they're unhappy, I'm unhappy, and I never did care for that."

"That's something I'll have to remember." Julia kissed her sister on the cheek. "I really do have to be going, but I'm so happy about . . . about Jason."

"And if it's a girl, maybe Julia?" Amelia said softly before she opened the door.

"For heaven's sake, don't do that. One of me is enough."

On the way home, Julia tried to get Clara to talk about her school work, about her day, but her daughter only answered in monosyllables. It wasn't until Julia had given up that Clara managed a complete sentence.

"Mama, why don't I have any brothers and sisters?"

"That's a hard question to answer, Clara. Your grandfather would have said because God wills it. They just never came."

"They could still come, couldn't they?" Clara asked wistfully.

Julia concentrated upon turning into the oyster-shell drive beside the house while she tried to think of an answer. It would be nice to give the child a hope, but truth was the only instrument Julia felt comfortable with.

"No, Clara. I'm afraid not. 'Tis too late now."

"You're not that old, Mama. Jenny Crowell's mother is older than you, and she's going to have a baby."

"Well, it's something you're too young to understand. Ask me again ten years from now, and I'll tell you."

"It's because you're too busy, isn't it? Other mothers aren't always away at some shipyard."

"No, Clara. That has nothing to do with it. I don't believe your Papa wants any more children. He thinks you're so perfect, anything else would be a comedown." Julia tried to make her voice light as she smiled at her daughter in the faint illumination cast by the buggy's lanterns.

"You always blame everything on Papa!" Clara said in a tight voice as she threw the fur robe off her lap. Before Julia could stop her, she had jumped down from the buggy and was running towards the house.

"Clara!" she called, but the child never stopped until she reached the kitchen door.

After young Ezra had taken charge of the horse and buggy, Julia walked wearily over the frozen ground to the front door. She tried to blame Clara's outburst on the fact that she was missing Robert, who had been like a younger brother to her, but Julia also realized she wasn't a good mother. The trouble was she didn't know what to do about it. When she thought back to her own childhood, it didn't help. She and Clara were so different. Maybe it would be best if she discussed her daughter with Amelia. She hated to admit to defeat, but she was defeated. I should have had a son, she thought. I'd have known how to bring him up.

As she hung her coat in the hall, the thing she noticed most about the house was its silence. Only the faint smell of supper cooking indicated that the house was inhabited at all. There would be bustle and chatter in the kitchen, but it was too far removed for sound to travel and there were too many closed doors in between. Julia understood why Clara had immediately gone there. She would like to do so herself.

She opened the parlor door, and although the fire was burning brightly and the lamps were lit, it was as neat, deserted, and lonely as the hall had been. Before she was able to enter the room, she heard the one sound she would have preferred never to have heard again. It was her mother's voice rising on a long, wailing note that ended in harsh sobs.

Reluctantly, she shut the parlor door and went to the stairs. The room behind her, which had felt barren only an instant before, now seemed a silent haven. She took the narrow steps slowly. Her feet felt so heavy, it was as though they were unwilling to reach her mother's room. When she gained the upper hall, she could hear Aunt Martha's low, soothing voice behind the closed door and so she bypassed it to go to the bedroom that had once been hers, then hers and Stephen's, and now his alone. The smell of rum and brandy seemed to have permeated the very woodwork. Cleaning never eradicated it. When she had found that even entering the room nauseated her, she realized that she couldn't continue to sleep there and had moved into the room that Megan and Robert had vacated. She found that she slept better now that she was not exposed to Stephen's restless nights and nocturnal prowling.

She took a deep breath before she opened the door and found what she had hoped not to find, although she had expected it. Stephen was sprawled with a glass in his hand in a comfortable chair in front of the fire and was staring at the coals. He had an old and stained brocade dressing gown on and there was a glimpse of nightshirt at its neck. His hair was unbrushed, and a few strands of the wayward lock that had once seemed so charming now hung limply over his forehead. His eyes were bloodshot when he looked up at her and they emphasized the strained lines in his flaccid face.

"Well, my lady, home so soon?"

"It's time for supper," she snapped. "Can't you even get dressed before evening?"

"What do I have to get dressed for?" he growled at her.

"You could have plenty to get dressed for if you set your mind to it. If nothing else, you might consider making a decent appearance for your daughter's sake."

"My daughter! My pretty little Clara. Even she's taken to avoiding me lately. Where was she this afternoon? I thought we might take a walk together, but she never came home."

"She was at Amelia's." Julia began to straighten the toilet articles on top of his bureau. "You've made so many promises that you've broken, I doubt she puts much stock in them anymore."

"I didn't promise to take her for a walk. I just thought I might when she came home from school."

"Well, she's home now. If you'd get dressed and come down, I'm sure she'd be delighted to see you."

"Too late now," he muttered and listlessly looked back at the fire. "I'm no longer in the mood for childish prattle."

"Her prattle wasn't exactly childish on the way home."

"What's that supposed to mean?"

"She wanted to know why we didn't have any more children."

"Don't try to put the blame for that on me, Julia. I gave you plenty of chances to conceive, and Clara was the only result. If I no longer find you attractive, I doubt the fault lies with me. Have you looked at yourself in a mirror lately?"

"Yes, I have." Inadvertently she glanced at herself in the walnut shaving mirror that sat on his bureau, but she already knew what she would find there. She was aware that she was no longer a young girl, that she looked tired at the end of the day, but she so often saw herself reflected in those other mirrors, the eyes of men, and knew she hadn't lost all of her charms. Angered, she struck back at him. "If you were still a man, you wouldn't find me so unattractive, but then I doubt you realize you're not. I doubt you've looked at *yourself* in a long time. If you had, you'd shave a little more often."

"And cut my throat? You'd like that, wouldn't you?"

"If your hands are shaking so much that you can't hold a razor steady, you'd best hire someone to do it for you . . . or hire a doctor to stop their shaking."

"I won't have any doctors tampering with me," he grumbled, and reaching under his dressing gown, he began to massage his chest. "They've done their damage, so don't try to fob me off on them. I wouldn't doubt you'd bring them in if you could . . . just as you've taken it upon yourself to hide all the liquor."

"I haven't hidden it. There isn't any left. You've drunk it all, and I don't intend to order any more. I'd like to know where you're getting it." She glanced at the bottle on the table. He no longer bothered to transfer it to a decanter.

"Oh, I'm sure you would. I know you've put out word not to sell me any, but I've still got a few friends left." He chuckled maliciously. "You'd never guess who they are, either, Julia. Not in a thousand years. You'd never guess."

"I have better things to do with my time. If you want to kill yourself, go ahead. There seems to be nothing I can do about it. Are you coming down to supper?"

"No. Send up whatever scraps you have left over."

"Oh, Stephen!" She banged his brushes on the bureau. "Don't act so maudlin. You've always been served the best food in this house. I can't force you to eat it."

"Just go downstairs and enjoy yourself, my dear lady. Forget about me. The rest of the world has. I don't know why you shouldn't."

"I just wish I could!" She took a last look at him and something in the way he held his head in the dimly lighted room reminded her of the young man he once had been. Caught between tears over their past joy and anger at him for what he was doing to himself, she quickly made her way to the door.

In the small bedroom, which she still thought of as Megan's, although it had originally been Sarah's and Aunt Martha had inhabited it for a while, she dashed water on her face and then held the cold cloth to her eyes to stop the burning, prickling sensation of eyes that had no more tears to shed. While she smoothed her hair, she studied herself in the mirror.

It was difficult to remember what she had looked like when she was young. She could only refer to the two portraits. She was familiar with them both, for the one Stephen had had painted of her in China hung in his bedroom, and the other, which Jason had commissioned, was in her father's study. However, despite the masses of black curling hair, the sapphire eyes, and the high, delicate bones, she wondered if they had been true likenesses. There was a resemblance, but the girls portrayed in them seemed like strangers who were separated from her by more than time.

Stephen's remarks had stung her more than she would care to admit. She took greater pains with her appearance than she normally did. As a final gesture before she went down to join Clara for supper, she pinched color into her pale cheeks.

When she entered the kitchen in search of her daughter, Clara announced, "If Papa and Gran aren't coming down, I'm going to eat out here."

"You will do nothing of the sort," Julia said. "You're going to eat in the dining room. You're almost eleven and it's time you learned how to behave like a young lady."

"It's cold in there."

"It is not. There's a nice fire going."

"That's not what I meant."

"I don't want to hear what you meant. You are coming now so Janet and Maryanne can serve." When Clara remained sitting obstinately at the old deal table with her lower lip stuck out, Julia stared at her imperiously and said sharply, "Did you hear me, Clara?"

Without waiting for an answer, Julia swept into the dining room and took her place at the table. The expanse of white linen was lonely with just two places set, and Julia understood only too well what Clara had meant by cold. It was.

Clara did come, but only when auburn-haired Janet brought the soup in, and then there was reluctance in every move the child made.

"Papa said to say hello to you," Julia said brightly, perhaps a little too brightly, but she was determined to make the meal a pleasant one.

"Why didn't he come down?"

"He isn't feeling too well this evening."

"I wish I could eat with him." Clara toyed with her soup, picking up a spoonful and then pouring it back into the bowl, but she made no attempt to eat it. "He feels better when I'm with him. He told me so."

"Yes. He thought you might take a walk with him someday soon. Have you been out with him lately?"

"Last week." Clara suddenly began eating with great rapidity as though to preclude conversation.

"Do you know who his friends are, Clara?"

"No." Clara seized a roll and chewed on it ferociously.

Julia had a feeling that Clara did know from whom Stephen was getting his supply of liquor, but she couldn't use the child as a spy. If, as she suspected, Stephen had sworn Clara to secrecy, she would only be dividing her daughter's loyalties by pursuing the topic any further.

After the soup course had been removed and platters of food had been put on the table between herself and Clara, Julia said, "You know, Clara, I really don't blame everything on your father. I don't know what I've said that would make you feel that way."

"It's not what you say. It's the way you look at him. The way you act," Clara said sullenly. "I wish I had a real mother."

"Clara!" Julia was truly shocked. "I am your real mother."

"No, you're not. You don't even know I'm alive half the time. You don't even care."

"But Clara, I do!"

"No, you don't. You don't care about anything except that dirty old shipyard of yours. I want a real mother like Aunt Amelia."

Julia felt as though a pit had opened up. It was so much worse than she had suspected. Aware that Clara was glaring at her with obstinacy mixed with fright, she tried to keep her own face and voice calm. She didn't realize how frosty her words were when she spoke.

"All right, Clara. If you still want to have your supper in the kitchen, I'll excuse you. You obviously don't have your dining-room manners with you tonight."

Clara quickly shoved back her chair and picked up her plate. With her head held defiantly high and her lips clamped shut, she stalked through the pantry door to the kitchen.

Julia tried to eat a few more bites of sea clam pie and then threw her napkin down on the table. She wandered into the parlor, but the fire had died down, and there seemed no point in raking it back to life. The house seemed full of lonely strangers, most of them related by blood or marriage, but none of them able to contact the others. How could the house be so full of people and yet echo with emptiness? If only she could hear her father's hearty laughter just once more.

Feeling a need to be close to him, she opened the door that led from the parlor to his study, and then, although she felt she might scream or faint, she did neither.

Chapter Sixteen

1855

At first, she was so stunned she couldn't believe what she was seeing, but the reality of it established itself with every passing second. The portrait of Jason, which had hung on the far wall since her marriage to Stephen, had been brutally and viciously slashed so that it hung in jagged pieces from its frame. Only one of Jason's arched eyebrows and his vigorous black hair remained attached to the top.

She went to it and tenderly tried to smooth the pieces back up into place, but it was impossible to fit them all together at once, and when a chip of paint flaked off, she stopped.

Even this he had to take away from me, she thought as silent tears poured down her face. What harm could a dead man do him? Still crying, she tried to get the portrait down from the wall. Although it was heavy, she somehow managed it.

Then she tried desperately to think of a place to hide it. She didn't know why she was trying to save it. It must have been damaged beyond any hope of repair. Yet save it she must. The only safe spot she could think of to store it even temporarily was in the carriage house or in one of the outbuildings. But she could never get it there by herself!

She hurried upstairs and found an old sheet in the linen chest. Once it covered the awful sight, she was able to dry her tears, but she found herself shaking violently. While she tried to force calmness into her body, she sat on the floor beside the picture. It was like sitting beside a coffin. Jason's coffin. Twice dead now. When it became unbearable, she wiped her face and went into the kitchen to fetch Ezra. She was relieved to find that he had not yet gone home.

Together they managed to carry it. As they approached the front door, Julia thought she heard a low chuckle from the upper hall. Once the painting was safely hidden on the floor of the sleigh, Julia left Ezra to saddle her horse. She returned to the house only long enough to snatch her coat from the hall. The house, which she had so loved and often yearned for during long months at sea, had become a hateful place full of shadowed minds and senseless acts.

Once she had turned her horse over to the watchman and told him that she didn't wish to be disturbed, Julia unlocked the office door. The last embers in the stove had long since died, but Julia preferred the chill she found here to the one she had found at home. It was easier to banish this cold, she thought as she built a new fire. It felt safer here, too.

Unable to contemplate a return to the house, she decided to spend the night. She pulled old quilts out of the chest where she had stored them a few weeks earlier. After laying them near the stove to warm up, she moved restlessly about the office. The shock that still tingled in every nerve made all consideration of work impossible.

As she paced the confines of the room, occasional, uncontrollable shudders shook her body. She couldn't think of Stephen. She mustn't! It was better to think of Clara. There must be some way she could reach the child.

Then she remembered the toys the men had made for her when she herself had been small. She would give them to Clara, and they might form a bond. They might even awaken an interest in the shipyard.

The last time she had seen the toys they had been pushed to the back of the wide shelf that ran around the room near the ceiling. But that had been years ago. She wondered if they were still there. Dragging one of the tall chairs over near the wall, she climbed up and stood precariously balanced on it.

At first her fingers encountered only dust, but then she felt something large made out of wood, which she pulled to the front of the shelf. It was the plane model of the *Crystal Star*. Occasionally she'd wondered what had happened to it, but had assumed that her father had given it to Captain Asa and that it had disappeared when the old man died. But here it was, covered with dust and smelling of age.

Forgetting about the toys, she took it from the shelf and carried it to the table in front of the fire. The lamp she had lit was flickering low. She turned up the wick so that she could examine the model more carefully. How far they had come since those days, she thought as she ran her finger along the flow of the lines.

While cleaning the model, she thought of the days when she had sculpted these lines. Her father had sat beside her and watched with pride. Together they had laid their plans and had turned them into reality. Those had been happy days, she thought. She had become as reconciled to Jason's death as she ever would be, and Stephen Logan was only a name she had heard from Aaron. Stephen. She remembered the day he had first appeared in the shipyard, the way he had been mesmerized by the sight of the *Crystal Star* sitting on the ways.

As though it were yesterday, she could see that carefree young man, with his cap cocked at a rakish angle on his tawny head, become suddenly, imperatively serious. She could hear the hunger in his voice when he said, "I want that ship."

The sob surprised her. The tears suppressed whenever she now looked at Stephen burst the carefully erected barriers and flooded her face as they pierced her heart. Pushing the model away, she laid her head on her arms and let the sobs, the tears, the anguish take control. Half an hour later, she was still crying with such abandon, she didn't hear the door open, but she felt the draft of cold air. She jerked her head up to look at the intruder with tear-blurred eyes.

"Julia!" David said, slamming the door shut behind him. "My love, what is it?"

In two long strides, he was beside her. He roughly pushed the table away from her, dropped to his knees on the bare-boarded floor, and pulled her into his arms. She clung to him, while her wild, racking sobs grew louder. She no longer cared whether anyone saw her cry or not. No pride could stand up before the onslaught of her grief.

"Oh, love, love." David held her close and stared over her head at the

247

black window on the other side of the room. "Go ahead. Cry. It's time you did. I've watched you hold it in for months and it's broken my heart. Oh, my sweet Julie."

"David . . ." she wailed, her voice was muffled in his greatcoat. "I can't stand it any longer. I can't stand any of it."

"You've been strong, love," he murmured as he stroked her back and dropped repeated kisses on the curls that were gathered on top of her head. "You've been so strong. But you can't keep on like that forever."

"David." She lifted her tear-streaked face from his huge shoulder and looked at him. "I really can't keep on. Take me away with you when your ship's launched."

"I wish I could," he said as he looked at the two vertical lines that drew her arched brows together and the black lashes that were stuck together with tears. "I only wish I could."

"You can." Her dark blue eyes were filled with imploring pain.

"You'll think different in the morning."

If only he could sweep her up, carry her home with him, take care of her, banish all suffering from her life. It was what he had wanted to do for so many years. But he knew Julia. He knew her as well as he knew the workings of a ship, as well as he knew the ways of the sea, as well as he knew the beating of his own heart and the blood that coursed through his own veins. She fought life on its own terms. Sometimes he thought her flat-footed and foolhardy in her refusal to bend. Yet it was something that ran deep to her core. She might think momentarily that she wanted him to take her away, to escape. Yet if he did, she would be miserable as long as she lived.

"You can't just run away, Julie," he said softly.

"I can!" Her fingers dug into the thick wool of his coat. "I don't care about anything else anymore. I don't care about anyone else. I just want to be with you."

"Oh, my love," he moaned.

All the self-control he had learned during the years of being near her and yet unable to touch her shattered in that second. His arms tightened around her and he pulled her onto the quilts that lay on the floor near the stove.

His kisses were gentle at first, and they comforted Julia with the protection of his strength and his love. But soon they became more abandoned. Their lips hungrily sought each other's eyes, cheeks, noses, and clung together through long moments of drowning ecstasy.

Without releasing his hold on her, David pulled off his greatcoat and flung it aside. They had to be closer, closer without the barrier of wool and linen. Blindly they fumbled with each other's buttons. Then there was the firm softness of full breasts and virile hairs of a strong chest. There was the twining of muscular arms with slender ones, of legs that somehow fit

248

despite their difference in length. There was the coming together of two who yearned to be one, who should always have been one. Together they entered a world that was eternal as the sea.

Then there was only the soft whisper of the star-encrusted universe.

"David," she whispered with love and awe as she opened her eyes and turned her head to look at him. "Oh, David."

"Sweet love." He raised himself on one elbow to look down at her. "My sweet Julie. It's you. Only you. There's never been anyone else."

"I know." She sighed.

"You should be *my* wife, Julie. No one else's. Never anyone else's." His eyes were filled with wonder. "We've belonged to each other. Always."

"Yes." She reached up and ran her fingers through his tousled dark blond curls. Constant exposure to the sun had kept them bleached to the shade of his boyhood. "Why was it we didn't know? When we were younger?"

"Maybe we did."

"Maybe." They were quiet for a moment, content just to gaze into each other's eyes. Finally she said, "I don't feel guilty."

"No," he said gently. "Nor I."

"I don't think I have an obligation to him anymore." She traced the line of skin beside the rough side whiskers that concealed some of the width of his awkward jaw. "Not after tonight. I've tried so hard. I really have. But tonight I've found how much he hates me."

"How?" His arms tightened around her as his muscles tensed with alarm. "What happened?"

"It was Jason's portrait. You know, the one that hangs in the study." She told him how she had found it, how she had discovered a virulent violence in Stephen she had never quite suspected.

"You can't go back to him," David said flatly after she had finished. "He's mad. No sane person would do a thing like that."

"I know. I'd planned to spend the night here."

"And tomorrow?"

"I don't know about tomorrow, David. I don't even want to think about it."

"I'll stay with you tonight." he said firmly. He snaked one arm out from under the quilts to run his finger across the soft skin of her cheekbone. The years and sea weather had left fine lines beside her eyes, but he saw them as an endearing sign of both her strength and her frailty. So far time had been kind to her, but if life continued to treat her harshly, how much longer would she retain her looks? "We'll think of something for the future."

"You know the launching's only a couple of weeks away." A foreboding of future sorrow tinged her earlier joy.

"I know only too well." He let out a short, hard breath and glanced down at her partially uncovered breasts. Raising his eyes he looked squarely into hers. "I don't know how I can go away and leave you here, but I don't know how I can take you with me. 'Twould ruin you. You'd have to leave everything you care about forever."

"No." Her smile was sad. "I can't leave Clara anyway. David, do you think I'm responsible for Stephen's becoming a drunkard?"

"You!" The surprise in his voice was honest. "Of course not. How could you have been the cause?"

"I often wonder," she said wistfully. "He wasn't when I met him. Maybe if I'd sailed with him after Papa died, if I'd given up the shipyard . . ."

"But it began long before that. Could be you didn't see it, but I did."

"I don't know. Maybe I did and didn't want to believe it. Still if I hadn't always been so stubborn, insisted on getting my own way. If I'd been more yielding . . ."

"He'd have hated you for it."

After a moment, David pushed back the covering quilt and got up to throw some wood chunks into the stove. Julia watched him, admiring the body that clothes always misrepresented. His broad chest rippled with muscles that ran down to his flat stomach and slender hips. His strong legs were covered with fine, curling blond hairs as were his arms. In the lamplight, his body had a golden haze. No one, not Stephen, not Jason, had ever lifted her to the heights where she and David had flown. As he had said, he was truly hers and she was his.

When he returned to slide under the quilt, he saw what was in her eyes and he smiled with the complicity of enjoyment.

"Julie . . ." he said, and then his face became more serious as he pulled the few remaining pins from her hair. "Please don't blame yourself. I've seen what the bottle can do to a lot of men. The pity of it is that it so often happens to the brightest, the best, the most charming. The men who are so eager to live life, they believe it will give them absolute happiness. Stephen's a perfectionist, isn't he?"

Julia thought about it for a moment, thought about the years they had spent together, thought about the way he ran a ship, thought of the demands he had made upon her.

"I reckon he is," she said slowly. "He never wanted anything but the best. Nothing else was worth having."

"Aye. And when men like that find there's no perfection in life, especially when they find there's a lack of it somewhere within themselves, they turn more and more often to the bottle. It makes the lines of life a little fuzzy, and for a few hours at least, it allows them to believe they're perfect."

"He can't believe that anymore."

"Maybe it's too late now."

"Too late?"

"After the wreck and the lives lost . . ." He paused as he thought of the horrors that Stephen had lived through. " 'Twould have been difficult for even the bottle to convince him of his own perfection."

Julia followed his thoughts, and a fresh grief for Stephen and his tragedy overcame her.

"You know, David, it's strange, but I still love him. Despite everything, I still do. And I'm so sorry for him."

"I don't doubt it." He tenderly kissed her eyelids as though, by closing them, he could shut out the sorrow of her vision. "You've got a lot of love in you, Julie. Maybe too much."

"Maybe." There was a catch in her voice as she spoke. "But it's hard to live without being loved."

"You know that *I* love you, don't you?" The dark blue rim that surrounded the grey-green of his eyes seemed more intense as he swirled her hair around her face. "That I always have? Ever since I first caught sight of you running around the shipyard with a smear of tar on your face and wood chips in your hair. Doubt you were more than five or six."

"I know," she said quietly. "The first I remember you, you were always hanging round the yard and eyeing the vessels as though you couldn't wait to get to sea. And then you were gone."

"But I always came back."

"Yes. I always cared for you, but I wish I'd known I could love you like this before . . ."

"Shh. Don't say it." He closed her lips with a light kiss. "Tonight we'll pretend all those years in between didn't happen. You're twenty again and I'm twenty-six."

"You look it tonight," Julia said and he did. His dark blond curls, which he usually tried to keep smooth, were rough and tumbled, and his skin had the color and tautness of youth.

"So do you." He sighed as his eyes darted over every feature of her face. "When I leave, you won't forget I'm coming back, will you?"

"As long as you don't forget to do it."

" 'Twould be difficult to forget." He rolled onto his side and pulled her close, fitting her body to his. After a moment, he said, "You've kept at me about the figurehead."

"And you always put me off. You said it was already finished."

"Aye. I wanted it to be a surprise, but I'll tell you now. I'd planned to have it brought down to the yard in a couple of days anyway. When the *Jewel of the Seas* was sold off for salvage, I bought the figurehead and carried it home. Been saving it ever since for the day I'd have my own ship."

The *Jewel*. Visions of her lost vessel swept through Julia's mind. She

251

was to have been Jason's ship, but he had died before he could claim her. David had been her first and only captain. She remembered the first time she had seen the ship underway. Somewhere near the equator in the Atlantic, and there had been David on her quarterdeck. How happy she had been to see him. Then a few years later, David had come on board the *Crystal Star* to report that the *Jewel* had been wrecked in a typhoon in Hong Kong Harbor. It had been a bitter time for both of them.

"David!" She drew a little away as she stared at him in astonishment. "You can't sail into every port in the world with that figurehead on your ship!"

"I don't know why not," he said with a lazy grin. "I did it for years."

"Yes. But the *Jewel* belonged to me. Everybody knows that figurehead is me."

"If anyone makes mention of it, I'll just say 'twas cheaper than having a new one made."

"You're not going to name the ship *Jewel of the Seas*?" she asked, suspicion showing in the way she narrowed her eyes.

"Nope." He stretched one arm and looked at her with amusement before he lowered his hand and laid it lightly on her waist. "Got another name. A better one. Had it a long time. Reminds me of someone I know. Someone who's bold as a gull, stubborn as a crab, curious as a porpoise, pretty as a double rainbow, and just twenty years old."

"I'm not certain I care for that description." She wrinkled her nose at him. "What's the name of the ship?"

"The *Yankee Girl*," he said with a grin.

"And what's Cynthia going to think of that? She's never set foot in America."

"I really don't care what Cynthia thinks."

"Have you seen her lately?"

"The last time I was in Liverpool. A couple of years ago. When I'm away from her, I can't believe it's as bad as it really is. Then, too," he said ruefully, "I reckon I'm lonely. My parents are getting older. I'd like to have a family somewhere. A wife and children I can think about while I'm at sea."

"You can think of me, David," she said softly.

"I always did."

"And I'll think about you." She smiled, but it was sad as she remembered how soon he would be leaving. "I reckon I always did, too. Much as I tried to avoid it. Oh, David, I can't bear for you to go."

"I'll be back."

"I know, and it will help knowing that there's someone in this world who's thinking about me, who really cares about me."

"Always," he whispered in her ear, pulling her so close their bodies met

252

in every intimate contact. "You'll come down to Boston to see about the rigging, won't you?"

"I hadn't planned on it. I'd arranged for Daniel to go," she said drowsily. "Somehow it's been hard seeing you every day. Arriving at the yard early, leaving late just in hopes that we'd have a few minutes talk together."

"All you'd ever talk about was the ship."

"I know. It seemed safer. I was afraid to talk of aught else. Afraid this might happen, I reckon."

"It worried me." He ran his hand up her back from the lovely cleft to the sweet curve of her neck. "You seemed so remote, more remote than you've ever been before. Sometimes I'd watch you cross the yard or maybe I'd look down into your eyes when we were discussing the work, and even with all the men around us, I wanted to take you in my arms, to comfort you, to break through that wall you built around yourself."

"The wall was necessary, David."

"Aye, but when I saw the pain in your eyes, the pain that never left them, I'd wonder how much more I'd be asked to take."

"I didn't know it showed. Is it still there, the pain?"

"A little." He tilted her head back so that he could study her eyes, which were now lazy with love. He smoothed the lines of her brows with his thumb. "There. That's better. It's gone now. Do you think you can sleep?"

"In your arms." She sighed and curled against him.

"I hadn't planned on doing it any other way." He held her close for a moment before he rose to extinguish the lamp, which had burned down to an edge of smoking flame. When he returned, she rubbed her cheek against his rough-bristled chin, nestled against the body that fit so well with hers, and sighed as she fell asleep.

David lay awake a little longer, then dismissed the worries of the future. He blessed the odd chance that had made him visit with the Halls that evening and catch sight of the light in the office as he passed by the shipyard.

When Daniel Sears saw the last glimmer of light fade from the window, he limped over to the watchman's shed to warm his hands before he went home.

"Everythin' all right now, Mr. Sears?" the hefty watchman, whose eyes were always a little vacant, asked him.

"Think 'twill do till mornin'," Daniel said tersely, discouraging further conversation. He hoped the watchman was still under the impression that he had been checking on some of the work. Most likely he did. He wasn't very sharp.

It had been hours since Daniel had glimpsed the light down the road.

253

Coming to investigate, he had seen through the window the sight of Julia weeping in David Baxter's arms. Cold as it was, he had maintained a silent vigil in the darkness at a discreet distance from the office. Captain Logan had occasionally been seen wandering around the yard at night. Although Daniel loathed violence, he had no scruples about forcibly preventing it especially when it might be directed at Julia.

David left when the night was still deep with only the blaze of winter stars to guide him, but Julia waited until a tinge on the eastern horizon told of coming day before she set out for home, where she could bathe and change her clothes before returning to work.

When the watchman, who was bundled up to his nose in old scarves and shawls over his shabby coat, had saddled up her horse and brought it to the mounting block by the office, she nodded and smiled at him.

"Thank you, Temple."

"Glad to do it, Miss Julia," he said as he pulled down a scarf to expose his mouth. "Busy night last night."

"Oh?" Her hand froze on the pommel. Was it possible that the man, noticing David's arrival and delayed departure, had decided to try a bit of blackmail. She tried to keep her voice casual. "What do you mean by that?"

"First you come along, then Captain Baxter had to go check out his ship. Never did see when he left. Must have been when I was makin' the rounds." The hefty man shifted his weight with embarrassment. "I'm sorry, Miss Julia. I know you want a full report, but I just plain didn't see him."

"That's all right, Temple." She bent to check the stirrup to hide her relief. "Captain Baxter has the right to come here whenever he wants."

"That's what I figured, Ma'am. Then Mr. Daniel Sears appeared not long after Captain Baxter. Must be somethin' terrible wrong with some of the work. Mr. Sears, he spent hours checkin' on it. Then while he was still here, Captain Logan come along."

"Captain Logan was here!" Julia could feel the blood draining from her face. She clutched the saddle tightly to steady herself.

"Yes, ma'am." In the dim light cast by the lantern, Temple didn't notice Julia's reaction to his words. "Like I was tellin' you."

"How long was he here?"

" 'Bout an hour, I reckon. He didn't do no damage, ma'am. After he left, I checked all around."

"You think he'd do some damage?" Julia asked coolly, but only three words echoed through her mind. Stephen was here! Stephen was *here*!

"Not on purpose, ma'am," the watchman said abashedly as though

254

apologizing for his remarks. After all, Captain Logan was her husband. "But he lit that fire down near the ship one night, you recollect, and forgot to put it out when he left."

"Yes." Although her hands were shaking, Julia managed to swing up into the saddle and fold her coat around her legs. "I'd forgotten. Thank you, Temple."

Julia was able to control her fright until she was well clear of the yard, and then she reined in at the top of the hill. From here, she could see the lanterns of the men who were beginning to converge upon the shipyard. It was such a normal peaceful sight, one she had seen hundreds of times, this beginning of a new winter's day. It had a slightly strengthening effect, but nothing could really calm her.

She tapped her horse with her heel and he started up into an ambling walk. As she passed her workmen, she was able to nod and wave to them. Yet all the while she feared the shortening road that led to her home. If only she had time to think before she had to face Stephen. But there was no place to go. The beaches would be too bitter with wind and night chill to linger on. The village was coming alive. Already the false dawn was giving way to the real one.

But what had he seen? What had Stephen seen?

There had been no noise other than the wind to indicate that anyone was prowling around the office. But she hadn't heard David before he'd entered the office, either. While David had been with her, there had been no outer world. Her world had begun and ended within the circumference of his arms. Oh, if only she were in them now!

There had been no face at the windows, but what if she had looked up instead of losing herself in David's eyes? Would she have seen a blurred, unshaven face? Would she have seen Stephen's tormented eyes?

Instead of bare trees and snow-patched stone walls, she saw once again the slashed and tortured portrait, and she shuddered. If Stephen was capable of that violence with no provocation, what would he do now? What would he do to her?

Then she rounded the bend, and there was the house with the rising sun reflecting red upon its windows and glazing pink upon its white walls. She guided the horse across the frozen lawn and around to the back of the house so that there would be no sound on the oyster-shell driveway. She dismounted and quietly led him into the stable, but she left his saddle on. She might need him again. Very soon.

She tiptoed across the back porch and slipped through the kitchen door. Only Janet, yawning and moving slowly, was in the room, since Julia was the only member of the household who normally rose this early and there was only one breakfast to be cooked. The woman jumped when Julia closed the door behind her.

"Miss Julia! Thought you was upstairs."

"Give me a knife, Janet," Julia said with no preliminary greeting. "A sharp one."

"A knife, miss?" The maid gaped at her.

"That's what I said," Julia snapped at her. "Can't you hear this morning?"

"Yes, miss." The woman hurried to the wall and took a medium-size knife down from the wooden board. She held it out to Julia. "This do?"

Julia picked up a loaf of warm bread that was lying on the deal table and plunged the knife into it. When she withdrew it, she nodded.

"Yes, Janet. This is fine. And don't mention it to anyone."

"No, miss. Not if you say so." Janet stared wide-eyed as Julia left the room. This house was becoming more like a loony bin every day. There were times when she thought about leaving it and looking for a new position, but she had been with the Howards since her youth. They had always been good to her. But now Miss Julia, too? She shook her head, then clamped her jaws shut as though to remind herself of her mistress's injunction.

As soon as she entered the dining room, Julia laid the knife on the table while she unbuttoned her coat and slipped out of it. She threw the coat over a chair and slipped the knife into one of the many pockets in her skirts. Then she tiptoed down the hall and crept silently up the carpeted steps. She went directly to Stephen's room and laid her head against the heavy paneling of the door. Heavy snores were clearly audible.

She sighed lightly as the tension that had gripped her began to dissipate. She went swiftly to her own room. With any luck, she'd be out of the house before he awakened, which was likely if he had been roaming around last night. She couldn't put off seeing him forever, but the longer the better, as far as she was concerned. At least it would give her time to put some kind of plan into effect.

After bathing and changing her clothes, she ate a hurried breakfast and escaped before anyone else had stirred. The relief she had felt last night when she had left the house was nothing compared to that which she now felt as she trotted to the shipyard. Stephen was quite capable of coming to the yard and making a scene, but there she could see to it that the men were around. They would protect her. However, he was equally capable of biding his time till he had her at a disadvantage and then attack. She couldn't trust him enough to be alone with him. For how long? she wondered. The rest of her life?

The first person she saw when she rode into the yard was Daniel Sears. In her agitation about Stephen, she had forgotten Daniel's presence last night. The watchman said he'd been there for hours. Although he often came over at night, it was unusual for him not to come into the office if there was a light. Could he have been spying on her? Daniel? No. If she couldn't trust Daniel, then there was nothing left in the world that she would ever be able to believe in.

She beckoned him over to her as she rode to the hitching post, and he limped after her so quickly he was there to help her dismount.

"Daniel," she said abruptly as she stepped down from the mounting block. "Temple tells me you were here last night."

"Yes, ma'am." His soft brown eyes were expressionless, and not a muscle moved in his swarthy face. "Just come over to check a few things out."

"I was in the office. You didn't drop by to see me."

He glanced down at a shattered ice puddle as though the frozen splinters would give him an answer. Then his eyes shifted to her face.

"Heard voices. Figured you was busy."

"What did you hear?" The fear that continued to haunt her gave an unexpected edge to her words.

"Just voices, Miss Julia," he said calmly and looked at her with quiet reassurance. "None of my business who was with you. Don't figure it's no one else's, neither."

She stared at him imperatively, trying to make him go on, but he only continued to look at her with sober honesty. Then she understood he was telling her without words that she had nothing to fear from him, no matter what he knew. Neither would he repeat it, not even to her.

"Did you see Captain Logan last night? Temple says he was here while you were."

"No, ma'am. I didn't see him." He jammed his hands into his pockets and looked nonchalantly across the yard. Then in a low voice that was almost a whisper, he said, "He didn't come nowhere near the office, Miss Julia. If he had, I'd have seen him."

"You would have! Daniel . . ."

"Figured he might be comin' round. Thought it best if I kept an eye out for him. That's how I know for certain he didn't come nowhere near you."

Julia closed her eyes for a moment as relief washed over her. It brought a weakness with it and she put out her hand to steady herself, but there was nothing to hang onto. Then her fingers met the coarse wool of Daniel's jacket. She opened her eyes to find that she was clutching the arm he had held out in front of her.

"Daniel, I don't know what's come over me."

"Not enough sleep," Daniel said tersely as he looked at the enormous blue eyes set in her pale and haggard face. "Too much worry. Best you come into the office and set a spell."

"Aye. I suppose," she said quietly as she let him guide her towards the office. "Are you absolutely positive about Captain Logan?"

"Be willin' to stake my life on it, Miss Julia," he said stolidly.

I hope you're right, she thought as she went up the steps, but it's more likely my life that's at stake.

After Daniel had Julia settled in an armchair, he watched her for a moment to make sure that she was all right. Then he said firmly, "Miss Julia, Captain Logan didn't see nothin'. He didn't hear nothing'. If he'd come near the office, I'd have done somethin' about it. There's nothin' for you to fret about."

"Thank you, Daniel. I don't know what I'd do without you."

"Well, you don't have to worry none on that score, neither." He seemed to be about to say more, but instead he shook his head. "Best I get back to work now."

An hour later when David Baxter found her, Julia was standing near one of the smaller ways, but she wasn't inspecting the fishing schooner that sat there. She was staring down Sesuit Creek towards the Bay.

The rasping of different pitched saws, the chunk-chunk of axes, the blacksmith's steady metal strokes that were interspersed by the tinkling of his mallet, all these formed a symphony more beautiful than David had ever heard in a concert hall.

The joy of the night still filled him, and he wanted to sweep Julia up in his arms. She loved him! She had said she loved him. She had shown him what such a love could be. After all these years, she was truly his. It was hard to restrain himself, harder still to dampen the radiance that he knew must shine from his face, but the workmen were everywhere. So many eyes to see what mustn't be seen. So many ears to hear what mustn't be heard.

"Planning the launching?" He managed to make his voice nonchalant as he came up to stand beside her.

"Launching?" She turned to look up at him, but instead of joy, he found the pain was still there and something else he hadn't seen before. "Oh, David. No. Not the launching."

"What is it, Julia?" he asked anxiously. His earlier elation was replaced by misgivings and dread. Was she already regretting the night?

"It's Stephen." As they walked to the banks of the creek, she told him about her husband's nocturnal wanderings. Her fear. The assurance Daniel had given her. "We can't meet alone again, David. He almost found us last night. If he had . . ."

Lapsing into silence, they watched but did not see the gulls hard at work in their winter hunger, the rocks disappearing under the flood tide, the morning sun sparkling on the waves and glinting off the ice that lined the sides of the creek.

"There must be a way," David said at last.

"None that I can think of," Julia answered with great sadness. " 'Twouldn't be worth the chance if there were. Stephen's always been jealous, usually for no reason at all. Now . . . I don't know what he'd do. It frightens me even to think about it."

David picked up a small flat green stone from the bank and skimmed it across the water as he thought over her words.

"What about Boston?" he asked when the pebble sank. "Come yourself instead of sending Daniel."

"I doubt that's too good an idea. A lot of people in Boston know us. They know Stephen, too."

David folded his arms behind his back. His face was stern when he looked down at her, and his eyes were bleak. The most beautiful morning of his life was turning into the blackest day.

"What you're really saying is that you don't want to come," he said tonelessly.

"No, David!" She laid one gloved hand lightly on his chest and looked straight up into his eyes. "That's not what I'm saying at all. You accused me of that once before years ago, and then you went and married Cynthia before I had a chance to make you understand. I'm not going to let that happen twice. I do want to come. There's nothing in the world would make me happier, but there's a lot more in this world than the things I want. It's a lesson it's taken me years to learn, but I'll never be able to forget it now."

"I understand." He brought one arm around and touched her hand, but even that touch was too overwhelming. He dropped his hand to his side. "I wish I didn't, but I do. You'll still think of me, though, when I'm gone?"

"Always." Her voice was choked with the tears that barely appeared in her eyes. "Every day. Especially at sunset."

He took a deep breath and then cleared his throat to check the emotions that were threatening to overwhelm him.

"Why at sunset?"

"Because that's the saddest hour." She began to walk slowly along the bank. "It's when the memory of all the people who've left you comes back, and the world seems very empty without them."

"And I'll be one of the people who've left you?"

"No. 'Twill make me happy to think of you because I'll know you're coming back to me."

"I will, Julie. That's a promise I swear I'll never break. Somehow, someday, we'll work things out."

"Will we, David? I don't see how. There'll never be another night like last night. We'll have to be friends. No more than that."

"We can never be just friends. Never again. But perhaps what happened last night isn't as important as . . ." Then he shook his head and there was a break in his voice when he rushed on. "No! It *is* important. It's the most important thing that's ever happened to me. But the main thing is for you to remember that I love you. I always have and I always will so long as there's breath left in my body."

"And I you, my love," she said softly in a voice that was no louder than the breeze.

His wide mouth that usually hovered at the edge of a smile broke into a grin. "And that's something I'll always find a wonder. Me with my ugly phiz."

"There's nothing ugly about you." She looked up at him, her eyes filled with adoration. No matter what others saw, love touched each plane and contour of his face.

"Then you've never looked into some of the mirrors I have," he said.

"They're the wrong mirrors." She stopped abruptly and tried to hide her feelings as one of the carpenters approached. After she had approved the cabinet fittings that he showed her, she turned back to David. "You will write to me, won't you, David?"

"I'll still be here for a couple of weeks."

"I know." Two weeks and then the world would lose all colors and become once again a grey bleak place. Only now it would be worse. Fear of Stephen would add a blackness and there would be only a blank void in the place that David had filled all these months. She had to have something to look forward to. "But when you've gone, you will write?"

"Is it safe? What if Stephen intercepts one of my letters?"

"You can write to me here at the shipyard. Send a cover letter complaining about the *Yankee Girl* or a report to me on how she's doing. It's not unusual. I get letters from shipowners quite often."

"Then I will. So long as it doesn't put you in danger." He looked across the yard at his ship, which was so nearly completed. Tomorrow the figurehead would be bolted into place, and in the months to come, it would be his only reminder of Julia. " 'Twould be nice to have someone besides my mother to write to. Someone who cares enough to really read my letters. Oh, Julie, it's you I want to write to. I've written you letters in the past, letters that said all the things I never dared tell you before, but I've always destroyed them the next morning."

"You won't have to destroy them. Never again."

"And you'll write to me?"

She smiled up at him. "Of course. There can't be any harm to it. Even if I can't say all I'd really like, it will be enough to know that you'll read the letters and hear all the unwritten words."

"I'll hear them," he promised her soberly.

With the approach of launching day, the work in the yard rose to its usual last-minute frenzied pitch. Julia and David had little opportunity for another quiet conversation, and then the day arrived. As soon as the paddle steamer towing the *Yankee Girl* behind her had left Sesuit Creek, Julia hurried to the top of the dunes, but it was something no one would remark on. She had always watched her vessels sail away just as her father

260

had before her. Some of the men even thought that by doing so she and he had brought luck to those vessels, and there were none who would disturb her.

It was just as well, for the desolation she felt showed in her face. The sight of the repaired and freshly painted figurehead in her blue gown with a whelk's shell in her hand and a porpoise playing underfoot did nothing to relieve her sorrow. So often when she and Stephen had entered a harbor she had looked eagerly for that figurehead. At the time, she had thought it was just in anticipation of seeing her ship, but now she knew there was more to it than that. And as she waved to the tall man who commanded the quarterdeck with such ease, she knew how very much more there was to it.

Her period didn't come that month. The only time she had missed one before was when she had been carrying Clara. At first Julia was alarmed, but then she put it down to the tensions of the launching and the fact that she was getting older. She'd be thirty-five come July. After years of trying to conceive a child, it couldn't have happened in one night.

When the next full moon arrived, though, and nothing happened, she began to worry. When the bodices of her dresses grew tight, she knew there could be only one explanation. As she faced the fact that she was with child and that Stephen would know without the slightest doubt that it was not his, her first instinct was to flee to Boston. David would still be there for another couple of weeks, and perhaps he would take her with him when he sailed.

Even as she made plans to go and stay with Megan until she was able to talk to David, she knew that she couldn't do it. Whether he cared for Cynthia or not, he was still married to her, and the scandal of such an elopement would prevent either David or herself from ever returning home. And if she were gone, who would look after her mother and Clara? Who would see that Stephen's needs were met? Who would keep the shipyard going? And who would defend her against Sarah's continuing, draining lawsuits?

But she couldn't stay, either. She would be able to draw her corsets tighter for just so long before her burgeoning body became obvious. She was thankful that she and Stephen no longer shared the same room and that he was so wrapped up in his own misery he rarely noticed anything apart from himself and his wishes.

Chapter Seventeen

1855

On a day when the air was thick with coming spring, Julia was sitting on a tall chair at her desk in the office. Unable to concentrate on the papers before her, she pushed them away impatiently. As she did so, the loneliness of her secret struck her with overwhelming force. Compulsively she pulled out a fresh sheet of paper and began a letter to David.

Her pen flew across the page as she poured out all her fears, the terror she felt every time Stephen's eyes lingered on her. She had reached the point of imploring David to return to the Cape before he sailed when she threw down her pen in disgust and tore up the letter.

There was nothing practical David could do to help her. It was wrong of her to burden him with the anxiety that such a knowledge would bring. He was going to drive a powerful ship crewed by unreliable men across the Atlantic, and he would need a free mind and a clear head to do it safely.

After throwing the shredded scraps of paper into the stove, she took out a fresh sheet and began a new letter. It was short and spoke only of his ship and the shipyard, for she was unable to lift her spirits enough to inject a note of gaiety. At least, she thought as she dropped the sealing wax on it, he would know she was thinking of him. For the moment that would have to suffice.

After she had impressed the letter with her ring, she sat idly at her desk. Through the open window, she could see the men at work. Everything was going well and for once there was nothing pressing that she must do. She suddenly realized how very tired she was, how worn down by fear and apprehension. She must talk to someone, and there was no one she could talk to at home. With Megan gone, only Amelia remained nearby. Megan, who had been through this herself, would understand, but would her sister? It was difficult imagining Amelia, who radiated such a loving goodness, ever getting herself into such a situation.

At least she could go and see her, Julia thought. Most of the children would be in school. It would be pleasant, too, to take a drive and see if the buds on the branches had begun to show green. It was so long since she had really looked at anything.

Yet as Julia drove the buggy to Amelia's house, she forgot to look at the trees and bushes. Instead she wondered how long it would be before Stephen noticed that she had given up riding her horse in favor of driving the buggy. Perhaps it would be safer to ride, perhaps it would be better for everyone if . . .

No! She pressed her hand against her still-flat stomach. She had wanted this child for years. If only it were a boy, it wouldn't matter that he came in an inconvenient way. Even if it were a girl, she would be David's daughter, and his longing for a child went even deeper than her own. No matter what happened she would protect her child.

The sight of Amelia, alone in her cheerful kitchen baking cakes, was distressing rather than comforting, however. Julia scarcely listened while Amelia chattered on, telling her about a letter from Samuel. Instead she sat and watched her sister's body and thought how soon she herself would begin to show the life she carried within her. But where Amelia carried it proudly, Julia would have to conceal hers as long as possible. The contrast was painful.

After putting the cake pans into the oven, Amelia closed the door with a flourish. "Julie, I don't believe you've heard a word I've said."

"I guess I haven't been paying too much attention," Julia admitted. "I was just thinking how well you look and how happy you are."

"I don't have any reason to be aught else." Amelia studied her sister's face quizzically. "Should I have? Is that why you're here?"

"No. There's no reason. It's just that you always seem to have life so well under control."

"Under control!" Amelia's dimples deepend as she burst into laughter. "Julie, I *never* have things under control. I always seem to have left ten important things undone in order to do one unimportant thing. I should be getting the children's clothes in order this very minute, but I started thinking how good the smell of baking would be while I was sewing and I ended up out here."

"Maybe the baking is the important thing."

"Maybe it is, but Julie, I wouldn't fret about having things under control if I was you. You've always been the efficient one in the family. Look at the way you've run that shipyard since Papa died."

"That isn't really what I meant." Julia brushed her hair away from her face with the back of her hand. It was hot in the kitchen. "Having things under control is a lot different from having life under control. My life seems to be scattered all around in pieces and I can't fit any of them together."

"You look right meeching," Amelia said as she sat down at the flour-sprinkled table. Her blue eyes were filled with concern. "What's wrong?"

"Everything," Julia said with a sigh. "I can't find much that's right."

"It's hard on you seeing Mama like she is every day," Amelia said sympathetically. "At least you've got to admit she's usually happy."

" 'Tisn't just Mama."

"I know. Stephen's been . . . difficult lately."

"He's going to be more difficult." Julia concentrated on a star she was drawing in the flour on the table. "Amelia, I want you to keep a secret. It could be bad, really terrible, if word got out before I'm ready to let it."

"Well, I'm right good at keeping secrets if you want to tell me."

"Yes. I'm . . ." She took a deep breath and looked directly at her sister. "I'm going to have a child."

"You are!" Amelia jumped up and threw her arms around Julia. "But that's not terrible. It's wonderful!"

Julia leaned her head against Amelia's breast for a moment. She wanted to go on, to tell her sister everything, to share part of the burden she carried, but the words wouldn't come. She couldn't admit, even to Amelia, the manner of her child's conception. She straightened up and shook her head.

"I just wish it was wonderful," she said glumly. "Stephen won't want this child, and I don't know what he'll do when he finds out."

"But you haven't told him yet." Amelia put flour-stained hands on the white apron that covered her hips and looked at Julia with a puzzled expression. "I'll bet when you do, you'll find he really does want it."

"No. I know Stephen, 'Melia." Julia put her elbow on the table and rested her chin on her knuckled hand as she tried to plan for a future whose visibility was shrouded by thick fog. "I may have to go away for a while . . . till the child's born. If I do, will you keep an eye on Clara for me? And Mama?"

"Julie! Things *can't* be as bad as all that." As though to emphasize her words, Amelia whipped off the white cloth that had protected her flaxen curls while she was baking and draped it around her neck. "You can't just run off. Where would you go?"

"Most likely to Megan. She'll help me, find a place for me to stay where no one will discover me." Even as she spoke, Julia's mind began to clear. Just being around Amelia gave her courage and a little optimism. Maybe she could work things out.

"You can stay with me, Julie."

"With Stephen just down the road? No. It would be too dangerous for you and the children as well as for me. I have to leave the Cape."

"Is he really that dangerous?" Amelia frowned as she thought of her brother-in-law. "I remember how good he was to me when I found out about Michael and the baby was born."

"He's changed. You saw what he did to Jason's portrait."

"Yes, but Cousin William thinks it can be fixed. That's what the painter in Boston told him when he took it there."

"I hope so. I dearly hope so." Julia paused as she thought of the wrecked painting. Even if it were somehow patched together, would she ever again be able to look at it or would it always be a reminder of the violence that could erupt at any moment? "The important thing, though, is that if Stephen was capable of doing that in one of his drunken rages, what else will he do?"

"Has he ever hurt you?" Amelia was shocked by the depth of Julia's apprehensions, and a very real fear for her sister's safety began to form.

"No. Not yet. Though what he'll do when he finds out about the child, I don't know. I have to keep my baby safe, Amelia. I can't take chances with his life."

"To have to keep a baby safe from his own father!" Amelia ran her hand over her stomach in a gesture that seemed to promise her own child a future of love and welcome. "I still just can't believe it. He's always seemed right fond of Clara."

"Yes. But she was born at a different time. *Everything* was different then."

"Yes. I reckon it was." Amelia sat down opposite Julia and took a deep breath. "If you're so set on this, I'll see to Clara and Mama, but what about Stephen?"

"There's not much anyone can do for Stephen," Julia said with a deep sadness for her husband. "Aunt Martha will see to it that he gets his meals and has fresh clothes."

"When do you plan on leaving, Julie?"

"Not till the last minute. But I can't put it off till too late." She looked down at the front of her rough grey-blue dress. "Will you tell me when you think I look as though I'm carrying?"

Amelia's eyes searched her sister's body. Julia had been so thin lately, but she was definitely filling out.

"Now that you've told me, I can see a little difference already."

"Really!" Julia's eyes widened in alarm.

Amelia leaned across the table and put her hand on her sister's arm. "Don't worry. I doubt anyone else would notice. I didn't till you told me."

"Don't let me wait till it's too late, Amelia."

"No. I won't. I promise." Amelia's dimples deepened. Perhaps a smile would make the world a little brighter for Julia. "Would you like a glass of milk?"

Lying awake on a stormy night in early July, Julia listened to the wind rushing through the spruce trees and elms. It was a sound that had comforted her since childhood, and she thought how much she would miss it when she left. She knew she would have to go soon and she dreaded it. She had left home so often, but this time there was none of the excitement of a new voyage, none of the anticipation of seeing a new vessel rigged in Boston, only the apprehension of an unknown place, an unknown life.

Tomorrow, she resolved, tomorrow she would begin packing. It would have to be done secretly, for she would be taking far more than she would need for one of her usual short business trips to Boston, which was the excuse she would give for her departure. No one but Amelia yet knew the truth, although Julia was aware that Daniel suspected something out of the ordinary was going to happen.

She had caught him watching her quizzically many times after she had begun to instruct him on the details of the next launchings and had gone over the specifications of the vessels that were to follow. However, being Daniel, he had said nothing, not even when she asked him to hold any letters David Baxter might send and to forward them to her at Megan's house in Boston.

As she went over her plans once again, she fell into a confused sleep where her father was waiting for her in Boston and was impatient because she hadn't arrived as soon as he had expected her. Then Jason stepped out of the torn canvas and began driving a nail into the wall to hang the portrait.

"Julie, Julie, wake up." Martha Chambers was shaking her shoulder. "I've been poundin' on the door, but I couldn't raise you. Had to find a key to your room, but you've got to get up."

Julia tried to shrug off Martha's hand and return to the dreams that seemed more pleasant than reality, but Martha was persistent. Finally Julia sat up. When she saw the older woman's face, she was alarmed.

"What is it, Martha? Mama? Clara?"

"No, it's Captain Logan."

"What's happened?" Julia asked as she threw the covers back and got up. She could hear the wind tossing the trees more violently than it had when she went to sleep. "What's he done now?"

"Dan Sears is downstairs, waitin' to speak to you."

"The yard!" Julia threw on her robe. Despite the impropriety of Daniel seeing her in it, there was no time to dress. "Is it the yard? Has he burned it down?"

"No, but best he tells you. That way you'll get the whole story," Martha said as she tried to hurry Julia along by handing her slippers to her.

"Oh, I can't be bothered with those, Martha," Julia said as she dashed out of the door barefooted.

Downstairs Daniel stood somberly with his cap in his hand. His oilskins were dripping puddles onto the carpet, but no one noticed it. His eyes were fixed on Julia as she came down the stairs, but he said nothing until she had reached the bottom. The hefty watchman from the yard stood beside him.

"Daniel?" Julia said. When she saw the tragedy and the pity in his eyes, she was afraid to hear what he had to say, but the suspense was intolerable.

"It's Captain Logan, Miss Julia. He took a dory that was tied up at the yard and put out into the Bay."

"I tried to stop him, ma'am." The watchman looked guilty as he broke

266

in. "But he got away from me. Said he had to go rescue the people. Said there was women and children out there screamin' for him. Miss Julia, I looked. Wasn't nothin' there. Just him tryin' to row out through them waves."

"Where is he now?" Julia asked Daniel.

"They're bringing him, Miss Julia," Daniel said sorrowfully. "Temple here roused me up, and I got some others to help me look for him. We found him on the rocks at the far end of the beach."

"Did you send for Doctor Willett?"

"No, ma'am." Daniel looked down at the hat he was turning in his hands. "Nothin' the doctor can do now."

Julia felt Martha's arms come around her from behind and she sagged back against the older woman, but she continued to stare incomprehensively at Daniel while she tried to formulate the words. Her lips moved but her throat refused to release a sound.

When he raised his eyes to look at her, Daniel said them for her. "He's dead, Miss Julia."

"Yes," she said and turned to go back up the stairs.

Martha, with her arms still around Julia, turned with her but looked back over her shoulder. "You two go along now," she said to the men.

"I'll wait to do what has to be done," Daniel said. "Temple, you'd best get on back to the yard."

The watchman nodded and then he blurted out, "Don't blame me, Miss Julia. Please don't blame me."

Julia, who was halfway up the stairs, paused and leaned on the banister while she regarded the men. "I don't blame you, Temple. No one's to blame."

Upstairs, Martha tried to guide her to her room, but Julia shook her head and walked on to Stephen's. One lamp was burning on the table near the empty fireplace. Beside it was a glass, but there was not a bottle or decanter in sight. The room smelled heavily of spirits, and the bed was so tumbled, the sheet was pulled away from the mattress. Pillows lay strewn on the floor beside it. It was impossible to believe that Stephen wasn't going to walk through the door and ask what she was doing there.

She walked to the fireplace and sat down in the chair he had so often occupied. Staring at the crumpled linen, she kept shaking her head. She couldn't think. No thoughts were possible now.

"Julie, come away, child," Martha said.

Julia looked at her blankly as though Martha were only an insubstantial shadow.

"Come, Julia," Martha said more firmly. "They'll be bringing him soon. No need for you to be here when they do."

"Not be here?" She looked at the older woman in amazement. "How could I not be here?"

"You're not dressed. You can't have those men gapin' at you. Come put some clothes on."

"All right, Martha," Julia said as she docilely rose from the chair.

"Julie!" Martha stared at her as she walked toward the door. The belt of Julia's robe had come untied, and her nightgown revealed the rounding of her body. "What didn't you tell me, child?"

"Tell you what?" Although her mind wasn't functioning, the words came automatically.

"That you've a babe started."

"Oh, yes. I'd forgotten."

Once Martha had seen Julia into her room, she watched her for a moment, but Julia sat down on the bed and stared at nothing.

"You goin' to be all right?" she asked. "If Dan Sears is goin' to hang around here, I might as well send him to fetch the women."

"What women?"

"To help with the layin' out, Julie."

"Oh. Yes."

While Martha was downstairs giving instructions to Daniel, Clara walked into Julia's room.

"Mama, what's happening? I went to ask Papa, but he's not there."

"Clara. Oh, Clara, come here." As though the the sight of her daughter had released her mind, Julia's thoughts began to race. Her first thought was that Clara mustn't see them bring Stephen in. If he had been battered against the rocks . . . She couldn't tolerate the thought of what might have happened. Quickly she got up and closed the door. Then she drew Clara to the bed with her.

"Mama! What is it? Why are you acting so strange?"

"Clara," Julia said as she held the child in front of her so that their eyes were on a level. "Your papa's had an accident."

" 'Twas his horse," Clara said. "I heard him take it out earlier."

"No, love. 'Twasn't the horse. He was in a boat. He had terrible nightmares, dear, and I don't think he knew what he was doing."

"He's dead! That's what you're trying to tell me, isn't it? Papa's dead." Clara screwed up her face and began to wail.

The high shrill sound tore at Julia's heart and she clutched the child to her.

"Hush, Clara, don't wake Gran."

But her words had no effect. Clara's cries went on and on until Martha opened the door.

"You two stay in here," she ordered. "I've got Maryanne in with Miss Lydia."

After the door was closed again, they could hear the tramp of feet on the stairs, and Clara tried to break loose from her mother, but Julia held her tightly.

"I want to go to Papa," Clara sobbed as she fought to break away from Julia. "I want my papa."

"I know, love, but you can't just now. He wouldn't want you to."

"He does. He always wants me."

"Not now, Clara. Not now." She pulled the child onto the bed and tried to make her stretch out, but Clara's body stiffened against her.

"You don't care about Papa. You never cared about Papa," Clara blazed at her. "It's because of you he's dead."

"Oh, Clara, you don't know what you're saying."

"I do know what I'm saying." Clara's tears subsided as her anger grew. "It's true. If it wasn't for you, Papa would still be alive."

Julia looked sadly at her daughter. "I loved him, Clara. I loved him more than you'll ever be able to understand till you're a grown woman and have a husband of your own."

When Martha returned, it was a relief. The older woman carried a bottle and a spoon. She showed them to Julia.

"I got Miss Lydia's medicine. She's had some and it's quieted her down. Now I want you both to take a dose. You'll need sleep for the days ahead."

"I can't sleep," Julia said as she released her hold on her daughter. "There's too much to be done."

"What's to be done is being done," Martha said with decision. "You're to sleep and care for that babe."

"No!" Clara said and jumped from the bed.

Before they could stop her, she had darted out the door, and they had followed her only as far as the hall when they heard her screams. Coming out of Stephen's room, Daniel Sears carried the struggling Clara.

"How can you let a child see a thing like that?" he demanded. His black brows were drawn together in fury.

" 'Twasn't our fault," Martha flared back at him. "Bound and determined to go in there, she was, and she run off from us."

"Well, take her and lock her in her room." Daniel tried to hand the squirming Clara over to Martha, but she glared at him.

"You take her there yourself," she commanded and pointed at Clara's door. "You seem able to hold onto her, which is more than we can do."

When he had done as she requested, Martha followed him in, still clutching the bottle and spoon in her hand. Julia stood alone in the hall for a moment, uncertain of what to do. Seeing her might only set Clara off again. Most likely it was best to leave the child to Aunt Martha. Yet there must be something she could do. She started down the hall towards Stephen's room, but Daniel, coming out of Clara's room, put a hand on her arm.

"No, Miss Julia," he said quietly but with determination. "It's not for you to see, neither. I'm sorry I spoke to you so rough."

269

"It's all right, Daniel, but I must do something."

"Just go lie down." As he tried to lead her away from her husband's room, he glanced down and saw that her robe had fallen open. With a furious blush, he pulled her away more forcibly. "You've *got* to lie down."

It was as though the laudanum Martha gave Julia that night sealed away her emotions, and she walked through the next two days in a trance. Cousin William came and stayed with them. A steady stream of visitors passed through the house to pay their last respects. As long as there were people all around her, Julia was all right. She dreaded the ordeal of the funeral and was determined not to think about Stephen until it was over.

On that day, Julia numbly followed her husband's body from the house to the church where they had been married. She fought memories every step of the way. When she stood in the cemetery, which looked down upon the marsh, she willed herself not to faint, not to cry out. She didn't think she was going to survive the moment when they lowered Stephen's casket into a grave not far from her father's in the family plot, but with Cousin William's arm around her, she was able to walk away.

Until evening, she was able to stave off those memories, but when darkness descended upon the weary house, they came flooding through her mind. There was no coherence to them. One second she would see Stephen beaming with pride for having broken a record, the next he was a bone-tired master rounding the Horn, and then she would remember him as she had last seen him.

She was trying to remain calm by brushing her hair when the sound arose, and as she doubled up on the carpet in agony, a primordial keening poured from the essence of her being. With one part of her mind, she was amazed at herself, knew that she should stop, but she had no control over her body, over the deep, rough wailing that terrified her. In that unexpected and uncontrollable dirge, she felt united with every woman who had ever lost a man and been taken over by the most basic and primitive method of grieving the body could devise.

It was only when Martha Chambers knelt beside her and pulled her up onto her ample bosom that the horrible sounds grew fainter, stopped, and the tears finally came. Gradually, Martha got Julia into bed. After she had given her a dose of laudanum, Martha climbed in beside her to pet and hold her through the night.

* * *

The next morning before Julia wakened, Martha summoned Doctor Willett to the house. He confined her to bed for a week. The constant nightmares she had of Stephen dying left her too weak to argue. If only the visions had been restricted to the description given her by witnesses, it would have been easier to live with, but she saw him being burned alive, being tortured to death by Chinese pirates, being buried while still breathing. Everything she had ever heard or read about death seemed to fuel her imagination, and she longed for sleep without dreams.

By day she could not avoid thinking about Stephen. She traced the course of his life and wondered about it. It was so unfair that one of his traits that she had cherished most, his integrity, had led to his deterioration and death. Without that integrity he would not have suffered so much guilt. Nightmares of screaming women and children would not have continued to haunt him all this time. The verdict at his trial might not have gone against him. He might still have been a respected master who did not have to flee at the sight of his fellow man. The waste of it! The waste of it! she would think as tears she was helpless to stem streamed down her face.

Once she was released from her bed, she had no desire to return to the shipyard. It was enough to give instructions to Daniel when he came by each evening. Clara avoided her, and the lassitude of grief was too great for her to make an effort to conciliate the child. Later, she thought, and she felt comforted by the knowledge that both Amelia and Aunt Martha were doing all they could for her daughter.

It was only Sarah who finally stung her to life.

The young crickets had given warning in the coolness of early morning that later the July day would be hot. Sitting on the front porch to catch the faint breeze that came over the marsh, Julia wondered if anyone would remember that it was her birthday. It didn't really matter, though. Nothing mattered that much anymore except the child within her . . . and peace.

She, who had always relished the long, warm summer days, could no longer enjoy their beauty. She regretted that her favorite time of year was passing by without her participation. In less than a week, it would be August. Then winter would come and it would be long and cold without the green warmth to sustain her. Yet even that regret was faint compared to the pain of grief that darkened all of life and refused to leave her.

When Sarah, and her son, drew up before the house in her smart carriage, Julia felt only a dull curiosity, but no real interest. Sarah and Aaron had attended the funeral and had been uncharacteristically quiet throughout. They had made no attempt to speak to Julia nor had they displayed any sorrow, but they had shown a silent respect just by being there.

"Hello, Julia," Sarah said, lowering her parasol as she came up the shallow steps. "I brought Thomas over to visit with Clara while I talked to you."

"I think she's up back in the cutting garden with Mama and Aunt Martha," Julia said without rising from her rocking chair. "Would you care for a glass of lemonade?"

"Not just now, thank you," Sarah said as she sat down in a chair next to Julia and tapped a bundle of papers she carried. "It's best to attend to our business first. Run along, Thomas, and find your cousin Clara."

When the boy, capering as though he rode a skittish pony, had gone, Julia watched her sister silently and wondered what ploy she was going to try now.

"Aren't you curious about these, Julia?" Sarah asked with lifted eyebrows and a smile that anticipated pleasure.

"Not especially. I think most papers are best dealt with by our lawyers," Julia said disinterestedly.

"Oh, I'm not certain you'd want your lawyer . . . or mine . . . to see these."

"Then I'm not certain I want to see them, either."

"Well, you'll have to see them sooner or later, Julia. Might as well be sooner. It'll save you paying some interest."

"All right, Sarah. What are they?"

Sarah smiled again, and with meticulous slowness began to untie the knots in the string that held the papers together. Julia had always considered it one of Sarah's more irritating mannerisms, but at the moment, she didn't care if it took her sister all afternoon to get them open. However, when Sarah removed the first paper and showed it to her, Julia caught her breath. There was Stephen's writing, tremulously formed in jagged lines across the page as it had become in the last few months of his life.

"Where did you get this?" Julia asked.

"Read it," Sarah said with every show of enjoyment and riffled the papers she still held in her lap. "There's plenty more."

As Julia scanned the page, she could see that it was a note of indebtedness for ten dollars and that it was dated only a few weeks earlier.

"Why should he have borrowed money from you when he had enough of his own?" Julia asked skeptically as the possibility of forgery entered her mind. Even as it did, she realized that shaky script wouldn't be easy to duplicate.

"Oh, he didn't borrow it from me. It was Aaron he went to, and it wasn't money Aaron gave him. It was rum, brandy, whiskey, gin, whatever was easiest to obtain. Seems you cut off your husband's supply, and the poor man had to go begging to the only friends he had left."

"Friends!" Julia tore the paper in half and then in half again. "Are you

272

aware that you were helping destroy him? Yes. You probably are. It's the sort of thing you enjoy, Sarah. Destruction."

"I was afraid you'd see it in the wrong light, Julia. I told Aaron you would, but it was a matter of family honor."

"Family honor? You never cared about this family or its honor or its welfare since the day you were born. All you've ever cared about was yourself, Sarah. You don't even care about that boy of yours or you'd let him *be* a boy instead of tying him to your side and treating him like a pampered pet."

"Must you always get personal, Julia?" Sarah took out her silk fan and wafted it in front of her face in the most unruffled manner possible. "I wouldn't consider allowing Thomas to play with the roughnecks we have around here. Thomas is going to be a gentleman like his father. But to get back to what I was saying, we *were* upholding family honor. How would it have looked if my brother-in-law had been groveling around cadging drinks from anyone and everyone? It may have been well known he was a sot, but there was really no reason to advertise it."

"If it hadn't been for you and Aaron, Sarah, he might not have been such a sot as you call him. If liquor had been more difficult for him to obtain, he mightn't have indulged in it so freely. I hold you largely responsible for his death, and I have no intention of paying you for those pieces of paper you're so fond of. You may frame them, for all I care." Julia stood up and dusted the torn scraps from her skirt.

"Oh, you'll pay for them, Julia. This is one case I'm going to win. The law of the land says that the estate of the deceased is responsible for his debts, and as far as I'm concerned, you're the estate. And everyone knows that a drunkard will always find some way to come by his liquor, even if he has to cheat or steal to get it. We did you a great favor in avoiding that."

"Sarah, I can't forbid you this house since it's Mama's home, but I never want to set eyes on you again as long as I live. I've forgiven you a lot in the past, but for this I will never, never forgive you . . . nor will I ever forget."

"Your forgiveness means nothing to me, Julia, but you *will* see me. Since you prefer to go through the lawyers, we'll meet in court. It's a pity. I'd hoped to spare you some grief when I heard you were feeling low after Stephen's death, but that's the last favor I'll ever try to do you."

"Well, that's one blessing," Julia said as she walked into the house and slammed the door behind her.

She wandered into the dining room. Sitting at the empty, polished table, she could see Sarah's carriage and a glimpse of the marsh beyond the screen of trees on the far side of the road. As she stared numbly at her empty, idle hands, she thought, happy birthday, Julia.

She tried to comprehend the utter viciousness of Sarah's actions, not just

273

in relation to Stephen but in her choice of this day to deliver the notes in gloating triumph. For so many years, Julia had tried to find some excuse for her sister, had tried to explain her to their father, to Stephen, to anyone who spoke against her, but there was no more explanation. There was an evil in Sarah that possessed her just as surely as the drink had possessed Stephen, and it was just as uncontrollable. Her sister. Her own blood. How could it be possible? Even more difficult to grasp was how Amelia and Sarah could be sisters. With the same parents, raised in the same home, how could they be so utterly disparate?

Julia was so completely immersed in her thoughts, staring at hands she did not see, she failed to notice the man who strode across the lawn. Neither was she more than vaguely aware of the knocker sounding at the front door and Janet brushing by on her way to answer it. It was only when Janet returned and spoke that she looked up.

"Miss Julia, it's Captain Baxter. Said he didn't want to disturb you, but he wonders if you'd favor him with a few minutes."

"Captain Baxter? Yes. Of course. Show him into the parlor," Julia said automatically as she pushed back her chair. "No. Never mind. I'll go myself."

When she entered the hall and saw David standing framed in the open door, she paused. There was a slight smile on his lips, but the triangular eyes beneath the brim of his tall silk hat were anxious. Seeing him so unexpectedly like this, Julia didn't know how she felt. Just a few short months ago she had been ready to throw everything over to run away with him, but now the numbness that overlay her life made him appear to be just a friend. A kind and good friend, but no more.

"Julia," he said, not moving from where he stood, "if you'd rather, I can come back another time."

"No." His words drew her forward and she held out both hands to him. "Come in, David. I simply didn't know you were home. You've taken me by surprise."

"I've just arrived. Left my luggage over at the station in Hyannis and came directly here. I had to be with you."

As he took her hands, Julia noticed the band of black on the sleeve of his dark suit.

"That's thoughtful of you," she said as she glanced at it. "Stephen would have appreciated it."

" 'Tisn't for Stephen. May I come in and tell you about it?"

"Oh, yes. Please do. I didn't mean to keep you standing here." As he removed his hat and entered the house, she added, "I don't mean to be rude, but I can't seem to remember my manners anymore."

"There's no need for manners with me, Julie," he said. There was great sweetness in his smile as he followed her into the parlor. "I came as soon as

I could. We had good air all the way, and I doubt anyone could have made it quicker. The *Yankee Girl's* one of the fastest clippers afloat, and she seemed to know she had to get me home quick to you."

Julia chose a straight chair, far removed from the others, and sat down. The distance was necessary for what she had to say. With all the doors and windows open, it was easy to see if anyone approached the room, and she felt there was privacy enough for their conversation.

"David, before anything else, I have to tell you that things aren't as they were before. Things between us. Stephen's death has changed everything."

"The way you feel about me?" He chose a large comfortable armchair from which he could see her, but he made no attempt to move it any closer.

"Yes." Her eyes were paler than their normal sapphire as she looked steadily at him. "The truth is that I can't feel anything. Not for you. Not for anyone. I've had so much emotion, there's none left. I'm empty of everything but sorrow and regret."

"I understand, Julie," he said with great gentleness. "I can wait. I only wanted to wish you a happy birthday . . . and to be with you. It's enough for now."

"There's still Cynthia, David," she said firmly. She must make him see the reality of the situation as clearly as she did.

"No. There isn't." He touched the band of crepe on his arm. "She died in late June. Bearing a child . . . or rather trying not to bear one."

"Yours?" She was shocked by the news and unconsciously laid a hand over the spot where her own child lay.

"How could it be?" He looked at her gravely. "I hadn't seen her for over two years. The news came to me in London."

"And the child?"

"It didn't survive."

"Oh." The full horror of the story struck Julia. That wretched woman. "I guess I should say I'm sorry, but I can't. She never gave you any happiness. All she ever did was make your life a misery. But now you know what it's like. To lose someone."

"No, Julie. I don't." He shifted in his chair as though he were about to rise, but then he settled down again. "I never had her, you see. I never had what you had with Stephen. When I heard the news, 'twas like hearing a stranger had gone. To be truthful, the only thing I felt was a little pity for her and a great deal of relief for myself. It's not something I'd tell anyone but you. They're not feelings to be proud of, but I have to be honest with you. I can't pretend to mourn her."

"No. We can't pretend, can we? Else all would be a lie."

He leaned forward with his arms on his knees. Julia watched his bowed

275

head with its smoothed-down dark blond curls as he studied the hands he had clasped before him. Then he raised his head to look at her. There was no mistaking the determination in his eyes.

"There's one important thing left, Julie. This time we mustn't miss each other. If it takes ten years, I'll wait for you. I want you to know that. Don't even contemplate marrying any other man but me ever again."

"You needn't worry about that," she said dully. "Marriage is the last thing I have in mind."

"Not now, maybe, but you felt the same way after Jason died, and fool that I was, I thought you could never care for me. I have no intention of making that mistake twice. I won't rush you, but all you ever have to do is say the time's come."

Julia rose and went to the window to see if Clara and her mother were on their way from the cutting garden, but the lawn was bare with only an almost imperceptible rustling in the tree tops. When she returned to her chair, she saw that he was staring with a startled look at her body. She hadn't realized that her cool, lightweight dress with only one petticoat was so revealing. Most people hadn't guessed her condition yet. When his eyes traveled to her face for confirmation, she nodded.

"It's true," she said as she sat down in the same isolated chair.

He started to speak several times, but when the question wouldn't come, Julia answered it anyway.

"It's yours, David. No one else knows it, and we can never let it be known, but it is your child."

David sprang up to go to her, but her coolness and the warning in her eyes held him off. Instead he put his hands in his pockets and stood looking down at her. Then he went to look out the window she had just quitted. Julia turned to watch him, but he stood immobile with his head leaning against an upper pane. Only his back was visible.

"Julie, you have to marry me now," he said without moving. His voice was very low, almost indistinct. "You can't keep my child from me."

"I won't, David." She almost rose to go to him, to touch him, to reassure him, but she couldn't. "You can come whenever you like, see it whenever you wish."

"I want more than that!" There was a harsh edge to his voice she had never heard before. Then he was in front of her with both of her hands gathered in his. "I want to be with you when it's born. When it first opens its eyes, I want it to look at me and say, 'That's my father.' "

"I'll teach the child to love you, David," she said earnestly.

"That's not enough. I'm not going to be Uncle David to my own child."

"David!" She abruptly pulled her hands away from his grasp. "We can't say it's yours. Not in front of the world. Do you realize what kind of name that would give him?"

276

"Yes. I know, but it's not necessary. I'll adopt him. Soon as he's born, I'll adopt him. From the day he can speak, he's going to call me Papa." He towered over her. There was no hint of a smile on his taut face, and his words rang out like an iron mallet striking an anvil. "And that's not all. I'm not going to let you go through childbirth alone. I'm not going to lose you. I'm going to be with you, and the only way I can do that is if I'm your husband. You're going to marry me, Julia Howard, whether you want to or not. And you want to. You just don't realize it at this moment."

Julia took a deep breath and stared at him in dismay. This was a David she had never seen before, one whose voice she had never heard. Then she straightened her back and lifted her chin at him.

"I've had some strange proposals in my day, but that's the queerest one I ever did hear. You don't *tell* a woman that she's going to marry you, David. You ask her."

"Well, I'm not asking you. I'm telling you. You're in no shape to make decisions for yourself just now, so I'll have to make them for you."

All desire to fight him left. She wouldn't submit to him, but she was not going to argue with him. He had meant too much to her in the past. Perhaps he would mean just as much in the future. But now he had to leave her in peace.

"All right, David. I'll marry you, but not now. Not for a long time. I wouldn't make you a proper wife till then anyway."

"I don't give a damn whether you make me a proper wife or not. I just want you to *be* my wife, proper, improper, or whatever the hell else you want to be. And you're going to be my wife before . . ." He paused to count off the months in his head. "Before December. That's when it's due, isn't it?"

"Yes. Near Christmas." Somehow she had to divert him from his course. What he proposed was completely out of the question. "David, it's not seemly for us to marry so soon. Neither one of us has been . . . alone that long."

"I don't give a damn whether it's seemly or not. It's done. It's done all the time." He crossed his powerful arms and glared down at her. "You have one child and another on the way who need a father. With all your responsibilities, you need a man. The most natural thing in the world would be for you to remarry. I doubt there's many who'd talk."

"Oh, David," she said wearily, "it's not really the talk I'm worried about. It's me. It's you. I don't have anything to give you. Someday I hope that I will."

Suddenly he squatted down beside her and took her hands again. His face became as gentle as his voice. "I'm not asking for anything, Julie. That can wait till after the child's born."

"That's not what I meant." She tried to withdraw her hands, but he held them firmly clasped. "Can't I make you understand? I'm not capable of *any* kind of love. In fact, whenever I think of you, I feel guilty. As though our love had something to do with Stephen's death."

"Did he know?" he asked with sudden alarm. "About the child?"

"I don't think so. No. I'm sure he didn't. He couldn't have kept it to himself if he had."

David looked relieved and nodded.

"Then it had nothing to do with his death. You've got to put that out of your mind. It was the wreck. He never did get over it. I've heard the story of how he went. Oh, Julie, he did enough to you while he was alive. Don't let him ruin our lives now. We could be happy."

"Happy?" She looked at him as though he had spoken a word in a strange language. "I hope so. I'd like to feel happy again someday."

"You will. I promise you that." He released her hands and stood up. "I'll give you till the end of November. After that, I'll listen to no excuses from you."

"What happens at the end of November?" Clara, standing in the doorway, looked at them suspiciously. Under her daughter's scrutiny, Julia felt the guilt in double measure.

"Nothing that we need be concerned about now, darling," she said more calmly than she felt. "Did you have a nice time with Thomas?"

"No. He pulled my braids, and when Aunt Martha made him stop, he said some bad words. Then he said Papa was a sot. What's that, Mama?"

"That's something Thomas should get a good hiding for," David said. "Which Thomas is that?"

"Sarah's son," Julia answered. "She came over to wish me a happy birthday."

"Oh, did she?" David looked at her skeptically.

"Yes. Run along, dear," she said to Clara. "Uncle David and I have some things we want to discuss. You may have tea in the kitchen."

"I'm going to have it with Gran and we're going to have it in here."

"Then go wash your hands," Julia said firmly. When they heard Clara skipping up the stairs, Julia looked at David. "Seems we're to be invaded. Will you stay for tea?"

"No. I'd best be getting on home. They don't know I'm coming, and since my father's ailing, I'm anxious to see him."

"I'm sorry. I didn't know or I'd have sent something over."

"He's getting on. Almost eighty-two now. I was born when he was just my age. Strange, isn't it?"

"I suppose." Julia rose to see him to the door.

After he had picked up his hat, he looked at her for a long moment but made no move to touch her. "You won't forget what I said? November."

"It's not likely I'll forget, but I still haven't agreed to it."

"You will. I'll be by tomorrow to remind you. And the day after that. And all the days that follow till I sail."

"How soon?"

"Depends on how fast we can get the work done, but no matter what, I'll be back come October and I'm not leaving again till you're my wife."

"David, what if I've changed?"

"You haven't." He clapped his hat on and strode off without another look.

Julia leaned against the door and watched him go, but it was only a moment before his long legs had taken him around the bend in the road.

Chapter Eighteen

1855

David was true to his word. Although he did not try to pressure her into agreement again, each day he spoke of his intention to marry Julia in November as though it were a settled thing. Then in early August, he was gone.

Once he had sailed, problems at the shipyard began to multiply. Daniel's requests that she return to work became increasingly urgent, and his distress finally forced her out of the lethargy of grief for a few hours each day.

At the shipyard she found she had to concentrate most of her wits and energy on keeping current with the modified designs produced by the leading naval architects. Competition was stiff and shipowners were demanding vessels with larger cargo-carrying capacities than the true clippers had. Speed was still important, but freight rates around the world were much reduced. There had been a ripple of concern in shipping circles last year when, for the first time, a merchant vessel using steam power had circumnavigated the globe. However, American shipping became complacent once more when it was discovered that the British-built *Argo* was a full-rigged ship, which used steam only as an auxiliary device. Furthermore, while she had made good time, she had not broken any records.

On a cold day in late October, when the northwest wind had swept the sky into a clear, dazzling blue, Julia sat with the plans for a medium clipper spread out on the table near the stove. Her child bulked large within her, and she was no longer able to sit with any degree of comfort at the tall desk.

As she went over the plans for a ship that was full above the waterline while still retaining the slightly concave lines below as well as the fair ends necessary for sailing speed, she wondered what her father would have thought of her use of plans in addition to a half model. The amount of mathematics now required to calculate centers of effort, gravity, buoyancy, lateral plane, and displacement was far greater than it had been in his day. She had little time now to spend out in the yard. All that, she had to leave to Daniel and Philip Sears while she labored over designs and went over plans with prospective customers. Correspondence and paperwork claimed the rest of her day.

Through the closed door and windows, she could hear the music of a busy shipyard. Above the hammering, sawing, pounding, ringing sounds of tools, men's voices could be heard shouting to one another. A man passed close to the office whistling a popular song. The sounds of childhood. The sounds of her life.

She leaned back in her chair and remembered the early days of her apprenticeship when she had chafed at being tied to the office by her father. How she had longed to be out there among the activity! She smiled as she thought of the look of intensity in her father's dark blue eyes as he explained to a restless twelve-year-old that the heartbeat of the entire business was in the office.

Now she was grateful to him for the discipline he had taught her. Of all his lessons, it was probably the most valuable. Without it, she would have found the long hours at the drawing board unbearably tedious.

Well, Papa, you taught me how to work.

She brushed her curls back from her face and lowered her eyes to the plans again, but the child stirred within her, reminding her of its father. David had promised to return in October, but it seemed that this was one promise he wouldn't keep. In three days, it would be November. His letters had begun to arrive a week after he sailed and had continued in a steady stream since then. 'Twas obvious why he hadn't broken any records when he'd stopped for every homeward-bound vessel in order to post a letter to her, she thought with amusement. His letters from England had been filled with complaints about the delays he was encountering.

However, Julia had felt nothing but relief with the news of each delay. His letters spoke of a November wedding as confidently as though she had accepted him even though each of her letters had contained a flat refusal. Yet once he was home, she wondered how long she would be able to hold out against him. As long as he stayed away, it was fairly easy. A fondness for him was returning, but she was still not ready for the emotional demands of marriage.

It was difficult to concentrate on the ship plans when she thought of what the next months would bring. She welcomed the distraction when the clerk, Roger Jackson, brought some papers over for her to check. She blamed her restlessness on the north wind that spoke of winter.

It must have affected Daniel Sears, too. He had taken to hovering over her lately. He had already been in twice this afternoon with hints that she should go home and rest. Now as she handed the last paper to the sandy-haired clerk, she glanced out the window and saw Daniel approaching again. When he opened the door, she unfolded a piece of linen and spread it over her drawings to protect them from the dust.

"All right, Daniel," she said as he limped into the room. "I'll go home, but only because you're not going to get any work done unless I do. I wish you wouldn't fuss about me so."

" 'Twasn't that, Miss Julia." Daniel's swarthy face was set in its most expressionless lines, which meant he was going to be stubborn. "Just thought you'd want to know the signals are up for the *Yankee Girl*. She's been sighted off Provincetown."

"Oh?" She picked up her coat and held it out to him. "Well, thank you, Daniel."

"Reckon that means Captain Baxter will be here in a few days," Daniel said as he helped her on with the coat.

"Yes. I reckon it does." She tried to sound indifferent, but she silently began to count the days.

"Maybe *he'll* be able to convince you to stop drivin' yourself. You've got to get more rest, Miss Julia."

"Daniel, you ever been a mother?"

"Me?" Taken off guard, his eyebrows shot up. Then he shook his head and said trenchantly, "No, Miss Julia, but that don't mean I don't know what a woman needs."

"Well, since you've never been married, either, I don't think you qualify as an expert." Julia softened the sharpness of her voice with a smile. "Now stop fretting, Daniel."

As she drove the buggy between the fields and houses on Sesuit Neck Road and then turned onto Bridge Street, where the northwest wind swept across the marsh and forced her to huddle deeper into the folds of her sable coat, Julia found herself resenting the return of the *Yankee Girl*. What little peace she had been able to attain would be shattered by David's presence in just a few days.

Yet she knew that she had looked forward to him being near when the child was born. She would need his strength then. He had become more than her old friend, more than her lover. He was the father of the life that stirred and stretched within her. She would need him when his child burst through her pain to enter the world.

But not till December. Not till it was too late to consider marriage.

A gust of wind flattened the golden marsh grass, and Julia shivered. But the wind was not her enemy now. It would be buffeting the *Yankee Girl*.

281

The ship would be pounding on waves driven by that northwest headwind. It would be some time before the ship was sighted from Scargo Hill. Time enough, Julia thought.

Out of habit, the horse slowed when he neared Amelia's house. Julia shrugged and then reined him in. She might as well stop. There was nothing waiting for her at home, and despite Daniel's concern, she wasn't all that tired. Besides, it would be a good chance to take another look at her youngest nephew.

Jason had come easily into the world a month ago, and although he was tiny, Julia was convinced that she could see a resemblance to his namesake. Perhaps it was only her fancy, but from the moment he had opened his eyes, which were growing greener every day, she had felt as though she knew him and he her. She had spoken of the similarity once, but after Amelia and Samuel, pointing to the golden down that covered the top of his head, had vigorously denied it, she kept her peace.

She only hoped she would get as much joy from her own baby, she thought as she knocked at the door. When there was no immediate answer, she opened it and walked in.

As she entered the parlor, she was surprised to find William Thacher alone, pacing up and down the room while he talked to his grandson, who was almost lost in his burly arms. When William looked up to see Julia, he gave her a sheepish smile.

"Telling him sea stories already, Cousin William?" Julia asked as she took off her heavy coat.

"Never too young to start, mermaid," William said. There was a twinkle in his green eyes as he used his pet name for her. It went back to her childhood, back to the days when she had been the one he had told his sea stories to.

Julia smiled at him with a love born of those early days. With each year, that love had strengthened and grown. No matter how her world threatened to come apart, no matter how other people changed or left her, Cousin William remained a steady and solid reality.

"Where's Amelia?"

"In her room." William beamed as he looked down at his grandson. He shifted the child in his arms into a position that he thought would be more comfortable. "I sent her in to rest up while the children are down to your house."

"What are they doing down there?" Julia rubbed her hands briskly before the fire. Her fingers itched to touch the child, but they were still too cold.

"Well, Levi wanted to try out my new rig, so I packed them all off with him."

"Do you think that's wise?" Amelia's eldest son, Levi, was apt to tease his brothers and sisters unmercifully or else to snap at them with irritation.

William shrugged his heavy shoulders, and then glanced down at Jason to make sure he hadn't disturbed him.

"The boy's twelve now. Time he learned to handle a little responsibility. Time he went to sea, too, but Amelia digs in her heels every time I mention it."

"Not everyone's meant to go to sea, Cousin William," Julia said with suppressed laughter in her voice.

"Maybe not, but that boy's of good seafaring stock." William shot a penetrating look at Julia. "Or are you planning on puttin' him to work in the yard?"

"No." Julia sighed as she thought of the many times she had tried to interest Levi in the shipyard. "I thought maybe he'd take an interest, but all he can talk about is the West. I had hopes for a while since he's Papa's oldest grandson, but none of the boys will have anything to do with it."

"Well, don't lose heart. Maybe this one will." He joggled the child in his arms. "Little early to tell yet, though. He's got the makings for something, I'll tell you that, and he's got the right name for it."

"Thacher's a name to take pride in."

"'Tain't just that. When you splice Jason alongside of it, then it's something the boy can really be proud of. You taken a good look at him yet?" William glanced at the child and then at the repaired portrait, which now hung on the wall of Amelia's parlor, before he looked at Julia pointedly.

"Yes. Samuel and Amelia think he's the living image of his grandfather."

"Nope. 'Tisn't me he takes after, nor Ben neither. I held that other boy in my arms when he was just this age. Only difference I can see is the hair. William leaned over the child and crooned to it. Jason caught the white curly beard in his fingers and gurgled back.

Julia moved across the room to him and looked down at her nephew with a smile. "I should be getting on home if the children are there, but I'm just as glad I stopped by. Are you going to let me hold that child, Cousin William? I've got some rights on him, too."

"You're not in any shape to go holding him," William said, "but you perch yourself on the sofa and I'll set beside you. Then you can play with him all you want. You gettin' in practice?"

"I'd better." Julia, sitting down in one corner on the damask-covered sofa, left plenty of space for William. "It won't be long before I've got my own little boy."

"So it's a boy, is it?" William grinned as he plumped himself down beside her. Before Clara was born, Julia had declared with great vehemence that she was going to have a son.

"Yes. It's a boy," Julia said resolutely. She leaned over the baby and smiled into his eyes. "He's got to be."

"Why? You plannin' to bring him up the way your pa brought you up?"

"Just what do you mean by that?" Her smile disappeared as she prepared to spring to her father's defense.

"The shipyard. Always the shipyard. You never had a chance, Julie. I told your pa as much but he'd never listen to me. 'Twasn't what you really wanted, was it?"

"I don't remember," Julia said as she ran her finger over the baby's silken cheek and smiled once again into his solemn eyes.

"Well, I do. Always planning to run away to sea, you were."

"I got there."

"And the yard brung you home again, too, didn't it? You wasn't ready to come. I've seen you down there on the beach, just starin' out to sea. Saw your pa, too, with the same look in his eyes. Why don't you sell the yard and get out of it?"

"It belongs to my son." When she touched Jason's lips with the tip of her finger, he began to smile. "Besides, what would I do without it?"

"Get married again . . . someday. Knowing you, you'll most likely marry a shipmaster. Go to sea again. Seems that's the only place you'll ever really be happy."

Julia froze for a moment and then looked at her cousin. He, however, was intently studying his grandson.

Without thinking, she blurted out, "David Baxter's asked me to marry him."

"Figured as much. The only question was how long he was goin' to take gettin' round to it."

"He wants me to marry him before the baby's born."

"Then do it. You've always appeared right fond of him. Your son's going to need his father."

"Cousin William . . ."

"Any child you have is likely to be hard-headed, and it's goin' to need a man to keep it straight. Seems to me young Baxter's just the man for the job."

"But what will people think? Stephen hasn't been gone four months yet, and Cynthia only a little longer."

"I doubt that's your problem." He shot her a penetrating look from beneath his full white brows. "You never did give a hoot in hell what people thought."

"No." Julia drew her hand back from the child. His eyes were beginning to close. Just as well to let him sleep. "I guess it's got nothing to do with other people."

"Funny. I always thought . . . Well, so you've decided he's not the right man for you?"

"It's not that. I reckon he's the right man. It's just the wrong time."

William moved the baby protectively in his arms. He cleared his throat before he spoke.

284

"You know Jason said something of that sort to me once. He thought maybe you were too young to marry him till I pointed out that, if someone's right, there's no such thing as a wrong time. You sorry he married you?"

"No. Of course not. But this is different." William's persistence in talking about David only reminded her of thirteen thousand yards of canvas that soared high above a deck that was over two hundred and fifty feet long. No matter what the wind, the captain of the *Yankee Girl* would not be long in making port. "It's Stephen. He's still there. I can't stop thinking about him, missing him."

"Stephen left you a long time before he died."

"Not really. And I didn't leave him." Julia rubbed her long, tapering fingers together. "I never stopped loving him even though I hated the drinking and what it was doing to him. We were bound together. In a way, we still are."

"Let him go, Julie. It won't do him any good to hang on to him. Won't do you nor your child any good, neither. You've got to keep on living. So has David Baxter. You might as well do it together."

"But Stephen would be there between us."

"Maybe. But that won't last. And I think young Baxter's got enough sense to understand."

"But that's not enough. I have to be free when I go to him . . . and I'm not free." She touched the baby's spun-gold hair. "Cousin William, the *Yankee Girl*'s been sighted. Ever since I heard the news, I've been thinking about him, but I've been determined to hold out for a while. Maybe a year or two. Now I don't know. Could be you're right."

William got up and carried his grandson carefully to the cradle near the fire. With gentle fingers, he tucked the child under its small blanket. Then he turned and looked at Julia.

"If it is a boy, what are you planning on naming him?"

"Benjamin."

"I figured that, too. You think your father wants his grandson born half an orphan? More important, you think he'd want you to deprive a father of his own son?"

"Cousin William!" The shock Julia felt was very real. That anyone should have guessed the secret she had guarded so well! David was the only other person who could possibly know it for a fact, and she was positive he would never betray it. Who else knew?

"Don't trouble to deny it, Julie." William crossed his arms across his burly chest and looked down at her with far-seeing eyes that the sea had trained so well. "There's not a word I'd ever say agin' you nor let anyone else say it, neither. But I know what shape your husband was in. I also know who was around when that child was conceived. And I've been watchin' you and Baxter for years, just waitin' for an explosion. You forget

285

I've known you for quite a spell. What's in your nature is in your nature, but when you've got it in your power to put things right, you almighty better do it."

Julia leaned back against the cushions on the sofa. The wind had certainly been knocked out of her sails. When she spoke, her voice was very low.

"And you think it's right for me to marry David as soon as he gets home?"

"Damn right I do."

"Do you think anyone else guesses?"

"Doubt it." He sat down beside her and took her hand in his. His voice was kind when he said, "There's not many who keep an eye on you close as I do. I'll admit now I was right worried when I watched you being worn down day after day with never a release in sight. I tried, but there wasn't much you'd let me do for you."

"You did a lot, Cousin William. You always have." She squeezed his big square hand. "I think Daniel knows."

"Daniel Sears?"

"Aye. He was at the yard that night. I suspect he knew what was going on."

"Well, if he's the only other one, then you've got no cause to worry. I've never seen anyone get more than two words in a row out of Daniel. And he's loyal. I'll say that for him."

Julia looked at the fire and then at the cradle where Jason lay quietly sleeping. The peace in the room contrasted sharply with the turmoil she felt within herself.

"But if I rush into marrying David, don't you think there'll be other people who suspect? I don't want to hurt my son."

"Nonsense!" William snorted. " 'Twouldn't make any difference if you waited five years to marry. Those who're goin' to think things will, and those who aren't won't. Marry him now and let the next scandal that breaks blow it clean out of everyone's mind. Before you know it, there won't be a soul who remembers when you married or how."

"Memories are long around here," Julia said with a sad wistfulness. "We have to think of Clara, too. She still goes into Stephen's room and wanders around, touching his things. I've been reluctant to have them packed away because of her. If she ever heard some gossip and believed . . ."

"Clara's not likely to hear anything," William interrupted. "And that child needs a father more than most. How does she take to David?"

"She always liked him before, but she started acting edgy around him when he was here after Stephen died." Julia reluctantly pulled out her watch and looked at it. "I'll just look in on Amelia and then I'd best be on my way. I'll see that Levi gets your rig back to you soon."

286

"Do that." He stood up as she rose. "Julie, you most likely think I'm an interferin' old man, and most likely I am. Do what you think best."

"First you try to tell me what I have to do. Then you switch tacks on me. You almost had me convinced."

"I told you what's right, but I don't want you to do it just because I say so. You've got to believe it yourself. At any rate, invite me to the wedding whether it's next month or five years from now."

"I'm expecting you to give me away, Cousin William. I wouldn't feel properly wed unless you were there." She glanced up at Jason's patched portrait, which Amelia and Samuel had hung. "Do you remember . . ."

"Yes, I remember," he said gruffly. "And now's no time to be talkin' about it. 'Twas nineteen years ago. You never could let anyone go, Julie."

"No, and I'm too old to learn now."

That night Julia vacillated from one decision to a compromise to a completely different decision, and swung the compass back again. Each time she turned in her bed, it seemed the baby turned twice within her as though reminding her that it needed sleep even if she didn't. When early morning brought a darkened sky and a northeasterly wind that scattered occasional showers in its course, Julia decided to stay home.

With Clara at school and Lydia in one of her gentle, otherworldly moods, the house would be more restful than the shipyard. If Daniel had any questions, he could send a message, and her fund of inspiration was at a low ebb.

She almost wished that David were here instead of battling the wind on his way to Boston. Once he was home, she would be able to tell him that there was definitely no chance she would marry him before the child was born. With that out of the way, her mind would be free to do the work that she wanted to accomplish before the baby confined her to the house.

Curled up close to the parlor fire, she had given herself up to the luxury of dreaming about her unborn child when a sudden gust of wind screamed around the windows and blew the front door loudly open. With a feeling of irritation at whoever hadn't latched it securely, she got heavily to her feet. It was most likely Clara, who seemed to leave everything half done these days, she thought as she opened the parlor door.

However, when she looked out into the hall, the front door was shut and David Baxter stood there, shedding dripping oilskins from over his rough clothes.

Julia stood frozen in the doorway. She was incapable of any words, any motion. All that she could do was stare at him.

"Hello." David grinned at her. He looked more like a schoolboy who had succeeded in playing truant than a captain home from the sea.

"How did you get here?" Julia asked and it sounded far more like an accusation than a welcome.

"Schooner." He shucked off his boots, and then in one swift movement, he had her in his arms. "Is that any way to greet your future husband?"

"David!" She stiffened and backed away from him.

He dropped his arms. This was not the homecoming he had envisioned, the homecoming he had looked forward to more than any other since he had been a boy. During the long days at sea, he had watched her figurehead dip and soar across the waves. He had relived the time when she had sailed with him on the *Free Wind,* and he had managed to convince himself that when he returned home, Julia would be waiting for him with a warm welcome. Now this.

He anxiously searched her face for an answer. Then his eyes traveled down her body. His child. The weight of it seemed too much for her slender body.

"Are you all right, Julie?" he asked with grave concern. "Daniel said you sent word you weren't going to the yard today."

"I'm fine." She couldn't bear his eyes upon her. They demanded too much.

Not yet, David. Not yet.

She deliberately turned her back on him and went into the parlor. "Just because I decided to take a day off is no reason for everyone to make a fuss."

"He says you're working too hard." He followed her into the room and closed the door behind him.

"Daniel Sears is an old woman," Julia said sharply. She carefully lowered her bulk into a comfortable wingback chair.

"All right, Julie, what is it?" He moved to the fire to warm himself, but he was careful not to block its warmth from her. "I thought you'd want me here. I hoped you'd need me. But you sound downright angry with me for coming."

"Well, you should give some kind of warning before you just burst in here. It's getting to be a habit with you. What have you done with the *Yankee Girl?*"

"She's on her way to Boston. I made arrangements with a fishing schooner to carry me home. I promised you I'd be here in October, and there wasn't much of it left." He chafed his hands in front of the fire and stared at the low flames that danced over the coals. When he looked at her again, he was frowning. "If you don't want me here, I'll leave."

She could see that he meant it. He *would* leave. If he did, when would he come back again? She needed him, but she didn't dare let him see how much.

"No, please. Don't go. I am glad you're home. I . . . It's just such a shock to see you so soon. When I heard the *Yankee Girl* had been sighted, I figured you'd be another week or so. Then you just suddenly appear. I've never heard of a master jumping ship before he made port. How could you just go off and leave her?"

" 'Twasn't any problem. Not when I wanted to be with you. Henderson's a good mate, and I'd already gone into everything with him. Soon as we sighted the Cape, I started praying I'd come across someone to ferry me home." He spoke slowly, almost absently, as he watched her. "You are all right, aren't you, Julie?"

"Yes. Maybe a little tired from toting this child around. I'd forgotten how uncomfortable it can be." She looked up at him and saw that his hair was clinging to his forehead in wet curls. The rough wool shirt that covered his broad shoulders was patched with damp. He was very dear to her, and his presence was reassuring. "You'll stay till after the baby comes, won't you? You said you would."

He studied her thoughtfully for a moment. Then he said, "Your letters, Julie. They were so cold. You couldn't have meant what you wrote."

"I meant it," she said quietly. "But just because I can't marry you doesn't mean I don't want you here."

Leaving the fire, he went to a side window and pulled the velvet curtains aside to look out.

"It's stopped raining. After I left the yard, I went home. I've got my parents' buggy outside so we can go see the parson. If we leave now, you won't get wet."

"Now!"

"Aye." He let the curtain drop and came to stand directly in front of her. "There's not much time. The banns will have to be read."

"David, what I said in my letters was no." She clasped the arms of the chair so tightly her knuckles whitened against the red damask.

"Maybe. But that's not an answer I'll listen to." He leaned over and cupped her chin in the palm of one hand. There was no way for her to evade the determination in his grey-green eyes. "I'll tell you this, Julie. If you don't come with me right now, I'm going down to Boston. I'm going to get the *Yankee Girl* unloaded and then I'm going to fill her up again with goods. As soon as I do, I'll be on my way to China."

"Before the baby's born?" She opened her eyes wide as panic filled her. He couldn't! She was no longer young. She suddenly realized how frightened she was of the childbirth to come. She had counted on his love to get her through it.

"Aye. Before the baby's born." And the set of that large jaw said that he meant it. "There's too many people, including me, who've put up with your nonsense for too many years."

"David, you promised!" As she pleaded with him, her eyes darkened to indigo and her voice was full of desperation.

"Are you coming?" He dropped his hand. A remoteness came over his face as though he were disassociating himself from her.

She drew a deep breath that sounded like a sob. He was really going to do it. He was going to go away and leave her when she needed him most. The child moved, and she instinctively laid her hand over her stomach. If she let David go now, her son might never know his father.

"You don't leave me much choice, do you?" she said in a low voice of acceptance as she looked down at the front of her black dress.

"No.". He leaned over and kissed her lightly on the forehead. Then he laid his hand on top of the one she rested over her child. "I didn't want to force you into it, Julie, but you didn't leave me much choice, either."

"Oh, David!" Suddenly she wanted to be in his arms, to feel the strength, the comfort of his large powerful body. With her free hand, she reached up to him.

He swept her up off the chair and carried her to the sofa. When his lips hungrily met hers, he broke through all the barriers that Stephen's death had created.

"You know I only did it because I love you, don't you?" he said in a voice that was husky with love and relief.

"I know." And she did. His love was everywhere around her.

Although she was aware of the shock that swept through the congregation the first Sunday the banns were read and of the smirks that followed, Julia went to church with David and sat determinedly proud beside him. As for David, he might never have known that they existed for all the awareness he showed. But at the end of each service, he swept her protectively out of the church before anyone could close in on them. Wherever she went, whether to the yard or to the beach or to visit Amelia, he went with her. He arrived at her house when she was still having breakfast in the morning and left her only after supper.

Instead of being annoyed by his continual presence, as she would have in years past, she enjoyed it. There was no need for constant conversation. It was enough for each that the other was there. Even the deep sorrow she still felt for Stephen was softened by David's nearness.

David chartered the *Yankee Girl* to an old friend as soon as all the cargo was discharged so that he was free to concentrate upon things closer to home. At the shipyard, he took an interest in Julia's designs and began to take a hand in some of her work. He would follow Daniel or Philip Sears as they made the rounds of the three vessels they were building. In a way that neither Jason nor Stephen had, he became profoundly involved in the business at the yard. Often he made suggestions in his quiet way, and Julia was glad to have a fresh eye that was not hypnotized by a routine that had built up over the years.

Once she realized that he would be able to handle affairs that were beyond Daniel's scope after she was confined to the house, she was doubly grateful to him. And she could see a great deal of wisdom in their approaching marriage. As her husband, he could deal with customers in a way only the head of a firm or a partner could.

David's parents welcomed the news, especially his mother, who immediately began to stitch delicate embroidery on tiny garments for the baby she had decided to adopt as her grandchild. When Julia saw them, she almost cried. She longed to tell the frail old lady that the child really was of her own blood, but she was afraid that she would only succeed in scandalizing her. As for her own family, they were unreservedly delighted except for Clara, who only watched and would express no opinion one way or the other. When Julia saw Sarah occasionally at a distance, she detected a disdainful smile, but since she no longer considered Sarah part of her family, she told herself it made no difference.

Their wedding was to take place just a month before their child was due. Although it had been necessary for the banns to be read publicly, it was possible to keep the date of the ceremony a secret. At first Julia had wanted just the two of them to meet at the church with the necessary witnesses, but David had been in complete disagreement.

" 'Tisn't just a matter between you and me, Julie," he had told her. "From now on, I'm part of your family and you're part of mine. They're going to have to put up with us and they might as well be in at the start of it. I know for a fact that my parents would be sorely hurt if they weren't included."

Julia finally agreed, even though she worried about her mother. More than that, she wondered how Clara would react.

Chapter Nineteen

1855–1856

It was November, but the sun shone brightly in the sky and a sweet south wind warmed the earth. Though a false promise of the spring that lay many cold months ahead filled the air, it felt like a true promise to Julia as she drove over familiar roads with William Thacher.

There were several buggies and a carriage lining the road in front of the tall-steepled white church, but a space had been left at the end of the walk for them. As William drew up before the church, Julia caught a glimpse of Clara going inside with Amelia and Samuel. Only Daniel Sears loitered at the foot of the steps. When he saw Julia and William in the carriage, he came limping rapidly towards them. He looked stiff and a little uncomfortable in his formal clothes.

"Wait till I get there to help you, Miss Julia," he called out. "Don't try to do it yourself."

"What in tarnation do you think I'm here for?" William growled at him and flung down the reins. "I still got both feet out of the grave."

"Well, it won't do no harm for the two of us to tend to her," Daniel said as he swung open the door of the carriage. "She don't take care the way she should."

"Daniel," Julia said, laughing as she gave a hand to each of the men, "you've got to stop that. I think you'd have this baby for me if you could."

Daniel's face suffused with color, and William looked at him speculatively before he firmly tucked Julia's hand beneath his arm.

As they went up the walk, Julia's earlier joy in the day evaporated. There had been another day, and it didn't seem that far in the past, when she had strolled here beside her father. The lawns on either side, now empty, had been filled with a boisterous, cheering crowd. There had been another man waiting inside for her then and all of life had seemed to lie ahead. A deep sadness took possession of her as she thought of the new mound in the graveyard that overlooked the golden marsh.

Till death do us part, she thought. And now I'll say it again. For the third time.

I shouldn't remarry. I shouldn't.

The child within her seemed to grow heavier. She shouldn't even be here. She was too tired to stand through a wedding. All that she wanted to do was to go home, lie down, and shut out the rest of the world. Her steps became slower.

"Come along, lass," William said when he felt her begin to lag. "No time for dallyin'. They're all waitin' for you."

She nodded and tried to smile as they went up the steps and into the vestibule. Daniel looked hesitantly at her with his hand on one of the inner doors.

"Go ahead, Daniel," she said.

"You goin' to be all right, Miss Julia? You look mighty pale."

"I'm fine, Daniel. Go find a seat. We'll be there in a minute."

"Well . . . If you say so." He looked at her reluctantly. Then he pushed open one of the double doors and let it swing shut behind him.

While she unbuttoned her coat, Julia was aware that William was studying her and it made her feel defensive.

"I reckon a bride has a right to be nervous," she said.

"You're not nervous." His voice was gruff as he took her coat from her and hung it up. "You got your mind too much on the past and not enough on the future."

"I needed more time." She smoothed the flounces of her heavy silk dress. Grey. What an awful color for a wedding.

"Well, time's just what you haven't got." After clapping his tall hat on the stand, he turned briskly back to her and held out his arm. "You ready?"

"Yes." She moistened her lips just before they entered the church.

Time slipped, and for a moment she almost expected the man waiting at the altar to be Stephen. However, there was no mistaking David's giant frame, which even the expert tailoring of his new frock coat could not conceal. His eyes were fixed steadily on hers, and he smiled as he watched her approach. She returned his smile and relaxed. There was no sense of the excitement she had felt in her two previous marriages. This man was not a stranger, but one she had known most of her life. David was the one she always should have married.

It even seemed strange that a ceremony was necessary, she thought when he held out his hand to her and welcomed her with an enormous grin that was far from solemn. He was a part of her. He always had been. And within her, she carried the physical joining of their two lives, which had been intermeshed in so many other ways years ago. As the Reverend Lamson began to say the words that would make them one in the eyes of the world, Julia thought that the best way to describe how she felt was comfortable.

After taking both of her hands in his, David looked down at her for a moment with the seriousness of his love shining clear on his face before he began to make his vows in a firm, quiet voice. Julia's voice rang true and clear through the church, but the words she spoke were for David alone. When he slipped the narrow gold band on her finger, her hand felt strangely light. The wide gold ring that had been Stephen's choice had been so much heavier.

There was another small moment of sadness when they turned to leave the altar together and she saw the faces that were smiling up at them in the sunlit church. The front pews were filled, but the faces weren't all the same. Instead of her father, it was Cousin William who stood beside her mother. Michael was gone from Amelia's side to be replaced by Samuel. Even Sarah's and Aaron's places were now occupied by Megan and Hiram Richardson.

Yet the places *were* filled, she reminded herself. The tides of life might sweep some away, but they washed others to her shores. And she saw love and affection in those faces that were turned towards her.

When they reached the second pew, David paused and Julia could see that he was looking down at her daughter. He held out his hand and said, "Clara, will you come with us?"

Clara, her fair hair concealed by a black bonnet, stood looking doubtfully up at the too-tall man, and when she tilted her head to one side, Julia held her breath. There was no telling what Clara might do. There was a strained hush throughout the church while David remained smiling easily down at the child. Then Amelia broke the tension by pushing Clara forward toward her new stepfather.

"Go on," she whispered.

Very slowly and very reluctantly, Clara put out her hand to touch the large one which David had never moved since he had first extended it. Then she gripped it with all her might and broke into a grin.

When they reached the vestibule, Clara tugged at his hand.

"I want to ask you something," she said in a hushed voice.

"Anything you like," David said as he bent down so that his ear was on a level with her mouth.

"What do I call you now?" Clara whispered.

"Why . . . whatever you like," David said slowly.

"But I don't know!" she said with distress. "You're not Uncle David anymore."

"Well, I figure you're my daughter from now on, and I'd be pleased if you'd call me Papa, but I doubt you'd feel comfortable doing it."

"No." She looked at him with great solemnity and greater urgency. It was obvious that this was a very important matter to her, one that had to be settled immediately.

"How about Dada?" he said, giving the most serious consideration to his words. "I've forgotten where, but somewhere in my travels I've heard children call their father that."

Clara silently mouthed the syllables. Then she said, "Yes. That might do. 'Tis a lot like David, too, so it won't seem too strange."

"It's settled then?"

"Yes . . . Dada."

David grinned conspiratorially at her as he straightened up. "Now we'd best get your mother home and off her feet, Clara. Why don't you run down and make sure the carriage is ready for us?"

Clara nodded and ran out through the doors, glad to be released from the adult world.

"Thank you, David," Julia said once the child had gone. "I've been fretting about that. How she was going to take all this."

"No more than I have," he said with a relieved laugh. "I've been certain all along that she resented me trying to take her father's place. Yet all she wanted was to find her own."

When they reached home, Julia was happy to sink down on the sofa while the family filled the room around her. The morning had been more of a strain than she had realized, and it felt good to prop her feet up on the needlepoint footstool, which Hiram Richardson carried over for her the minute she sat down.

"I'm getting in a little practice, you see." His face was radiant when he sat down beside her and he looked much younger than his years. "Has Megan told you our news?"

"No. There's been too much going on ever since you arrived yesterday for us to have a chance for more than a few words." So much pride was shining in his light blue eyes, Julia decided to venture a guess. "Are you trying to tell me you're going to become a father?"

"Precisely," he said and beamed at her. "At last. Though I really shouldn't say that. The baby may carry my blood, but Robert's my first child. I adopted him, you know."

"Yes, I know." Julia wondered how she had ever so misjudged this man. But perhaps she hadn't. Perhaps he had changed under Megan's influence. Whatever the truth, she found herself liking him very much. "It was good of you."

"Not good *of* me. Good for me. That boy has a joy of life I can taste, and when I look at him, I can see a little of Megan there, too. I recognize that you always thought I was too old for her, Julia, but I've tried to be good to her and the boy."

"And you've succeeded." Megan's voice was light and silvery. "What are you two doing? Sitting there gossiping about me?"

"Hiram was just telling me your secret."

"Oh, he wasn't supposed to. I wanted to be the one to tell you. Just for that you can go fetch me a glass of sherry." Megan smiled at her husband. When he rose, she sat down in his place. "It won't be for a long time yet. Almost seven months."

"Between you and Amelia and me, we seem to be trying to populate the state of Massachusetts." Julia studied her friend's face. She was no longer the slender sylph she once had been. Marriage and her comfortable life in Boston had added a little flesh to her bones. Yet there was still an elfin sparkle in her black eyes. "And we're none of us all that young anymore."

"We're not so old, either. Oh, Julia, Hiram's so happy about it. Though he never said so, I believe he thought he was too old to be a father."

"And obviously he isn't."

"No." Megan giggled mischievously. "He certainly isn't. That was one time you were wrong, Julie, and I was right. And I never want to hear you say anything about someone's age again."

"You're happy, too, aren't you, Megan?"

"Yes. Extraordinarily happy. I look back on those last days in Tahiti and it all seems like something terrible that happened to someone else. If it weren't for Robert, I don't think I could believe it did happen."

"You were someone else for a little while, Megan, and it's no wonder after what you'd been through. But now you remind me of the girl I first knew. Remember the rock pool and Mama Omemema?"

Julia could still see Megan with a pink flower in her hair tossing aside her role as a missionary's wife as easily as she had tossed aside her black stockings. With two native girls as their only companions, they had swum almost naked many times in that hidden pool. However, they had visited the old Tahitian woman only once. They had sat in her small house, and the palm leaves had rustled in the breeze as an accompaniment to Omemema's liquid voice.

"I'll never forget them. Do you remember her predictions? I can still hear some of her words." Megan frowned slightly as she tried to recall them. "As the clouds rise together from the sea to fall upon the mountain streams, so will our thoughts and lives touch and meet, separate, and meet again time after time. She was right, wasn't she?"

"Yes. She was right about a lot of things." Julia's eyes darkened to a deeper shade of blue as she heard the old Polynesian woman's voice and the young Megan's interpretation overlaying it. You will live a long, long life, but you will die many small deaths before the big one.

Megan, too, remembered the words and she caught Julia's hand. "Don't think about that, Julia. Just remember she promised you much joy, and today should be a joyful one for you. It is for me, just seeing you and David together. I know you'll be all right as long as you have him to take care of you."

"Yes. I think I will be." Julia looked across the room at her husband, who was standing with one arm draped around Clara's shoulders while he talked to Cousin William and Samuel. "He's so solid. Like a boulder. And just about as immovable."

"And Amelia's done wonders with Samuel," Megan said as she followed the direction of Julia's eyes. "Why, do you know he actually smiles nowadays? I couldn't believe it when he smiled at me the first time this morning, but he's done it five times already. I've counted."

"Oh, Megan." Julia giggled. "You haven't."

"I most certainly have. Now you see, you were wrong there, too. I could never have lifted that blackness he carried around with him, but Amelia's just too sunny for anyone to resist. I must go talk to her and find out how she does it," Megan said as she rose supplely from the sofa. "We have to set out early tomorrow morning, and I want a chance to talk to everyone before we go. After all, this is my family as well as yours. You gave them to me."

"You've never heard from yours?"

"Never, but it doesn't matter so much anymore. I think perhaps I have a better one now." She looked fondly over at her husband.

For a moment, Julia enjoyed simply looking around the room at these people who were so dear to her. Her mother and David's parents were gossiping in one corner, while Amelia and Megan were in another. Clara was carefully offering a tray of sandwiches around under Aunt Martha's watchful eye. Even Daniel and Philip Sears, whom Hiram Richardson had engaged in conversation, looked at ease.

"I know you said you didn't want anything to drink," David said as he sat down next to her and offered her a glass, "but I doubt one glass of sherry will harm the child."

"Maybe a few sips." Julia smiled as she took the glass from him.

"For a girl who told me she had no intention of marrying me a few short weeks ago, you look right happy," he said, raising his glass to her. "I've been watching you and I don't believe you've stopped smiling once since we left the church."

"Does it show that much?" She let her hand drift to his leg to feel the solid reality of him. "I am happy, David. Very happy."

"They say brides are always beautiful, but I doubt there's ever been one as lovely as you."

"In my shape? Hardly."

"You are, Julie, you really are." He draped his arm along the back of the sofa behind her and looked at her with eyes that were shining with love. Then he made a wry face. "It's the groom in this case who's sadly lacking. You've always married good-looking men. I never have been able to understand why you took to me."

"Haven't you, David?" She squeezed his thigh. The hard muscles in it moved under her touch. "You're better-looking than you give yourself credit for, but even if you weren't, it wouldn't matter. I've been building vessels long enough to know that it's not so much what's above the water-line that counts. It's what's below."

Once the wedding was over, Julia gave in to David's persuasions. She no longer went to the shipyard, though she continued to receive reports from Daniel and David. For the first time in many years, she allowed herself to relax. The long nights spent with David beside her gave a stability to her days. The entire household seemed to bloom under his warmth and never-failing cheerfulness. While Julia sometimes found Clara looking wistfully at Stephen's portrait, the child nevertheless seemed to accept and even rejoice in David's presence in the family.

Julia was impatient with the slowness and clumsiness her burden imposed upon her and looked forward to the day when the baby would begin to lead its own separate life. At the same time, she was in no great hurry for it to happen, for soon thereafter David would return to sea. She didn't know how long he planned to remain at home. It was a question she

297

didn't raise. The answer would give her a date to dread, and she didn't even want to contemplate life without him.

When the first pains came, she was reluctant to send for anyone. She tried to conceal them from her mother and Martha Chambers, who were sitting in the parlor with her. However, with the second wave she gave a gasp, and Martha, who had been covertly watching her for several minutes, was instantly on her feet.

"Best I send for Mrs. Fuller and Doctor Willett," Martha said.

"No, Aunt Martha, it's too early. It's not due for more than a week."

"Due or not, from the looks of you, it's comin'.'' Martha rubbed both hands down the sides of her stiff black skirt as though she were preparing for work. "Now you get yourself upstairs while I send word."

"What's happening?" Lydia looked up from her needlework with a bemused smile.

"Nothin' to fret about, dear," Martha said soothingly. "Julia's babe's on the way."

"Well, don't just stand there, Martha!" The announcement stimulated Lydia to an energy she rarely showed these days. "Send for Benjamin. He'll want to be here."

"I'll do that, Miss Lydia. Now you just stay here quiet till you're needed."

As Julia rose, she gave another gasp. She started to double over when Martha caught her.

"Hurry," Julia panted. "I think he's impatient to get here."

"Bein' yours, he would be. Come on then. I'll get you upstairs," the older woman said. Once they were in the hall, she shouted in a stentorian voice, "Maryanne! Janet!"

Before she and Julia were halfway up the stairs, the two maids burst out of the dining-room door. Janet still carried an empty pot in her hand, but she grasped the situation immediately.

"I'll get Ezra. Where do you want him to go first?"

"Mrs. Fuller's. Then Doctor Willett's," Martha said decisively. Although she was well into her seventies, there was nothing Martha enjoyed more than being in command during an emergency. "After that, he can go fetch Captain Baxter. You go find Miss Amelia and tell her what's happening. And Maryanne, after you set some water to boil, you stay in the parlor with Miss Lydia. Don't let her get het up."

When they reached the door of the large front bedroom, which she had moved back into after her marriage to David, Julia pulled away from Martha's comforting arms and held onto the bedpost. She took a deep breath and tried to stand very straight. The pain had gone.

"I'm all right now, Aunt Martha. May just be a false alarm. I'll lie down for a bit."

"It's certain you'll lie down, but we'll get these clothes off you first," she said as she began to work on the buttons of Julia's dress. "How was it with you when Clara was born?"

"Not bad, I think. It's hard to remember, it was so long ago."

"Aye. Could be different this time," Martha said as she thought of Julia's age. Thirty-five was a good long way from twenty-five, and with all Julia had been through, she wasn't exactly blooming with health. "We'll not take any chances," she added firmly.

Julia was well tucked into the feather bed with layers of towels beneath her and Martha had the coals blazing in the fireplace when the waters burst. Within a few minutes, David was in the room. When Ezra had arrived at the shipyard with the news, David had not taken the time to put on his hat and coat. An early snowfall had dusted the shoulders of his black suit with flakes, and his dark blond curls had been rumpled by the wind during his wild gallop to the house. He grasped Julia's hand in his cold one and looked sternly at Martha.

"Where's the midwife?" he demanded.

"She's on her way, I reckon," Martha said calmly. "Ezra was supposed to go for her and the doctor before he went to the shipyard."

"Aye. He said he'd left word with them. But why aren't they here?" He looked as though he were going to rush from the room and drag them back bodily.

"David," Julia said as she squeezed his hand, "these things take time. As long as you're here."

"I promised, didn't I?" He smiled down at her and tried to will some of his own strength into her. All of the normally high color had left her face and she looked terribly frail to him. He had gotten her into this and somehow he had to pull her through it.

"Don't leave me, David," she pleaded, clinging to his hand. "Please don't leave me."

"I won't." His voice was very steady.

"Doctor Willett's goin' to have somethin' to say about that!" Martha was scandalized and showed it by putting her fists on her plump hips. "A bornin's no place for a man. 'Tis woman's business."

"It's my business," David said firmly as he released Julia's hand just long enough to carry a straight chair to the side of the bed. "I'm staying, and it'll take a team of oxen to move me."

"We'll just see about that," Martha said as the doctor and the midwife came into the room. "Doctor Willett, Captain Baxter says he's stayin'."

The doctor went to the walnut bureau and put his bag on its top. While he opened it, he peered over his glasses at the man who had his large jaw set and was staring resolutely back at him.

"Well, Martha, looks like Captain Baxter's stayin'. Never did believe in disputin' a man twice my size. Don't pay. Don't think it's something you want to see, though," he added to David as he walked casually to the bed. "Strong men been known to faint."

"No doubt," David said impassively. "Don't reckon I will."

"Then move that chair up closer to the head of the bed. We've got work to do here."

It was worse than she remembered. Far worse. And yet as long as she could stare into David's eyes and pull against his strong hands, it was bearable. When the sounds were driven from the depths of her body, she learned to shut her eyes because she saw her agony reflected in his. At times she almost told him to go, but she couldn't. In this pain-wracked world, he was the lifeline to which she clung.

And then her scream was echoed by a smaller one and the doctor was approaching her with a pad of cotton and the dropper. Even as she smelled the sickly sweet odor of chloroform, she fought against it.

"Tell me!" she demanded.

"Boy," Doctor Willett said.

"Benjy." She sighed, and as the room and the people in it grew hazy, she smiled.

When she woke up, her mouth tasted as fuzzy as her head felt, and it took her a moment to focus.

"You awake, Julie?" David said softly when he saw her eyes begin to blink. "Benjy wants to say hello to his mother."

She turned her head towards his voice and found her husband sitting on the bed beside her. He cradled a small bundle of blankets, which looked tiny in his powerful arms. Yet the pride that showed on his face as he glanced down at it said that it was his son he held.

"How about his father?" she mumbled. "Has Benjy said hello to him yet?"

"Aye." The words *father* and *son* sang in his heart. "We've had a long conversation. Mrs. Fuller says he was born smiling, but he let out an almighty yell right after. I can vouch for that. Good lungs for a quarter-deck."

"I'm glad he smiled," she said dreamily. She still couldn't shake the effects of the drug.

"So am I. He hasn't opened his eyes yet, but he's got your hair."

"Let me see him." She stretched out her arms. She had to touch him, feel him, make sure of his reality.

"Here, Julie," Amelia said from her other side. "Let me get these pillows under your head."

Julia looked up at her sister, who was smiling through her obvious

300

weariness. Yet she couldn't spare more than a glance for Amelia. Her eyes were too hungry for the sight of her son.

When David was satisfied that she was propped up securely and that she was comfortable, he laid the child in her arms and with gentle fingers pulled the blanket away from around his face.

Julia took a sharp breath. My son, she thought. After all these years, you're finally here. Oh, I'll give you everything, teach you all I know. You'll grow into a man who'd make anyone's heart proud. Mine. David's. Papa's. Oh, my handsome boy.

"He is smiling!" she said aloud. "He doesn't know what he's just gotten into, but he looks happy to be here. He's so beautiful!"

"Looks a mite red to me," David said skeptically, but his face was radiant.

"Oh, babies almost always look like that," Amelia reassured him. "You'd be red, too, if you'd just gone through what he has, but it'll go away soon."

Julia fumbled with the blanket as she tried to unwrap him. She had to make sure that he didn't have some awful defect. But no, he was perfect from his tiny toenails to the ears that were set flat against his head. There was very little hair on his head, but it was a true black.

The joy she felt in touching this child, in feeling the flesh that was of her own was a joy she had never experienced before. Not even when Clara was born.

"He looks like you, Julie," Amelia said as she bent over the bed to admire her nephew.

"You can't tell with a baby," Julia said, but she hoped it was true. It would be disastrous if he resembled David too much.

"I can tell," Amelia said. "I've had enough experience along that line."

"You're just seeing what you want to see." Julia smiled up at Amelia and then noticed that no light was filtering through the drawn draperies. "What are you doing here at this hour? Feels like the middle of the night. You should be home taking care of Jason."

"Jason's asleep in the other room. Only three months apart, and cousins, too. Just think what friends they'll be."

"Yes. I hope they like each other," Julia said as she continued her search of her son's long, slender limbs for any imperfections.

"They will," Amelia promised.

"Has Clara seen him?" Julia asked, carefully pulling the blankets around her child to shield him from any draft that might wander through the room.

"Aye," David said. "She came home about half an hour after Benjy arrived."

"I hope she was happy. She's wanted a brother or a sister for a long time."

"Well, I think she was a mite disappointed when she found it was a boy," David said with teasing laughter in his eyes. "But she was excited even so. 'Twas hard enough to convince her to go to bed."

"She kept asking if he was really hers," Amelia hastily added.

"And Mama?" Julia tickled Benjy's lips with the tip of her finger, and when he wrinkled his mouth at it, she unbuttoned her nightgown and held him to her breast.

"Mama's a trifle confused," Amelia told her. "I think because we told her you were going to name him Benjamin."

"She wasn't upset?"

"No, no. Nothing like that."

"I hope not." The pull of his small mouth sent joy streaming through her body. "I want everyone to like him. I've waited for him for so long."

In January and February of 1856, the Atlantic coast was plagued with violent storms, and many fine vessels were lost. As the wind howled around the house and drove everyone close to the fire, Julia was content to stay at home with her child. There was a comfort, too, in knowing that David was either at the shipyard or at her side. It was not a happy winter for women whose husbands were at sea.

In late February, the weather eased. On the first mild day, Julia wrapped her son up well and slipped from the house with him. No one but Ezra, who had readied the horse and buggy for her, knew where she was going. She had made no mention of her plan, for she knew the protests it would draw. But she was determined to take her son down to the beach and show him the sea. Her father would have understood, she thought, but she wasn't so certain of David's reaction.

When she neared the dunes, Julia reined in and reached into the large basket on the floor of the buggy. At two months, Benjy's eyes were wide open, and Amelia's perception had been a true one. His eyes were a deep blue beneath the finely arched brows, and his black hair had begun to wisp into soft curls. But Julia wondered if she had ever looked at the world with such acceptance, and although his lips were as finely molded as her own, she suspected that the smile was inherited from his father.

"Well, Benjy," she said, lifting him up. He smiled the toothless grin that was his greeting. "It's about time you two met. It's a shame you couldn't have been born at sea, but it couldn't be arranged."

At the top of the dune, she paused and searched the horizon until she finally sighted a far-off cloud of sails. Then she shifted him in her arms and turned his face gently in that direction.

"See that ship out there, Benjy? That could be one your mama or even your grandpapa built. And I'll teach you how to build them, too. It won't be too many years before you're ready to come to the yard."

She made her way very carefully down the shifting path that led to the beach. As they neared the water and the tinkling of the pebbles grew louder, the baby cooed with pleasure.

"Isn't it pretty, Benjy? And isn't it clean and free after spending all your life cooped up in a house? See, taste it." She rinsed her hand in the ice-cold water and shook off all but a few drops. Then she drew one finger across his lips. He smacked his lips and looked puzzled at the strange taste, but then he smiled at her as though it were a tremendous joke.

"If you're planning on christening him, I hope you don't favor the immersion method," David said from behind her.

"How did you know I was here?" Julia, startled, whirled around.

"If Aunt Martha hadn't told me, I might have guessed it anyway. She saw you driving off and bludgeoned the truth out of Ezra. Then she sent word to me."

"And you've come to take us home."

"No." He bent over his son and their smiles met. "Just as long as you're not planning to teach him to swim, a little sea air won't harm him. Want to walk a ways?"

"Yes. I'd like that. I seem to have been cooped up in that house forever. Till today, I didn't realize how much I'd been missing it. The sea. Then I smelt it in the breeze."

"I know," he said. "Did you notice the ship out there?"

"Yes. I was showing her to Benjy. I wonder who she is."

"She's *Yankee Girl*. Word came in earlier this morning."

"You going to take her to sea?" Julia asked the question quickly as though she were plunging into icy water. Since there was no way of avoiding it, she wanted the answer immediately.

"I should." As he looked towards the horizon, a certain longing entered his eyes.

"I suppose so," Julia said reluctantly. She knew that look too well, had seen it in the eyes of too many men. The day that had seemed so bright became instead a harbinger of a spring that would see him far away.

"I wish I could take you with me, Julie, you and Benjy." He glanced down at his child with the same intensity of longing. "Clara, too."

"I wish you could. I miss the life at sea, but not as much as I'll miss you."

David narrowed his eyes to stare again at his distant ship. Then as they resumed walking, he jammed his hands into the pockets of his greatcoat and scuffed at the multicolored pebbles that covered the sand.

"There's another thing I sometimes wish, Julie," he finally said.

"What?"

"That you were a nice normal woman."

"Oh, David!" Her arms involuntarily loosened and then she clutched Benjy closer to her. "I am, aren't I?"

"No. Here, let me take him. He's too heavy for you to carry around like that." Once he had his son in his arms, he continued. "Normal women don't run shipyards. On the other hand, if you were like them, you wouldn't be Julia, would you?"

"I guess not." She looked miserably down at the sea wrack left by the receding tide. "I'm sorry I can't be what you want, David."

"But you are. Never seen any other woman I really wanted. You haunted me all those years." He smiled at her reassuringly, but almost immediately his eyes saddened with a foreshadowing of loneliness. "It's just that I don't know how I can leave you behind."

"I'd come, but I can't leave the yard. You've seen that, David. You've seen the work that piles up. Daniel's good, but he's not very imaginative. I suppose I could hire a naval architect. But even then, who would deal with the customers?"

"I know. I've been turning it over in my mind ever since the word came. The only way you can get out of it is to sell the yard, and I know you can't do that."

"I'm glad you understand, David. Everyone's always been telling me to sell, but I can't, especially not now."

"It's for Benjy, isn't it?" He looked down at the child who now slept placidly in his arms.

"If he wants it. I hope he will."

"Most likely he will. And if he does and you'd sold it, 'twould be as though you'd robbed him?"

"Yes. Papa meant it for him."

"That's what I figured." He glanced once more at the horizon. The ship had disappeared. Shifting Benjy into one arm, he reached down and took Julia's gloved hand. "Well, if you can't come with me, I reckon that means I'll have to stay with you."

"Do you mean it, David?" Julia stopped and swung around so that she could look up into his eyes. There was an amazed smile on her face as she clutched at his arm. "Do you really mean it?"

"Aye," he said soberly. "I've thought it all out. On one side of the scales, I balanced all those years I spent without you and how I'll hate not being here to see Benjy grow up, and on the other I put the price of a master's salary. They were weighted pretty heavily in one direction. I'd pay a master's wage twice over to be with you and Benjy. Might not get as rich that way, but we'd have enough."

"Oh, David, I'm so glad." Julia laughed joyously. "I shouldn't be. I know you'd like to be back at sea as much as I would."

"No." He grinned at her fondly. "Not as much as you. You're a little daft when it comes to that. Maybe I should sign you on as master. I'll run the yard and you go to sea."

304

"No, thank you. I'll stay with you."

"Well, that's another thing I've taken into consideration. If I'm home, I'll be able to take over most of your responsibilities. 'Twill give you time to spend with Benjy. I'd like him to have his mother around when he needs her."

"I could take him to the yard with me." She would miss the yard if she were exiled from it. So much of her life had gone into it. The men there were her friends. She hoped that wasn't what David had in mind.

"Aye." He grinned down at her with understanding. He knew that there was no way he could tie Julia to a house without making her miserable. "Most likely, you'll be instructing him in the art of shipbuilding before the year is out and start him as an apprentice before he's two. Nonetheless, if you don't feel like going down to the yard, I don't want you to feel you have to. Daniel's right when he says you work too hard."

"You're good to me, David." She tucked her hand under his arm. "Maybe too good."

"Think so?" He laughed down at her. "Then maybe I'll have to reconsider."

"You wouldn't!"

"No. I wouldn't. We'd best turn back. I think Benjy's had enough fresh air for one day. He's fast asleep."

Chapter Twenty

1857–1858

The humming of bees and the scent of the honeysuckle in which they swarmed drifted through the open windows, bringing with them the essence of late July. There was a drowsy peacefulness in the summer afternoon, Julia thought contentedly as she looked up from the plans she had been studying. David was sitting by the open doorway with his long legs stretched out in front of him. Sunlight glinted on the golden hairs of his muscular forearms as he carved the model for the ship to come. Beside him on the floor, Benjy was playing with two crudely fashioned boats that had paper sails attached to their sliver masts.

The years of sadness and care seemed far in the past, and having lived with David's placid influence for over a year and a half, she felt herself growing younger. In a few days, she would be thirty-seven, but he made her feel as though she were twenty-five again.

Aware of her eyes on him, David looked up and smiled with a lazy contentment that matched her own.

"Wool-gathering again, Julie?"

"No. Just thinking this is a moment I'd like to capture forever. If I could just stop time, this is where I'd stop it."

"But then you'd forestall all the years ahead." He reached down and rumpled his son's black curls, and the boy looked up and smiled at his father. "We'd miss seeing Benjy grow up, and the best half of our lives is yet to come. No, I wouldn't stop time just now if I was you."

"I don't want to think about the future," she said with a sigh as she rolled up the plans. "Every time I do, I start fretting about the yard. We were lucky to get the order from Moses Blake to lay down a ship come fall, even if it is only six hundred forty-eight feet, and we've got one more fishing schooner to build for Jake Carnway, but after that what? As it is, we've got one of the ways sitting idle now."

"What we've got will get us through the winter, and something's bound to turn up come spring." His knife flashed in the sun as he concentrated upon the model.

"With ships sitting empty in Boston and New York, who's going to invest in another? You yourself said Donald McKay hasn't got anything in hand at all."

"Nope. He thought best to close down temporarily. Understand he's out scouting the streets."

"And so are Hall and Webb and Briggs. Half the yards on the East Coast are closed down."

"Well, that just means if anyone wants a vessel built, they'll come to us. We're open, and I've made certain everyone knows it."

"But how long can we stay open? We had to cut the men's wages once in order to get costs down, and you saw how many left. If we have to cut them again, we won't have anyone to build even a dory." She sighed as she got up and went to the large cabinet she'd had built, and as she slipped the plans into place, she looked at the rows of empty holes waiting for future plans. She shook her head.

David raised an eyebrow as he watched her. Then he said quietly, "When we need more men, we'll get them from the yards that are closed."

"Well, we'd best move fast. From what I see in the papers, half the men in the country are heading West."

"Come, Julie, don't ruin your perfect moment," he said soothingly as he tilted his chair and rocked on its back legs. "We're doing better than most. There's not many ships have gotten a tea charter from the British lately, but *Yankee Girl* should be well on her way to England now. The vessels you've got shares in are at least eking out their expenses, and as long as you've got that railway and factory stock, we won't starve. There'll be a demand for ships again."

"I'd like to know when," she said sharply. Hearing the edge to his mother's voice, Benjy looked up and cocked his head. She smiled at him reassuringly.

"Oh, just let someone discover more gold somewhere in the world or let the Europeans fight another war," David answered. "The Treaty of Paris may have ended the Crimean War, but the British and French get restless when things get too peaceable. The rest of the country is prosperous. All we have to do is wait it out."

"I guess so." Her smile grew rueful as she turned it on her husband. How well he kept her on an even keel, she thought, and how much she loved him for it. He saw things through a longer glass than she did. "Maybe I make too much of things. It's a good thing I have you around to straighten me out."

"Aye." He laid the model on the table and carefully put his knife into the fitted instrument case. Raising his arms above his head, he stretched luxuriously. "I've been sitting still too long. Care to take a turn around the yard?"

"Yes." Julia jumped at his suggestion. The summer day was too enticing to spend it sitting in the office.

As they approached the ways where a small brig was nearing completion, they found Moses Blake staring across Sesuit Creek. He was a tall, gaunt man with a crest of black hair. When Julia saw the somber look on his face, she paused and clutched Benjy's hand more tightly. Was it possible that Moses had come to cancel the order for his new ship?

"Morning, Moses," David called out as he strolled up to their customer. "Trying to picture how your vessel's going to look sitting there?"

"No, no. Tryin' to picture somethin' else. You're the one I come to see."

Moses glanced significantly at the nearby men stirring a pot of tar and at others who passed close by carrying newly sawed planks. He nodded his head to a narrow stretch of shoreline farther up the creek. "It's what you might call a private conversation."

David followed Moses along the narrow path between tall reeds. Julia was determined not to be left out of the conversation, but Benjy slowed her pace. When she caught up with them, the two men had their hands stuck casually in their pockets and were looking at the church spire on the distant hill.

"We've got a new shipment of goods," Moses was saying. "Five of them stashed in the Randalls' barn. Think they're safe enough for a few hours. Problem is how to move them on out."

"Nehemiah Kelley's taken them north before," David said and nodded at a black-hulled fishing schooner that was bobbing calmly at the wharf across the creek. "Think he'll do it again?"

"Aye. He's willin'. Says if we can get them on board by midnight, he'll take them direct to Canada. It's the gettin' them from the Randalls' barn to the schooner that's a worry. Lots of folks hold that Southerners have a right to own slaves. Lots of others lookin' for a reward for catchin' the escaped ones. Hard to know who to trust."

David nodded glumly. "I know. It's gotten so half the people round here aren't speaking to the other half. There's bitter feelings and they're running high."

"You willin' to help out?" Moses glanced at Julia and Benjy. "I know you done it before, but there's some danger to it. You got your family to think of. Maybe I don't have the right to ask again."

"I'll do what I can," David said without a moment's hesitation. "What's your plan?"

"Well, we reckon the *Annie Snow* over there is bein' watched. Word's out that Kelley is part of the Railroad. He'd feel safer takin' them on board out in the Bay. Good thing there's a late moon tonight."

"And how do you plan getting them on board?"

"That's where you come in. You and your men. You must have some you can trust." He looked at David questioningly.

"There's a few," David said as he thought of the Sears brothers and three others who had been outspoken in their support of the abolitionists.

"Shipyard's never been used before. Figure we can smuggle the goods here after dark. It'd be up to you to clear the yard of all those except the ones you trust. Then if we can row the shipment out in one of your workboats . . ."

"Sounds like a good plan," David agreed. "I can handle my share of it."

That night Julia sat on the front porch alone and waited for David to return home. The waning moon had just risen and shone dreamily over the marsh, where frogs were singing their nightly chorus. The moon worried Julia. By now the people should be aboard and the schooner on her way north. If they were still in the shipyard or in the workboat, then David was in greater danger.

She longed to go and meet him, but she didn't know which route he would take. Restlessly she began to pace the porch. Then she wandered out onto the lawn. Standing at the foot of a chestnut tree, she looked up and down the road. The moon had risen high enough to see that it was empty.

There was a crackle of twigs to her left. She looked around sharply.

When David emerged from the trees on the far side of the lawn, she gave a great sigh of relief.

"David," she called softly, knowing that she was hidden in shadows cast by the tree.

"I told you not to wait up for me, love," he whispered when he reached her side.

"I was worried." As she looked up at the rugged features that took their shape more from familiarity than from the dim light, she realized just how anxious she had been.

"Nothing to worry about," he said casually, but the eagerness of his lips when he kissed her told her that he had been more concerned than he wanted her to know.

"How did it go?" she asked as he straightened up.

He listened to the whisper of a breeze stirring the tree tops and searched the shadows for movement before he nodded.

"Just as planned. For once there were no hitches." He put an arm around her and together they turned to look across at the moonlit marsh.

Through the trees on the far side of the road, they could see streams whose scattered reflections were silver in the green darkness. An occasional bird gave a startled call that could be heard above the steady harmony of frogs.

"Seems peaceful, doesn't it?" David said, his voice hushed. "Wonder how long it'll last."

"The night, the season, or our world?"

"Our world. I listened to those people tonight, and all the time they were talking, I could hear Kansas posses riding and the crackling of rifles carried by both border ruffians and free-staters. The homesteaders out there live in a nightmare world, never knowing when an attack will come from either a group of pro-slavers or some abolitionists led by John Brown and his sons. Think what it would be like to hear gunfire from over there," he said as he pointed across the marsh, "and not know which of our friends was being attacked, nor who was attacking them."

"Did the slaves come all the way from Kansas?" Julia asked as she tried to imagine the long, trackless way and the fear that would lie along it.

"No. From Georgia, but they're the reason for the fighting in Kansas."

"Well, it has nothing to do with us. We're a free state. All we can do is help those who escape continue on their way."

"I wonder if it doesn't have something to do with us." David sighed and was silent for a moment. Then he pulled her closer and put his other arm around her. "Come. Let's go in. It doesn't seem so peaceful out here anymore."

309

$$* \quad * \quad *$$

As she unbuttoned her dress, Julia curiously watched her husband wash his face. The experiences of the night seemed to have given him something weighty to consider.

"What were they like?" she finally asked.

"People. Poor and uneducated. Frightened people. Their owner died and they were to be sold off. Likely they would have been separated, man from wife, child from mother. They were all related. A family." He turned with the towel in his hands to look at her, and his eyes were troubled. "And they might never have seen each other again. Not as long as they lived."

"Well, they should be in Canada soon. Then their troubles will be over," Julia said, her voice muffled as she slipped her nightgown over her head.

"Aye. God willing *they* will be." He turned the lamp out and got into bed beside her. His arms were tight around her as though he wanted to assure himself of her reality when he added, "But what of the others? Hundreds of them. I listened to those people talk and I thought of you and Benjy and Clara. I thought of my parents, your mother and sisters. What if it had been us who'd been born with black skins and were going to be separated forever?"

"It would be like death."

"Yes. And all the time I was listening, I was thinking of you and Benjy and the moment you wanted to capture. I began to think you were right. We should capture each happy moment and let time stop for a little while till we've caught that moment so well it can never be lost."

He loosened his hold on her as his lips traced her features and settled for a moment at the hollow of her throat, which was always so sweet to his tongue. As he lowered his mouth to her breast, he murmured, "This is a moment to be captured, caught, and held forever."

It was a night they both captured and held dear, for that night another child was conceived. When within the month the Ohio Life Insurance and Trust Company folded and brought the subsequent panic that rippled across the nation, the thought of the child to come gave them a mutual strength they might not otherwise have had.

In newspapers, they read accounts of bank after bank closing its doors as the alarm was spread by telegraph. Twice there were banks in which they had deposited money. Then even financially sound factories went into bankruptcy. Far-flung railroads, which would not have the population to support them for many years, became defunct. They watched the turmoil of the country and their disappearing investments with a feeling of utter helplessness.

The reality of the shipyard became ever more important to David as well as to Julia. It was a solid thing that could be seen and heard and touched. As long as there were enough funds to keep it running, they were determined that it would continue. Fortunately, neither Moses Blake nor Jake Carnway showed a disposition to cancel the building of their vessels.

Yet even as the keels were laid that fall, Julia prowled around the workmen and watched them restlessly. David, riding in after a morning spent with bankers and lawyers, was disturbed to find her wandering nervously around the yard from the sawyers to the ways to the blacksmith's shop to the office and back again. He dismounted quickly and strode across the yard after her.

"You've got to calm down, Julie," he said when he finally caught up with her near the ways where the ribs of Moses Blake's modified clipper were beginning to be placed. "You're doing the child no good the way you keep going on."

"I can't help it." She impatiently brushed the hair away from her face with the back of her hand as she watched the carpenters at work. "I keep wondering how far we're going to be able to build these vessels. When will the money stop? What's the point in laying keels when we may never be able to launch them?"

"You know both Blake and Carnway have guaranteed funds."

"Yes, but how long's their money going to hold out? Are they any better off than we are?"

"Julie, look at it this way." He glanced around the yard and saw the constant movement of workers who went steadily about their various jobs. There might be less activity than in the past, but there *was* activity. "Even if we can't complete the vessels, at least our men are working. They can provide food for their families, which is more than many can. I was reading the other day how the streets of Boston and New York are filled with unemployed men. Healthy, able men begging."

"Yes." Julia's shoulders sagged as she thought of the wretched, ragged men she had seen. "Our men may be working, but I've had to turn a lot away. Everyone who loses his livelihood comes here looking for work. We don't have anything for them. The best I can do is give them a little money, and that won't carry them far."

"All we can do is take care of our own." He struck sharply at his boots with his riding crop. "Don't give money to anyone you don't know. It's in too short supply."

"I don't." Julia wandered towards the bank where she could hear more clearly the sparkling voice of the creek. When David followed, she continued. "I give more advice than anything else, and I doubt that's worth much. I wish I could do more."

"Well, the *Yankee Girl* should be home soon. With her profits, things will be a little easier."

"Oh!" Julia put her hand to her mouth. "How could I have forgotten? She's been sighted. There's a telegram in the office from Provincetown reporting her. She's coming home in ballast."

"Damn!" He slashed with his crop at a clump of tall golden weeds that clung tenaciously to the bank. "I wrote Captain Parr he might have to do that, but I'd hoped he would hold out a while longer and find some kind of freight for her. I wish they'd get that Atlantic cable they're always talking about laid. I'd best go down to Boston and see what I can do about getting her away again. Come home with me while I pack."

"I'd best stay here." What she really wanted to do was to climb over the dunes to the beach. There, hidden from most eyes, she could walk beside the sea, which was now at high tide. It was always soothing, even if it held no solution for their financial problems. But with David going to Boston, she would have to stay close to the yard.

"There's nothing here that Daniel and Philip can't handle, and I want you to rest." He tucked her hand beneath his arm and guided her towards the office. "I have half a mind to take you down to Boston with me. That way I can keep an eye on you. You know you're not a young woman anymore, Julie."

"Well, that's a fine thing to say to me!" Her dark blue eyes flashed with indignation.

"I'm talking about childbearing," he said patiently. " 'Twas bad enough when Benjy was born, and that'll be more than two years in the past by the time the new one arrives." He paused in front of the office door. "You want to get anything from in there before we go home? I'm going to have a word with Daniel. If he lets you spend more than three hours a day around here while I'm gone, I'm going to fire him."

"You can't fire Daniel. He doesn't fire." Julia had to smile as she pictured David trying to fire Daniel. She could just see the stubborn set of that swarthy face. "Uncle Josiah tried it a few times, but Daniel doesn't pay any attention."

"Well, I have a little more authority than your Uncle Josiah did. And if *you* don't mind better, I'm going to fire you."

The look of mock ferocity he gave before he turned away made her laugh in spite of herself. She paused for a minute as she fondly watched him striding across the yard. Then as she went into the office to give last-minute instructions to the clerk, she realized once more how much she depended upon David to lighten her darker moods. How deeply she would miss him when he went to Boston!

She was tempted to go with him, but the city was an unhappy place now with windows boarded up and vessels swinging idly at anchor in the harbor. The search for cargo would most likely be depressing, too. It was best to stay home where there was at least some activity.

It took David well over a month to secure enough cargo to fill the holds of the *Yankee Girl*. By the time she sailed for California, the freight rates had been so reduced, profits from the voyage would only be minimal. Yet as long as she was working, she would be well cared for, and David was satisfied that she would be sound when the future he optimistically expected brought higher rates.

The weeks while he was gone seemed endless to Julia. She wondered how she would ever manage a longer separation if he should someday decide to return to the sea. She had grown accustomed to having his powerful arms around her each night while she slept. With David beside her she had no bad dreams. When he returned from Boston, he brought with him a happiness that not even their financial concerns could completely dampen.

That winter, while the small ship rose on the ways at a laggard pace due to the slow disbursement of funds that was all Moses Blake could afford, a sickness invaded many homes. The infection was not a severe one and was easily shaken off by the young and hearty, but when William Thacher came down with it, it lingered in his chest. Amelia became so concerned about him, she wanted to move him to her house.

At first William obstinately refused to give up his independence and leave even temporarily the home in Brewster that he so loved. When Samuel arrived in port in January and put the *Neptune's Dragon* into dry dock for a complete overhauling and recoppering, he drove over to Brewster and, without listening to his father's protests, bundled William into the carriage and brought him to East Dennis.

When Julia first spoke to David about it, he was reluctant to let her visit her cousin for fear that she would catch William's disease, but Julia persuaded him that she must go. After all, she pointed out, Benjy had been down with the same thing for about a week in December, and she hadn't caught it from him. Despite the fact that she was in her sixth month of pregnancy, she had never felt healthier.

The day after Samuel brought William home, Julia left the shipyard early in the afternoon to call on him. It was a sharp, clear day with very little wind. After the dampness of the past couple of weeks, she hoped that the change in weather would begin to mend William's health.

As soon as she opened Amelia's front door, she could hear his harsh, tearing cough.

"Amelia, is it all right for me to see him?" she asked when her sister came out of the sick room into the small hall to greet her. Amelia wore a cheerful rose dress, but strain showed in the lines beside her eyes.

"Best you do," Amelia said with relief when she saw it was Julia. "He's been asking after you ever since we got him here."

"Why didn't you send for me? I'd have come," Julia said with some feeling of alarm.

"I figured you'd stop by sometime today, and there didn't seem to be much point in upsetting you."

"How is he?" Julia took off her coat and hung it on a peg on the wall.

"He's not good, Julie," Amelia said sadly. "Doctor Willett stopped by and checked on him. If only I could have carried him over here earlier, maybe he wouldn't have sunk so low."

"There wasn't anything you could do about it, Amelia." Julia put her arm around her sister's shoulders and gave her a squeeze. "Cousin William's a stubborn man, and all the while he kept insisting he was well cared for by that housekeeper of his. He most likely was. She's a good woman."

"That's what Samuel says, too. And you're right. He is stubborn. I can't even get him to stay in bed as much as he should."

"Well, I'll see what I can do." Julia straightened her shoulders and tried out a smile before she opened the door to the bedroom on the first floor, which Amelia and Samuel had vacated for William.

He was sitting in an armchair close to the fire with wool shawls draped around his shoulders. When he saw her he started to rise, but Julia went swiftly to his side and kissed him on the cheek just above his vigorous white beard.

"Well, mermaid," he said after he had returned her kiss heartily, "you come to take me home to Brewster?"

"You look fine just where you are," Julia said as she pulled up another chair close to him.

She tried not to show the concern she felt as she examined his face and frame. Just a couple of months ago, he'd had the springing step of a young man. His white hair and beard had only set off his high color and the sparkle in his green eyes. Now, although the room was hot, he sat with his arms protectively around himself as though to ward off the cold, and his once-robust body seemed frail. Age, which had never been able to touch him before, had suddenly descended to deaden the color and tone of his skin.

"You bring Benjy with you?" he asked and the effort to speak sent him into a paroxysm of coughing.

314

"No. I was just on my way home from the yard and stopped in to check up on you. I hear you've been right stubborn. You listen to Amelia, Cousin William, and get more rest. She says you won't stay in bed."

"You always did take pleasure in tellin' people what to do. Never thought I'd see the day you'd start on me."

"Never thought I'd see the day I'd have to."

"Well, at sixty-five, I'm not going to have a chit of a girl like you tellin' me what to do." He paused until another spasm of coughing had passed. Then he said, "Julie, I want to go home to my own bed. I can't get comfortable here."

"Do you want to come over to our house? Maybe you'd feel more at home there." Julia knew it would throw the house into a turmoil, but it didn't matter how much it might inconvenience anyone. She loved her cousin too much to consider anything but his comfort when he was so ill.

"Nope. If I can't go home, I'll stay put. No point upsettin' Lydia."

The cough came again, and this time he seemed unable to stop. Julia got up and rubbed his back in the hope that it would help his racked body.

When he finally caught his breath, she said, "I'd best go, Cousin William. Talking doesn't improve that cough of yours."

"No! Don't do that." He caught her arm and held it firmly with something of his old strength and looked up at her. His eyes implored her to stay. "I won't talk. You just sit with me a spell. Maybe do a little talkin' yourself. Tell me about the yard. Benjy. Clara."

"All right. Just a little longer," she promised, and he released her arm.

After she had resumed her seat, she began to tell him all the things he might want to know, but every time he began to speak, she held up her hand and went on. Finally she left him with the promise to look in the next afternoon.

Each afternoon when Julia stopped by Amelia's house to visit with William, she saw the toll another twenty-four hours had taken. Sometimes she was able to convince herself that he was better, but as the weeks went by, it became obvious that his strength was deserting him. Finally the fever and the cough were too much for him, and he kept to his bed.

Early on the afternoon of the first day of February, Amelia's oldest son, Levi, arrived at the Howard house with the news that William was asking for her. When he added that his mother thought she ought to come quickly, Julia snatched up her coat, and despite the burden of the child she carried, she practically flew down the road.

When she walked into William's room and heard the gurgling wheeze that had replaced his spasms of coughing, she fought to keep the tears from her eyes. She didn't know how long she could hold them back, but she didn't want him to see her cry.

Samuel and Amelia, standing beside his bed, looked pale and strained. With their eyes, each warned her what to expect. Then they moved away to stand by the far window so that she could have a few private minutes with William.

"You wanted to see me, Cousin William?" she said gently, bending over the bed and taking his frail hand in hers.

When he opened his eyes to look at her, it seemed that all other shades had been washed from them, leaving only the clearest lake green.

"Aye. Reckon I'm . . . goin' to be seein' . . . your pa soon. Jason, too." It was painful to listen to the words that came through his constant battle for breath, but Julia knew that whatever he had to say was important to him, and she didn't try to stop him. "Thought I'd best . . . take a good . . . long look at you so's . . . so's I can give them a full report."

"You're not going to see them for a long time," she said emphatically as she squeezed his hand.

"You never was one . . . run away . . . from truth. Don't start now."

He closed his eyes as he tried to concentrate upon renewing his energy. Julia sensed that he had more to say. Standing quietly with her hands clasping his, she waited until he would be able to speak. She knew that whatever he said would be as important to her as it was to him, for she was certain that this would be their last conversation. When he opened his eyes again, there was a slight smile sketched on the lips above his white beard.

"Won't mind seein' . . . Ben again. Do a little . . . yarnin'. Maggie, too. Seems half a lifetime . . . she's been gone. Been ashore too long. Time to make . . . another voyage."

As he looked at her, he seemed to have trouble focusing. Then he closed his eyes, and she leaned over to kiss his weathered brow.

"I hope it's a good voyage, Cousin William," she whispered softly in his ear so that none but he could hear her.

He squeezed her hand, and when he let his relax, she allowed the silent tears to come. Even when Amelia came to prop William's head up higher on the pillows in an attempt to ease his labored breathing, Julia continued to stand beside him with his hand in hers. It was only when Samuel came and took her by the shoulders that she released it.

"He'll sleep awhile now," Samuel said in a hoarse voice. "Why don't you go wait in the parlor and have a cup of tea. I'll call you if . . . when he wakes again."

Julia, blinded by tears, was only able to nod as he led her from the room. After all, Samuel was William's son. It was only right that he be the one to hold his father's hand and stand vigil at his bedside.

316

Through hours that seemed endless and yet passed too swiftly, Julia sat in the parlor near the fire. She was vaguely aware of children's muffled voices in the kitchen, of the maid who brought tea and tended the fire. Occasionally Samuel or Amelia would come out and sit with her for a few silent moments, but for the most part, she was alone with grief and memories.

Two cups of tea had gone cold in her cup and a golden red sunset filled the winter sky when Samuel came into the parlor. The bleak, lost look on his face told Julia it was over.

"He's gone, Julia. We didn't have time to call you," Samuel said as he looked directly at her. "I'm sorry."

"It's all right, Samuel," she said quietly even as the pain of his words ripped at her heart. "We'd already said good-bye."

He started for the door, then turned back. His normally guarded brown eyes were moist as he tried to find the words.

"After you'd gone, he opened his eyes only once. 'Twas just before the end." His voice broke and he struggled for a moment to regain control.. "His last thought was of you. He said, 'Take care of my mermaid.'"

"Oh, no, Samuel." Julia covered her face with her hands to smother the sound of her sobs and to hide the tears that threatened to drown her. It was too much. Too much. She couldn't bear it. But Samuel was here. She must bear it. William should have spoken of his son, his grandson, not of her.

It took a few moments for her to regain control. Then she grabbed the already wet handkerchief from her sleeve and wiped at her face. When she looked up, she found that Samuel was watching her.

"I'm sure it wasn't his last thought, Samuel," she said. "He just didn't have a chance to say all the rest. He would have been thinking of you and Amelia and little Jason."

"It's all right, Julia." His jaw was clenched and his lips were tight, but there was compassion in his eyes. "I don't mind. Never did. You were closer to him somehow than either Jason or me. Maybe because we were boys. Maybe because you'd spent more time with him than we ever did. Whatever, it doesn't matter. We knew he loved us in his own way."

"Oh, Samuel . . . how are we going to manage without him?" Julia wailed, and then she and Samuel were holding tight to each other. His racking sobs and tears mingled with her own.

When Amelia came in, she found them still there, clutching at one another. She put an arm around each of them and guided them to the sofa.

"You two sit down," she said, and though she was not far from crying herself, she was not going to be gainsaid. "I'm going to fix you each a brandy. One for me, too."

* * *

The funeral was held in Brewster a few days later. Despite the bitter cold, the number of people who attended from all over the Cape as well as those who came from Boston and New York attested to how much William Thacher had been loved.

Julia and David had taken Clara to the funeral with them at her insistence. When they returned home from Brewster, they found Lydia sitting in the parlor with Aunt Martha and Benjy.

While they stood about the fire trying to thaw out, Lydia intently studied them one by one. She gave special attention to their black clothes. After a few minutes' consideration, she spoke very calmly.

"Well, who's gone now? Must be William. Haven't seen him for a spell. You might have told me."

Clara looked at her grandmother and gasped. Then she ran out of the room and up the stairs. Lydia seemed completely unaware of her granddaughter's reaction as she continued.

"I'd like to have gone to the funeral," she said in an aggrieved tone. "I always was right fond of William."

"Mama, don't get upset now," Julia said soothingly.

"Well, if it wasn't William, who was it?"

"It was Cousin William, Mama."

"Just as I thought," Lydia said triumphantly. "So he's gone, too. Sea didn't get him, did it?"

"No, Mama. 'Twas a cold in his lungs. He couldn't shake it and it went into pneumonia."

"Died in his bed, did he?" Lydia nodded her head as though in agreement. "That's good. Then he went peaceful. They put him next to Margaret?"

Julia was amazed at the coolness with which her mother accepted William's death. They had gone to such pains to conceal even his illness from her.

"Yes, Mama. Next to Margaret. Come spring, you'll have to go over and see him."

"No," Lydia said placidly. "Think I'll see him sooner than that."

"Better wait till the weather's warmer, Mama. You don't want to risk catching cold yourself."

"Don't fret about it, dear. I'll see him when the time comes." She put her needlework very precisely on the table beside her and rose from her chair. "I've been a mite tired today. Think I'll go up and rest awhile. Martha, you coming?"

When the two older women had left the room, Julia looked with bemusement at David and said, "You never know how she'll take things. I'd have sworn it was going to send her into one of her bad spells."

"I know." He chafed his hands even more vigorously in front of the fire. "May yet send her into one. You notice she didn't mention your father? Seems strange."

A few hours later when Martha Chambers took a supper tray up to Lydia, she came down the stairs almost immediately with the untouched tray still in her hands. As she walked into the dining room where the family was gathering for the meal, she looked directly at Julia.

"Your mother's gone," she said bluntly.

"Gone?" Julia threw her napkin down with alarm and shoved her chair back from the table. "You don't think she tried to get over to Brewster all by herself? We'd best go look for her."

"No, Julia." Martha put the tray down on the table and sank heavily onto the nearest chair with a deep sigh. "You won't find her. 'Twasn't that I meant. She's decided to join your father and Captain Thacher. She was sleeping peaceful last time I looked in, and she still appears the same, but there's not a breath left in her body."

"Grandma!" Clara shrieked. She started to rush from the room, but David caught her before she reached the door.

"You can't help Grandma now, Clara," he said softly.

"You don't care!" She struggled to get away from him. "She's not your grandma."

"No, but I loved her all the same. She was a gentle old lady, and now she's got her dearest wish. She's gone to join your grandpa, and he won't be make-believe to her anymore."

"But she left me! I want to go see her. Everyone leaves me."

"Not everyone, Clara." David retained a firm grip on the girl, but he tried not to hurt her. "We're still here. Stay with us."

"No. I want to say good-bye to her." The tears welled up in her angry grey eyes and she looked at Julia pleadingly.

Through her own shock, Julia was aware of her daughter's very real grief. Clara had been closer to her grandmother than any of them and had perhaps loved her more than Lydia had ever been loved, even by her own children and her husband. And Julia remembered the awful time when Clara had seen Stephen's drowned and mutilated body. It was a terrible memory for the child to carry.

"I'm going up, David. Let her come with me." Julia glanced at Martha, who nodded her head in agreement. "If Mama went peaceful, it won't hurt Clara to see her. Might hurt her a lot more if we don't allow it."

"You want me to come with you?" he asked.

"No. Just Clara and me." She held out her hand to her daughter. "We'll just go up and say good-bye. We won't be long."

Chapter Twenty-one

1858–1859

That winter took a heavy toll, and by the time spring arrived David, too, had suffered his share of losses. In early March, his father died from pneumonia. Within the month, David found himself an orphan twice over, and he laid his mother to rest next to his father's fresh grave.

His greatest consolation was that his parents had known a child of their own blood was on its way into the world even as they left it. It was a consolation to Julia, also, for she, like David, had always regretted that they could not tell them that Benjy was the grandson the old couple thought they had only adopted with all their hearts.

When the full spring moon brought the vernal tides, only the schooner was launched. The trickle of funds had kept the ship growing, but at such a slow pace, she would not be finished for some time to come. For once, it made no difference that the largest of the ways would be tied up for a full year with one ship. Despite all of David's efforts to secure business, no orders had been forthcoming. What had been a panic in 1857 had settled into a full-scale depression in 1858. By April, another small fishing schooner was ordered, and they felt themselves fortunate to have the yard at least solvent. So many had been bankrupted.

With May came the birth of Daphne, whose thick blond curls and triangular eyes left no doubt as to who her father was. Clara, now fourteen, became so entranced with her half-sister it was difficult to persuade her to let anyone else hold the baby.

Business at the shipyard dwindled even more and in the year that followed, many men had to be laid off. With the recent deaths in their families, David and Julia, Samuel and Amelia found themselves to be the older generation. Although they had carried the responsibilities of that generation for several years, there had always been someone to look up to, someone who had been an adult when they had been children. Now it was they who stood on that upper step.

Despite their problems and their sense of loss, or perhaps because of them, David and Julia together with their three children found themselves growing into a solidly knit family. There was a feeling of endurance and a calm happiness Julia had not felt since the days of her own childhood.

However, in the spring of 1859, long before David mentioned it, Julia began to see the signs. Thinking himself unobserved, David frequently climbed the dunes that sheltered the yard from the Bay and searched the open sea that was too often empty of traffic. Julia, watching him from afar, was all too aware of the eagerness with which he scanned the pages of each newspaper for signs of returning prosperity.

Papers which had once featured the arrival and departure of the clippers on their front pages and which went to press early to announce the setting of a new record, now relegated such matters to brief statements in the marine columns. Shipmasters were no longer the golden heroes of an exuberant age.

The *Yankee Girl*, stripped of her yards and topmasts, lay idle in Boston with only a shipkeeper to watch over her. She was in good company. With the reduced freight rates and the small cargoes to be found, many of the most famous ships were too large to pay their way at sea. Captains, who could show the greatest patience when beset by the vicissitudes of headwinds, gales, and doldrums, chafed at their enforced leisure, and the shipyard became an informal meeting place where they could gossip and catch up on the latest news.

It was there that David and Julia first heard about the American ships that had cleared China for England with cargoes of tea. When Amelia showed them Samuel's letter telling of his arrival in Liverpool with a cargo of Japanese goods, Julia held her breath and waited for David to broach the subject.

As spring passed and summer arrived, David spent an inordinate amount of time with Benjy and Daphne, as sea-bound fathers so often do before they leave the land. More and more often when Julia awoke at night, she would find him leaning over her with his eyes fixed on her face. Finally, the strain became more unbearable than the postponement of reality, and Julia herself brought up the subject.

The summer day was hot, with a few cumulous clouds hanging their low reflections on a placid sea. Julia had stayed home that morning, but Benjy, who had discovered that it didn't require much cajolery on his part to convince his mother to take him to that magic world of shells, pebbles, and sand, had begged to go down to the beach. After seeing that Daphne was safe with Martha and Clara, Julia hadn't hesitated. Since she rarely missed an opportunity to take her son to the shipyard, she decided on the beach that lay just beyond it.

After a leisurely stroll through the yard, where they picked up Benjy's small shovel and pail, they climbed the dunes. As they topped the rise, Julia saw David sitting on the lower path with his arms resting on his long legs. He was staring out at the sea, so immersed in his thoughts that he wasn't aware of their arrival.

Benjy, upon spotting his father, let out a whoop and plummeted down the path. He landed on David's lap with a scattering of sand and all of a three-year-old's enthusiasm. With the pail and shovel in her hand, Julia hurried after her son.

"Benjy!" She laughed. "That's no way to greet your papa. Here. Take these." She handed him his toys. "Go on down to the beach and see what you can do with them."

"You come, too, Papa," Benjy said, his dark blue eyes sparkling with enticement. "Come play with me."

"Not just now, son," David said ruffling Benjy's blue-black curls. "Maybe later."

"Then I'll wait." Benjy might have his father's smile, but he also had his mother's determination to achieve his own ends.

"No, Benjy," Julia said firmly and pulled him up by one sandy hand. "I want to talk to your papa. You go play. Look. Isn't that a large shell I see down there?"

Benjy searched the beach for the shell. Then he nodded, and without another word, he was off. Julia sat down on the sand beside her husband.

"When are you leaving, David?" she asked with no preliminaries.

"Soon." He showed no surprise at her question, but instead of looking at her, he stared out at the water made distant by a low tide. "I can't put it off much longer if I'm to commission the *Yankee Girl* and get her round the Horn in the best weather."

"I wish we could go with you." Her voice was wistful as she plucked a blade of beach grass.

"Why don't you?" He turned his head to see what effect his words would have. "Time Benjy got his feet wet, and it won't hurt Daphne. She'd get along anywhere."

She was silent for a moment. Then she lowered her eyes to the piece of grass, which she tried to split with her thumbnail.

"There's the shipyard," she said quietly.

"There's little to do there. All we have building is one small packet. I don't see why Daniel and Philip can't handle it."

"They won't bring in new business."

"No."

The sharp edge of the grass sliced her finger and brought an easier pain. As she dropped the blade and put her finger in her mouth, David pulled a handkerchief out of his pocket. He took her hand and examined the cut.

She watched him frowning over her finger. Then she said, "Still, if it was just the yard, I think I'd go. But there's Clara."

"No reason Clara can't go." He wound the handerchief around her finger and held it tightly. "She can even have her own stateroom. There's

322

plenty aboard, and we'll be lucky if we can find passengers to fill them."

With his right hand holding hers, her arm was bent at such an awkward angle, it caused a strain, but she didn't want to take her hand away from him. Too many months without the warmth his touch always brought lay ahead. She moved towards him to ease the strain. As she did, he put his other arm around her and pulled her closer until her head was resting against his shoulder.

"Clara's like Mama," Julia said with a sigh of regret. "She hates the sea. Remember? Even when she was little, she was sickly till we brought her ashore to live."

"Then leave her home. You did it before. Aunt Martha can look after her and Amelia's close to hand if anything comes up."

Julia looked down at the beach. Benjy was showering sand all over himself as he dug with great enthusiasm. If only she could take him to sea. How she longed to go! The one passage she and David had made together had been such a sad one, and this time, it could be so glorious. If only life were more simple.

"I can't leave her, David. She's lost too much. Her father, her grandmother. Maybe when she's older. She's fifteen now. Maybe after this voyage, we could go."

"Maybe. If there is another voyage."

"What do you mean?" She stiffened, thinking of Stephen threatening her with words, very like these.

David scattered kisses over her hairline until she relaxed. He didn't know precisely why she was suddenly tense, but he did know that some things triggered strange responses in Julia, and he was certain he knew their cause.

"All I meant was, if business picks up, you'll need me back here. Then I'll be able to hire a master again. Just now we can't afford one, and I'm not necessary to the yard. It's the only solution I can come up with. God knows, I've racked my brain to find another."

"I know," she said sadly.

"The *Yankee Girl* won't bring in what she once did, but it's better to have her working. An idle ship is only a drain. I'd sell her if I could, but there's no market."

Julia straightened up and looked at him with amazement.

"You couldn't give up that ship and you know it!" she said emphatically. When she leaned back against him, her voice was sympathetic. "Besides, you've been away from the sea for a long time now. It's been hard on you."

Benjy caught their attention by excitedly jumping up and down on the beach. He was waving something in his hand, but his words were drowned

323

out by the breeze and the light surf of the incoming tide. David dropped her handkerchief-bound hand long enough to wave, and Julia waved, too. When Benjy went back to his play, David shook his head.

"Leaving you and the children's going to be a lot harder than leaving the sea ever was. I've been waiting, hoping that something else would turn up, but the only good thing that's happened is that foreign commerce is showing some signs of life. I'd best go get my share of it." He unwrapped her finger and looked at it. Although there was a spot of blood on the handkerchief, only a thin line showed on her finger where the grass had sliced it. He brought her hand to his lips and tenderly kissed the wound. "I don't know who's going to look after you when I'm gone."

"I'll look after myself." She tried to smile confidently when she saw the concern in his eyes. If he had to go away, then she would send him off with as few worries on his mind as possible. "I've done it before. And I had a lot of other people to look after then. Mama. Megan and Amelia. All their children. Now there's just our children and Clara."

"Don't separate Clara from our children, Julie. She's your daughter. That makes her mine, too."

She squeezed his hand and they sat in a mingled silence, their minds filled with thoughts of that lonely future.

"Are you going straight to China or will you go to San Francisco first?" she finally asked.

"If I can get a cargo for California, I'll go there first." He trailed a finger over the vein of her bare arm.

"It makes a long voyage. Maybe a year."

"Maybe longer. From what I hear, it sometimes takes months to find a cargo no matter what port you put into. Josh Sears has had the *Wild Hunter* out for over two years now. Last I heard he was in Singapore and had to sail from there in ballast for Hong Kong."

"Don't stay away that long, David."

"I'll try not to." The smile that touched his wide lips was a promise.

Julia was determined not to be parted from David until he weighed anchor. When he went down to Boston, she and the children accompanied him. They would at least have the fitting-out time together.

The heat, noise, and soot of the railway cars made her wish that they had waited for the packet, but the packet's sailings were more sporadic now that the railroad had taken over so much of its business. Benjy, however, was delighted with the speed, and it was impossible to make him stay in his seat. In the past few weeks, David had tended to spoil him, and now he made no effort to restrain his son when Benjy, running up and down the aisle, imitated the sound of the engine and the click of the wheels upon the tracks.

By the time they reached the Richardson's house on Louisburg Square, Julia was wishing they had brought Aunt Martha along. She was the one person who could make Benjy really listen, for if he didn't he was apt to find himself turned over her knee. It was something Julia could never bring herself to do. She remembered her own youthful high spirits too well. Yet, fearing that Martha would be relegated to an uncomfortable servant's room, she had hesitated to bring the older woman with them. At home she was a member of the family, and a very important one at that. Julia would wait and send for Martha when they found quarters of their own.

Almost immediately after David had let the polished brass knocker fall, Megan herself threw open the door to reveal Hiram Richardson striding down the long hall with a broad smile on his face. The skirts of Megan's yellow muslin dress were pushed slightly aside, and Edgar's face with light blue eyes topped by golden brown hair peered out at Benjy, who was the elder by six months.

Robert, with his flaming carrot crest, came running from another room. When he saw them, he lost all of his ten-year-old poise and flung his arms around Julia. Then he turned and assaulted Clara, who laughed with glee upon seeing him. The years they had spent growing up in the same house had formed a close bond between them.

"Julie, you're here at last," Megan said, her black eyes sparkling. After a quick embrace, she held her friend back and gave her a thorough inspection from her flower-sprigged straw bonnet to her full-skirted lavender silk dress. "Eddy was up at dawn this morning, and all day he's been asking how soon Benjy was coming to play with him."

"Well, he's here now, and Eddy's welcome to him." Julia presented her cheek for Hiram's kiss and then she glanced down at her son. He was standing close beside her while he eyed Eddy. "I just hope you don't mind having a railroad train complete with engine in your house."

"They can go out into the garden and play," Megan said and reached out for Clara to give her a light kiss. She admired the girl's rose dress and smiled. "Clara. You've become quite the young lady. You've been growing up behind my back. And there's that sweet thing. Isn't she dainty?" She held out her arms to Daphne, whom David still held. "Let me have her."

While Megan was fussing over Daphne, Julia untied the lavender satin ribbons of her bonnet and looked around the high-ceilinged rooms that had once seemed so formidable. Now, with Megan's touch everywhere apparent and filled with the laughter of children, they had mellowed while losing none of their luxury.

"It's so good to be here," she said. "Like coming home."

"Well, that's the way we want you to feel." Megan glanced up and noticed that Hiram and David were disappearing through the large double doors that led to the dining room. Robert had abandoned Clara to tag along behind them. "Looks like the men have gone off to find a little liquid refreshment, but I'd be willing to wager that what you want is to wash off some of that soot."

"I hope I don't look that bad." Julia laughed and pulled out a lace-edged handkerchief to wipe her face.

"No. You look beautiful, but I know how I feel every time we take the railroad to visit you," Megan said as she led the way to the graceful curving staircase. "Where's Aunt Martha?"

"I thought it best to leave her home till we get settled in our own place."

"Settled in your own place? What are you talking about?" Megan paused on the first step and looked at Julia with astonishment. Then she noticed that the boys were still hesitantly eyeing each other. "Eddy, you take Benjy out to the garden. Show him your new ball."

After they had gone scampering down the wide hall, she looked over Daphne's mop of honey-gold curls indignantly. "Julie, I won't hear of you staying anywhere in Boston but here. And Hiram would be mortally insulted."

"We'll most likely be here a couple of months. Maybe more," Julia said as she and Clara followed Megan up the stairs. "We can't impose on you for that long."

"Nonsense. Isn't that right, Clara? You don't want to go anywhere else, do you?"

"No, Aunt Megan." Clara's long, silky curls swayed as she shook her head and her grey eyes lit with a smile for the adopted aunt she loved.

"Now, you see, Julie," Megan said. "You can't take Clara away from me. Besides if you want to talk about imposing, seems to me I remember staying with you for a matter of years."

"But there's five of us!" Julia looked down the hall at the row of doors. It had been one thing when just she and David had come to visit, but this was another matter. "I don't know how you're going to find room for us all."

"Well, you and David are going to sleep in here," Megan said as she led the way into a bedroom whose walls were covered with a Chinese wallpaper patterned with exotic birds perched on flowering fruit trees.

"But, Megan, this is your room!"

"Oh, I don't sleep here very often." Megan glanced mischievously at her friend. "I find Hiram's bed a sight more comfortable."

Julia put her bonnet on the gilt-decorated white dresser and glanced around the room. The bed was hung with pink silk and the windows were draped with the same fabric. She remembered so well the first time she had seen it. Hiram Richardson had then told her that it was for the wife he would someday have. It seemed strange that she had seen it before Megan had; stranger still that it had been before she had even met Megan. She felt as though they had been friends all of their lives.

"You're directly across the hall, Clara. Why don't you go on over and wash up? Everything's ready for you," Megan said as she put Daphne down on one of the pale green Oriental rugs that covered the floor. "And this sweet one and Benjy can go in with Eddy. His nursemaid's right next door to him, and she'll be able to keep an eye on them. There's still a room ready for Aunt Martha. I never dreamed you'd come down for a long stay and not bring her along."

"Well . . ." In her embarrassment, Julia poured water from the pink-flowered porcelain pitcher into its matching bowl. It looked so cool and refreshing in the heat of a city afternoon. "Aunt Martha's used to her comforts."

"Why, Julie!" Megan stared at Julia's back in complete amazement. "You don't think I'd send Aunt Martha up to the servants' rooms, do you? I lived in your house long enough to know better than that."

"I wasn't sure," Julia said hesitantly. She immediatley began to wash her face so she wouldn't have to look at Megan's eyes. It was true she kept expecting Hiram's wealth to affect her friend, even when Megan persisted in remaining unchanged.

"Well, your luggage should be up any minute now. As soon as you've changed, we're going to send a telegram to Aunt Martha and tell her to get on the very next train," Megan said emphatically. She plumped down on the floor near Daphne and peeked around her raised hands to make the little girl laugh. "You know she's going to miss the children terribly if you keep them away from her too long. How old is she now?"

"No one knows. She won't say, but I figure she must have passed her eightieth birthday. Not that you'd know it to look at or listen to her, but she's finally agreed to take things a little easier."

Julia dried her face and hands on a fine linen towel, then sat down on a white brocade slipper chair to watch her friend and her daughter. Although Megan doted on her two sons, she would dearly love to have a little girl.

"How's Robert doing?" Julia asked.

"Robby?" Megan took Daphne's tiny hands and began to play pat-a-cake, much to the child's delight. "Oh, he's fine. Last year he got top grades in his class, though I declare I don't know why. He never seems to study. He's building a model railroad down in the basement, and when he's not there, he's down at the counting house with Hiram. Hiram may be getting close on to seventy now, but you'd never know it. When he and Robby get together, they're into everything. I get plumb worn out just watching them."

"And Robby gets along well with the other boys? They don't tease him about being . . . different?"

"They spend so much time trying to keep up with his latest ideas, I doubt they've ever noticed that there is anything different about him. They just follow along behind him." Megan's laughter was filled with pride. Then she said more seriously, "His father's blood really isn't all that noticeable, Julie, except to those of us who know about it."

"Have you ever told him?"

"No. I don't intend to and Hiram agrees with me. As far as Robby's concerned, he was born Robert Fairfield, and he's now Robert Richardson. He's pretty happy with the father he's got. I think it's the best present I ever gave him. I know Hiram's mighty proud of him."

With Aunt Martha settled in at the house on Louisburg Square, Julia was free to accompany David as he set about recommissioning the *Yankee Girl*. Occasionally she supervised it herself when he went the rounds of the counting houses looking for cargo or charters. It often seemed a hopeless task, and he sometimes wondered if he were right to plan on taking the ship to sea again. However, as summer deepened into autumn and the *Yankee Girl* became seaworthy once more, David, with Hiram Richardson's help, began to find small loads of freight for California, and he became more cheerful. But sometimes in the evenings as he watched the boys playing on the carpet or dandled Daphne from his knee, a sadness lingered in the lines of his face.

The days were growing shorter by October, but Benjy was allowed to stay up late on David's final night ashore. When they had finally tucked him in beside Eddy, Julia and David went slowly down the long hall hand in hand.

"I don't think he knows what's happening," David said thoughtfully.

"No. Not completely. He won't be four till December."

"I wonder how old he'll be when I come home? I've enjoyed it, Julie. Enjoyed these years of staying home with you and watching my children grow up." He opened the door to their bedroom for her and followed her in. "Not all men are able to do that. I must be thankful for what time's been given me."

"Oh, David!" She turned to look up at this giant of a man she had

328

married. At forty-five, his hair had begun to recede slightly from his low, broad forehead, but it still gathered into tight curls. Two deep lines were etched between his eyes, which were now filled with sadness. As she looked at him, she realized that she loved him more than she had ever thought possible. "If only . . ."

"Hush," he said as he raised her hand to his lips. "If only's don't count. Remember?"

When he dropped her hand and turned away to shed his coat, Julia, watching him, raised her hand to her own lips to touch the spot his lips had brushed. After he had draped his coat neatly on a chair, he picked up the buttonhook from the dresser and came to her.

"Need some help?"

"Yes, David." She tried to keep the tears from her eyes. This was the last time. It would be an eternity before he performed that familiar task again. "I do need help."

While he unbuttoned her dress, she gave herself over to the sensuous enjoyment of his large hands as they lightly traveled down her back. Memories. She must store them for the future.

As they undressed each other, their eyes clung together, saying those thousands of things that must be said again and again. When her pink satin dress lay on the floor surrounded by her petticoats, chemise, corset, and stockings, she stood straight before him so that his eyes and his hands might wander where they wished. David, too, would need his memories.

"You're still a lovely woman, sweet Julie," he said in a hushed voice as he memorized her body in the dim lamplight. New stretch marks had been imprinted on her torso since their first time together. His own children had put them there. He bent to kiss them. "There's none other like you in all the world."

"Well, don't go shopping to check it out." She tried to laugh, but there was a quaver in her voice.

"I won't," he said as he swept her up and carried her to the bed. "Oh, my love, I won't."

Three times that night they became one, and there was no sleep for either of them as the dark hours sped towards dawn. The fire was kept burning and the lamp was kept lit so that nothing would be lost to them in those final hours.

Once during the night when they were resting, lying side by side with their hands clasped, David said, "At least this voyage will be different from any other I've ever taken."

"Different?" Julia asked dreamily. "How?"

"All those lonely passages with only a cold, brittle woman who wouldn't even wait for me in England. All those regret-filled years that I spent thinking of you and of what might have been. Years with few letters, no true wife, no children. Years with no memories to relieve those eternal days

329

and nights when there was no one to talk to. This time, I sail a rich man."

"Rich? I'd say that's the last thing you are or you wouldn't be going."

"Oh, I am rich." He stretched his long legs and put his free hand behind his head. "I have a wealth of memories to take with me. I'll relive every day of our lives together. And I'll be able to think of you and Benjy, Daphne and Clara at home waiting for me. Best of all, I'll know that you're thinking of me just as I am of you."

"Yes, David." She rolled over and propped her arm on his far shoulder. He never minded her weight. Her thick black hair swept across his chest, and she smiled as she looked into his eyes. "That's something you can always be certain of. At any hour, whether it's day or night, when you think of me, you can be sure I'll be either thinking or dreaming of you."

"Remember once when I asked you if life had any meaning?"

"When we were building the *Free Wind*?" She pushed her fingers through his curls, which had become tousled in the night. "Yes. I remember."

"You said then that there was a God who watched over us. That I had the sea and a ship. Those weren't the answers I wanted, but for the past four years, you've given me the answer I had to have."

"Aye." She smiled as she nestled down beside him. "I've had moments of doubt myself, but not since the day we stood at that altar together. God has been good to us."

"And He'll continue to be." Bringing his hand out from under his head, he began to stroke her smooth back. "Don't worry about me while I'm gone, Julie. I'll come back to you, and when I do, I'll be the same man who left."

"Asking me not to worry about you is like asking a crab to fly, but I'll try not to. I won't let the children see if I am."

"The children." There was a catch in his voice. "Don't let them forget me, Julie."

The autumn morning was crisp and the trees were flying their bravest colors when the family and Aunt Martha climbed into the Richardsons' carriage. David's sea chest took up so much of the space they were cramped together. The carriage would have to return to the house to fetch the Richardsons, who wanted to be on hand to see David sail.

David was dressed in his best black frock coat, as befitted a master on sailing day. It reminded Julia of the time when she had sailed with him, and she knew that once the ship had passed the Roads, he would change into rougher clothes. But she didn't want to think about that.

330

She wore a bright blue coat trimmed with black braid that she'd had made just for the occasion. She knew that it was an extravagance when money was so scarce, but it was cheerful and she wanted him to carry away a memory of her looking her best.

The ride seemed so short, and when the carriage clattered down the stone wharf it was too soon over. As they drew up beside the *Yankee Girl* and Julia saw the figurehead, she caught her breath. It was really happening. David really was going to sail away and leave her. Although she had seen the ship a hundred times during the fitting out, there was something very final about the sight of the tall topmasts and the yards all in place. The sails were furled tightly in their gaskets, but the men who would unfurl them were on deck. There had been no problem in finding a crew in this hungry world. A few of the men who had signed the Articles were ones they had been forced to lay off at the shipyard.

Julia found herself trembling when David helped her from the carriage. He held her arm for a moment, and his soft green eyes misted as they looked into hers. She managed a small smile and he nodded. Then he looked up at the quarterdeck and cupped his hands beside his mouth.

"Is she ready for sea?" he shouted up at the mate, who had come to attention at the rail as soon as the carriage arrived.

"Aye, aye, sir," the mate shouted back. "Ready for sea."

"What time's the tug due?"

"Tug's due at three bells, sir."

David took his gold watch from his pocket and looked at it. He glanced regretfully at Julia.

"It's just after nine," he said. "That leaves us less than half an hour. I don't know whether the Richardsons will be here by then or not. I hate the thought of leaving you and the children stranded."

"It's all right, David. I'll see you out of sight." She moved aside as two seamen advanced to pick up the chest the coachmen had hurriedly unloaded onto the wharf.

"Do you want to come aboard for a moment? There's time enough for that."

"No. I don't think so. 'Twould just make me want to stay."

"Aye. Best not to," he said soberly. Then he turned to Aunt Martha and took Daphne from her arms. He pushed back her bonnet and ruffled her curls.

"Well, little princess, you don't know what's going on, do you?"

"Yes," she said with a wide smile and grabbed at his chin. Yes was one of her favorite words and she used it for almost everything.

"Can you give Papa a kiss?"

"Yes." She tilted her face and when David raised her up to his own level, she implanted a loud kiss on his cheek. He grazed her forehead with his lips. When he handed her back to Martha, he blinked a couple of times.

"Martha, good-bye. Take care of them all for me."

"I'll do that, sir." Martha was fond of this big man who had brought peace to a troubled household. She'd miss him as much as the others. "May you have a safe voyage, Captain Baxter."

"Thank you, Martha."

Then he looked down at Clara, who was standing as close to him as she could get. She was inspecting the ship with frightened eyes.

"Clara," David said gently. "It's going to be all right."

She looked up at him, pleading for reassurance. "You will come back, won't you, Dada?"

"Of course I will," he said in a voice he tried to make jovial. "If for no other reason than to see how many beaux you've collected. Now don't you go getting yourself married before I've had a chance to inspect the young man."

A blush instantly stained Clara's fair skin and she lowered her eyes to the ground. He had guessed her secret thoughts, thoughts that at fifteen she wasn't supposed to be entertaining. But it was all right. Dada would never betray her.

"I won't," she said earnestly as she looked up at him. "I'll wait for you to approve them."

"And you'll write to me? Tell me all that you're doing? You can talk to me in letters, you know, just as much as though I was here."

"Yes. I'll write." She caught his hand and clung to it, then lifted her face to him as he bent over to kiss her.

"Take care of your mother," he said, straightening up.

"I will."

He smiled and then he turned to Benjy, whose dark blue eyes sparkled with excitement as he watched the men aboard the ship going about their duties. David held out his hand to his son.

"Benjy?"

The boy immediately went to his father, and David scooped him up.

"So you like the *Yankee Girl*, do you?" David asked.

"Oh, yes, Papa!" Benjy clutched at his father's neck with one arm, but his eyes never left the ship. "Take me with you."

"I wish I could, son." David pressed his lips together and shook his head. "How I wish I could."

"I'll be good." The boy turned the full intensity of his black-lashed eyes on his father.

"It's not that, Benjy." His voice choked and he held the child tighter. "I know you'd be good. Maybe next time."

"Next time? When?" Benjy demanded.

"Well . . . Maybe a year from now."

The glow left Benjy's face as he thought of that enormous, endless time. A year. It was forever.

David kissed Benjy on his soft cheek and started to put him on the ground, but then changed his mind. He shifted the boy higher with one arm and held out his other to Julia. She came quickly to the shelter of his body. They looked into each other's eyes for those long silent minutes. There were no words left to be said.

Then they heard the engines of the tug as it approached the wharf. The mate was shouting orders. Lines were being taken aboard. The pilot strolled up the gangway.

David gave Benjy a final squeeze and set him on the ground. As he straightened up, he took Julia in both his arms. The last kiss was short, but it was layered with past sweetness and future hope.

"Julie . . ."

His voice broke and tears appeared in his eyes. She tried to speak, but couldn't. As he dropped his arms, he caught her hand. Even as he took a step away from her, he held it. Then he broke the contact and ran up the gangway.

The last lines were cast off. Water opened up between the wharf and the *Yankee Girl* as the tug towed her out into the harbor. Benjy's eyes were on the ship, but all others were on the big man who stood easily on the quarterdeck. Although all his attention appeared to be on the ship, he occasionally glanced back at the wharf.

The first sails were beginning to blossom on her yardarms when the Richardsons drove up. Robby jumped out of the carriage and ran up to the group who stood on the wharf.

"They've gone!" he said, utterly disappointed. "I wanted to say goodbye to Uncle David, Aunt Julia."

"I'm sorry, Robby," Julia said, but she barely glanced at the boy.

Hiram Richardson came up behind his son and laid a hand on his shoulder. "Don't bother Aunt Julia now, Robby," he said in a quiet voice. He looked over at Martha, who was showing signs of weariness from holding Daphne. "Martha, why don't you take Daphne and go sit in the carriage. Better yet, you go on home with Mrs. Richardson. Eddy and Benjy can go with you. I think there's room enough for Clara, too. Robby and I'll stay here with Mrs. Baxter until the carriage returns."

"No!" Benjy said emphatically. "I want to stay with Mama."

"Let him stay, Hiram," Julia said softly.

"Me, too." Clara moved to Julia's side and slipped her hand into her mother's. "I want to watch till he's gone."

When the carriage drove off, the ship was moving more swiftly, and David was discernible only because of his size. He towered above all other men on deck.

Then the lines to the tug were cast off. All but the royals were set and drawing. Julia was scarcely aware of Clara's hand clutching hers. Her eyes and her heart followed the *Yankee Girl*.

Oh, God, keep him safe. Bring him back to me. Bring him safely through the storms. Then the *Yankee Girl* was gone.

Chapter Twenty-two

1859–1860

Ship *Yankee Girl*
Atlantic Ocean
October 22, 1859

My dearest wife,

My thoughts have been with you since my last sight through the glass of you and Clara and Benjy standing on Long Wharf. Now that we are well clear of land, I will take this opportunity to begin a letter, which I will send off by the first homeward bound vessel we sight. The weather has been fair and the crew are working well. . . .

October 29

A week since I have been able to sit down with pen in hand. The seas are beginning to calm, but for four days, it blew a gale, fortunately sending us in the right direction. It made me realize that I was growing soft and comfortable. Well, this voyage should go a long way towards hardening me up again. How I wish you were here in the cabin, Julie. There is good light for reading or sewing. If I close my eyes, I can pretend that you are beside me as you were in those sad days aboard the *Free Wind*, but this time I should make you happy. . . .

November 3

A few days of head winds and rough seas, which God in His wisdom has sent to try my patience. He knows that I will need a great fund of it during the months to come. A voyage just begun and already I find it a sore trial to be parted from you and the children. . . .

With affection,
Your devoted husband,
David Baxter

East Dennis, Cape Cod
Massachusetts
October 22, 1859

My dear husband,

We have just arrived home from Boston. The Richardsons were kind

334

and wanted us to stay on a few days, but there seemed to be no point in remaining without you. Now that we are home, I find our bedroom is just as empty as theirs. But I think of you in your cabin and know that it is lonelier. At least here, I have the children and friends while you have no one to talk to.

All the way home, Benjy was convinced that you would be here when we arrived. No one could persuade him otherwise, though Clara and Aunt Martha and I all tried. He was a very disappointed little boy when he discovered that we had told him the truth. He has gone to bed trying to hide his disappointment. . . .

October 28

I have been busy with the yard, trying to settle all the matters that have come up in our absence. Things are very much as we left them. Daniel has taken good care. Yet it is discouraging to find that there has been no one interested in building a large vessel since Daniel's last letter to us in Boston.

Though I've not had the time to write you these past few days, you've never been far from my thoughts, David. I glance at the globe and try to trace your course. I have the logs from the *Crystal Star*, and when I read a little from them to Benjy each evening, I tell him that is most likely what your day has been. He seems to enjoy them, and I hope it will keep you fresh in his memory till you return. . . .

October 29

I am posting this to you today so that I'll be certain there is at least one letter waiting to greet you in San Francisco. May God keep you in his protection and send you fair winds to bring you home safe to me.

Your loving wife,
Julia Baxter

Ship *Yankee Girl*
November 5, 1859

My darling wife,

The winds which treated us so well at first have deserted us. I have never suffered so from impatience as I do on this voyage, but then I never had a loving wife and dear children waiting at home for me before, either. . . .

November 10

Today we saluted old Neptune as we crossed the Equator. Now that we are 1°14′ South of the Line, I feel both further from you and nearer to you, Julie, for with each league that parts us, we are one league closer to home. . . .

335

November 11

This has been a beautiful and warm day. Reminded me of a June day at home. At sunset, I longed to show you the reflections the sunset cast upon the sea. I doubt I have ever seen it lovelier. All windows and ports are open. The wind is fair and the sea is calm. . . .

November 12

Tell Benjy there are whales in plenty here and they are great barnacle encrusted monsters. . . .

East Dennis
November 24, 1859

My dear husband,

Your first letter arrived yesterday, and I feel as though the sun is shining after weeks of clouds and rain. No orders save those for a few small fishing boats and dories. I will wait till after Christmas, but if we have nothing more in hand, I shall have to lay off a few men. I can see no way out of it.

I read your letter to the children, and Benjy had me repeat parts of it over and over again. Clara listened with equal interest. I hope you will find space in some of your letters to mention her. . . .

November 27

It has been raining the past two days and Aunt Martha is moving stiffly because of her rheumatism. . . .

November 29

Captain Jackson paid a call this afternoon to tell me that on his way home he had sighted the *Yankee Girl* and that she was flying signals to say that all was well aboard. He sends his regards and begs you to excuse him for not stopping, but his wife was expecting a child and he was trying to rush her home before it arrived. Their little boy was delivered in New York and both he and Mrs. Jackson are doing well. Oh, how it made me long to be with my husband aboard his ship. . . .

Ship *Yankee Girl*
December 9

My sweet wife,

My last letter went off to you yesterday aboard the *Giraffe*, Captain Gaines. I trust it will find you well. I know you have never thought Cape Horn beautiful, but today it is. How I wish that you could see it, my dearest. Placid seas, fair winds, the sun shines on the earth and water. Old Cape Stiff has decided to relax for once, but I shall not trust it till we are safe in the Pacific. . . .

December 14

As Christmas approaches, the men's spirits grow lower. I will have two pigs killed for their dinner on Christmas Day. There cannot be a man aboard who is bluer than I am, and the thought of a pig does little to cheer me. . . .

December 16

It must be growing cold at home though it is as hot as Hades here. I worry about you. I know you will see to it that the children are well bundled up, but do take care to wear your thick shoes and your warmest coat when you go to the yard. . . .

December 27

The men have cheered up now that Christmas is past. Was Clara's dress finished in time for Christmas Day? Tell her I think she must look pretty in it and that I wish that I was there to see her all decked out. What did Daphne think of her second Christmas? I doubt she remembered the first very well. It is hard to think that she will be two years old when I next see her.

I thought of you and home constantly that day, but we have been beset by squalls from every point of the compass and so there was no time to write. I did open your present and I think my new vest will look very fine on the streets of San Francisco. . . .

East Dennis
December 25, 1859

My dearest husband,

This day began bright and sunny. At church, the pastor said a special prayer for all of our men at sea, and he especially mentioned those aboard the *Yankee Girl*, so you see the thoughts of the entire congregation were upon you and your men. Even though I write this by lamplight after having brushed out my hair and donned my nightgown and robe, I am still wearing the garnet earrings you left for me. It was such a pleasant surprise to open your small package and find them. I felt that you were very near. . . .

December 28

I have told the men who must leave by the middle of January, and it was a very sad occasion. They have been loyal to us and the yard, and I told them so. I also told them that, as soon as we get more work, I want them all back, but I hoped they would find gainful employment more immediately. How I wish you were here to lift my spirits. . . .

December 29

Clara has come down with a cold. I don't believe it is a very severe one, but Aunt Martha has her tucked up in bed and is coddling her. I worry that the little ones will catch it, but they have stronger constitutions than she does.

Benjy wants to know if you have seen any flying fish yet, and I have told him that I was sure you must have. The whole idea of a fish that flies is fascinating to him. . . .

December 30

Dear Dada,

I am cozy in bed with a pile of handkerchiefs beside me. Mama says that I am not to worry you and to tell you that I am better. You are not to worry about the beaux, either. No one has come courting nor are they like to if they see me with my red nose and running eyes. I miss you. . . .

Ship *Yankee Girl*
January 1, 1860

My dearest Julie,

A new year that begins with days that take us further apart, but I trust the end of it will see us together once more. I am driving this ship as hard as I know how, and I hope to reach the San Francisco pilot grounds in record time. I am certain there will be a letter from you there. It has been very hard all these months with no word of you. We crossed the Line yesterday, so you can see how anxious I am. . . .

January 4

Light airs and baffling. We have lost ground these past twenty-four hours, and a fine rain soaks us all. Have put the men to scrubbing the outside of the ship. It seems I boasted too soon and now I am to be taught a lesson. When I think of the letters that are waiting for me with news of my dear ones, it makes me long to jump overboard and tow the ship to California. I almost think I could do it. . . .

January 6

Still no wind and I despair of ever reaching San Francisco or seeing my home again. . . .

January 7

Breezing up so strong, I had the skysails in. Your letters will soon be read. Has there been any sickness at home? I remember too well that winter two years past. Makes me wonder who will be gone when I return home. Don't drive yourself too hard, my dearest wife, and be sure to stay home if you feel the least bit poorly. If work doesn't go well, don't let it put you in the doldrums. . . .

January 18

We took the pilot on board at eight this morning and are now at anchor in San Francisco Bay! The pilot brought me your letters. There are five of them and the sight of your handwriting went a long way to cheering me. I've had no time to do more than glance at the end of your last letter to assure myself that you were all well, but they will be read before the lamp is out. The mail goes first thing in the morning, so I will close this letter in order that you may receive it as soon as possible.

I am in good health and have not had a sick day since I left home. Always remember that I love you as much as any man ever loved his wife. Maybe more.

Your devoted husband,
David Baxter

East Dennis
January 20, 1860

My dearest husband,

The men I laid off have gone and the yard seems lonelier than ever with the few that are left. It is terribly quiet. The wind is louder than the sound of tools. How I wish you were here. . . .

January 25

Since John Brown's execution, there is more hard feeling amongst people than ever. I have heard that every member of both the House and the Senate in Washington goes onto the floor armed with a gun. I look at Benjy and am afraid. . . .

January 28

Daphne speaks so clearly now. She prattles on about her papa. I wish you could see her. She is so dainty and so pretty. . . .

January 30

The letter you entrusted to Captain Gaines arrived today. You sound very lonely. How my heart aches for you and my arms long to hold you. I trust that you are in San Francisco now and are feeling cheerful. It comforts me to think that we walk the same continent even though on opposite shores. . . .

San Francisco
February 2, 1860

My darling wife,

I have read your letters again and again and am afraid that I will wear them out with too much handling before the voyage is over. Another one arrived today. Don't be low about the men you have to let go. It is the only thing you can do. . . .

339

February 5

Tonight I have just returned from a most elegant dinner party given by your friends, the Courtneys. They have built a magnificent house on a high hill overlooking San Francisco Bay, and the food was very fine. The best I have eaten since leaving home. Mrs. Courtney asked to be remembered to you and to tell you she hopes to see you with me the next time I sail to San Francisco. She only echoed my strongest wishes. . . .

February 8

There is nothing to be found in this town but discouragement. No one has goods they want shipped and every day the prices of goods I might wish to buy on my own account rise. . . .

February 12

Today I saw Paul Kelley and we had dinner together. He was only here for a couple of days on business. I must say he looks very prosperous. He says his mother is well and enjoying her new house in Sacramento. He was glad to get first-hand news of home. We spoke of you so often, your ears must have been burning. . . .

February 27

Still no business to be done. I was a fool to leave my home if this is all I get for my pains. . . .

March 2

I can wait no longer for trade, but must go seek it. I am buying a few things on my own account. Some flour and wheat, shrimp skins and fish fins, old bones. But for the most part, I will be forced to sail in ballast. I wouldn't mind so much if you and the children were sailing with me. . . .

March 13

We sail with the morning tide. All the crew, if you can call them that, are aboard. Three white sailors, nine boys, one carpenter, two Kanakas, four Malays, and two Manila men. All that I brought out with me have left the ship. It is the fashion here. I have left instructions for my mail to be forwarded to Hong Kong. I will miss your letters. Oh, my Julia, how lonesome I am for you and my family. . . .

East Dennis
March 14, 1860

My dear husband,

Benjy has pestered me so much lately to begin reading the logs to him again, I started today with the account of my one voyage from San Francisco to China. He has a lively imagination for such a little boy. He quite surprises me with some of his questions about life aboard the *Yankee Girl*. . . .

March 20
Philip Sears came to me this morning and told me that he was leaving the yard. He plans to pack up his family and move to Cincinnati come spring. It is hard to see him go, but I cannot pay him what he deserves. I worry about Daniel leaving. . . .

March 28
I think Clara has a beau. Young Jim Parker has taken up hanging around the house. However, Clara stoutly denies it. She is nearly sixteen now. It does make me wonder. . . .

April 12
Philip has gone and so have many of our best craftsmen. They have found other occupations. I cannot blame them, but I get very low when I walk through the yard. Papa trusted me. He left me his affairs to manage and I have failed him. Oh, David, I need you here. There are so many things I want to talk over with you. . . .

April 14
Aunt Martha has told Daphne that she must put her feet solidly on the ground when she walks, but Daphne thinks that toes are sufficient. . . .

Ship *Yankee Girl*
Pacific Ocean
March 15, 1860
My dearest wife,
'Tis good to be on blue water again even with a crew that is still well soaked with rum. They'll be dry enough in a few days. The mates have confiscated the bottles smuggled aboard. I saw the last of the American continent with a great feeling of relief. Not much good came to us out of California. . . .

March 17
We logged four hundred and eight knots today! The *Yankee Girl* has never been in better form than she is now. She seems to love the Pacific, but perhaps she is just trying to speed her master home to his loved ones. . . .

March 19
The moon was full tonight and I wondered if it shone on your face as

341

it made its passage across Cape Cod. My bed aboard never seemed too large before, but now I find that I sleep on one side of it, leaving room for you. Then I wake and you are not there. . . .

March 20
A day when the weather was not. The wind blew from not one point but puffed occasionally from every direction. It is not raining, but it is not clear either. Just a soaking mist. It is too stifling to stay below, but too raw to enjoy the deck. How I long to reach the trades and leave all this behind. . . .

March 21
A heavy swell from the West contributes to our misery. The ship rolls with no wind to relieve her. . . .

March 22
No other sail in sight. Would like to sight just one. Misery loves company. Oh, for the humblest shack ashore. . . .

March 25
Finally the trades. The *Yankee Girl* is taking to them like the true lady she is. To while away these tedious hours, I have begun to make a small ship for Benjy. I shall name her the *Clara Daphne*. . . .

March 28
A moderate breeze these twenty-four hours and pleasant weather. The men have begun to shed their clothes and expose their bodies to the sun. Oh, my dear wife, sometimes I feel your presence so strongly, I expect to find you standing near, but then I turn and you are not. . . .

April 1
Several of the men have reported that they are missing personal possessions. Clothes and such like. We have done a thorough search of the sea chests, but have come up with nothing. I knew the thief would be wiser than to stow everything in his chest, but I hoped for one small thing he might have overlooked to betray him. Tension is high aboard. . . .

April 3
Tell Benjy that the *Clara Daphne* is shaping up nicely. . . .

April 8
Today I saw a land bird, and either his navigation is wrong or mine is. I think the fault is his. . . .

342

April 16

Calms these three days. If this keeps up, I will be an old man before I see my wife and children again. . . .

April 17

Calms. Have the men employed in making boarding nets, but unless we get more wind than we have had these past four days, the cord will rot before we have occasion to meet with any pirates. I am lonesome, blue, and disconsolate. . . .

April 18

Calm and hot enough to heat Aunt Martha's blood. The men have stripped down to the bare essentials, and they eye each other constantly. The mood aboard is not pleasant. . . .

April 20

Good air with all sails out. The clothes have been found, but the culprit has not. . . .

East Dennis
April 15, 1860

My dearest husband,
Today I caught Benjy and Jason in Mama's room. They had a sheet draped over a broom handle, which was stuck in the rocking chair. The two boys were rocking and shouting, "Land ahoy! Ship ahoy!" They each claimed to be captain of the ship, but depending upon whose account you heard, the chair was either *Yankee Girl* or *Neptune's Dragon*. 'Twas most unhealthy for the chair, but I didn't have the heart to stop them. . . .

April 18

How can time pass so slowly? Not quite six months and already it seems a lifetime. I don't know how I will manage another six. Jane Farnham, who is newly married with her husband out to sea on his first voyage since their wedding, said to me the other day that it must be easy for me since I've experienced it before. She told me that it must be nice to be older and *settled*. I managed to smile. My dearest, how could I tell her that this is the hardest voyage of my life? . . .

April 25

A pleasant day. I took Benjy and Jason to the beach. Daphne and I watched them cavort on the sand like a pair of puppies. 'Tis good to get them out of the house after the rain of the past week. Yet all the while I was there, I found myself watching the sea for a suit of sails I knew was half a world away. . . .

April 28

Am feeling more cheerful today. I broached the subject of his leaving with Daniel. It's been fretting me ever since Philip left. Daniel swore that he would never leave so long as one wood chip remained on the ground. I don't believe he would. . . .

Hong Kong
April 28, 1860

My darling Julia,

Having made port today, I feel that I am closer to you. There are a number of familiar ships here. Samuel was the first to board, eager for news of Amelia and his family. He looks well if a little tired. He says there is not much business to be had for ships the size of ours. . . .

May 1

Tell Clara I say she is too young to entertain serious notions. I know you did at her age, but I thought you far too young even at the time. . . .

You mustn't feel guilty about the yard and your management of your father's finances. After all, much that was lost was due to his own choice of investments, and that wasn't due to his lack of wisdom. No one could have foreseen the economic disasters that were to come. . . .

May 3

Daphne's birthday. How I wish I could hold my little girl on my knee once more. Six months have most likely made a great change in her. Is she still the happy child I left behind? All I have to do is think of her and it gladdens my heart. Tell her that I have made a doll for her. . . .

May 12

I saw your friend, Mrs. Kirkwood, today. As you know, her husband died three years ago, but she seems quite content living with her daughter and son-in-law. He resigned his commission in the British Navy and is in business here. She thinks very highly of you. But no more than I do. . . .

May 14

I have disposed of what little cargo I carried at a reasonable profit. There is nothing to be had here, but from what I have been told, there is not much activity anywhere on the China Coast. I shall have to employ patience, but it seems a hard thing. . . .

My dear husband,

It is a beautiful day today, but I am low. Maybe I've caught it from Clara. I haven't seen Jim Parker for a while, which I suspect is the cause of her blues, but she won't discuss it with me. I wish you were here to talk to her. You always did have a way with Clara. . . .

June 20

Amelia came over today with a letter from Samuel. He says you are not in Hong Kong as yet nor has he heard of your being reported anywhere on the China Coast. My heart quite dropped when she read it to me, but then I discovered the letter was dated more than two months ago. I tell myself that you must be there now.

June 30

Daphne reminds me more of you all the time, and that does *not* mean she is ugly. She's the prettiest little thing I ever did see, and she's a good child. They have all been very good in your absence, but I think they need their papa. . . .

July 5

I know you will be sorry to hear that Aaron Martin's father died on the 1st. The funeral was held two days later, and I went with Amelia. Sarah did not speak to either of us. In fact, she pretended not to see us. Aaron saw us even if he didn't speak, but I feel very sorry for him. It must have made a dreary Fourth of July for him. Did you celebrate the Fourth in China? I know you must be there. . . .

July 12

Your first letter from Hong Kong arrived today. It much relieves my mind to know that you are safe and well. I said a special prayer of thanksgiving. . . .

July 25

I am forty years old today. 'Tis a bleak thought without my dear husband beside me to tell me how pretty I am and that I still don't look a day over twenty to him. You lie so charmingly. All day I have kept repeating the words you said the night before you sailed. Would that you were here to say them now. . . .

July 28

I am glad to hear that you are able to employ patience. 'Tis something I have in short supply. . . .

August 1

Benjy has pestered me so much about the *Clara Daphne*, I have had to make a sketch of the *Yankee Girl* for him. I hope that is what you are modeling his ship after. He carries it around in his pocket and shows it to everyone who will listen to him. He proudly tells them that his papa is building that ship for him. . . .

August 5

I have written little about the yard because there is no good news in that department. I leave the running of it mostly to Daniel so that I may spend most of my time with the children. . . .

Hong Kong
June 13, 1860

My beloved wife,

A ball was held aboard the *Foxfire* last night, and if you had been here you would have been much in demand. Only fifteen ladies present, and some of the husbands so jealous, they followed anyone around who had the temerity to dance with their wives. You would have outshone the fairest face to be seen. . . .

July 1

We employ our enforced leisure with boat sailing, though I am sure that all of us would prefer to be racing our larger craft. I have not done badly. . . .

July 12

I sail for Foochow today. I understand that I may get a consignment of tea for Liverpool if I make haste. . . .

Foochow
July 20

Nothing here to do but kick our heels. One day they say they will have something for me, the next day they don't know. No one knows what date the tea will be available. . . .

July 25

Your birthday. Don't feel low. I can tell you forty is not such a bad thing to be. After all I arrived there six years before you. And I would not trade you for any other woman. My dearest, I wish I was there to give you the present I bought for you in Hong Kong. I will not spoil it for you by telling you what it is. . . .

July 27

We began loading today, and my heart is a hundred times lighter. Only two more passages and then I will be holding you in my arms. So often I think of you standing on Long Wharf in your brave blue coat, and I can almost believe you will be standing there just so when I return. . . .

East Dennis
August 20, 1860

My dear husband,

I took Benjy and Jason to the yard with me today. They enjoy it so, I hoped it would cheer me to see their pleasure, but the sight of our handful of men working on the small craft that once were only a sideline of the yard made me feel terribly blue.

Even the sea sounded sad when I took the boys to swim in it. For no reason at all, I felt like crying. It is as though I have lost something that can never be recaptured. Is it because of the yard? Or is it because I feel my youth is truly over? I sound like a silly middle-aged woman. I need you here to tell me what a goose I am. Still I cannot shake the feeling.

When we were leaving the yard, Daniel brought me a letter that had just arrived from you. What happiness that gave me! But for some reason, it didn't last.

After getting the boys home, I have come up to my room and locked the door. My gloom is so deep, I don't want to infect the children with it. All I want is to be held and comforted in a way that only you can. The next best thing is to read your letters and write to you. I may decide not to mail this because it most likely would depress you, but even so, maybe you will hear my words across the miles. . . .

I love you so much, David. . . .

Even with all this writing, I feel no better. Janet has brought me a tray of light supper, but I have no appetite. . . .

I pray that you are homeward bound, because I don't know how much longer I can do without you. Just come home safely. I'll never let you out of my sight again. I'll go anywhere with you. 'Tis better to leave Clara ashore than to suffer again these past months. She is more confident now that she has two suitors. . . .

It is past midnight, and I watch these pages pile up beside my hand and wonder why I keep on. I know I can never send this letter. Perhaps I will show it to you when you return home. 'Twill prove to you how much I love you. . . .

The sky is growing lighter in the east. I hear a few sleepy birds trying out their morning song, but it doesn't feel like dawn to me. All night has been spent in reading and rereading your letters and then going back to my desk to write more.

I pray that you are on the final passage of your voyage. If only I could know that you would be home again before the year is out, then I could go on.

Oh, David, I love you. . . .

Foo Chow
August 6, 1860

My darling Julia,

We sail in a couple of hours and my gladness knows no limits. Homeward bound! The words keep pounding in my head and beating in my heart as they must in those of every man aboard. We have to deliver the tea to Liverpool, but if I can find no cargo there for America within a week, I am determined to sail home in ballast. I will not be kept away from my wife and children any longer.

With any luck, I'll be home for Benjy's fifth birthday. The *Clara Daphne* is launched and rigged, all ready for him to sail. Don't let Daphne grow too fast. Tell her she must wait for me. And remind Clara of her promise.

Oh, my love, to be with you again, to see you, to hold you. 'Tis hard to believe the day is coming when you won't disappear with my dreams, but will be there beside me when I waken. To feel your warmth. To see your smile. . . .

This was the last letter from David. There were no more. Ever.

Chapter Twenty-three

1861

As best Julia could piece the story together later, the *Yankee Girl* had sailed with her cargo of tea from Foo Chow on August 6, 1860. Two vessels reported seeing her later in the South China Sea, but she never reached Anjier. A typhoon had been traveling over the sea, but no one could say whether David's ship had been in its path or not. No debris had been found. The ship, her cargo, and her complement of men had simply vanished.

* * *

That winter and through the following spring, Amelia watched with concern as her sister's figure dwindled and the dark shadows grew deeper under her indigo eyes. Whenever she tried to speak about David, Julia cut her off and withdrew into herself. A sheath of ice seemed to encase her.

However, when summer came, Amelia was determined to break through that barrier. One day in late June, she asked Julia to walk with her up to the cutting garden in back of the family home. With Aunt Martha suffering from rheumatism and the maids too busy to tend it, the garden would have ceased to exist if it hadn't been for Amelia. Knowing how her mother had loved that flowering spot, she tended it in her memory, and often it was Clara who helped her.

Today Clara was visiting with some friends in the village, and Amelia had lured Julia up there on the pretense of asking her advice about some chrysanthemums. She had found occupations for all the children so that she might talk to her sister alone. Even before they reached the white picket fence that surrounded the garden, Amelia broached the subject.

"Julie, about David . . ."

"Yes?" Julia stiffened. Her face was stony with unwept tears and the need to keep the sorrow she suffered from her children.

Amelia looked uncertainly at her sister's averted face, but she was determined to continue this time.

"I've been talking it over with Samuel, and he says nobody really knows anything. He says men have turned up a year later, even five or ten years after they've disappeared at sea. Don't give up on him, Julie."

"No, Amelia." Julia put her hand on the gate. She remembered another day. It had been late spring, and David had come to seek her out. He had stood with his hand on this very gate and she had refused to speak to him. So long ago. Twenty-one years. She bit her lip and deliberately swung the gate wide open. Once inside, she turned to face her sister, who had followed close behind her.

"I won't harbor any false hopes, Amelia. He's gone. I could even tell you which day it happened."

"Oh, Julie, you can't!" Amelia's light blue eyes widened with dismay as she stared at her sister. "No one knows."

"I do." Julia stood very erect with her chin held high. The soft morning sunlight touched the white that was beginning to appear at her temples. "Remember the night Jason died, Amelia?"

"Aye." Amelia remembered that night all too well . . . and the events that had followed. Julia couldn't break down again. She couldn't. It had been bad enough in their youth, but now with the children so young and

349

with Aunt Martha growing old, it would be disastrous. "I'll never forget it as long as I live," she said quietly.

"Well, David came to say good-bye, too. I didn't understand at the time. Now I do." She looked towards the house, where one of her bedroom windows was visible through the early-summer green of the trees. "I spent that night writing him a letter. A long letter. It wasn't finished till dawn. And then I was alone. So terribly alone. I still am."

Amelia looked into her sister's eyes and saw the truth there. It was impossible not to believe her. She reached out a hand to touch Julia, but there was something in her expression that forbade it. Instead she continued the movement of her hand to the pins that bound her own flaxen hair and patted at them. There had to be some way she could reach Julia. Some way she could touch her.

"You're not alone, Julie," she said softly. "You have the children. You have me and Aunt Martha."

"I don't have David. Not anymore. I should have taken the children and gone with him."

"Then you would all have disappeared, too."

"Would we?" Julia's brows drew together in a puzzled frown. When she continued, her words were thoughtful. "Mama once told me she was sure the sea was a woman who jealously took our men from us. But I don't think she was right. The sea's not a man or a woman. The sea is simply the sea. Maybe Mama was right about one thing, though. Maybe the sea is jealous. Maybe I loved it too much, and when I loved a man . . . I don't know. But it took them all."

"And now you hate it?"

"No. I can't hate the sea. But David and I were supposed to grow old together, Amelia." All of her careful coldness dissipated as withheld tears came to her eyes. "Why couldn't it have spared me at least David?"

Finally Amelia felt that she could touch her sister and she put an arm around her.

"Maybe it has, Julie. Please keep on hoping."

"I can't hope." Julia closed her eyes for a moment and took a deep breath. Then she knelt down and began to examine a bed of petunias. One by one, she pinched off the spent blossoms. After a while, she said, "Have you heard what Sarah's been running around saying about me?"

"Don't pay any attention to Sarah, Julie." Amelia sat down on the warm grass and folded her hands in her lap. Her wide skirt of sprigged muslin touched the black of Julia's dress. "She'd do better if she'd tend to her own business. From what I hear, Aaron's doing none too well. Ever since his father died, the saltworks have been going steadily downhill and Thomas is running wild down in Cambridge. He's not only drinking, but he's gambling, too. Aaron's been down there twice to get him out of scrapes. If it keeps up, they'll ship him home."

"I suppose, with all her troubles, I should excuse her. Yet whenever someone tells me that she's saying, 'Well, Julia's going to have to wait seven years this time. That should slow her down a bit,' I can hear that awful laugh of hers, and I want to throttle her."

Amelia saw the accumulated suffering of all Julia's losses in her eyes, and she glanced away. Looking in the direction of Sarah's house, she made up her mind.

"I'll stop her," she said determinedly. "I'm going to have a long talk with Sarah, and I'm going to spread a few tales of my own."

"I don't know of anything that would stop Sarah when she's set on something. What tales could you possibly tell that would bother her?"

"Evidently Aaron isn't husband enough for her. She has time and to spare for other women's."

"Oh, Amelia, she's not . . ."

"Oh, yes she is. Half the township knows it. You'd know it, too, if you listened to gossip once in a while."

"Well, I don't see how you can threaten her with something half the township knows."

"I doubt Sarah's aware that her little secrets furnish such delightful conversation over tea. I won't tell her about that. I'll just tell her that *I* know."

"Oh, leave her alone, Amelia," Julia said as she accidentally tore a living plant from the ground. "It won't help anything, and from the sounds of it, she's got enough problems or she will when Aaron gets wind of it."

Chapter Twenty-four

1863

The months eventually became years, and the pain of immediate loss was blunted even though there were moments when memory could lacerate her. If there had ever been any reason to hope, Julia knew that it was gone when David's chronometers turned up in a shop in Hong Kong. Captain Bradfield had seen them there and had sent them home to her. Pirates or moonrakers in the infested waters of the South China Sea had somehow stripped them from the ship. Julia only hoped that David had already gone when the brigands boarded the *Yankee Girl*. The sea would have given him a clean death.

As she drove the buggy towards the shipyard one day in early August, she waved to Daniel, who was inspecting the bogs where the cranberries grew. It was odd work for him, but there was no other. When she had finally had to close the shipyard, he had gone to New York to ply his trade, but within two months his loyalty had brought him home again. That had been a year ago, and now together they were culling the vines for a living. At harvest time, he could still supervise the workers with their wooden scoops, but they were not the craftsmen who had once respected him. Nor were they young men.

Benjy and Jason, now seven years old, tumbled from the buggy almost before she had reined in the horse and were running across the yard to the beach while she lifted Daphne down to the ground. As she watched the boys disappear over the dunes, she was thankful that they were too young to be affected by the war that racked the country.

Sarah's son Thomas had been listed as missing at Shiloh a year ago April, and Amelia's Levi was fighting in some unknown Southern place. Samuel had received a commission in the Navy, and he, too, was in Southern waters, where the North tried to blockade the enemy's ports. Whether Aaron had joined the fight or whether he had gone West, no one knew. One day, he had simply disappeared with no word to Sarah.

As soon as her feet touched the ground, Daphne spun away from her mother. Julia thought of Clara, who sat at home and mourned the boy she would now never marry, for he, too, had fallen. She wished that she could give Clara a little of Daphne's gaiety. Julia walked slowly after her daughter, and the deserted yard seemed haunted by lost echoes of axe and hammer, mallet and saw.

Now there were only the screeching gulls plummeting over Sesuit Creek, which babbled with the ebbing tide. In the distance, the soft shush of the summer surf could be heard. The buildings had been auctioned off along with all the tools, and tomorrow the dismantling would begin. What had once been a blacksmith's shop, an office, a wood shop, or a caulkers' shop would become a barn, a house, or a stable. The tools had been carried away by the various people who had attended the auction.

While Julia had told herself that she had come on a final inspection, she knew that she had come to say good-bye. The land was still hers and she would keep it just as she kept Stephen's bluff for Clara. Someday Benjy might want to build another shipyard here, but she doubted it.

Steam and iron were replacing the winged wooden ships. Stephen had been right when he had urged her to go into it. He had been right about so many things.

As she walked up the three short steps to the office, she thought of the hundreds of thousands of times she had mounted them before. The first time, she had been close to Daphne's age. And this was the last time. Pushing open the door, she found that the only thing that was the same was slant of sunlight across the dusty boards. All of the furnishings had been removed. Yet in her mind, she could see it so clearly, see her father pacing it with the stride born of the quarterdeck, see him sitting beside the stove with his legs stretched out before him on a cold winter's day, hear again his voice telling her of the sea, its ships, and the building of them.

She could see a young Julia there, too, with her unruly black curls pushed behind her ears as she nibbled on a pen with a frown of concentration. She watched the girl who stared with longing through the grimy window at the strident activity of the shipyard.

Benjy had been conceived in this room on a night of unbearable pain that had turned into joy and comfort. She could see David rising up from their nest of shared quilts and the golden haze the lamplight had given his body, heard him say once again, "You do know that I love you, don't you? That I always have?" And she saw the loving compassion of those triangular grey-green eyes.

Her throat tightened and she hurriedly swept across the room to the door. No. It was best that the office would be torn down and its wood put to use in another building, one which would hold no more memories. Was it the sun or were they tears that blinded her as she called to Daphne, who had wandered too close to the banks of the deep, swift-running creek?

When she reached her daughter, she looked across the creek at the wharf, which was being kept in good repair though it was not so much used now except by the fishing boats, and she remembered a day of giddy joy. It was the day Jason had finally returned to her from the sea. The first and only time. She could see his tall, lean body poised on the rail of the packet as he prepared to leap ashore even before they had docked, and she could see the radiant happiness in his emerald eyes.

Daphne spun away from her again and was pirouetting in the middle of the yard. When she tripped and landed on the hard pebbled sand, Julia hurried to her, but before she could reach her, Daphne was already up and skipping towards the largest of the ways. Knowing that they were rotten, Julia sped after her. Yet when she reached them, Daphne was already intent upon her search for nails that had once been carelessly dropped and that, after being buried for years, had worked their way to the surface.

As she stood beside her daughter, Julia thought of the long, proud line of ships that had slid down those ways, each one more beautiful than the last. There had been the *Belle of Canton, Jewel of the Seas, Neptune's Dragon, Free Wind, Star of Gold, Yankee Girl,* so many others. And of course, there had been the *Crystal Star.* That day, when they had set out on their first voyage with all the hopes of their future and their youth, had Stephen, with his tawny hair exposed to the sun, really been as vibrant and as masterful as he seemed in her memory?

Abruptly she decided that her inventory was finished. There was only pain to be had here in this shipyard peopled by ghosts. Taking Daphne firmly by the hand, she mounted the winding path of the dunes. Yet even from here, she saw a burly figure with his golden hair and beard pacing the hard-packed sand below. Mermaid, Cousin William had called her that day for the first time. And he had called her that all her life till the moment of his last breath. In his own way, he would always remain her own personal vision of Neptune.

All my captains are gone, she thought. And she looked up at the clouds that raced across the summer sky. Were they racing, too, her captains, with sleek clippers whose sails rose higher and more tautly drawing, more beautiful than clouds could ever be?

Daphne, pulling at her hand, brought her back to a world where there was still joy to be had.

"Mama, see the gulls!" Daphne said with her mist-green eyes sparkling and her too-wide mouth curved upwards above her daintily triangular chin. "Oh, if only I could fly."

"Maybe someday you will," Julia said, smiling back at her daughter.

"Did you ever fly, Mama?"

"Yes, Daphne. Not till I was a lot older than you are. But I did fly."

"Tell me about it."

"I flew on clouds of canvas and dreams come true. You'll find your own way, Daphne."

"Will I, Mama? Truly?"

"Yes. I promise."

While Daphne stood silent, following the birds with entranced eyes, Julia looked down at the beach again. Blue pools lay scattered over the sand, a promise that the outgoing tide would return. Water still lapped at the base of the stray, scattered boulders, and only the highest points of the rippled bar showed the lightness of drying sand. Where the sandpipers scurried at the water's edge, there was a line of dampness.

Jason was busily scooping up sand with a clam shell at the side of one tide pool, and he packed it into a castle that would resemble one only in his imagination. The golden hair that glittered in the sun he had inherited from Amelia or William, but those clear emerald eyes that slanted slightly up on finely molded cheekbones could have had only one source.

Then she looked to his right at another tide pool, where Benjy knelt with a piece of seaweed dangling in front of a whelk's shell. His face, however, was turned towards the water, and Julia could guess what dreams he was dreaming. His thirst for sea stories was insatiable. Oh, my son, she thought, the sea will never harm you, but God help the people you love.

Slowly, so as to savor the moment of their youth that was too quickly passing, she walked down the face of the dune, but Daphne scampered ahead of her towards Jason and his sand castle. Julia, however, was more intent on her own son.

"Benjy," she said softly as she approached him. " 'Tis time to go home."

354

He brushed a blue-black curl away from his forehead with a sandy hand as he looked up at her, and she caught her breath. For that fleeting second, it seemed that her own father looked at her with those indigo eyes. The cleft in Benjy's chin was David's, but the lift of that chin, the level eyes, the straight determined shoulders reminded her of the older Benjamin. Then she shook her head as the illusion passed. No. He was not Papa. He was Benjy. A very unique and different person. Her son.

It goes on, she thought as she held her hand out to him. Just as the sea goes on, ever changing, ever the same, so does the ebb and flow of life.

AFTERWORD

Perhaps no better commentary on the early merchant marine of America and the quality of men engaged therein, can be suggested than the remarkable part played by tiny villages and men of obscure origin. From Maine to Georgia few localities failed to produce ships or men or records which added measurably to the glories of the day of the sail. Frankfort, Damariscotta, Cape Elizabeth, Medford and Mystic were small communities, yet all produced not one but many ships whose names were once familiar the world over. In the matter of men no similar area produced more deep water masters of outstanding ability than Cape Cod. . . .

Carl C. Cutler
Greyhounds of the Sea

Ships Built by the Shiverick Shipyard
East Dennis, Cape Cod, Massachusetts
Revenue
Hippogriffe
Belle of the West
Kit Carson
Wild Hunter
Webfoot
Christopher Hall
Ellen Sears